PRAISE FOR KELLEY ARMSTRONG

"Armstrong is a talented and evocative writer who knows well how to balance the elements of good, suspenseful fiction, and her stories evoke poignancy, action, humor and suspense."
The Globe and Mail

"[A] master of crime thrillers."
Kirkus

"Kelley Armstrong is one of the purest storytellers Canada has produced in a long while."
National Post

"Armstrong is a talented and original writer whose inventiveness and sense of the bizarre is arresting."
London Free Press

"Kelley Armstrong has long been a favorite of mine."
Charlaine Harris

"Armstrong's name is synonymous with great storytelling."
Suspense Magazine

"Like Stephen King, who manages an under-the-covers, flashlight-in-face kind of storytelling without sounding ridiculous, Armstrong not only writes interesting page-turners, she has also achieved that unlikely goal, what all writers strive for: a genre of her own."
The Walrus

ALSO BY KELLEY ARMSTRONG

Rockton thriller series
City of the Lost
A Darkness Absolute
This Fallen Prey
Watcher in the Woods
Alone in the Wild
A Stranger in Town

A Stitch in Time time-travel gothic trilogy
A Stitch in Time
A Twist of Fate

Standalone Thrillers
Wherever She Goes
Every Step She Takes

Past Series
Cainsville paranormal mystery series
Otherworld urban fantasy series
Nadia Stafford mystery trilogy

Young Adult
Aftermath
Missing
The Masked Truth
Darkest Powers paranormal trilogy
Darkness Rising paranormal trilogy
Age of Legends fantasy trilogy

Middle-Grade
A Royal Guide to Monster Slaying fantasy series
The Blackwell Pages trilogy (with Melissa Marr)

CURSED LUCK

KELLEY ARMSTRONG

This is a work of fiction. Names, characters, businesses, places, events and incidents are either the products of the author's imagination or used in a fictitious manner. Any resemblance to actual persons, living or dead, events, or locales is purely coincidental.

Cover Design by Cover Couture www.bookcovercouture.com
ISBN-13 (print): 978-1-989046-29-6
ISBN-13 (ebook): 978-1-989046-28-9

AUTHOR'S NOTE

Cursed Luck began life as a quarantine project. I was writing a thriller when the lockdown hit in March 2020, and I suddenly struggled with the tense and serious tone of that book. I needed something light and fun, and I suspected readers did, too. I decided to start a free serialized urban fantasy.

If you read the free online version, that was my first draft. This version has been fully tweaked and smoothed, copyedited and proofread. While there are some minor plot changes, it remains the same book readers saw in the summer of 2020...just a cleaner version!

CHAPTER ONE

AIDEN CONNOLLY IS MAKING me an offer I can't refuse, even when I know I should.

For the past two years, I've run a small antiques showroom in Boston. Business isn't exactly booming. I recently downgraded to a micro-apartment tiny enough that my cat is ready to serve me an eviction notice. So when this guy walks in and offers me a "unique opportunity," it's hard to say no, though if my gut warns me his job is a million miles out of my league.

Also, in the last five minutes, I've formed a very definite opinion of Mr. Connolly. He's kind of an asshole. He strode past my By Appointment Only signs as if they didn't apply to him, marched up and said, "I'm Aiden Connolly," as if I should recognize the name. I do not.

He stands there, looking down at me. Way down. He's not overly tall—maybe five eight or nine—but Connolly is one of those guys who could manage to look down their nose at someone standing at eye level. The smell of old Boston money wafts from him like fine cologne, and from his expression, my perfume is clearly eau de working class.

It doesn't help that Connolly is a ginger. I know that's usually an insult, but I have a thing for redheads, especially ones like this with red-gold hair and eyes the color of new grass and just the barest suggestion of freckles across the nose.

Combine "rich asshole" plus "hot young guy" plus "job that's beyond my skill set," and I should send him packing. I really should. And yet, well, I'm reaching the point where I drool every time I pass the fresh fruit stand but have to count my pennies to see whether I can buy my apple a day.

"My office needs redecorating," he announces.

I look around my dimly lit showroom, crammed with antiques. "That . . . isn't really—"

"You are not an interior designer," he says. "But I believe you could be, of a sort. I'm envisioning a different process, one that begins with set pieces and builds around them."

It takes a moment to understand his meaning. "Start with antiques and design an office to suit?"

"Yes. Someone else would do that design, of course. What I want is an expert to select the base pieces. Roger Thornton tells me you have a unique collection and an eye for quality."

I brighten at that as Connolly's odd offer begins to make sense. Roger Thornton is one of my best customers.

"My collection is indeed unique," I say. "Every piece is one of a kind. Not a single factory-produced item."

"I will take your word for that. I've collected a few antiques over the years, but I wouldn't even know their period of origin."

This admission could come with chagrin or self-deprecation. It could also come with pride, someone wanting to be clear their brain has no space for such mundanities. From Connolly, it's a simple statement of fact, and I grant him a point for that.

"Now what I'd like—" he begins.

My front door opens, bell tinkling. I wait for the intruder to notice the By Appointment Only signs. Instead, a man strides in clutching a box. He looks like a professor. Maybe forty, tall and slender with wire-rimmed glasses and silver-streaked hair. He even wears a tweed jacket with leather patches on the elbows.

"I'm sorry," I call. "We're open by appointment only."

He keeps heading straight for me.

"I'm sorry," I say again, a little firmer now. "If you have a piece to sell, you'll need to make an appointment. I'm busy with—"

The man thrusts the wooden box at me. "Fix this."

I glance down at a hanging hinge. "I'm afraid I don't offer repair . . ."

I trail off. The box is a tea caddy. Regency period. Rosewood. Perched on four cat paws, with a mother-of-pearl inlaid top showing a kitten playing with yarn. That yarn seems to slide off the box and snake toward me, whispering a soft siren's call of devilry. Joker's jinx.

I clear my throat. "I do purchase damaged items, but if you want me to take a look at this, you'll need an appointment—"

He thrusts the box into my stomach. "I mean the curse. Fix *that*. Take it off."

I force a light laugh and try not to cast a nervous look at Connolly. "I'm afraid that's a whole other level of repair. I'm not sure why you think this is 'cursed'"—I air-quote the word with my tone—"but that is definitely not my department. Maybe you have the wrong address? There's a psychic two doors down, upper apartment."

"Are you Kennedy Bennett?"

"Er, yes, but—"

"From the Bennett family of Unstable, Massachusetts?"

"It's pronounced Unst-a-bull," I murmur reflexively.

"Owners of 'Unhex Me Here,' also in Unstable?"

"Er, yes." I tug at my button-down shirtfront, straightening it. "But I . . . I'm not part of the family business."

"Your sisters sent me. They say this curse is a joker's jinx, and that's your area of expertise. Now unhex my damn box, or I'll leave a one-star review."

"Go," Connolly says.

The man turns and blinks as if Connolly teleported in from an alternate dimension.

"I said, go," Connolly says. "Ms. Bennett clearly has no idea what you are talking about. Just as clearly, she has another client. Now take *that*"—his lip curls—"piece of kitschy trash and leave."

The man's face flushes in outrage. "Who the hell are you?"

"The person Ms. Bennett is currently dealing with. The client with an appointment."

"Y-yes," I say. "Mr. Connolly absolutely had an appointment, and I must insist that you make one yourself if you're interested in selling that box. As for anything else you think I can do with it, my sisters have a very weird sense of humor. I'll totally understand if you one-star *their* business."

The man's jaw works. Then he plunks the box on a sideboard. "Fine. You know what? You just bought yourself a curse, young lady. *That's* my one-star review."

He stalks out, leaving the box behind. As the door bells jangle, Connolly murmurs, "That was interesting."

I force a laugh. "Right?" I ease the cursed tea caddy off the sideboard and tuck it safely out of reach. "So tell me more about this job, Mr. Connolly."

I AGREE to stop by Connolly's office after lunch so I can see the space. Once he's gone, I exhale and slump over the sideboard. Then I lock the door, place the tea caddy on my desk and peer at it.

While Connolly called it kitsch, it's actually a valuable antique like everything in here. As I told him, all my goods are one of a kind. That's because they're cursed. Formerly cursed, I should say. The *former* part is very important.

I come from a family of curse weavers—a gift said to stretch back to the Greek *arae*. While we can weave curses, we can also unweave them, and that's our true calling. Most times we're asked to uncurse an item, though, we fake it. Not that we leave the curse on. That would be wrong. The problem is that those who show up on our doorstep rarely suffer from an actual cursed object. Instead, they suffer from an anxious mind that needs settling, and for generations, the Bennett women have provided that service, pretending to uncurse some heirloom or other.

People who have a real cursed object usually don't realize it. They may only know Great Aunt Edna's jewelry box gives them the creeps. Worse, no one wants to buy it because it gives *them* the creeps, too. That's where I come in. I will take that box off your hands. I'll even pay you for it. Then I'll uncurse it and resell it.

One might think that the ethical thing to do would be to offer to uncurse the object. I tried that a few times. The owner stared at me as if I'd sprouted a turban and hoop earrings. Lift a *curse*? What kind of wacko was I? They just wanted to sell their dead aunt's weird jewelry box.

A couple of times, when I felt really bad about buying an heirloom, I tried quietly uncursing the object and giving it back. Didn't help. They wanted it gone. That explains the tea caddy suddenly in my possession. While the owner obviously believed in the curse, he decided dumping it on me was safer than keeping it. Or he just got pissy and wanted to storm off with a grand gesture . . . which ultimately benefited one of us more than the other.

I'll uncurse the caddy tonight, and if the former owner returns, I'll buy it from him. Fair and square. Right now, though, I have a far more important task: texting my sisters to tell them I'm going to kill them in some fresh new way that is totally different from the other two times this week I threatened to do it.

Kennedy: Suffocation. Inside an antique tea caddy.

It only takes a moment for my younger sister to reply.

Hope: I don't think we'd fit.
Kennedy: Oh, you will when I get through with you.

Our older sister, Turani, joins in.

Ani: Pfft. I'm not worried. To kill us, you'd need to come to Unstable. Which apparently has fallen off your GPS.
Kennedy: I missed one weekend. ONE. Also, the highway runs both ways. You could come here.
Ani: To that den of iniquity?
Kennedy: We call it 'Boston.'
Hope: Can we go pub-hopping?
Ani: Yes. When you're twenty-one. Now what's this about a tea caddy?
Kennedy: Joker's jinx Regency tea caddy. Guy barged in during a client showing.

Ani: I didn't send him. Hope?

Hope: Hell, no. I learned my lesson. I hate you, by the way, K. I had a date last week. Made the mistake of offering to drive, forgetting that every time I sit in the driver's seat, it makes a fart noise. 🐱

Kennedy: Unhex it. Oh, wait, you can't. Jinx.

Hope: Hate. You.

Kennedy: Well, whoever sent the guy, please just don't do it again.

Ani: We didn't, K.

Kennedy: Confer. Get your story straight. Gotta run.

They don't text back to protest. They know better. One of them sent that guy, and I don't care which—I just want it to stop.

My sisters aren't trying to ruin my business. They just don't understand why I need to run it in Boston rather than Unstable where I'd pay a fraction of the rent and have a steady stream of tourist clients. Except I don't want bargain-hunting tourists. I also don't want to live at home. Not right now.

Mom died of cancer a month before I fled to Boston. Three years earlier, a car accident claimed our father. That time I fled in the opposite direction—quitting college to come home and be with my family. After Mom died, I needed out. I needed to breathe, to be somewhere that didn't have my parents—our family, our memories —imprinted on every damn blade of grass.

Besides, I'm twenty-five, and if there is an age when I should be living wild, this is it. Yes, there are times when I miss Unstable and my sisters so badly I could cry. Times when I must admit that "living wild" means "going to a bar, telling myself I'm going to hook up with a hot guy, and then spending all night chatting with the bartender instead." But I just . . . I want to give this a shot. I want to prove that I can make it on my own, even if I don't need to prove it to anyone but myself.

CHAPTER TWO

THIS IS . . . not what I expected.

Those words keep cycling through my head that afternoon as I sit in the reception area of Connolly's office. I did my research on the guy. As I guessed, he comes from old money. His family arrived in America even before mine. Connolly himself runs one of those vaguely named companies whose actual line of business remained unclear no matter how hard I searched. Something about securities. Stocks, maybe?

From that, I thought I knew exactly what to expect from his place of business. It'd be old-school Boston. Dimly lit hallways linking a warren of tiny offices, the stink of age permeating the building. That fit with someone looking to redecorate with antiques and recreate the kind of office his great-grandfather might have had. Massive carved-oak pedestal desk. Swivel desk chair with buttoned red leather. An antique globe for the corner. Maybe a few mismatched Tiffany lamps. Bookcases full of first editions that will languish, unopened, for the rest of their lives. Aiden Connolly will sit in that leather chair, his loafers perched on a desk worth more than I make in a good year, as he sips single-malt whiskey from a cut-glass tumbler.

That is what I expect. Instead, his offices are in a modern skyscraper, the rooms all steel and marble and glass. I have no idea where I could even put an antique without it seeming as out of place as a wet dog in a formal parlor.

I'm in the reception area, perched on a glass chair that, with each fidget, threatens to send me sliding to the floor like a penguin on a ski slope. Speaking of penguins, I wish I'd worn the black pencil skirt and white Oxford shirt I'd contemplated when I slipped home to change. So far, I've seen three people, all of them dressed in shades of black and white. The Nordic blonde behind the desk wears a pearl-gray dress that I keep expecting to tinkle like crackling ice when she moves.

Forget antiques. What this place needs is a splash of *color*. Technically, my red dress provides it, but I feel like an open wound ready to ooze onto the white marble tiles.

"Ms. Bennett?"

I jump and see Connolly waiting at an open door. His fingers tap the doorframe, impatient at this two-second delay. I leap up . . . and my heels promptly slide across the marble. Connolly's PA shakes her head. Her boss, fortunately, has already retreated into his office. I find my footing and follow him with as much dignity as I can muster.

When I step into Connolly's office, he's at his desk, leaning over it to rustle through papers. Earlier, I'd squashed Connolly into the narrative I created for this job—and into the wood-paneled office I imagined—but seeing him here, I realize I'd been deluding myself. I cannot actually imagine him lounging with his shoes on a big antique desk. His surroundings here suit him perfectly. Chilly, austere, stylish and haughty. His personal office is no different. I'm sure it's gorgeous, in a Scandinavian way. It just makes me long for a warm, woolly sweater and a crackling fire.

"Mr. Connolly?" I say as he rustles through papers.

Green eyes lift to mine as one sandy brow arches. He does not say "Call me Aiden, please." He could be talking to someone ten years his senior, and he'd still insist on the formality. Old money, old ways.

"I . . . think there might be a misunderstanding," I say. "This doesn't seem like the . . . environment for antiques."

"No, it's not, is it?" he says. "Which is precisely the problem."

He opens a side door and strides through. The door half shuts behind him before he grabs it and gives me a sharp wave, lips tightening in annoyance that I didn't follow.

I walk in and—

"Oh," I say, my breath catching.

We're on the fourteenth floor, and until now, I haven't glanced out a window. I can't avoid that here—one entire wall is glass, jutting out to form the curving nook of a solarium. Sunlight streams through, bedazzling a view that overlooks the Common.

"This is the room I want to redecorate," he says. "The sunlight made it too warm most of the year, but thankfully, the air conditioning has been upgraded."

Upgraded is definitely the word. The room is about sixty-five degrees, AC pumping an arctic jet stream. I inch closer to the sunny windows.

"I wish to repurpose it as a staff area," Connolly says.

"A lounge?"

That lip press again, as if the word is too informal, conjuring images of employees actually relaxing, possibly in real chairs.

"A staff *area*," he repeats. "I understand that my choice of decor may invoke . . ."

"Antarctica without the penguins?"

The faintest narrowing of his eyes. "I was going to say it invokes a sense of asceticism that some find off-putting."

"Asceticism is great," I murmur. "If you're a monk."

He continues as if he hasn't heard me. "Personally, I *like* clean lines and simplicity. Clutter in one's environment produces clutter in one's mind. However, I am aware that employee productivity may suffer in a setting that is not comfortable. So I wish to remodel this room in a more traditional style."

He walks to a built-in bookcase of glass shelves. That's when I notice the antiques. Three pieces small enough to fit on those shelves: a snuffbox, a cigarette case and a mahogany triptych mirror.

I'm drawn to the cigarette case first. It's art deco, the silver lid inlaid with jade showing a twenties-style flapper smoking oh-so-elegantly.

"This is beautiful," I say, curling my fingers against the urge to touch it.

"I won it in a card game."

My glance must be sharper than I intended, thinking he's joking, though I'm not sure which is harder to picture—Connolly playing cards or Connolly telling a joke.

"I have an excellent poker face," he says.

He points at the snuffbox. "I won that on the same night. I have a bit of luck now and then." His lips twitch, as if this is indeed a joke, albeit a personal one I am neither supposed to understand nor pursue.

"And this—" I stop short, fingers extended toward the mirror. I wasn't going to touch it. I know better. I was just gesturing. Still, the moment I do, I yank back.

Curse.

I hesitate and then give myself a mental shake. Obviously, my brain is misfiring, because the irony there would just be too rich. This morning, Connolly dismissed the guy with the cursed tea caddy . . . only to have a cursed object himself.

I glance at the mirror again and those tendrils of magic snake out, whispering . . .

Nope, definitely cursed.

Damn.

I inch closer and let the first notes of that hex wash over me. A lover's lament. Better known as an ex-hex. Hell hath no fury like a lover scorned. And from the vibes rising from this mirror, someone felt *very* scorned.

"Did you win this one?" I ask hopefully.

"No, that was a gift from a woman I was seeing. Quite surprising, actually. I'd long admired the mirror, and when we had a falling out, she gave it to me. A peace offering to show there were no hard feelings."

He waves away his words. "Which is more than you care—or need—to know. But of the three, it's my personal favorite, and whatever you suggest for this room, that one piece must stay."

Of course it must. He couldn't just say, *Oh, I don't really care for that particular piece, perhaps you'd like to buy it from me?*

Connolly clearly doesn't realize it's cursed—it takes a psychically attuned person to pick up even just "bad vibes."

I can see why he likes the mirror. Of the three, it's the simplest piece. Edwardian. Gleaming red mahogany. Original mirror glass, only faintly warped. The center piece is oval with brass fittings that allow it to tilt.

I will admit I have a predilection for more ornate items—gaudy, Ani would say—and the cigarette box is more my style, but I must appreciate the sheer artistry and elegance of the mirror. A truly perfect piece . . . flawed by a nasty little curse.

Two hexed items in one day?

It's been a year since I last stumbled over a cursed object "in the wild." And yet, technically, I've only stumbled over one today. The tea caddy was brought to me after my sisters sent the owner, which they do with irritating regularity.

Also, let's be blunt, I am not the least bit surprised that Aiden Connolly has earned himself an ex-hex. Something tells me his romantic history is a Christmas-light string blinking red with angry exes. He's young, attractive, successful and single. He'll have no problem finding companionship, and I suspect he'd have no problem moving on a month later, probably via breakup text. He's also exactly the sort of guy who'd see nothing suspicious about an ex offering a lovely parting gift.

"Ideally, I'd want a dual-purpose area," Connolly says, and I tear my gaze from the mirror to find him across the room. "A place for staff to decompress, but also a place to entertain clientele. A more traditional meeting room."

"Got it. Now, I must admit I wasn't able to find a lot about your company online. What, uh, exactly do you do?"

"Insurance."

My soul drops. I'll admit, I'd held out hope for something a little more interesting, a little sexier. But no, this fits. Sadly, this fits.

"What sort of insurance?" I ask, struggling to sound intrigued.

A wave of his hand. "This and that. Now, I only have a few more minutes before my next appointment. Do you have any questions, Ms. Bennett?"

Any chance you'll let me take that mirror home? Fix it up for you?

That is a problem to consider later. I ask to take photographs of the room, hoping to get a little more face time with the mirror. Connolly stays right where he is, watching. I snap my shots and leave with a promise to call later this week.

CHAPTER THREE

I'M HOME, my mind still churning through my dilemma. As I'd been leaving Connolly's building, I'd texted and called my sisters. I'd tried again, walking home from my showroom. They aren't answering, which could mean they're annoyed at me, but it more likely indicates cell service is down in Unstable. That's the problem with living in a place where the average resident is still on dial-up internet. The psychics of Unstable have a direct line to God, Fate and the future. To Boston? Not so much.

I push open the door to my apartment to see a black cat on the kitchen counter and my favorite bone china mug resting precariously on the edge. One small kitty paw rests against the mug. Green eyes meet mine . . . and the mug creeps toward the edge.

"Don't you dare, Ellie."

Another nudge.

"Yes, we ran out of wet food, and you hate kibble." I reach into my shopping bag and hold up a can. "Better?"

She considers. Then another nudge sets the mug teetering.

I snatch out a can of tuna and wave it. "There. Happy? I felt bad, so I bought you a treat."

She sniffs and hops down to wait by her dish. As I push the mug back, she's purring as loud as a buzz saw. I shake my head and open the can.

I've had Ellie nearly four years, ever since someone dropped her off at our Unstable home, claiming she was cursed. Ellie was the thirteenth cat in her litter, and she's completely black except for a white spot that bears an uncanny resemblance to the evil eye. She isn't cursed, though. She's just an asshole. In other words, as Ani would say, she's a cat. True, but Ellie inherited the asshole gene more than most of her species. Hence her full name of Elohssa.

Once Ellie is fed, I start pacing the apartment, which takes about ten strides. With each revolution, I check my phone. Nothing from Ani or Hope. My texts are delivered but unread. Damn it.

I plunk onto my sofa. Ellie takes her spot on the armrest. She isn't the world's cuddliest cat. Oh, she acts like it, rubbing up against your legs with that buzz-saw purr. It's a trap, one that has left scars on both my sisters. I've learned the pattern. Two pats are acceptable. A third will draw blood. Mostly, she just sits nearby. And she listens. Say what you will about Ellie, but she is an excellent listener.

"So I have a problem," I begin, and she stretches out, getting comfortable.

I tell her about the ex-hex.

"I want the job," I say. "Connolly's paying well. It would look good on my resume, and it might lead to more work. The guy is about as warm and cuddly as you, but I can work with that."

She rumbles in sage agreement.

"The thing is, a poorly woven curse can fray and infect those in the vicinity. My love life already sucks. What if I catch the curse, and I'm doomed to a life of lonely celibacy?"

Her look tells me I'm overreacting. Or, possibly, that I'm already on that path, so don't go blaming it on a curse.

"Yes, I suppose the chances of me catching the hex are slight. The problem . . ." I thump my head back into the sofa. "Arghh! The problem is that I'm a nice person who wants to do the right thing."

Ellie gives a disdainful sniff.

"Hey," I say. "Be thankful for that, or you'd be living in a barn. Or with a houseful of small children with grubby hands that love to pull kitty-cat tails. While I can complain about catching Connolly's curse, the truth is that I should fix it. Like seeing a loose floorboard nail when I have a hammer in my bag. I want to fix it before anyone gets hurt. If that makes me a sucker, so be it."

Ellie cleans one paw.

"Fine. Yes. That settles it. I need to uncurse Connolly's mirror. The next problem is how. I need time alone with it. Time when no one's going to walk in and ask what I'm doing."

I pull my legs up under me and consider the matter. "Clearly, the answer is that I need to break in tonight. I'll take my lock picks and disarm his security system . . ."

Ellie's eyes narrow.

"That was a joke," I say. "I can barely open the bathroom door when the lock sticks. This is going to require finesse."

I don't fail to catch the cat's look then, the one that says, if finesse is what's required, this mission is doomed from the start. I stick out my tongue and push up from the sofa. Time to grab my kit. I have a curse to unweave.

———

It's seven p.m., and I'm outside Connolly's office building, wearing the best disguise for the job: no disguise at all. While I'd only seen a few employees flitting about earlier, they were all under forty. That means at least a few will be ambitious enough to work later than the boss.

Most I saw earlier were also male, and I'd caught a few admiring glances as I walked through. I'm not the prettiest Bennett sister—that would be Hope. I've been told my skin is my best feature, which always feels like groping for something nice to say. I *am* blessed with clear light olive skin, though. Straight black hair swings past my shoulders. Guys have called my eyes everything from mahogany to chestnut to rich oak. In other words, brown. And apparently wooden. I have an average figure, unblessed by Ani's curves, but if women compliment my skin, for guys, it's all about my legs, and tonight I'm showing them off in my shortest skirt and highest heels.

My first stop is the building's parking garage, where I find the numbered spots for Connolly's business. I presume he gets the first, but one through five are all empty, and the two cars remaining in his section are a pickup and an old smart car. Neither strikes me as his style.

An elevator ride takes me to Connolly's office suites. The main door isn't locked, and I walk in to find a janitor mopping the floor. A female janitor. Not ideal but . . .

"Oh my God," I say, breathlessly, as if I've run up thirteen flights of stairs. "Thank God someone's still here. I need access to the solarium."

"The *what*?" she says, leaning on her mop.

I wave my free hand. "The—the atrium. The solarium. The room with all the windows. I'm redecorating it, and I got home to find my cell phone pictures aren't enough. I need this." I gesture to the camera around my neck.

Her wrinkled face pinches. I raise my voice a little, letting it echo through the empty halls.

"Cell phones just aren't good enough. They don't have the right f-stop and lens aperture and exposure rate." I throw out random camera terms and pray she isn't an amateur photographer. "I need proper photos and— Oh!" I bounce on my toes and wave at an employee leaning from his office. "Hello! Can you help me, please?"

Now this guy is exactly what I was hoping to find here. Late thirties. Average appearance. Slightly harried. Staying late at the office because no one is waiting at home. Hopefully, not gay, but if so, I can appeal to any big-brother sense of responsibility toward a young career woman.

I wave frantically, and he comes out, hesitantly at first. Then his gaze sweeps over me, and he straightens and runs a hand through his hair before he strides out.

"May I help you?" he says, his voice lowering an octave with each word.

I explain the situation so far.

"Also measurements." I hold up a tape measure. "I need the width of the doorway, to know what size of furniture I can get through, plus the distance between outlets and immovable obstacles and . . ."

I exhale, drooping. "I know I should have gotten all this earlier.

Or made an appointment. But this . . . It's not my usual gig. I'm an antiques dealer. A job like this is huge, and I got frazzled, and Mr. Connolly . . ." I lower my voice, as if the man himself might be watching through a security cam. "He's kind of intimidating."

The employee chuckles. "*Kind of?* I've been here a year, and I'm still afraid to ask for a key to the washroom."

"Well, then I don't feel so bad. I just . . . I got nervous, and I snapped a few cell phone shots, and then at home, I realized that wasn't nearly enough. I just need, like, thirty minutes in there. Or even twenty. I know the room attaches to his office, but I'm presuming that door is locked."

"I don't think his PA even has a key to his office."

"Then there's no security issue just letting me into the solarium." I turn to the janitor. "Do you have the key for *that*?"

She shrugs. "No need. Just a few pieces of old junk on a shelf. Mr. Connolly's office is the only room he wants locked." She turns to the employee. "Including the washroom."

"Er, right. I . . . knew that." He gives a strained chuckle. "Well, no more running downstairs to the coffee shop for me." He sweeps an arm along the hall. "Come along, Ms. . . ."

"Bennett," I say. "But you can call me Kennedy."

He beams. "Let's get you situated in that room, Kennedy."

CHAPTER FOUR

MY FAMILY HATES to call what we do *magic*. That conjures, well, conjuring. Casting spells and manipulating elements, possessing the power to smite one's enemies and conjure cupcakes from the ether. Given the choice, I'd probably take that last one. A good thing it isn't an option.

Lacking more accurate terminology, we do refer to our wider community as a *magical* one, but people in it are only blessed with a single ability, like curse weaving or dream shaping or luck working. Even in Unstable, the average psychic doesn't possess any power beyond the skills of a very good entertainer. Those who have actual abilities live in harmony with those who don't, and there's no ill-will or envy. Let's face it, even those of us *with* powers fake it most of the time, like pretending to uncurse perfectly ordinary objects.

We aren't witches or wizards, though I may have convinced Hope otherwise when she was six, in bed with chicken pox, and I read her nonstop books about magic schools. I then borrowed Mrs. Salazar's pet owl to deliver Hope's invitation to one, sending my sister into tears thinking she was about to be packed off to a boarding school. I staunched those tears with the reassurance that hers would be an online education, and I recruited Ani to devise lessons. Ani still grumbles about it, and Hope still has her magic-school achievement certificates framed on her bedroom walls. I call that a win both ways.

If actual spellcasters exists, even Jonathan doesn't know about them. Jonathan King is the local librarian and Ani's best friend since toddler-hood. After Hope and I marathoned *Buffy the Vampire Slayer* during a dual bout of mono, we started calling him Giles. No one in Unstable knows more about our secret world than he does, and he has declared there is no such thing as witches or wizards. Also, to Hope's eternal disappointment, no brooding vampires or ripped werewolves, either. Just families who've inherited one specific power.

All those powers, though, have one thing in common. Balance. You cannot create in a vacuum. Weave a curse on one object, and you must unweave another. To uncurse an object, you must cast another curse, preferably on a different object. If this sounds simple, let me assure you, it is not. Ani keeps actual spreadsheets to track cursed and uncursed objects. My method is a little . . . less rigorous.

Once the solarium door is firmly closed, I prepare. Then I cautiously approach the mirror and pick it up. Even through my gloves, the ugliness of the curse throbs.

Damn it, Connolly, what did you do to this woman?

The answer comes slowly. The mirror doesn't speak, of course. That would be weird. Although, there is an old story about a doll that actually *did* tell a curse weaver her secret. I turned that one into a bedtime horror story for Hope . . . who now has an entire collection of formerly cursed dolls.

This mirror, thankfully, does not talk. Instead, it sends out little tendrils of psychic power that slide through me and reveal their truth in sibilant whispers.

He would not stay.

And now he will.

Whether he wants to or not.

Ah. That makes sense. Connolly failed to provide the commitment his lover desired. He doesn't seem like the smooth-tongued devil type, so I'm guessing he didn't lead the woman on with lies and empty promises—she just wanted more than he was willing to give.

It's a nasty curse for a relatively minor relationship "crime." But Mom always said curse weaving is like selling someone a gun. You can ask what it'll be used for . . . or you tell yourself you're just the broker and sell it without question. This is why Bennetts weave curses with great reluctance. We feel obliged to ask for the reason and then make a judgment call.

Connolly's lover wanted a commitment. He didn't. As the curse suggests, he refused to "stay." Perhaps the fitting curse would be that when he finds a woman he *does* want to be with, she'll leave him. But that's risky—what if he never finds that woman or what if he sells the mirror before then? Instead, the curse causes him to "stay" with whatever he deemed more important than his lover. If he refused to move in with her, he'll be stuck in his current residence forever. If he found their relationship interfered with his career, then he'll be trapped in his position, his business never expanding. An insidious curse, particularly for an ambitious young man like Connolly.

I set to work unweaving the curse. By the end, I'm dripping sweat and mentally wiped out.

"You'd better appreciate this, Connolly," I mutter as I clean up.

Which is ridiculous. He'll never know the mirror was cursed, much less *un*cursed. Which is for the best, really. Just call it my good deed for the month and—

The door opens. The *locked* door into Connolly's office. It swings open, and the man himself walks through, still dressed in his funeral-director-gray suit.

"Ms. Bennett," he says. "What a surprise."

I stammer my excuse about camera shots and measurements. I barely get out a line before he waves me to silence.

"I know why you're here," he says. "Unweaving the lover's lament on my mirror."

"W-what? Lover's—?"

"I believe curse weavers colloquially call them ex-hexes? Very kind of you, and much appreciated, even if I actually paid to have it cursed. A little test to discover whether you really are what they say you are. Whether you'd recognize a cursed object. You didn't seem to, which was terribly disappointing. But now you've returned and unhexed it for me. I appreciate that."

"You . . . set a trap for me?"

"A test," he says. "As a prospective client, I needed to verify your credentials."

"Prospective client . . ."

His lips curve in what he must consider a smile. I see only teeth. "Yes, I have a job for you, one that suits your particular talents far more than redecorating." He gestures through the door into his office. "Come have a seat, and we'll talk."

CHAPTER FIVE

I DO NOT FOLLOW Connolly into his office. I grab the rest of my supplies and shove them into a bag.

"You may leave that for later," he says. "No one will disturb your belongings."

I keep packing. Then I toss the bag over my shoulder and head for the hall door.

"Ms. Bennett? My office is through here."

"And the elevator is through here. I'll send you an invoice for my time earlier today and for the unweaving. You may also just give me the mirror. I'm tempted to stuff it into my bag and walk out, but unlike some people, I believe in playing fair."

"I have a job that will earn you far more than that mirror—"

"Not interested." I grab the hall doorknob.

"You haven't even heard what it is."

"I've met the guy who'd be my boss if I took the job. That's all I need to know. The answer is no. Hell, no."

I twist the knob. Nothing. I yank, panic prickling through the anger. When it doesn't budge, I force calm and turn to him.

"Open this door, Connolly."

"I just want to—"

"Hello!" I shout against the door. "Hello!"

"No one's here. I sent them home."

The panic crystallizes. "You—you're holding me hostage?" I

steady my voice and channel Ani. "You do realize you're threatening a *curse* weaver, right?"

"It isn't a threat. Just hear me out—"

I grab the only chair in the room, march to the window and swing the chair back. He catches it in one hand.

"That seems extreme, Ms. Bennett. Also, unless you can fly, it's a thirteen-story drop."

"I thought we were on the fourteenth floor."

"Only because buildings never call it the thirteenth. It's bad luck, don't you know." His lips twitch as if in another private joke. "Either way, jumping from that window would definitely be bad luck."

"I have no intention of jumping. I'm just going to smash every window in this room. That'll set you back about . . ." I eye the huge panes of glass. "Ten grand?"

"Probably twenty."

"No job is worth that kind of loss *plus* the curse I'll slap on your ass."

"People can't be cursed."

"It's a figure of speech," I say. "Unlock this door. Now."

"Just give me five minutes—"

"I'll give you five *seconds* to unlock the door."

"Or you smash my windows?"

"Nope, we've moved beyond that. Let me out, or you're getting *this*."

I march to my kit and snap on gloves. Then I withdraw a radioactive-grade bag, unzip it and remove a black ball.

"Is that an . . . eight ball?" Connolly says.

"No, it's a Magic 8 Ball. And it says,"—I hold it up—"outlook not so good."

"Cute. I know your area of expertise is the joker's jinx, but I believe you need to up your game, Ms. Bennett."

"Oh, this is no joke, sir. This right here is a curse bomb."

"A cursed Magic 8 Ball?"

"A cursed Magic 8 Ball *bomb*." I lift it to his eye level. "How much do you know about curse weaving?"

"Enough to know there's no such thing as a curse bomb."

"It's my own creation. See, when you uncurse an object, you need to curse something else. There are lots of workarounds. This is mine."

He frowns at the ball, sandy brows furrowing. "I don't understand."

"Think, Connolly. To uncurse an object, I must curse something else. Now, I could cast a practical joke on some random inanimate object, but that's only fair if it's a minor curse. Your mirror had a major hex. For those, I cast them all onto one small object." I lift the ball. "Curse bomb."

He takes an involuntary step back before stopping himself. "You're joking."

I turn the ball on the tips of my gloved hands. "Would you like me to leave it here so you can find out?"

"You cast *all* your balancing curses onto *one* Magic 8 Ball? That's —that's—"

"Unwise? I'll give you my sister's number. You two can vent your concerns together. For now, the point is . . ." I heft the ball. "Let me out of this room, or I unleash hell."

"I just want—"

"Five. Four. Three."

He throws open the door. "Fine, but you are being very unreasonable, Ms. Bennett. I also do not appreciate the dramatics."

"And I do not appreciate being held hostage. Is that what *you* consider reasonable, Connolly? Locking a woman in a room until she does what you want? Guess you deserved to keep that ex-hex whether it was meant for you or not."

Color suffuses his cheeks. Then he clears his throat. "I apologize. I see how detaining you could be construed. I only wished to speak to you, and I went about it in the wrong way. If you would just give me five minutes of your time, Ms. Bennett, I'm sure it will be worth your while. Whatever you decide, you may take the mirror as compensation for your time."

I lower the Magic 8 Ball. "Thank you. But I still don't want to hear about the job. I'm sorry. After this, I don't trust you, and I don't want to work for you."

"Perhaps your sisters would do the job, then."

"You can ask them, but you can bet I'm going to tell them what you did."

"Understood."

When I eye the mirror, Connolly says, "At least allow me to have that packed properly. You can pick it up tomorrow."

I glance at him.

"I promise I will not bother you again, Ms. Bennett. I'll hope, of course, that you'll change your mind and want to hear my proposal, but I will not withhold the mirror until you do. Just . . . consider hearing me out. Please."

I shake my head and throw my bag over my shoulder. As I stride toward his office door, Connolly steps out of my way and doesn't say another word as I go.

I'M DREAMING of Aiden Connolly . . . and not in a good way. After what happened tonight, I don't think he's ever entering my dreams in a remotely positive light. I'd be upset enough about the trap with the mirror, but what he did after that doubled down on the deception.

I'll give him the benefit of the doubt and say he didn't think it through. The fact remains that he trapped me, and my stomach still tightens thinking about it. I didn't know him well enough to guess what he intended. In that moment, I felt helpless and frightened.

I don't dream about that moment of fear, though. I dream about what he said after that.

Perhaps your sisters would do the job, then.

It sounded as if he meant he'd try hiring them. But he'd seemed unconcerned by my warning.

Unconcerned because he knew my sisters would never get that message?

By the time I bolt awake, gasping for breath, sunlight seeps around the blinds. Ellie sits at the foot of the bed, as if she's been watching me toss and turn all night.

"Ani and Hope," I whisper. "They never got back to me."

I scramble for my phone and flip to the text messages. Delivered but unread. I stab Ani's number. It rings through to voicemail just as it did last night.

I pull up Jonathan's number. If he doesn't answer, I'll know Unstable's lines are down.

Or he might not answer because he's still asleep, as most people are at . . . I check the clock. 5:50 a.m.

My fingers move down the list to our Unstable neighbor's land-line number. Mrs. Salazar is always awake by five.

And what am I going to ask her? Whether cell service is down? She doesn't have a cell phone. Or internet.

I just want to know my sisters are okay.

So what would I ask Mrs. Salazar to do? Run next door and bang on our door?

I'm overreacting. I know I am. Cell service is down again, which is further ammunition for my argument that Ani needs to reactivate the damn landline. I can bitch about that, but it's really my own fault for not e-mailing her last night. Also, Aiden Connolly's fault for jamming this worry into my brain.

Perhaps your sisters would do the job, then.

Was that a backup plan? Or a threat?

The sensible part of my brain says I'm being silly. My fear is sleep anxiety, nothing more. Something happens when we go to bed and shut down the logic centers of our minds. That freedom can be marvelous—Michael Fassbender joining me in my nonexistent hot tub on my nonexistent back deck.

Turn down the logic dial, though, and you also unseal the anxiety pressure cooker. Last week, I got so busy chatting with the fruit-stand lady that I didn't pay for my apple. Instead of my sleeping brain just nicely reminding me to pay the next day, it sent me a nightmare of the police breaking down my door and hauling me off to a Victorian debtor's prison.

In this case, instead of nicely suggesting I should e-mail Ani, my sleep anxiety has me scrambling to pull on clothing, ready to run the sixty miles to Unstable to check on my sisters.

Ellie hops onto the dresser and watches me send another text, which goes into "delivered" status and stays there.

"I'm going to e-mail them now," I announce.

As I do it, she keeps staring.

"There." I set my phone aside with a decisive clack. "That'll be enough."

Her narrowed eyes call me a liar.

"Fine, yes, I'll call Jonathan after breakfast. See whether cell service is out." I rise and tug on a T-shirt. "But I am not driving up there this morning. I have two showings, and I need to uncurse that tea caddy. I also need to pick up my new mirror from Connolly's office."

I drag a brush through my hair. "You know what, I might even keep the mirror. I could use one in here."

Ellie's eyes narrow more.

"Fine, yes, I can't afford to keep it. And no, don't give me that look. I'm not changing the subject. I've made my decision. I'm not renting a car and driving to Unstable this morning. That would be crazy and paranoid. Ani and Hope are fine. Just fine."

———

AN HOUR LATER, I'm walking out my front door, cell phone in hand as I reserve a ShareCar for the drive to Unstable. I've canceled my appointments. The cursed tea caddy isn't going to get any more cursed stashed in my showroom. As for Connolly, if my sisters are missing and he has anything to do with it, our next conversation will be a little more involved than "Hey, I'm here for the mirror."

I don't honestly think they're missing. I certainly don't think Aiden Connolly kidnapped them. But my brain can't help leaping to worst-case scenarios, and if I don't make the drive to Unstable, I'll spend the entire day clutching my phone, blasting Ani and Hope with texts and e-mails.

I'm stepping from the apartment, phone raised as I confirm my car reservation, when I stumble over something in my path. My phone goes flying, and I would have followed if strong hands didn't catch me.

I suppose I should scream, being grabbed by a guy in a dimly lit hallway. Or I should lash out, calling on that single summer of karate lessons twelve-year-old me just had to have. Maybe it's the fact I recognize that grip. Or maybe it's just the fact that my "attacker" kept me from falling rather than throwing me against a wall. Either way, I only squint against the near darkness as a burly figure retrieves my dropped cell phone.

"Jonathan?" I say.

He doesn't answer. Obviously, it's him. Even in the dim lighting, his figure is unmistakable. If there's a stereotype of a librarian, Jonathan cannot be crammed into it by any stretch of the imagination. He's six feet tall, broad shouldered with muscles that suggest he bench presses entire shelves of encyclopedias. Dark skin, dark eyes, and dark hair cut to his scalp.

"Seems fine," he says as he hands me my phone. "Sorry about that."

I'm still blinking in confusion when I catch the smell of fresh bread and fresher coffee. I follow the scents to the floor and see a bakery bag and two takeout coffees, one already opened.

"Wait," I say. "You were sitting outside my door? How long have you been here?"

He checks his watch. "Couple hours maybe? I didn't want to wake you."

"Why are you . . ."

My gut freezes.

"Ani," I whisper. "Something's happened to Ani. She's missing, isn't she? She wasn't answering my texts or calls and—"

He lifts huge hands to stop my babble. "If I thought they'd been kidnapped, I'd be at the police station, K. It's just . . ." He lifts the coffee and bakery bag. "Can we step inside?"

I nod and open my door.

CHAPTER SIX

As soon as we step into my apartment, Ellie comes running. Well, her form of running, which is moving slightly faster than a stroll. She sees Jonathan and stops short. Then she launches into a full-throated purr and begins rubbing against his legs.

As he bends to pet her, I start to warn him and then remember that isn't necessary. This is Jonathan. His size might make grown men step aside, but animals—like small children—see right past that. A smile from Jonathan makes toddlers stop screaming. Ellie tolerates his ear scratches without even a raised warning paw.

I don't invite Jonathan into the living room. It's a miracle we're not still out in the hallway with me yanking on his shirtfront, screaming "Tell me now!"

"They're missing, aren't they?" I say as he tries to hand me a morning bun. "Ani and Hope are missing. They must be. You drove all the way from Unstable in the middle of the night—"

"I'm concerned," he says. "Yes, concerned enough that I couldn't sleep. If I went to the police, though, they'd tell me to go home and chill."

"What's happened? I was texting yesterday and calling—"

He motions for me to lower the volume. "Cell service went out midday. It's still out. I saw Ani early yesterday afternoon. I was supposed to come by for dinner and a board-game night, but there was an emergency town-council meeting to discuss, not coincidentally, the cell-service issue. I still expected to swing by and see Ani afterward, but the meeting went on forever. You know how it is."

I do. One problem with having a town full of psychics is that you also have a town full of residents convinced that a closer cell tower will microwave their brains.

Jonathan continues, "The meeting ended just before midnight, and I swung by to see if Ani was still up. The house was dark. I went back to my place and got an hour of sleep before bolting awake. Something at your sisters' place had been poking at me."

"What?"

"Their car was gone."

Our mom's old car rarely leaves the driveway. Unstable is a walking town, and we live on the main street.

"I ran back to the house," Jonathan says, "and found a note on the business entrance. It said they had an emergency job, and the shop would be closed for a day or two."

It's a plausible explanation. Other curse weavers call us in for urgent cases. Legend says we're descended from the leader of the *arae*, which makes us stronger weavers. We also get calls from other magic workers who stumble over a cursed object.

"But Ani wouldn't leave without telling you or me," I say. "If she had an urgent call . . ."

When I don't finish, Jonathan nods. "If that call came at night, she'd wait to tell us in the morning."

"But she was supposed to see you last night. She'd find a way to let you know she'd be gone."

He shrugs. "She must have forgotten."

"Nothing is urgent enough for Ani to forget you're coming over."

"Well, then, she knew I'd see the car gone and read the note on the business door."

I don't like that answer. I really don't. Ani is as conscientious as Jonathan. She'd have e-mailed a full explanation so he didn't worry.

"This isn't an urgent situation, K," he says. "I just wanted to let you know. Now we'll sit down, have our healthy breakfast and wait for Ani to wake up and text us from wherever she is."

That resolution lasts about as long as my decision not to grab a ShareCar and drive to Unstable at dawn. Jonathan and I manage a few sips of coffee and two bites of our muffins. Then it's 7:30, an hour past Ani's morning alarm.

A new text goes unread. Two calls go unanswered. Same with my texts and calls to Hope, and Jonathan's texts and calls to Ani. While it made sense that she didn't get my texts at home, there's no way her emergency just happened to take her to a cell-free zone. She's in trouble.

By 7:50, I'm outside the door to Connolly's office, with Jonathan downstairs, ready to intercede in case anything goes wrong. Connolly is the first person there, and as he steps off the elevator, he's reading a newspaper. The financial section, not surprisingly. He's so engrossed in it that he walks up to his office, reaches for the knob and nearly grabs me in a very inappropriate place.

Seeing where his hand is heading, he jerks back, paper rustling. In a blink, he recovers and nods. "Good morning, Ms. Bennett. Dare I hope your early arrival means you're willing to hear my proposal?"

"No, but I am willing to hear what the hell you meant about my sisters last night. In fact, I'm going to insist on it."

"Good. I'm glad you're finally seeing reason."

He folds the paper and then walks to his office with such nonchalance that my hands itch to grab him around the neck and shake him.

When he takes off his overcoat and begins to smooth it, I snap, "Are you trying to piss me off?"

"I am composing myself for what is obviously going to be an antagonistic conversation while wondering whether it would be rude to make a coffee before we talk."

"God, you really are an asshole, aren't you?"

He turns a cool gaze on me. "You've pounced on me as I come into work. Not only have I agreed to speak to you, but I'm acknowledging that coffee—which I desperately need right now—should probably wait. Now may I please hang up my—"

"My sisters are missing. They disappeared sometime yesterday. Likely around the time you offered me a job, and when I refused to hear you out, you said maybe they would do it instead."

He pauses, as if processing my words. Then his brows rise. "Are you suggesting I *kidnapped* them?"

"I'm suggesting they are missing right after you mentioned going to with this job. And when I said I'd warn them first, you seemed very unconcerned."

"Because I—" He glances toward the front door. "May we speak somewhere else, please? Perhaps in your showroom? My staff will arrive at any moment."

I march to the reception desk, scribble something onto a large sticky note and slap it on the front door. Connolly walks over to read it.

"Fumigation?" He shakes his head. "Please hand me that marker and a new piece of paper. I'll simply ask them to stay out—"

"Fumigation or biological contamination," I say. "Your choice."

He sighs. "May we at least adjourn to the staff room where I might make a coffee? I had a very long night, and I have a feeling you'll need me to be more coherent than I can manage right now."

I haven't taken a close look at him, being too freaked out about my sisters. Now I notice the purple underscoring his eyes and the first hint of lines at his mouth. Two bright red acne-like spots are, on closer inspection, shaving nicks. His freckles, barely visible yesterday, weave a connect-the-dots pattern across his nose and cheekbones.

While Connolly looks exhausted, he also looks far more human than he did yesterday. Like an actual person rather than an automaton programmed to piss me off.

"Fine," I mutter. "Get your damned coffee."

His shoulders sag in visible relief. "Thank you."

I follow him into the staff room, which is just as ice cold—in decor and temperature—as the rest of the office suite. That reminds me that he'd been considerate enough to plan a more comfortable staff room, and some of my own chill thaws . . . until I remember that was a ruse. A lie to trick and test me.

Connolly walks to the coffee maker, one of those expensive espresso jobs. At the click of a button, it begins grinding beans for a single serving.

"Would you like one?" he asks, raising his voice to be heard over the whirring.

"No, what I'd like is to talk about my *missing sisters*. You don't seem surprised that they're gone."

He fusses with the machine. "If you'd let me explain last night—"

"Don't condescend to me, Connolly. I had every reason to get the hell out of here after you trapped me. Do you know what happened to my sisters?"

"If you're asking whether I personally kidnapped them—"

"Of course, you didn't. Guys like you don't do your own dirty work."

"True." His tone stays infuriatingly calm. "I hire people to perform tasks outside my area of expertise. As I tried to hire you last night." He lifts the mug, takes a sip and exhales in satisfaction. "Are you sure you wouldn't like a cup?"

I unclench my teeth enough to say, "I'd like to have this conversation. Start talking. Now. Or else . . ."

I open my purse.

"Let me guess," he says. "You brought your Magic 8 Ball."

That *is* what I was about to pull out, but when he glances into my purse, he goes still.

"Is that . . . a gun?" he says.

I flip out the tiny derringer. "Cute, huh? It was a going-away gift from my sister's friend. To keep me safe in the big, bad city."

When I glance up, Connolly has inched back.

"Really? *This* scares you?" I wave the gun. "Believe me, my curse bomb is way worse. Look how tiny this thing is. It'd barely put a hole in you."

"That gun is quite capable of killing someone."

"Is it? Huh. Then maybe we should try this again." I aim the derringer at him. "Do you know where my sisters are?"

He swallows and then visibly pulls himself together, his gaze wrenching from the gun barrel and lifting to meet mine. When he speaks, the words come slow and careful, so I cannot misunderstand them.

"I did not kidnap them, and I don't know who did. However, I believe I know why they were taken. That's what I was going to discuss with you."

"When? After you drank your whole damned coffee? These are my *sisters* we're talking about."

"I understand that, and I apologize if it seemed I wasn't taking this seriously. I am."

"Good." I lift the gun. "So where are my sisters?"

"I just told you. I don't have them."

"Are you sure?"

"Yes."

"Really, really sure?"

"Yes. Now please lower the—"

I pull the trigger. A spot of red explodes on the wall behind Connolly. He stumbles against the coffee maker and stares down at his chest.

"I aimed beside you," I say.

He squints at the bright red spot on the wall, far too crimson to be blood.

"Jinx," I say, twirling the fake gun. "It's a nice piece, though. Specially made just for me. *So* much fun in paintball. Do you play?"

Connolly's expression suggests he really wishes he had a gun right now. And not a fake one.

"Did you really think anyone would buy me a real gun?" I say. "Hell, *I* wouldn't buy me one. But thank you for confirming that you don't have my sisters. Now let's talk about who does."

"I am not talking to you about anything, Ms. Bennett. You just—"

"Shot *beside* you with a *fake* bullet? I wouldn't have pulled out the gun if you hadn't noticed it in my purse. At that point, if I *didn't* threaten you with it, you wouldn't have taken me seriously. My sisters are missing. I'll keep saying that until you get it."

"I do get it. I apologize if I seemed to be stalling. I was collecting myself and preparing for what is likely to be a long conversation."

"Ready now?"

"I am."

"Good. Get yourself another coffee, and we'll talk in your office."

CHAPTER SEVEN

"Are you sure I can't make you a coffee?" Connolly asks as we walk into his office.

"Yeah, no. Weirdly, not in the mood."

He pauses, cup to his lips, and then lowers it and nods. "Yes, of course. I'm sorry. That was thoughtless of me."

I settle myself into the visitor's chair, fussing more than necessary so he doesn't see my expression. I don't know what to make of Aiden Connolly. I've called him an asshole more than once. Yesterday morning, though, my assessment was "kind of an asshole," and I think that's more accurate. In many ways, he's your stereotypical successful young businessman. Condescending and overconfident to the point of arrogance. Yet whenever he's about to tip over into full asshole-mode, he has the grace to admit he's overstepped. It's as if his brain doesn't process "how would this make someone feel?" as fast as mine does, and his emotional wiring needs an extra surge to leap the gap between self-concern and empathy.

Or maybe he's just a clever asshole who knows his target isn't going to put up with that bullshit, so he's dialing it back and feigning contrition.

As I settle in, struggling to mask my confusion, I text Jonathan. I tell him all is well, and I'm certain Connolly doesn't have Ani and Hope because he stuck to his story even when I held him at gunpoint. Jonathan pops back a thumbs-up, as if there is nothing the least bit alarming in that statement.

As I lower my phone, Connolly says, "First, are you absolutely certain your sisters are missing?"

"I'm certain they aren't home. I'm also certain that they aren't answering texts, calls or e-mails. Is it possible I'm overreacting? Sure. So you can skip that part."

"I wasn't going to suggest that. If this is unusual behavior for them, then yes, I believe there's a very good chance they've been taken."

"Because you knew they were in danger. Yet you failed to mention that last night."

He steeples his fingers on the desktop. "If you'd listened to my job offer—"

At a look from me, his hands shoot up. "That was uncalled for. I apologize. If I actually thought they were in danger, I would have warned you."

"You wanted to hire me for a job. Presumably, unweaving a curse. If my sisters have been kidnapped, and you think it's connected, that's because there are other parties involved. You're working for someone who needs an object uncursed."

Connolly fixes me with a cool look. "I don't hire myself out like a common laborer, Ms. Bennett."

"Ah, right. Common laborer. That'd be me, right? The chick you *were* trying to hire."

He hesitates. Then he picks up a silver pen, fidgeting with it before realizing what he's doing and setting it back down.

"You have a knack for twisting words and intentions, Ms. Bennett."

"Not sure how else I could have interpreted that one. What you really mean is that I have a knack for calling you out when you're being a dick. People don't generally do that to you, do they? At least, not people you consider common laborers."

He lifts the pen again. "Shall I write 'I apologize for being a dick' and just hold it up at regular intervals so we can move this conversation along?"

I can't help smiling a little at that. "Or you could try not being a dick."

"Genetically impossible. If you ever meet my parents, you'll understand. No one has hired me. I'm one of several people pursuing an object. The most famous cursed object in history."

"And you accuse *me* of being dramatic."

He opens a desk drawer, withdraws a folded newspaper and extends it. As I take the paper, I realize it's actually a supermarket tabloid. Below the fold is a photograph of a woman in a coffin. She's about my age, and even post-embalming, she's drop-dead gorgeous. According to the headline, the dead woman—one Josephine Hill-Cabot—is . . .

"Ninety-seven?" I say.

"Exactly," Connolly says smugly.

"Uh, I hate to break it to you, Connolly, but this is a tabloid. It also has articles on . . ." I flip pages. "Hillary Clinton's alien love child and a man whose sneeze blew off all his wife's hair."

Connolly reaches into the drawer for another folded paper. This one is the *New York Times*, with a much smaller article stating that the wealthy Hill-Cabot clan is embroiled in an inheritance scandal after claiming that a deceased woman in her twenties was their reclusive matriarch, Josephine. The article also notes that DNA results confirm their bizarre story, and so police are now investigating the possibility of a larger scam involving medical personnel.

"Damn," I say. "Huh. But eternal youth wouldn't be a curse, not unless . . ."

My head shoots up. "The Necklace of Harmonia?"

Connolly's lips twitch. "The most famous cursed object in history. Or is that being overdramatic?"

My attention snaps back to the articles, devouring the words now.

He continues, "I'm not sure how much you know about the necklace and the mythology surrounding it."

I point at my face.

"Yes," he says. "It's Greek myth, and your mother was Greek. Your father partly Greek, too, if I'm correct. That doesn't mean you know the mythology."

"I didn't mean my cultural background," I say. "I mean what I am. A curse weaver. The living embodiment of Greek myth. So yeah, I know all about the Necklace of Harmonia. Short version: the wearer is blessed with eternal youth and beauty but cursed with great misfortune. Some say it also confers wealth, but others argue the eternal youth and beauty help amass wealth. Either way, you'll be young and healthy and rich . . . and your life will suck in every possible way."

"As it did for Josephine Hill-Cabot. Three marriages. All three husbands died, all in tragic accidents."

"So you think Josephine had the Necklace of Harmonia."

He passes over another photograph, a black-and-white shot showing Hill-Cabot as a bride. Around her neck, two serpents clasp a jeweled sun between their mouths.

"Either that's the real necklace, or it's a gorgeous reproduction," I say. "Let me guess. You said there were other interested parties. After Josephine's death, you've all realized she had the necklace, and now you're madly racing to steal it from the Hill-Cabot vault. I think I've seen this movie."

"Do I look like a thief, Ms. Bennett? I'm a businessman. As you saw, the family isn't able to claim their inheritance, given the suspicious circumstances of Josephine's death. So they've discreetly put several items up for sale. One is the necklace. They had several interested buyers, so it's being offered in a very exclusive auction in just a few days. All those buyers are part of the magical community, where it's theorized that a skilled curse weaver could remove the hex."

"Leaving only the charms: eternal youth and beauty."

He leans back in his chair. "You'd consider eternal beauty and youth a blessing then?"

"Pfft. No." I wave at the photo. "That kind of beauty is nothing but trouble. And eternal youth? How long did Josephine manage to live in the real world before she went all Howard Hughes? At some point, you can't keep crediting genetics and moisturizers . . ."

I trail off. "You think it's *all* curse. The beauty and youth part is a trick. A trap. The wearer thinks they're getting an awesome gift in return for a bit of bad luck. Instead, it's all bad." My gaze lifts to his. "Joker's jinx."

He smiles, and it isn't his usual smug smirk. It's a genuine smile, his green eyes crackling with summer's warmth where, a moment ago, there'd been nothing but winter chill.

"That's why you wanted to hire me," I say. "Others are looking to combine a weaver with a charm caster, and you think they've got it wrong. What they need is an expert in one particular curse. The joker's jinx."

"Exactly."

I shake my head. "I'm flattered, but I'm still not sure it's enough. That is one serious curse. The biggest of them all. It would take more than just skill to unweave it. It'd take—"

"Luck?" He smiles again, that summery blaze of a smile. "That's where I come in."

I have a bit of luck now and then.

"You're a—" I begin.

"I am indeed." He leans back in his chair, that smug look back.

"Wow. I've never met an actual leprechaun."

He sits upright so fast the chair squeals. "A what?"

"Leprechaun. I should have guessed. You mentioned luck. You're Irish. You have red hair. You're not overly tall."

He straightens. "The average American male is five foot nine, I am five nine and a half."

"That's . . . oddly specific. Also, interesting that you know that particular piece of trivia. Still, I didn't say you were short. Just not overly tall. Which I'd expect from a—"

"I am not a leprechaun. There's no such thing."

I eye him. "Are you sure? Because you—"

"I'm a luck worker."

"Mmm, luck workers are Italian. Descended from the Roman goddess Fortuna. Leprechauns, on the other hand—"

"—do not exist," he says, his voice chilling. "If you are at all familiar with Celtic history, you will know Britain was invaded by Rome."

"Yes, but not Ireland."

"There was still a mingling of bloodlines. The Connollys trace part of their lineage to Rome. The part that makes them luck workers."

I open my mouth, but he cuts me off with, "I can bring the required luck to your weaving. That is all that matters."

"Mmm, no. What matters is that my sisters are missing. I presume you're implying they've been kidnapped by someone else hoping to unweave the curse."

He nods. "When I went to research curse weavers, your family was the first name to come up. That is, apparently, what happens when you run an actual business removing curses."

"Are you suggesting that if they're kidnapped, it's our own damned fault?"

"Not . . . really. Although one could say—"

"One could, but one should not."

He raises his pen for emphasis. "My point is simply that it seems unwise—"

The pen bursts, ink spraying his white shirt. He startles back and then looks from the pen to me.

"That was my favorite pen."

"Tragic. Now—"

He hesitates. "Did you jinx it earlier?"

"That would be wrong. I need a reason."

"But you didn't touch it. Curse weaving requires physical contact with an object."

"Does it? Well, then, the exploding pen was a coincidence."

He turns it over in his hands. "It's true, then. Your family has a little extra. That's what the rumors say. You're the direct descendants of the leader of the *arae*."

"Maybe. Or maybe you're just really *un*lucky. At least when it comes to favorite pens."

"You can weave minor curses from a distance without any materials. That is definitely a show of power. It's also the real reason your sisters were targeted. Well, that and the fact they're very easy to find, running a business—"

"You do like that pen, right? And you'd eventually like it *un*cursed?"

He sets the pen down.

"Yes," I say. "My family openly practices unweaving. Has for centuries. Do you know how many times it's led to kidnapping?" I make a zero with my forefinger and thumb. "What's the point in forcing us to uncurse something when we do it for a living?"

"If it's a famous and potentially dangerous curse? On an object so valuable that any gifted curse weaver would insist on full profit sharing?" He glances at the pen. "I will concede your point, though."

"And refrain from suggesting that the victims had it coming? That if they didn't want to be attacked, they shouldn't be flaunting their stuff, strutting around in a mini-skirt, metaphorically speaking?"

Spots of color heat his cheeks. "I . . . did not intend it that way."

"Then stop saying it. Please."

"I will. Yes, hiring your sisters is the obvious solution. Obvious to me but"—he shrugs—"perhaps they tried. Perhaps they skipped that step. Whatever the reason, our course is clear. We need to find your sisters—"

"Really hoping that *we* is also metaphorical."

His brows knit. "I don't see how it could be."

"I can find my sisters. Just give me the information."

"I don't have information. I have vague leads. Which I will share as we hunt for your sisters together—"

"Metaphorically together?"

"I have the information you need. I also have the contacts you need. You have the curse-weaving skill *I* need. We'll find your sisters, and if I win the auction, you'll uncurse the necklace, for which I will pay you twenty-five percent of the original purchase price."

"I don't want the money. I just want my sisters."

He waves away my words. "You're concerned for them now. Once you have them, you'll want the money. It's obvious you could use it."

"*Excuse* me?"

"Unless you want me to find your sisters alone. That would drop your share to ten percent, but I'm willing to consider it."

"I don't give a shit about the money. But I'm not going to sit on my hands while you search for my missing sisters, either."

"Excellent, then we are agreed. I'm hiring you—"

"No. You aren't *hiring* me for anything, Connolly. I'm not your employee."

"Of course you aren't. This is only a contract position—"

"Not an employee."

"A service provider, then, and I am your client—"

"Nope." I cross my arms. "Employer or client, either way, that'd make you my boss. That ain't happening. Equal partners or nothing."

He shakes his head. "I don't have partners, Ms. Bennett. I have employees and service providers." He lifts his pen and pulls out a checkbook. "Let me write you a retainer. Proof of my sincerity as your new employer—"

Ink explodes, splattering his shirt again. He turns cool eyes on me.

"Would you please stop doing that?" he says.

"Would you please stop deserving that?" I say. "I'm not your employee. Not your service provider. We are partners, or I walk away and you find another experienced curse weaver who specializes in the joker's jinx, one who will put up with your shit. That last part's going to be toughest."

He hesitates, pen still poised over the ruined checkbook. "I have no experience with partnerships and—"

"Step one, stop calling me Ms. Bennett. You may mean it to be respectful, but it sounds condescending. My name is Kennedy."

Another hesitation, longer this time. "I suppose then that you may call me Aid—"

"No need. I like Connolly. Now, let me call in my associate. He's waiting downstairs."

Connolly's brows rise.

"You trapped me here last night," I say. "I wasn't coming alone. Jonathan is an old friend from Unstable."

Connolly frowns. "Does he have a magical power?"

"He doesn't need one." I take out my phone. "He's a librarian."

CHAPTER EIGHT

I want to hit the road ASAP. Roar out of here in hot pursuit of my sisters. Which would require a) a car, b) some sucker willing to look after my cat, and c) a vague notion of where to actually find Ani and Hope. Having none of these, I must yield to Jonathan's suggestion that we discuss it with Connolly over a real breakfast. Not that I want breakfast. Really, absolutely, definitely do not want breakfast. But Jonathan insists, and when the server brings out the breakfast sandwich he ordered for me, on fresh-baked focaccia, I must admit my stomach rumbles.

We're eating in the courtyard behind a coffee shop. Inside, it's wall-to-wall pre-caffeinated zombies. Out here, we're the only occupied table. That doesn't keep Connolly from grumbling about discussing this in a public place.

"It has heat," I say, pointing to the sun. "Which is more than I can say for your office."

Connolly turns his cool stare on me. I'm not even sure it's the courtyard he disapproves of as much as the company. He hasn't said a direct word to Jonathan beyond hello.

Some men are like that around physically intimidating guys. Connolly hasn't struck me as that type, though, and despite his penchant for business wear, he obviously spends some time at the gym. I decide he just really doesn't like bringing someone else into this. That would explain why he keeps looking from Jonathan to me and back again, as if assessing.

"So you're a luck worker," Jonathan says with an easy smile. "I should have figured you weren't just a guy who knows about curses. If I'd done my research,"—he lifts his phone—"I'd have put two-and-two together. Boston. Connolly. Magic. Luck workers."

Connolly leans to look at the screen. "Where did you find that?"

Jonathan shrugs. "In my files." He peers down at the screen. "Connollys, originally from Cork, Ireland. Arrived in Boston in 1825. There are several branches in the area, but you'd be the son of Liam, who's married to Marion O'Sullivan, also from a family of luck workers. They have two sons, Aiden and Rian."

"You have our file on your phone?" Connolly says. "A file identifying my *family* as luck workers?"

"It's secure," I say. "Without a passcode, even the owner can't unlock an iPhone. I learned that the hard way last year. Got so accustomed to using facial recognition that I blanked on my code. Lost a year of photos."

"Backups," Jonathan says.

"Yeah, yeah. I came up with a better solution. Now I carefully catalog all my passwords in a notebook."

Connolly stares at me.

"She's kidding," Jonathan says. "Or, if she's not, it's a cursed notebook, and the ink will turn invisible if the wrong fingers touch it. As for my phone, I have an extra password on my custom-made file app. The data is also encrypted." He turns a deceptively bland look on Connolly. "I do know what I'm doing."

"I still think—"

"Don't," I say. "Or if you must, then stick with thinking and not saying. Jonathan's data is secure, and even if it wasn't?" I throw up my hands. "The Bennetts run a business uncursing objects. We're listed in the Better Business Bureau with an A+ rating. No one's banging down our door to burn us as witches. No one cares."

"Except the people who kidnapped your sisters."

I pause. "Touché. Can we talk about that now? Please? This sandwich is delicious, but I really want to get moving."

• • •

I TOLD Connolly that I know the story behind the Necklace of Harmonia. True, though, later I'll run my recollection through the Jonathan-wiki to be certain I'm remembering everything correctly.

I also told Connolly the Bennetts are the living embodiment of Greek myth. That's a bit of a boast, though not far off. You won't find the *arae* in your elementary school primer on Greek and Roman mythology. It takes some digging to get to them, and even then, details are sketchy. They're curse spirits best known for punishing the living on behalf of the dead.

Our family version is a little different. Mom and Yiayia—her mother—always debated the exact nature of the *arae*. Were they gods? Minor deities? Or just women who had a special talent and were elevated to semidivine status for it? We'll never know.

Back to the Necklace of Harmonia. It has the sort of history you expect from Greek myth with innocents suffering for the gods' inability to keep their togas wrapped. In this case, it was Aphrodite, goddess of love, shacking up with Ares, god of war. That'd be fine if she didn't have a husband at home and, apparently, no open-marriage contract. Hephaestus, understandably, was a bit annoyed that his wife was off gallivanting with a hot young god while he slaved over a hot furnace fire and vowed revenge.

Aphrodite and Ares's first child, Harmonia, grows up to marry a prince, and Hephaestus gives her the wedding gift of a gorgeous necklace he made himself. The Necklace of Harmonia.

In the myth, the curse doesn't begin life with the full eternal-youth-and-eternal-misfortune hex, maybe because the earliest owners were gods. Instead, it turned Harmonia and her husband, Cadmus, into serpents, but only after a long life together. Harmonia's daughter, Semele, inherited the necklace and died after insisting on viewing Zeus's true form.

Fast forward a few generations, though, and the curse takes on its current form. Queen Jocasta enjoys youth and beauty . . . until she accidentally marries her son, which is, really, the epitome of misfortune. From there, the necklace passes in and out of human hands, bringing beauty and destruction wherever it goes.

In myth, the necklace's last-known location was around the neck of an ancient Phoenician tyrant's mistress as she perished in a fire set by her own son. In the magical world, though, stories about the necklace continued. The last I heard, the necklace had been bought by a rich American at the turn of the twentieth century. Curse weavers love to speculate on the buyer's identity. Jack Astor, purchasing it just before setting foot on the Titanic? Benjamin Guggenheim, who also died on that ill-fated ship? Joe Kennedy Sr., whose descendants continue to be plagued by misfortune?

So it's no surprise that it ended up around the neck of Josephine Hill-Cabot, who in her youth had been the debutante of the decade, the gorgeous and accomplished heiress to the Hill fortune. Jonathan confirms that both the Hill and Cabot families were on the list of those suspected to own the necklace.

When Josephine's death sparked tabloid stories—and then her necklace appeared on the black market—the magical community took one look at the design and knew what it was. Connolly might have dismissed my comparison to those old-school Hollywood capers, everyone jockeying to steal or swindle a rare object, but I wasn't far off. Interested parties *are* assembling their crews. But instead of safe crackers and demolitions experts and computer hackers, they're hiring curse weavers, charm casters and luck workers.

"So why hasn't anyone else tried to hire us?" I ask.

"Timing," Connolly says. "When multiple buyers expressed interest, the Hill-Cabots switched to an auction. That gives everyone time to plan. I was able to move quickly, having already determined that a strong candidate lived in my city."

"You came to me with a fake job, hoping to test me for a real one," I say.

"Exactly."

"Treating me like a poseur instead of a responsible member of the magical community, which my reputation would tell you I am."

When Connolly's mouth opens, Jonathan cuts in with, "But it seems you weren't the only one moving fast."

"No," Connolly says. "Whoever took your sisters obviously didn't waste time negotiating to hire them properly."

"Do you know who that might be?" I say.

"I know possibilities."

"If you give me names, I'll compile dossiers," Jonathan says.

"First, I'm going to have to ask for proof that there is an auction. Whatever you can supply. I don't mean to sound suspicious . . ."

Connolly nods. "Understandable."

Connolly takes out his phone, and I don't know what he shows Jonathan, but it's obviously satisfactory. They start talking. I know all this is important, but I want to shout "Just give me a name, damn it!" Toss one of those possibilities my way and let me run with it. Which is entirely the wrong way to go about this.

As they discuss names I don't recognize, I check my messages, trying to focus on something other than the fact that my sisters are missing. I end up in our text thread, staring at yesterday's exchange as tears prickle.

Such a normal conversation. That's the way it goes, though, isn't it? I still have my last texts from Dad. I'd been running to class, and he'd sent me plans for Mom's birthday. I'd popped back "Can't talk! Later?"

Later.

Sometimes, later never comes.

This will be different. Whoever took my sisters just wants them to uncurse the necklace. Hope might balk, but Ani will be reasonable. She'll keep them safe, and by next week, I'll be sending them another text just like this one, giving them shit for directing another potential client my way and . . .

"Joker's jinx," I whisper.

"Hmm?" Jonathan says, fingers poised over his cell phone as if he'd been typing.

I turn to Connolly. "That guy yesterday. The one with the tea caddy."

"Tea . . . ?"

"The box with the cat on it. He said it was cursed with a joker's jinx and that my sisters sent him. They insisted they didn't."

Jonathan nods. "Ani mentioned that. She said she didn't send him. She figured Hope did, but Hope swore otherwise. Ani decided to drop it unless you brought it up again."

"Which I wouldn't have. I figured Hope did it, and I moved on. If they didn't send him . . ."

"Then some random guy just happened to show up with a joker's jinx?" Jonathan says.

"*Not* random," I say. "I didn't presume my sisters sent him. He said they did. He brought me that box on purpose."

"Testing you," Connolly murmurs. "As I did. I would have preferred a jinx, but the weaver I visited had a very limited repertoire."

"So two people tested me in one day? That doesn't make sense."

"What other answer is there?" Connolly says. "He knew it was a joker's jinx. He brought it to test you, and I frightened him off."

"*Frightened* him off?" I say. "Uh, no, sorry. You *pissed* him off."

"Then he stormed out and left the box. Does that make sense if it was a test? He left too easily. Almost as if that was what he planned to do all along."

I shove to my feet and whisper, "The *box*."

I'm striding out as Jonathan catches up. Connolly takes an extra moment to realize we're leaving the cafe entirely. I wait until he's with us before I continue.

"He *planned* to leave the box," I say. "He probably expected I'd agree to uncurse it, and he could leave it with me. When Connolly told him off, he used that excuse to abandon it."

"But you've uncursed it by now, haven't you?" Connolly asks.

"I didn't have time."

"You left a *cursed box*—"

"It's a minor curse," I say. "I intended to fix it last night, but your mirror seemed more important. I was going to unweave it today." I glance at Jonathan. "Can you give me a ride to the showroom?"

"Absolutely."

Connolly lifts a key fob. "My car is closer."

I shake my head. "Thank you, but Jonathan and I can handle this."

"That wasn't an offer. We have a deal. I've shared valuable information, and I'm not letting you two ride off and leave me on the sidelines."

I open my mouth and then stop. Bickering isn't going to get my sisters back. I need to grit my teeth and get through this. "Fine.

Jonathan? Would you mind getting Ellie? We'll need to hit the road after this."

"Ellie?" Connolly says.

"My cat."

Connolly opens his mouth, but Jonathan cuts him off with. "Got it. Anything else?"

"Just the cat. Thank you." I hand him my keys. "I owe you one."

He smiles. "Never. Friends don't keep score, remember?"

My breath catches at that. They're Ani's words. *Friends don't keep score. Family doesn't keep score.* That's how our parents raised us.

Where are you, Ani?

Are you safe? Are you okay?

"Ms. Bennett?" Connolly says, glancing at me.

"It's Kennedy," I say. "Now let's go see what's up with that tea caddy."

CHAPTER NINE

I'M STANDING in my showroom, and I think I'm going to throw up. Double over and vomit, and then curl up on the floor and sob. I've been holding it together. Fighting every impulse to grab Ellie and my toothbrush and hit the road, searching for my sisters.

To quell panic, my impulsive mind needs plans. They are the guardrails for my bumper-car brain, restraining its wild pinging and keeping me on track. First, I would investigate the cursed tea caddy, which was almost certainly not a random drop-off and therefore could be connected to the Necklace of Harmonia auction and my sisters' disappearance. In the interest of further efficiency, Connolly had dropped me off while he parked. All I needed to do was find the tea caddy. I walked into my showroom and . . .

I walked in and found *this*. It's as if someone has slammed a wall into my path. I want to throw up and cry and say "I can't do this." My sisters have been kidnapped, and their lives depend on me—*me!* —and I am not the sister for this. I should have been taken, and Ani should be hunting for us.

The bell over the showroom door announces Connolly's arrival. His footsteps stop short, and I feel his gaze on my back.

"Did you forget where you put the box?" he asks.

I don't answer. I just stand there, staring at the destruction all around me.

"We need a more methodical way of looking for it," he says.

"You can't just go ripping things up, Kennedy, however upset you might be. Someone will think you've had a break-in."

And there it is. A beacon in the darkness, showing me the way back. Giving me a target for everything I'm feeling right now, my despair solidifying into a lightning bolt of rage.

Before I can get out a word, he takes another step and sees the ruination. Really sees it. Not just one dresser with its drawers pulled out or a single vase accidentally toppled and shattered, but smashed china and splintered wood covering my showroom floor.

"Oh," he says. "You *did* have a break-in. I hope you have insurance."

Something inside me snaps, and it must show on my face because Connolly has the sense to inch backward before he stops himself and pulls up straight.

"Good insurance is—"

"Finish that sentence, and I swear I won't shoot past you this time," I say. "And if you dare—*dare*—to try selling me insurance right now, I'll use real bullets."

His eyes chill. "I would never be so gauche. I was simply saying that if you do have insurance, it will be covered, and if you don't—" He stops there, wisely clipping off the rest.

"I have insurance," I say, "but I have no idea whether it covers someone breaking in to my showroom and intentionally—" I look around, the words seizing. I blink back tears. "I don't know whether I'm covered, and right now, it doesn't matter. It just . . ."

It hurts. I'm looking at the destruction of pieces I nursed back to health, uncursing and repairing and polishing. Now they are corpses around me. That shouldn't matter. My sisters are so much more important. This just feels like gasoline thrown on a fire I've kept tamped down to a manageable size.

"It doesn't matter," I say, turning away abruptly. "It can't."

"But it still does."

His voice is soft, and it startles me. He stands in the dim light, watching me. Just watching, not judging, and that single droplet of kindness feels like a wave of it, and I want to throw my arms around his neck in gratitude. I imagine how he'd react to that, and a bubble of laughter rises, chasing away the despair.

"Thank you," I say.

I survey the damage and exhale. "Insurance should cover it. I have a good policy. More than I could afford, honestly, but this isn't the best neighborhood."

"I doubt this is random vandalism, Kennedy. That would be highly coincidental."

"I know." Another deep exhale. "Let's just—" I stop short. "The tea caddy. What if they were looking for that?"

As I run through the debris, Connolly strides toward my tiny office.

"The door has been jimmied open." He pops his head in. "If the box was in your office, I'm afraid it's gone. The room has been thoroughly searched."

"Then it's a good thing it wasn't in there."

"You don't lock up cursed objects?"

I ignore him and drag aside a toppled armoire. Under it, the floorboards seem no different from the rest, but my practiced fingers find the latch. A section of the floor springs up to reveal an ancient safe door. I enter the combination and open it. Inside is a large cavity, big enough to hold pretty much any antique smaller than that armoire. Clutching the edge, I reach down until my gloved fingers touch the tea caddy. I lever up and hold it overhead. Connolly bends to inspect the hidey-hole.

"This place was once a jeweler's shop," I say. "The safe was a selling point for me. A place to store objects awaiting uncursing. Marginally more responsible than putting them into my office, right? Or leaving them just lying about."

He dips his chin in what might be an apology. I don't needle him further. He'll ease off, or he won't, and I'll just keep reminding myself this is a very temporary partnership.

I take the tea caddy to my workbench, which had once stood discreetly behind an antique dressing screen, now in pieces on the floor. Connolly nudges a broken wood panel with his shoe.

"This destruction seems more than someone searching for an item. It's not as if you could have hidden a box within these panels."

"First, we don't know they were searching for anything. Second, if they were, how better to cover their tracks than to make it look like vandalism?"

"True. But I was thinking this seems more like a statement. Or a threat. Did you have any unusual appointments lately? Someone offering you an atypical job?"

"Besides you?" I set the caddy down. "You think someone else might have been trying to hire me. Someone I refused to see or a job I refused to take. No, nothing like that. But . . ." I open the tea caddy. "Grab my phone out of my back pocket."

He hesitates. I sigh and start to close the caddy, but he waves for me to continue and removes my phone with all the care one might use to remove a bomb from its casing.

"Raise it," I say as I shine a penlight into the caddy.

He does, and the phone registers my face and unlocks.

"Go to my calendar," I say. "Check my appointments from the last few days. See whether any of those names look familiar in case someone else *was* scoping me out for this job. Or scoping out my showroom, hoping I kept my unweaving kit here."

"Would the kit help anyone without your abilities?" he asks as he thumbs through my appointments.

"No, but it *would* help another curse weaver. You can give my family shit for practicing our craft openly, but it means we've been refining that craft for hundreds of years. My kit is worth more than anything in this shop."

I glance over at him. "I don't suppose you offer insurance for that?"

"I could." He doesn't lift his gaze from my phone. "While I mostly sell the standard sort, I do insure magical objects, as well as offering more . . . general insurance."

"General? Ah, that's where the luck working comes in."

"Hmm."

I want to ask more, but this isn't the time, and his vague response suggests he wouldn't answer anyway. Later, then.

"Find anything?" I ask.

"Not in the last few days, but you do have an appointment this morning."

"I canceled it. Left her a message earlier."

"When did she make the appointment?"

"Yesterday evening." I glance at him. "After you'd been here. You think she could have been someone planning to bid on the necklace?"

"I don't recognize the name, and yet . . ." He shakes his head and glances toward the front of the shop. "Does your door alert keep a record of when it goes off? That might tell us what time someone broke in."

"It's just a bell. I had to choose between a security system and insurance, and Ani said insurance was more important."

"She's correct." He walks to the front door and examines it. "It's been jimmied open. That would be easy enough to do with an old lock like this. Which is an observation, not a criticism."

"Thank you. Yes, it's old and shitty, and it would have been easy to break." I poke at the inside of the tea caddy. "About that canceled appointment. Would you mind searching the name? Get more info on her? In case she's connected."

"Good idea." He takes out his own phone. "Finding anything there?"

"Not yet. I'd already determined the curse yesterday. Minor joker's jinx, but honestly, I considered leaving it on out of respect for the weaver."

He glances up to frown at me.

"Curse weaving is always a craft," I say. "But the joker's jinx is special, at least in my opinion. Ideally, it should be fun. Maybe a little wicked, but never outright cruel. To me, that'd make it a misanthrope's malice."

"A particularly savage curse that isn't aimed at a specific target. A net cast wide to ensnare the unwary."

"Yep. Cursing innocent people just because you can. That ultimate asshole move, bordering on psychopathy. The joker's jinx is different. It can be a prank played on a certain person, or it can just be a prank, like this one."

"A random joke aimed at anyone who owns it."

"Not the owner exactly. This is an object-based curse, which means, technically, I don't need these gloves, but I'm being safe. The Necklace of Harmonia carries a curse that falls on the owner. The only way to reliably lift it is to uncurse the object while it's still in that owner's possession. If Josephine Hill-Cabot gifted the necklace to someone else, she could have passed on the curse . . . or she could have been stuck with it *plus* given it to someone else—like a communicable disease. In the disease-curse scenario, if the next owner uncursed it, that might not have helped Josephine. Just like giving medicine to the person who caught it doesn't help the person who communicated it. But, in some cases, it's a magical cure that undoes the curse all the way back down the line. So many permutations, all depending on the intent of the weaver. This, though, is an object-based curse. I can't 'catch' it. Like your leaking pen. It would leak for anyone who used it, and you could use any other pen just fine. Now that I've uncursed it, it's harmless."

"Which I appreciate."

"Oh, don't thank me yet. That which is uncursed can easily be recursed." I tap the tea caddy. "This is the same principle. The curse is a practical joke, playing on the design itself. The cat is the key."

"The cat . . . ?" He notices the cat on the lid. "Ah."

"It's a cat tea caddy," I say. "And what happens if you drink tea in a house that has a resident cat?"

His blank expression tells me he's never owned a pet.

"Hair," I say. "Cat hair everywhere." I gesture to my outfit. "I have a black cat. I also have three pairs of black jeans. These things are not unrelated. And I have lint rollers—" I grab one from under the workbench. "Everywhere. Also, before you point it out, yes, I know black cats are considered bad luck."

"It depends on the culture. Many consider them *good* luck."

"Well, Ellie never got that memo. So yes, cats shed, and no matter how hard you try, every now and then, you get a cat hair in your coffee." I nod at the caddy. "Or your tea. Store your tea in this, and it's a guarantee. Free cat hair with every cup."

"Joker's jinx."

"A minor one, which is the best kind, and it's why I was debating whether or not to remove it. With the jinx, the caddy is a fun conversation piece. Without it? It's just an antique tea caddy and, as you said, a little kitschy."

"Is there anything else about it?"

"Well, it's a helluva curse weaving, I can tell you that. Reason number two why I hesitated to remove it."

He frowns. "I thought you just said it was a *minor* jinx."

"It is, but it's an expert weaving. Seriously top-notch. I bow to the weaver."

"Is there anything else about the caddy that might attract attention?"

"Like a secret hatch? That's what I was checking." I lift the box and turn it over in my hands. "Nothing. I can't find any reason why someone would break in to steal it. You mentioned the possibility this was a test, but if so, I don't know what the guy hoped to achieve. I never confirmed that I recognized it as jinxed—you overheard our entire conversation. Sure, he could storm in today, demand it back and see whether I fixed it, but the jinx is so tiny it's hardly a test of my skill."

I set the tea caddy down. "I hate to assume this was a coincidence . . ."

"It can't be."

"Then we presume there's some meaning to the box I don't understand." I glance over. "Did you get anything on that name?"

He gives a start, as if reprimanded, though my tone was light. "No, sorry. I was distracted. Let me . . ." He hits a few icons on his phone. "Nothing. Nothing at all, which is odd. *Erin* isn't an unusual first name, and *Concord* . . . Wait." Furious tapping. "*Concord* isn't even a surname. It sounds as if it could be, but it's not."

"*Concord*," I say, picking up my own phone. "Concordia. Isn't that—"

He stops, finger poised over his phone. "Of course. It's the Roman name for Harmonia, goddess of harmony and concord. I thought something about the name seemed familiar. I've been reading everything I can find on the myth."

"*Erin* is significant, too. Concordia's Roman opposite is Discordia, goddess of discord and strife. In Greek, she's Eris. So *Erin Concord* is definitely a fake name, and definitely someone coming to see me about the necklace. Someone who apparently couldn't resist the urge to be clever."

"Hmm," Connolly says. "I may know who that is."

"Then why don't I call and say I can make the appointment after all."

He shakes his head. "She wouldn't have shown up on her own." He glances around. "This damage is . . . not what I'd expect from her, but her hirelings could have taken the initiative. In any event, there's no point speaking to her associates when I can contact her directly."

"You have a number?"

"Better than that. I have her home address and a standing invitation to visit."

I arch my brows.

"Not like that," he says. "She's long been interested in what I have to offer."

"Oh, I'm sure she has," I murmur, too low for him to do more than arch his brows in question.

"It's a bit of a drive," he says. "But she's also someone I'd like to speak to about your sisters."

I tense. "You think she could have taken them?"

"No, but she'll help us narrow down that list of suspects."

"Because she's interested in what you have to offer?"

"Precisely."

I have a feeling that is not what he seems to think it is, but either way, this seems like a very good first step. I'm about to pocket my phone when I see the tea caddy. "What should I do with this?"

"I'll bring it along," Connolly says, reaching for my gloves. "I suspect it means something. We just need to figure out what."

CHAPTER TEN

WE MEET up with Jonathan just outside the city. We've decided he'll take Ellie and return to Unstable to see what he can learn about my sisters' disappearance. In a town that small, someone must have seen something. The stop is really just a chance for me to reassure Ellie that Jonathan hasn't cat-napped her. She doesn't care. She's with Jonathan. That's all that matters.

"He's clear," Jonathan says as Connolly waits in his idling car. "I ran a basic check, made a few calls. I'd stay away from his parents, but no one has anything bad to say about Aiden Connolly. He's definitely the white sheep of the family."

"Thank you."

"Background check. Friend-finder tracking. Emergency codewords. I think you're ready to ride off into the sunset with a stranger." He pauses. "Have you asked anything about this person you're going to meet?"

"Vanessa Apsley is the name, but don't let on I told you, please. She's a dream shaper. Part of something he calls the magical gray market—not totally legit, but not a criminal enterprise, either."

"Wow. You asked for details before getting into a car with a total stranger. I'm impressed."

I sock him in the arm . . . and don't mention that I didn't ask until we'd already been in the car. Then I hug Jonathan and whisper, "You doing okay?"

He makes a face. "I'd rather be chasing Ani's kidnappers. That's a lot more heroic than cat-sitting."

"If you want to come with us—"

"No." A quick embrace. "I'm just venting. Someone should ask around town and gather data. Just"—he lowers his voice, mock-conspiratorial—"when you find Ani, tell her I got a flat tire or something. Otherwise, I'd totally have been there, busting down the door to rescue her."

I smile and squeeze his arm. "With any luck, no door-busting will be required. Ani and Hope were taken to uncurse the necklace. That makes them valuable. They won't be mistreated, and once we know who has them, we can negotiate for their release."

One last hug, and one last goodbye to Ellie—who totally ignores me—and then we're off, heading in opposite directions down the highway.

———

WE'VE BEEN on the road for an hour, and I'm ready to throw myself into traffic. Not that Connolly is a chatty driving companion. I'd be fine with that. I'd love to ask him about luck working and his insurance business. But he's busy talking . . . to other people.

He's been on the phone since we got in the car. He dug up an old Bluetooth earpiece, so I don't even get the mild entertainment of listening in on his calls. It's all business. He tells employees that the fumigation was a false alarm, but they may work from home today, and then he proceeds to conduct several appointments he's missing.

I don't do well with boredom, especially when I'm ready to scream with panic and frustration. Lacking headphones, I put my cell against my right ear and play a podcast. I have it as low as possible, but Connolly must still catch a murmur of voices—far softer than the "murmur" I'm catching through his earpiece, let me say—and he casts annoyed glances my way until I shut it off.

We're on a very dull stretch of highway. There's nothing to do. Nothing to see. Just time to worry and fret, not just about my sisters but about whether I'll survive Connolly's driving long enough to rescue them.

As I expected, Connolly drives a very nice car. High-end luxury sedan with a logo I don't recognize, but honestly, I don't know which logos I would recognize. Still, I can appreciate a fine ride with a smooth suspension and buttery leather seats that can achieve more positions than a yogi.

Connolly, sadly, drives exactly like the sort of entitled asshole who owns a car like this. He sticks to the fast lane, even when other vehicles get on his back bumper and flash to pass. If cars don't get over fast enough for *him*, he passes on the right. And I swear that with every lane change, another vehicle beeps to warn him that they're in his blind spot. He still makes his turn.

Finally, my frayed nerves can't take it anymore. I wait until he's between calls and say, "Why don't you let me drive?"

He shakes his head and starts hitting buttons on his phone.

"You have business to conduct," I say. "Business I pulled you away from. I get that. So at least let me drive while you handle it."

"I'm fine, thank you."

"It's not really a request, Connolly. I'm being polite while insisting that either you stop making calls or you let me drive."

"*Can* you drive? I thought you didn't have a car."

"Doesn't mean I don't have a license. Or that I'm not a good driver. And with a car like this, it practically drives itself. All you need to do is listen to the warning signals, like the ones telling you someone is in your blind spot."

A frown suggests he's learned to tune out that particular sound as Hope learns to tune out the alarm of every clock we buy her.

I continue. "You have insurance. The best insurance, I bet. It will cover another driver and any scrapes she gets into. It will *not* cover the damage you cause by being on your phone."

"My calls are hands-free."

I glance down at the phone, clutched in his hand. He jams the cell into the center console.

"I was trying to minimize noise," he says. "I can operate it by voice."

"It's the operation of the motor vehicle I'm concerned about. I really am insisting, Connolly. Either you let me drive, or I'll rent a vehicle. I want to live long enough to rescue my sisters."

His mouth opens, and I know an argument is coming. Then he snaps it shut and veers onto the next off-ramp.

———

For ten minutes, Connolly sits like Dad during our first driving lesson, his back ramrod straight, hands clutching whatever they can find. Then, like my dad, Connolly relaxes, if somewhat awkwardly. I'm sure he expects I'll be all over the road, chatting away, only a quarter of my attention on the car. For me, though, driving is like weaving a curse. It requires—and deserves—my full focus.

Once Connolly realizes I'm fine, he starts responding to texts and e-mails. We're nearly two hours into our trip when my phone rings. I glance over to see an unknown number.

"Could you answer that?" I ask. "Just take a message, please."

He lifts the phone, and I unlock it with a glance.

"Hello," he says. "You've reached Kennedy Bennett's phone. She's busy right now. May I take a message?"

I half expect him to beep after that. Instead, he listens and then hangs up.

"Uh, when I said 'take a message,' I didn't mean it quite so literally."

"It was phishing," he says. "They asked if you'd accept a collect call from Tehran."

"Turani?" I say, my voice rising.

"Perhaps? I thought it was Tehran, but either way—"

"Turani is my *sister's* name. Ani. Turani. After the Turani Atok curse. We're all named after famous—" I cut off the explanation. "Give me that phone."

"You're driving."

I veer onto the shoulder. "Not anymore."

"I don't think you're supposed to pull over here."

"My kidnapped sister just tried to collect call me."

I grab the phone from him. As he reaches over, I expect him to snatch the phone back, but he only turns on the hazards.

I nod my thanks as I hit redial. It rings. Rings. Rin—

"Hello?" a voice says.

"Ani? Is this Ani?" My words come out in a barely intelligible rush. "Someone called me from this number saying—"

"It's me, K."

"Oh—oh, God. Oh, God."

Tears stream down my face, the dam breaking in a tidal wave of relief, complete with hiccuping sobs as I clutch the phone, barely hearing my sister's soothing words. Connolly tries to hand me something. A handkerchief? Is that an actual handkerchief?

I wave it off and squeeze my eyes shut as I gulp breaths.

"I'm okay," I say. "Which is what I should be asking you. Are you okay? Is Hope okay? What happened?"

"I'm fine. Hope . . ."

"Is she all right?" My voice rises to glass-shattering octaves. "What's going on? Where is she?"

Connolly gestures, asking if I'd like him to take the call, presumably so we can get more coherent information. He's trying to help, but there's no way in hell I'm letting go of this lifeline to my sister.

"May we switch spots?" he asks. "Tell me where she is, and I'll start driving."

I lift a hand to brush him off. Then I stop. He's right. I interrupt whatever she's trying to tell me to ask where she is.

"I-I don't know," she says.

"Is she safe?" Connolly asks. "Is she someplace safe?"

I relay his words, and that calms her a little, the ever-practical Ani returning. "Yes. I'm safe. I'm at a gas station, where I miraculously found a payphone. The sign says Redmont Gas and Tires."

Connolly already has his phone out, typing into the search engine, hearing her before I can pass along her words. In that moment, I forgive him for at least fifty percent of the shitty things he's said and done. Maybe even seventy-five.

Before I can speak, he's out of the car and walking around to the driver's side. I scramble over the console.

"We've got it," I say. "We're on our way."

Connolly gets in and hooks up his phone to the car, the map appearing on the screen, GPS already running. I tune that out and focus on my sister.

"You were kidnapped, yes?" I say.

"I thought I heard a man's voice. Is that Jonathan?"

"Jonathan is the one who realized you were missing," I say. "He showed up at my doorstep at four a.m. because the cell tower was down at home."

Which isn't what she asked, but she interprets it as answering her question. I can explain about Connolly later.

"Yes, we were kidnapped," she says. "We were at home and—"

"Just tell me about Hope. If you're safe, then I want to know about Hope."

"I . . . I don't know. She isn't with me. I escaped and—"

I miss her next words as Connolly, obviously eavesdropping, glances over. "She escaped and left your sister behind?"

A lethal glare shuts him up and turns his attention back to the road. On the other end, Ani didn't hear him, and she's still talking.

"—thought she was in the same place. We were sedated, so all I knew was that I woke up in this rundown shack. I managed— Right. No details."

A deep breath. Part of me wants to say just go ahead and give me the full story, but a bigger part wants to shove her toward the finish line.

"I got out of my ropes," she continues. "I figured Hope was in the next room. Except there *was* no next room. Apparently, I didn't Houdini-wiggle out of my bonds. Our captors must have only half-assed secured me. Left me in a one-room hunting shack and took Hope."

"Is she sure Hope wasn't there?" Connolly asks. "Did she search the area?"

He gets another glare, and again Ani thankfully didn't overhear his words. No one is more responsible or careful than my sister, and even if she did everything possible, she's already going to blame herself.

Even without hearing Connolly, she tells me how hard she searched—looked for a basement, checked the outhouse, searched the woods for an hour before finally making her way to this gas station.

"Our captors ditched me because I was being difficult," she says. "I said we'd do whatever they needed. It was curse weaving—I knew that much. But I asked too many questions, made too many demands. I wanted them to treat us like professionals and make a business deal. I was trying to be reasonable."

"And Hope let you do all the talking. Which made them think she was the pliable one, the easily intimidated one."

Ani makes a noise that's half sigh and half growl of frustration. "You know how she is. When I take over . . ."

"She steps aside. She was letting you bluster and negotiate while she worked on an escape plan. They mistook her silence for compliance, and they decided they only needed one curse weaver."

"If I'd foreseen that, I'd have shut up. Or I'd have insisted *she* do the talking."

That isn't true. Ani couldn't have sat quietly by. Nor would she have pushed Hope to talk in case their captors did something far worse than abandon the "difficult one" in a hunting shack.

"You were rejected," I say, forcing levity into my tone. "Now if I'd been there, they'd totally have kept me. I'm the shiny, vibrant, irresistible sister."

That makes her laugh. "If you were there, K, they'd have dumped you at the first off-ramp like Dad threatened to do on every road trip. Now how far out are you?"

"Less than an hour. Plenty of time to give me all the details."

CHAPTER ELEVEN

ACCORDING TO ANI, their trouble started yesterday morning, around the same time Aiden Connolly walked into my life. Our family business is appointment only, like my showroom. There are exceptions, such as town festivals and busy summer weekends, but at this time of year, you need an appointment.

Yesterday morning, Connolly strode into my showroom —*without* an appointment—and offered me a fake job. At nearly the exact same time, Ani was weeding the back gardens when someone strode into our yard—without an appointment—and wanted her to uncurse an object.

The woman had been a middle-aged version of Connolly. Demanding, condescending, arrogant. Which works better if you're a hot young guy. Well, no, that's just for me—Ani wouldn't care. And what lured me to Connolly's office yesterday was the promise of a job, not the guy himself. Money doesn't matter to Ani. My sisters live in a mortgage-free house, run an established business and live in a town where the cost of living rivals that of rural Maine. So when this woman demanded Ani's services, my sister decided she didn't need her bullshit and turned her down flat.

The nature of the job didn't help matters. The woman wouldn't say what object needed unhexing. Just that it was a famous curse, and if Ani would agree to attend a secret meeting, all would be revealed.

Mysterious object. Mystery buyer. Definitely suspicious.

Worse, it wasn't just Ani they wanted. Hope had to come along, too, or there wouldn't be a meeting. So Ani decided there wouldn't be a meeting.

By that time, Hope had come out to hear what was going on, and she agreed with Ani. Now, if the woman had spoken to Hope alone first, my little sister might have been unable to resist the temptation of a delicious mystery, but once Ani pointed out the perils of gallivanting off to secret meetings, the woman would have no chance of persuading Hope, even if she approached her later.

When Ani and Hope refused the job, the woman wanted to know if they could recommend another curse weaver. The woman mentioned me. Not by name—if she knew that, she wouldn't need Ani's reference. But wasn't there a third Bennett sister? One who'd moved away?

With that, Ani's defenses flew up, and she asked her to leave. The woman did, and Ani didn't think of it again until I texted an hour later, accusing her of sending the guy with the jinxed tea caddy.

Ani had someone pop by, out of the blue, wanting a mysterious object uncursed and then asking about me. And now I was saying someone wanted a jinxed object uncursed and claimed my sisters referred them to me.

Ani is furious with herself now for not seeing it was suspicious, but our brains do that. They see a connection, realize it's not possible and move on. Later, Ani *did* think she should warn me about the woman, but by then, cell service was down, and so she made a mental note to talk to me when she could.

That night, as I already know, Jonathan was supposed to come by for board games. Ani watched a movie with Hope while keeping an ear open for Jonathan's rap on the door. When she heard the back doorknob turn, she figured his knock had been swallowed by an on-screen shootout. Ani hadn't bolted the door yet. It's Unstable—you don't lock up until you go to bed.

Ani called a greeting to Jonathan, footsteps approached and . . .

Two strangers in balaclavas walked in. Ani dove for the fireplace poker, and Hope grabbed a vase, and after that, it's a blur until they woke in the back of a van, bound, blindfolded and gagged.

A man was in there with them. He ungagged Ani, and they talked. Which consisted of Ani demanding answers and the man giving some variation on tough-guy movie dialogue like "I'll give you answers when I want to give you answers" and "I'm the one in charge here." Which he really wasn't once he removed Ani's gag.

While Ani argued, Hope lay there, awake but still, and their captor mistook that for submission, which he definitely wasn't getting from her big sister. Next thing Ani knew, she was waking in that hunting shack . . . alone.

I ask what the man said. It hadn't made much sense to Ani at the time. He knew she was a curse weaver, and she hadn't argued the point. We aren't vampires or some other impossible creature. We fall under the same blanket as psychics and mediums. For those who believe in our powers, we're a valuable addition to the parapsychology world. For those who don't believe, we're harmless entertainers or deluded new-agers, neither anything to fear.

So when this guy called Ani a curse weaver, she didn't argue. She figured he wanted a curse woven and that's why they'd been kidnapped—the Bennetts are known as reluctant weavers. But no, he wanted an unweaving. That's when she set about negotiating.

Negotiating made sense. She unweaves curses for a living. Just give her more information, and they could settle on a price. If he'd refused to pay, well, she would have argued, but in the end, she was smart and reasonable, and she would have agreed to exchange an uncursing for their freedom. The conversation never got that far, though. When she tried to negotiate, he decided they'd chatted enough. He knocked her out, and she woke up in the shack.

———

WE FINALLY ARRIVE at the gas station. Or what used to be a gas station. It closed recently enough that the fuel price on the old sign is still accurate. But from the looks of the place, it'd been on life support for decades before they pulled the plug. Its death can be squarely blamed on a new highway five miles west. With no reason for drivers to come this way, it's an empty road in the middle of nowhere.

Connolly barely pulls into the weed-choked gravel lot before I throw open the door. He manages to call a warning. I'm gone, though, staggering out as soon as it's safe to do so. Then I'm running along the front of the boarded-up station, shouting for my sister.

There's no one here.

We're too late.

Ani's captors didn't abandon her in that shack. They stashed her temporarily, came back, found it empty and knew she'd gone looking for a phone. She'd been watching for me. Instead, she got her kidnappers.

Why did I tell her to wait here? Why didn't—

A shadow peeks around a corner. Then that shadow becomes my sister, and I run to her and launch myself into her arms, as if I'm a toddler again, my big sister home after an endless day of kindergarten.

I hold her as tight as I can, clinging and inhaling the herbal smell of her. She hugs me back and smooths my hair and whispers words of comfort, and for one moment, she isn't Ani. She's Mom. Her hair is the same texture as Mom's, falling onto my cheek as I hug her. Her soft and fierce embrace feels like Mom's, as does that gentle hand in my hair and those words in my ear.

I kinda lose it then, as I did when I heard her voice on the phone. I break down, sobbing, and it doesn't take a shrink to tell me this has been about more than my sisters being taken. It's about losing my family, the dull pain from Dad's accident and the raw pain from Mom's death. I hadn't allowed the thought to form, but somewhere in my deepest despair, I'd seen a vision of a life where I am the only Bennett left, and that rushes out, the fear and the relief.

I sob until my throat hurts, and then I pull back, snuffling. Ani does look like Mom, more than any of us. I have our mother's skin tone and her dark hair and eyes, but it's Ani who has her curls and her curves and her features. Through my tears, her face blurring, I could mistake her for Mom.

"I look like hell, don't I?" she says.

I shake my head. "You look perfect."

She blinks, as if she's misheard. There might be only two years between us, but it always feels like more. I am the annoying little sister always ready with an insult.

Ani's face softens, and she pulls me into another hug. Then she glances over my shoulder, and I twist to see Connolly walking toward us.

"Ah," Ani says, looking him over. "Now I know why Kennedy hasn't come home for two weeks. Something you forgot to tell me, K? Someone new in your life?"

"What?" I look from her to Connolly. "*Ack*! No! Definitely not." I catch his expression. "I mean, umm, no, we're not— No. We just met. Like yesterday."

"You caught a lift with a guy you met yesterday?"

"What? No. Well, yes, but not like that. Geez, Ani. What do you take me for?"

"Umm, the girl who showed up after her first week in Boston, dropped off by some guy she met the night before."

"Hey! That's not fair. If you're implying that I slept with some dude to get a free ride—"

"Of course not. You met him. A neighbor or something, I recall, and you start chatting, and you mentioned going home to Unstable the next day, so he offered you a lift. As guys do."

She looks at Connolly. "Sorry, Red. If you thought you were racking up points, you don't know my sister. She presumed you were being nice. Because, golly gee, guys are just so sweet about stuff like that. Or they are if you're Kennedy."

I sputter. "That is not—"

"Blame small-town living," she continues to Connolly. "She's used to people doing nice things for no reason other than being neighborly. Not that she'd take advantage of you. She'll totally owe you one—which means she'll dog-sit for you, maybe run an errand or two. Anything else is off the table."

Connolly's gaze has gotten increasingly cool as Ani talks. I expect him to tell her off. Instead, he turns that icy gaze on me.

"You accept rides from young men you've barely met? That is extremely unsafe, Kennedy. You could end up—"

"At a closed gas station?" Ani says. "Miles from the nearest town?"

"Precisely. You—" He stops as his gaze lifts to the storefront sign. "You mean me?"

Now Connolly is the one sputtering. I cut in with, "It isn't like that, Ani. This is a business arrangement. Remember that woman who tried to hire you yesterday? That's what he did."

"You're the guy with the tea caddy?"

"No, no, he shooed him off. Connolly—Aiden—tried hiring me for a job, only he was really testing me with a cursed object. I snuck back to unweave the curse, and he admitted it was a test. I got angry and stormed out, but not before he said something about you and Hope. When you two disappeared, I went back to him."

"He threatened us? After he *tricked* you?"

"It wasn't like—" Connolly clears his throat. "Yes, it was a bit like that, but I have admitted my mistake, and Kennedy and I are partners in this venture."

"Partners, hmm. Great. So, whatever you people are trying to uncurse, Kennedy gets half of the profit, right?"

Connolly's mouth opens. Stays like that for a moment before he closes it and adjusts his tie. "I would be open to renegotiating a fair—"

"Half."

I shake my head. "I already told him I don't want his money."

She stares at me and then cradles her forehead against one hand. "Oh, K. Of course, you did." She wheels on Connolly. "You are taking advantage of my sister's kindness—"

"It's not kindness, Ani," I say. "The deal is that he helps me find you and Hope, and in return, I uncurse an object. I don't care what he does with it after that. I only care about finding you two."

She pulls me into a one-armed embrace. "All right. Understood. But now that I freed myself, I think we can agree that whatever deal you had with him isn't necessary."

"Hope is still missing," Connolly says. "And I'm still your best chance of finding her. I'll renegotiate the terms of our deal, but you need me—"

"I don't need you. I don't know you, and after you tricked my sister, I don't trust you."

Connolly looks over, as if expecting me to step in. How can I? Ani's right that I'm a little too trusting, but I'm not gullible or naive. There have been things Connolly has done that I appreciate. But there are even more things he's done that make me wary.

And if a little part of me says this is a man that I'd like to know better, I'll chalk it up to my taste for gingers, even if I know it's more than that. I keep thinking I have Connolly figured out, and then he says or does something that suggests I don't, and that intrigues me. This isn't the time to be intrigued by a guy, though. It really isn't.

"Ani's right," I say. "I appreciate your help, Aiden, but I think we can take this from here. I'm sorry."

His jaw works, and I brace myself. Then he says, "Don't be sorry. I've given you reason to mistrust me. I do, however, honestly believe I am your best chance of finding Hope." He turns to Ani. "Fifty percent."

"I don't even know what this is about." She lifts her hands against his explanation. "And I don't want to. Kennedy, you say he mentioned us before we were kidnapped, and he says he's your best chance of getting Hope back. Does that not suggest he knows exactly where to find her . . . because he's part of this?"

"Set a price," Connolly says. "A bond, if you will, surety that I am not involved in your sister's kidnapping." He glances around and then points at his car. "If I'm lying, you may have that."

I shake my head. "I don't want your—"

"I know. You don't want my money or my car. However, I am loath to part with either as you may have guessed. My family is wealthy. I'm personally comfortable but not to the point where I can blithely hand over the keys to a seventy-thousand-dollar vehicle."

"Seventy—" I choke. "Who spends seventy thousand dollars on a car?"

"Successful young Boston entrepreneurs." Ani looks at Connolly. "My sister is more accustomed to guys who inherited their dad's Ford pickup."

"Nothing wrong with that," I murmur. "I appreciate frugality."

"Fine," Ani says. "Sign a bond on the car—"

I clear my throat. She understands my meaning right away, but it still takes her a moment to hand over the reins.

"I'll take the bond," I say. "First, because, as you said, the car means something to you. Second, I don't see the point in you continuing a charade of 'helping' me find someone you kidnapped when I've already agreed to lift the curse. Third, I had Jonathan run a basic background check on you, and it came up clean."

"As it should. My reputation—" Connolly stops. "Wait. Background check?"

I look at Ani. "Also, Jonathan says to tell you he was right behind us, coming to your rescue, but he got a flat tire. Truth is he took Ellie for me and went home to investigate the scene of the crime."

"As he should. I'm far more impressed by him doing the practical thing. Men." She shakes her head.

My phone buzzes. "Speak of the devil." I whisper, "Flat tire, remember?" and then hit Accept.

"K?" Jonathan says before I can speak. "K, tell me that's you."

"No, sorry," Ani says. "Kennedy's busy. You're stuck with me."

"Ani? Ani!" Jonathan's voice rises in a way that makes my heart soar. "Oh, thank God. I pulled off to get gas and saw a message from Kennedy saying to call her right away, and then I saw I'd gotten a call from an unknown number, no message. I had this image of you at a phone booth in the middle of nowhere, using your last quarters to call me when my damn phone's auto-set to Do Not Disturb while I'm driving."

"Which is the sensible thing to do."

"Not when your best friend's been kidnapped."

"Well, you were oddly right about the payphone in the middle of nowhere. Are you sure your mom isn't really psychic? Wrong on the last quarters, though. I was kidnapped from my couch. I grabbed the fire poker, not spare change. Which, in retrospect, was a bad call. Anyway, I was phoning collect. When you didn't pick up, I moved on to Kennedy."

"Wait," I say. "I was your *backup* choice?"

"You don't have a car. Purely a practical decision."

I grumble and wave at her. "You two catch up. Connolly and I will scout around."

As we walk away, Connolly whispers, "What are we scouting for?"

"Hell if I know. I'm just giving them a few moments alone." I glance back to see my sister clutching the phone to her ear, her face glowing as she talks. "They're adorable, aren't they?"

"Are they . . . together?"

"Not yet. But I'm working on it. I'm *always* working on it."

He looks back toward Ani. "So, you and Jonathan aren't . . . ?"

"What? No. Eww. Where would you get that idea?"

"You seemed close."

"Uh, yes. Because he's been Ani's best friend forever."

Something like a smile warms his eyes. "Also, I apologize for saying she left Hope behind. Ani didn't hear that, did she?"

I shake my head.

He continues, "Even if she had left her, it'd be understandable. Practical even. Get away and phone for help."

"Maybe. I'm not sure I could do it, though."

We walk to the edge of the parking lot, and he squints against the sun, his eyes dazzlingly green but distant.

"I'd like to think I would," he murmurs. "But I'm not sure I actually could."

"You have a brother, right?"

"Younger. Maybe that's the key. Younger siblings. I swear I've spent half my life getting mine out of scrapes. I wouldn't dare leave him behind. He'd leave me, though." A wry twist of his lips. "No doubt about that."

"Maybe," I say. "Or maybe he'd think the same about you. When I left for Boston, I figured my sisters would be happy to see me go. I can be a bit . . . much."

That twitch of his lips, his eyes warming. "I can't imagine."

"Right? I figured they'd welcome the break, and maybe they did, for a week or two, but now it's all about how to get me back to Unstable. Whether it's moving away or fleeing a kidnapping, sometimes logic says you should strike out on your own, but it's hard. It's really hard."

"Well, in my brother's case—"

"K!" Ani calls, waving. "Let's hit the road."

I motion that we're coming and then glance at Connolly as we walk. "You were saying?"

"Nothing important. We need to get your sister home. She's had a shock."

I snort. "If you think she needs a bed to swoon in, you haven't been paying attention. It'll hit her later, but for now, she'll want to move forward. Step one, I believe, should be checking out that hunting shack."

"Good idea."

CHAPTER TWELVE

On Connolly's GPS, Ani pinpoints the rough area of the hunting cabin. It's in a forest, not surprisingly. While we don't see a road, presumably, there's one close to it if they carried Ani from the car. We analyze the region using satellite imagery maps and spot the area we're looking for.

Along the way, I explain the situation to her—Necklace of Harmonia, auction in four days, multiple interested parties all jockeying to hire curse weavers. Also, before she dismisses it as nonsense, I tell her Jonathan has investigated and declared it legit.

We arrive at the road to the shack. Calling it a road, though, grossly overstates the matter. It starts off as gravel, and then becomes dirt and finally narrows to two grassy tracks into the forest. That's the point where we abandon the car, to Connolly's obvious relief. This is why I respect guys with second-hand pickups. There are enough stressors in life without fretting over every scratch and ding.

Ani spots landmarks that tell her we're on the right track and help her gauge distance. It's a testament to her level-headedness that, while fleeing captivity, she'd had the presence of mind to note landscape features. That doesn't keep Connolly from asking, "Are you certain?" every time she recognizes something.

"You could go search on your own," I say.

"That seems unwise."

"Cell service works out here. You can call us if you find it first."

"You shouldn't be alone in the forest, especially when there could be kidnappers nearby."

It's a lovely excuse, but I suspect *he's* the one who doesn't want to be alone. He walks along the hard dirt paths as if they're quicksand, sucking at his designer leather shoes, and he bats aside every twig as if it's crawling with spiders.

"The dirt will come off your shoes," I say. "Guaranteed. Also, those branches aren't poisonous. Not the vines, either."

"I noted three leaves on that last one, which I believe indicates poison ivy."

"Poison ivy is *that* right over there." I point to a patch. "The vines are Virginia creeper. That tree is a yellow birch. That other one is a white ash. The bush is hawthorn. Beware of those. They won't rip your shirt, but they can scratch."

Connolly eyes the vine. "You're certain this isn't poison ivy?"

"Yep."

"Listen to my sister," Ani calls back from up ahead. "She spent two summers as a park ranger."

"Caught the bug in Girl Scouts." I glance at him. "I'm going to guess you were never a Boy Scout."

"No, my parents said that was for the mid—" He stops short.

"Middle class? Along with hiking and camping and all outdoor activities, I'm guessing."

"We did sail," he says. "And I row."

"Rowing? Ooh, I love shooting rapids."

"There . . . aren't many rapids where I boat. I'm on a sculling team. A group of us continued after college."

"Harvard," I say. "For business, right?"

"Yes. How—? Ah. Jonathan must have found that in his research."

"Nope, just a wild guess."

Ani glances back and looks between us. "I have nothing to worry about."

"What would you worry about?" I ask.

"Nothing," she says with another look from me to Connolly. "Nothing at all."

———

CONNOLLY IS ACTUALLY the one who spots the cabin first. I think his brain sees a familiar shape and screams "Civilization!" His steps definitely lighten. Then he gets a good look at the building.

As advertised, it's a hunting shack. A single room with walls that waffle in the wind. Bone wind chimes and decorative animal skulls give it a nice *Texas Chainsaw Massacre* touch.

"People live here?" Connolly says.

"If they're lucky," I say. "Do you know how much these cottages cost? We used to dream about getting a summer place like this, watching the stars through the holes in the roof, playing with the families of mice living under the floorboards. It's only a ten-mile walk to the ocean. Paradise."

Silence.

"She's kidding," Ani says. "And the fact that I need to clarify that says so much. No one lives here, Aiden. It's a hunting shack."

"For hunters, yes?" he says. "They live here while they hunt."

"That's not how a hunting shack works," I say. "See, a place like this has been passed down, generation to generation. When the weekend comes and the wife gives you a list of chores, you say you're going hunting with the guys. You come out here, shoot a grouse or two and then head inside. Light the fireplace. Pull out the lawn chairs. Drink beer until it's safe to go home again."

"I don't understand."

"You know the men's lounge at your country club?" Ani says.

He perks up. "Yes."

"Think of it as that."

He nods. "When we were growing up, my father spent a lot of Saturday afternoons there. And your father went to places like this, right?"

"Our father was a small-town doctor," I say. "If he got an actual weekend off, he spent it at home with us. Now, we're supposed to be scouting for clues, right? There's a path over there with broken undergrowth and twigs. That shows where they carried Ani through. We can follow it back later and see where it goes, look for any clues along the way."

"You're quite good at this," Connolly says. "Do you watch a lot of crime shows?"

"She reads books," Ani says.

I shrug. "Small town. Big library. We didn't have cable growing up, and the internet's too crappy to stream. I read a lot."

"Your parents encouraged you to read," Connolly says. "That's good."

"And very middle class?" I say.

"No, I just meant that it's good you picked up the hobby. Reading expands the mind, and literacy of any sort, even mystery novels . . ." He catches my look. "That's condescending, isn't it?"

"Yep. Good catch, though. Now, let's split up and look around. We'll save the cabin for last."

———

I'VE EXAMINED AS MUCH of the surrounding forest as I can. Now I'm standing at the front door, studying it. I step forward and—

A figure leaps from the bushes, slamming into my side and knocking me to the ground. I jab up, my elbow making contact. The figure grunts, and I try to shove him aside, but he's holding me down, his back arched over me, arms out as if to shield us. I'm about to slam my elbow into him again when I catch a flash of red-gold hair.

"Connolly?" I say. "What the hell?"

A throat clears behind us. "That's my question," Ani says. "Perhaps even more strongly worded. Please tell me there's a valid reason why you're lying on my sister. I have no idea what that reason could be, but I'm hopeful."

"Get away from the door!" he says, waving. "It's armed."

"Uh-huh," Ani says. "Try again, Mr. Connolly."

He rises as I push up to my feet.

"The door is armed," he says coolly. "Your sister was about to open it when I saw the device."

"You mean the one in the top right corner?" I ask. "The black box that'll trigger when the door opens?"

"Er, yes. So you saw it? And you were still opening the door?"

"Did you see my hand anywhere near the knob?" I shake my head as I walk over. "I was getting a closer look. It's like the entry alert on my showroom. Not triggering a bomb or a shotgun but a signal, one that tells someone—in this case the kidnappers—that the door has been opened."

Ani stands on tiptoes to peer at the trigger. "Huh, she's right. It's a battery-operated signal device."

"Presumably operating on cellular service," I say.

"So you triggered it when you left," Connolly says to Ani. "Meaning your kidnappers know you're free and could be combing the forest right now."

"I crawled out a window."

I nod. "If you're being held captive in a cabin, you aren't going to waltz out the front door. You could walk right into your kidnappers, having a nice cup of tea. Or you could trip an alarm. The sensible answer is to find another way out."

"Then why put that on the front door?" Connolly asks.

"Because they didn't expect Ani to be sensible. The trigger was to notify them when she escaped. Which means there's only one thing to do."

Connolly nods. "Stay far away from—"

"Open the front door."

I reach for it. Both Ani and Connolly jump to stop me.

I pause. "You're right. We should go in the window, take a look around and *then* open the front door."

"Or not open it at all," Ani says.

"But if it brings them running, isn't that what we want? They still have Hope."

After a moment, Connolly says, "That's actually a good idea."

"One of these times, you will stop sounding so shocked when you say that. Now, Ani, show us how you got out, and then we'll summon the demons who stole our sister."

CHAPTER THIRTEEN

ANI HAD CRAWLED out through a window after prying off rotted boards, which cost her two fingernails and earned her three splinters. Meanwhile, from up close, we can see that the front door is both unlocked and not quite shut, a literally open invitation to escape. She'd sensed a trap and taken the hard way.

There's nothing inside the shack. I'd joked about hunters bringing lawn chairs, but that must be exactly what they do. Ani's captors dumped her on the floor without even a bottle of water. As she points out, her bonds were obviously loose on purpose, and the front door is unlocked, so she wasn't in mortal danger. I can still be furious on her behalf.

Ani and I check the interior while I ask Connolly to scope the exterior, mostly so he doesn't need to squeeze through a filthy window and I don't need to endure his silently palpable agony as he ruins a second shirt in one day.

Once outside, we stand ten feet from the front door.

"I'll open it," Connolly says. "I'd like you both to take cover. While it certainly seems to only activate a signal, we can't take chances. You two—"

I pitch a rock at the front door, hitting at the right angle to swing it open. A light on the black box flashes red.

"Or we could do that," Connolly says.

"Nice throw," Ani says. "The Unstable Unicorns miss you."

To Connolly's raised brows, I say. "Softball team. Also the name of the local soccer team, the bowling team and the knitting club. The unicorn is kind of the town mascot." I look around. "We should withdraw to a safe spot to watch—"

My phone vibrates. I lift it to see a blocked number. Connolly reaches out.

"I can handle my own spam calls," I say.

"I was thinking it might have something to do with the necklace. Another potential buyer looking for a curse weaver."

"All the more reason for me to take the call myself."

I hit Answer. "Hello?"

"Miss Bennett?"

The voice sets my teeth on edge. It's mechanically distorted, which is creepy, but the tone still comes through, and that's the part I react to. A rough, patronizing growl that no filter can mask.

"It's Ms.," I say.

Silence. Then, "What?"

"You called me Miss. I prefer Ms. Just establishing that right away since this seems to be a first contact. I'm Ms. Bennett, and you are . . . ?"

It's a moment before he responds.

"You don't know what's happened to your sisters, do you?" he says. "Otherwise, you wouldn't be quite so impudent."

Impudent? Something tells me that by the time I finish this call, Connolly's condescension will feel positively heartwarming.

"You mean because my sisters are missing," I say.

More silence, and I get far too much satisfaction from throwing him off-kilter again. Then I realize Connolly can overhear, and I expect him to wave wildly, telling me to take it down a notch. He's only listening, though, same as Ani. I ease the phone from my ear to make that easier.

"You seem less concerned than one might expect," the man says.

"Oh, I'm concerned. They're my sisters. I'm presuming you know something about their disappearance, and if so, you'll tell me, because that's why you called. But bear in mind, please, that there's a reason you're calling *me*. I'm the one who doesn't live at home. The one who left. I love my sisters, but we don't get along."

Ani looks confused. Connolly nods, as if he understands what I'm doing.

When the man doesn't answer, I say, "I know something's stirring in the magical world. People keep trying to hire me to undo a curse. Something about an auction? A necklace? I never listen long enough to get the details. I'm not for hire. Neither is Turani, and if someone came waving a blank check, she'd still send them packing. Hope, though? Hope's a little different."

He's quiet. I could think he's hung up, but whatever is distorting his voice is also amplifying his breathing. He's listening. Learning. I'm making a point here with my lies, and I must spin them to Hope's advantage.

"Hope's a kid," I say. "Twenty years old. Never lived outside Unstable. She was going away to college, but then our mom died, and there wasn't any money."

Not true. Hope had been on a gap year to help with Mom, and she extended that to rethink her future.

I continue. "She's desperate to get out of Unstable, but Turani holds the purse strings tight, and curse weaving is the only job Hope's ever had. So if someone tried to hire her, she'd have gone for it. But they'd need to get past Turani first. Anyway, that's neither here nor there since you have them both. But I'm guessing you're calling me because I'm the curse weaver you actually want."

He's going to tell me that Ani is free—as he knows from that door signal—but if I want my other sister, I need to uncurse the necklace.

So when he says, "No, Ms. Bennett, I don't want to hire you," I'm the one thrown off-kilter.

I manage a strained. "All right."

"You aren't part of the family business," he says. "You can call that a choice, but from what I hear, it's a lack of ability."

I open my mouth to protest and wisely snap it shut just as both Connolly and Ani turn warning looks on me.

"Don't fall for it," Ani mouths.

She means he's trying to get a rise from me and make me eager to prove my worth. I pretended I wasn't freaked out by my sisters disappearing, and he's pretending he doesn't really want to hire me.

"What's your specialty again?" he says. "The jester's joke?"

"Joker's jinx," I say before I can stop myself.

He snorts. "Pranks. This is the most famous cursed object of all. The Necklace of Harmonia. It's not a child's hex."

Connolly's sharp look warns me not to share his theory. My responding look politely asks him to give me more credit.

The man's insults remind me of one of our neighbors in Unstable. She writes children's books, and people are always asking when she'll "graduate" to adult fiction. Same goes for the joker's jinx. As curses go, it's usually the most benign. Playful. Lighthearted. Even childlike. That does not mean it's easy to weave. It also doesn't mean it can't be wicked, like granting the "blessing" of eternal youth while punishing you for your vanity.

"It's obviously a lover's lament," the man says.

"An ex-hex?"

He sniffs. "The fact you even use that phrase betrays you as an amateur, *Miss* Bennett. The proper name is *lover's lament* for a reason. It's a category of hexes designed to punish an inconstant lover. That may be an ex. It may also be a current partner. All that matters is that the party requesting the curse feels betrayed by a lover."

Connolly is definitely benefiting from this conversation. In comparison, it's going to be *so* much harder to accuse him of treating me like an idiot.

"I'm sure you aren't familiar with the background of the necklace," the man says.

I clamp my jaw against a rejoinder. Or worse, sarcasm. That would feel good. So would reciting the entire history of the necklace —or the origins of the term *lover's lament* and the full breadth of the curses both it and the joker's jinx cover. But I'm quickly realizing this will go better if he feels he has the advantage.

He proceeds to blah-blah about the background of the necklace. I roll my eyes, and Ani rubs my back, telling me I'm doing fine.

Connolly could leap into the silence to pantomime a new plan. But he just listens, and their tacit approval helps.

"Fine," I say when he finishes. "You're right that it sounds like an ex—a lover's lament, and you're right that it's Hope's specialty. I presume then that you're calling to negotiate for Ani's release?"

"No, your sister is already free. I'm sure you'll hear from her soon. This is about you."

"I . . ." I glance from Ani to Connolly. Both shrug their confusion. "I thought you didn't need my skills."

"I don't, but as you said, you've been contacted by other interested parties. I believe one is Aiden Connolly. Yes?"

Connolly snaps upright, his face tensing. I motion to ask whether I can admit it. He considers and then nods.

"You'll have to be more specific," I say. "I've had a few offers."

"You couldn't miss Mr. Connolly. Only a few years older than you but acts like he's twice that. Thinks very highly of himself and his abilities while forgetting the silver spoon wedged in his mouth from birth." A pause. "No, in Aiden Connolly's case, that spoon is definitely wedged up his ass. He's a sanctimonious prick."

With every word the man says, Connolly's eyes harden. By the end, I have to pedal backward to keep him from grabbing the phone.

"Right," I say. "Aiden Connolly. The cute ginger. Kinda uptight, but I'm not sure sanctimonious is the right word if he's trying to score an infamous cursed necklace."

"Which is why young Mr. Connolly doesn't belong anywhere near this auction. That's where you come in."

"You want me to . . . do what? Convince him not to bid? We're not exactly drinking buddies. Hell, I'm pretty sure he doesn't *have* drinking buddies. Unless you count knocking back single malts at the old-boys' club."

I mouth a "sorry" for Connolly, but he waves it off.

"I'm not asking you to go out for a beer with him, Miss Bennett. Though I'm sure you have a few seductive wiles to fall back on."

Wiles? Now I know why this guy wants the Necklace of Harmonia. He's almost as old as it is.

"Hey, now," I say. "I don't do that kind of stuff. You have my sister, so I'm willing to negotiate—"

"Use your charms at your discretion, Miss Bennett. I only pointed out that Mr. Connolly is preoccupied with furthering his business interests. He'll be susceptible to girls like you."

I chomp down on everything I want to say. Ani's expression says she's doing the same on my behalf.

He continues, "Men like Mr. Connolly are so busy scrambling up the corporate ladder that they don't have time for unpaid companionship."

Connolly's brows furrow, as if he's heard wrong, unable to put *unpaid companionship* in context. I see the moment it hits, the horror and then the outrage as he gestures and shakes his head. I bite my cheek to keep from laughing. Seems whoever this bastard is, he's an equal opportunity insult artist.

"Yeah, no," I say. "Aiden Connolly doesn't strike me as a guy who needs to pay for it. But whatever. You're proposing . . ."

"That you accept his offer. Promise him the uncursing. Convince him you can do it. And then, when it's time to bid, back out."

"Quit once it's too late for him to find a replacement. Which forces him out of the auction."

"Exactly. Then your sister will unweave the curse, and I'll release her with adequate payment."

Somehow, of everything he's said, that last bit outrages me the most. Paying her says this is a valid business transaction. Not kidnapping. Not blackmail. Just business.

"I want to speak to my sister."

"I thought you might. Hold on."

As I wait, Connolly gets my attention. I pretend to mutter into the phone, "This better be a private line," and he nods. That's what he wanted to tell me. That it won't be. Watch what I say.

A few clicks and then, "Hello?"

"Hey, kid," I say. "Finally got that ticket to a magical school and left us, huh?"

A hiccup, and then she breaks down like I did when I saw Ani at the gas station.

"Whoa, sorry. Let's retry that. What did you get yourself into now, Hopeless?"

More sobbing, as if my "mean big sister" act only makes her miss me more.

"It's okay," I murmur, channeling Ani. "How are you? That's what I need to know here, Hope. Are *you* okay? They want me to back off and let you uncurse this necklace."

"You should do what they want," she says. "I'm fine. Really. They've got me in a nice place." She pauses. "Remember when you took me to New York for my eighteenth birthday, just the two of us, and the guy at the desk thought you were cute so he upgraded us?"

"Pretty sure I'm not the one he upgraded for."

"Pretty sure you were. Anyway, the room's like that. The windows are boarded up, of course, but I have a bedroom and a sitting area and any food I want. Plus Netflix and an Xbox. They asked if they could bring me anything, and I said I'd like a copy of that book you recommended, the one based on a Russian fairy tale. They said they'll get it."

As she talks, her voice breathless as a tween's, Connolly's frown deepens. I swear I can hear his thought process. *Is this girl really as ditzy as she sounds?*

"Code," I mouth.

Ani catches my eye, and I shoot her a thumbs up. Hope really is fine. That's what she's telling us—that this isn't a lie she's been fed by her captors.

Tell your sister you're okay. Tell her you're in a comfy suite and all is good.

My sister has anxiety. Nothing major, but one way it manifests is seeing articles about an accident or a crime and needing to find a personal solution, in case it ever happens to her. A month ago, she mailed me a keychain window breaker, and I knew she must have read something about people drowning in cars.

Before that, there was an article about a girl whose live-in boyfriend wouldn't let her leave the apartment and forced her to tell her family all was fine. For that, Hope wanted a code. A way we could let each other know whether we were speaking freely or under duress. If we talk about our shared past and tell the truth, everything is fine. If we lie, something's wrong. Everything Hope said here is true.

She's fine.

Held hostage, yes, but if there's a danger meter to such a thing, she's at the bottom of it. At least for now.

"Hey, someone here wants to say hi," I say.

Both Connolly and Ani look over sharply. Connolly waves a "cease and desist," gesturing at Ani.

"She can't actually talk," I say. "But she is listening. Say hi to Sophie. You remember Sophie, right? My cat."

Connolly's brows furrow in comic confusion. Ani reaches out and squeezes my hand. Sophia is Ani's middle name, after our maternal grandmother.

"Oh!" Hope says. "Sophie! Hey, kitty-kitty. You being good for Kennedy?"

"She's fine," I say. "She got out last night, and she looks a little worse for wear, but she just needs some kibble and a good brushing. I'll take care of her."

"I'm sure you will. You take care of Kennedy, too, Sophie."

We talk a little more after that. We don't say anything important. We can't. If Hope knows more—her rough geographic location or information about her captors—she chooses not to share it, and I understand that.

Hope doesn't want us coming after her. That's as much for her sake as ours. Right now, she's sitting on a ledge, as comfortable and secure as can be. If we climb up—or throw a rope down—we *might* be able to rescue her. Or we could fall. Or she could fall. She just needs to sit tight and do as she's told, and then her captor will eventually put up a ladder for her to safely descend.

That's what she's been told. Just wait a few days, uncurse the Necklace of Harmonia and they'll let her go. She doesn't know anything about Connolly or the "mission" I've been given to guarantee her safety, and I'm sure as hell not adding to her anxiety.

"We just need to wait this out, K," she says. "I don't like the way they went about it, obviously, but we'll get through this, and then we'll protect ourselves so it never happens again."

Her captor cuts in, and then Hope is gone.

"I want daily calls," I say to him, "to be sure she's okay."

"Proof of life?" His mechanically distorted voice snorts.

"I'm considering this a hostage taking. You're holding her to ensure we both do as we're told. I need that call."

"Your sister will be fine, but yes, I will telephone this number once a day and let you speak to her."

CHAPTER FOURTEEN

When I disconnect, I glance at Connolly, who's deep in thought. I give him a moment and then clear my throat.

"Did you recognize anything about the voice?" I say. "I know it was distorted."

"It's definitely not the woman we were going to see. As I said, I didn't think she'd resort to kidnapping, but this confirms it."

"Could she have hired someone to call us?"

"No, she would insist on doing it herself. Otherwise . . . I'm relatively new to all this, as he said. Besides, I only know gray-market players enough to point them out at a party, and I have no idea which ones are bidding on the necklace."

"Can you give me more insight into what's happening here?" I ask.

"No need," Ani says. "You've heard the terms, Mr. Connolly. Dare I hope you have enough decency to back out of the auction?"

"It . . . isn't that simple."

Ani surges forward, but I stop her with a look. Connolly's hesitation and his sidelong glance tell me he's not being an asshole. It really *isn't* that simple.

"How much?" Ani says.

He frowns.

She presses on. "How much profit would you expect from this

necklace if you were able to buy it, uncurse it and resell it. Name a figure."

"It isn't about the money."

"Then what the hell is it about?"

"It's . . . complicated."

"Aiden," I say. My use of his first name must startle him. He looks up, eyes meeting mine, clouds swirling in his. "You know we can't accept that as an answer. This is Hope's *life*."

"No one is going to kill her. That's not how anyone operates in this world."

"Fine. I'm not forcing your hand right now. I want to get Ani home. I want to talk to Jonathan and see what he's come up with. And I want to think. Mostly, I want to think. Before we go further, though, I'm going to need a better explanation than 'it's complicated.'"

"Understood."

"Can we leave?"

He nods, distracted, as if he's already faded back into his thoughts. Then his head jerks up, and he turns toward the shack.

"That transmitter," he says. "If it's connected to a cell service, there might be a way to trace the number. I suspect it would lead to a dead end, but I should bring it."

He does that. Then we continue on. We take the path I believe Ani's captors used to carry her to the shack. I let Connolly walk ahead while I search for clues. In a movie, one of her captors would have dropped a lighter with his name engraved in it. Better yet, a stray business card would have slid from his pocket. I find only broken twigs and scuffed shoe prints.

I've caught up with Connolly when his arms shoot out, holding me back. He pauses, head tilting as he listens. Then, without a word, he strides forward. I jog after him and try to grab his shirt, but he strides at a remarkable pace.

"Please get off my car," he says.

I hurry out to see three guys. One lounges on the hood of Connolly's car like a neighborhood thug. A glance across the trio, though, makes me wish they *were* neighborhood thugs. They wear dark suits filled out with muscular builds. Short hair. Clean-shaven.

While they look like federal law enforcement, menace swirls thick around them, the air of men who intimidate their way through life.

We should have been more careful coming out of those woods. Yes, the signal triggered that call, but it could also have recalled Ani and Hope's kidnappers.

Connolly strides out, not the least intimidated, and normally, I'd find that hella sexy, but this is one case where I'd have argued for a bit more caution. It's three of them against three of us, and that'd be better odds if I were armed with more than my fake derringer.

Connolly walks up to the guy on his car hood. The man is bouncing on it, grinning. He's about Connolly's age and Connolly's height. Stocky bordering on beefy with a wide face and a pug nose that I'm sure was a lot cuter when he was five.

"Do I need to ask you again?" Connolly says. "I don't think you want that."

"Oh, I want it." The guy meets Connolly's gaze, his thick lips curving in a sneer. "I really want it."

"Are you sure?" Connolly stops within striking distance. "I seem to recall the last time we had this discussion—"

The guy hops down, his hands slamming out as if to shove Connolly, but he doesn't actually make contact. At a wave from Connolly, the other two men retreat silently to their car—a black SUV parked twenty feet away.

"Friends of yours?" I say to Connolly as I walk from the woods with Ani behind me.

"Friends of *yours*?" the guy says. He whistles as his gaze travels over us. "Please tell me they aren't sisters. If you're banging sisters, I might actually need to be jealous."

Connolly's eyes chill. "Show some respect—"

"Respect?" the guy says as he strolls toward us. "Girls like this don't want respect. That's where you always get it wrong, Aiden. This one here?" He waves at me. "What she really wants is someone to grab her pretty hair and—"

Connolly moves fast, but I move faster, getting between them so quickly Connolly's fist glances off my shoulder.

I turn to face the other guy. "That's where *you* get it wrong. Girls like me love respect. Can't get enough of it. Can't get enough of guys who show it, either. My sister and I were driving along with Aiden here, and we just couldn't help ourselves. Insisted he pull off for a threesome in the woods over there. *That's* where respect gets you."

The guy pauses, not quite knowing what to do with this. Insulting women with sex talk isn't nearly as much fun when they join in.

Finally, he says, "Well, if you're into threesomes, you should try me on for size. I'm sure Aiden here didn't quite scratch the itch."

"Mmm, no. He scratched it very well." I step back to run my hand up Connolly's arm. "When a guy knows how to treat a woman out of bed, it's a sure sign he knows how to treat her *in* bed."

The guy snorts. "Yeah, that's not what I heard. Remember Tiffany in sophomore year, Aiden? She told me—"

"*Sophomore year?*" I say. "Sex at sixteen is the starting point of a very long learning curve. Or it's supposed to be." I peer at the guy. "Please tell me you know that."

"Wanna find out?"

I shudder. "God, no. That'd be like going from that"—I wave at Connolly's car—"to a moped."

Connolly moves forward. "And now that you two have met, perhaps a more complete introduction is in order. Travis, this is Ms. Bennett, Kennedy, this is Travis."

"Let me guess," I say. "He works for your father."

"Mother, actually."

I make a face. "Ugh. Sorry. That was sexist of me."

Travis saunters back to Connolly's car and hops onto the hood again.

I wince. "Really? You have a very limited repertoire, don't you, Travis?"

"I don't think we resolved this," Travis says, chin rising.

"Yeah, we kinda did," I say. "Aiden discreetly threatened to kick your ass, and you decided to get off his hood."

"K," Ani warns under her breath.

"Kick my ass?" Travis says. "Like hell. He was threatening to run to Mommy, as he always does."

"As I *never* do," Connolly murmurs. "All right, let's go with that, Travis. I'm threatening to tell my parents. Now get off my car—"

"It's not yours. It's Mommy and Daddy's."

"No," Connolly says. "It is mine. Bought with my money. Which I earned."

"From a business Daddy bought you."

Connolly's mouth opens, and then he pulls back. He glances my way. He wants to defend himself, but he knows Travis is baiting him.

It doesn't take a scrying ball to see the past between Connolly and Travis. From Travis's cracks, they've known each other for years. I'll go out on a limb and say they weren't childhood buddies. Their families know each other. Most likely, Travis's works for Connolly's.

They're the same height now, but Travis carries himself like a man who thinks he's bigger, and Connolly getting defensive about his height suggests it's a sore spot from his youth. Connolly was a small kid, and Travis was a big one. I picture Connolly as studious and quiet, but with the arrogance of privilege he still carries. Travis would have felt compelled to use his size to prove his superiority. Connolly might have been smarter and wealthier, but he was just a little redheaded punk, easily pushed around. That's changed. Connolly's *still* smarter and wealthier, but now, in a fair fight, I'd put my money on him.

"What do you want, Travis?" Connolly says, enunciating each word.

"Your mommy was wondering what you're doing out here. You canceled lunch—oh, I'm sorry, *brunch*. She saw where you were and had me come find you."

Travis smirks, as if waiting for Connolly to flush in embarrassment. Not even a touch of pink brightens Connolly's cheeks.

"Tell my mother that I'll call her," Connolly says. "Thank you for the message. You may leave now."

With that dismissal, it's Travis who colors. He covers it by crossing his arms and walking up to Connolly. "If she trusted you to tell her what you're doing, she'd have called you."

"Yes, and perhaps someday we'll no longer need to play this

little game, but for now, we are both stuck with it. My mother doesn't expect me to tell you what I'm doing. This is business. Family business. Your only job was to show up and report where you found me and what I seemed to be up to. And to convey the implicit message that I may have stepped beyond the circle of my mother's trust, but I cannot escape the circle of her influence. Message delivered. Now leave."

Travis spins to face me.

"No," Connolly says. "You have no parting words for Ms. Bennett or her sister. You've insulted my guests enough. If you feel the need to toss one final insult, please aim it at me."

Travis directs his glare my way, as if I'm puppeteering Connolly. He opens his mouth again.

"No," Connolly says, the word harsher now. "That is your last warning. And before you say it, I *won't* tell my mother on you. I'll tell yours. That is always so much more effective."

Ani stifles a laugh that has Travis starting to turn on her before muttering something about Connolly, incoherent but obviously unflattering. Then he stalks back to the SUV where the other two men wait.

CHAPTER FIFTEEN

I SIT UP FRONT, and Connolly drives. He might seem calm, but as a kid, I endured the female version of Travis—the girl who decided it was her mission to grind my confidence into the dirt. As an adult, I look back and realize she'd been envious. She was the only child of divorced parents, both of whom seemed to want a child-free life. I had what she didn't, and she took it out on me. Yet even though I understand and feel sorry for her, my stomach still clenches when I see her around town. Connolly may act as if he was immune to Travis's insults, but that doesn't mean he is.

He's quiet, focused on his driving, which is actually really good once he's not trying to multitask. He checks his blind spots and uses signals and everything. We've been on the road for about twenty minutes when he says, "I'm sorry you were subjected to that."

"I loved the part where you were about to knock him flying."

His lips twitch. "More like knock him staggering."

"I suppose I should say that violence doesn't solve anything, but I kinda like guys defending my honor. I'm old-fashioned that way."

Ani makes a noise in the back seat. I ignore her.

"Moving right along," I say. "Any chance Travis could be involved with our kidnapper? He doesn't like you very much."

"If not liking me very much is the criteria, our suspect list will be very long indeed."

"Made a few enemies, have you?"

He goes quiet.

"I was kidding," I say.

"I almost wish I could say yes. With power comes enemies, and I can't claim more than disgruntled business rivals. In this field—the trade in magical objects and skills—I'm still a novice. Right now, I don't intimidate more than hapless employees, and that's unintentional. If anyone actually dislikes me, it's because of my background."

"Your family."

"For some, yes. With most, though, dislike stems from my station in general. I have money. I was raised in a certain way, with certain expectations, and it can make me"—a sidelong glance as his eyes twinkle—"a bit of an asshole."

"Hey, I didn't say it. This time."

"But I can be. The point is that I would be more surprised if Hope's captors liked me. In fact, I'd be disappointed. You saw how Travis behaves. He has always felt threatened by me, and he has always lashed out. Now that I can hit back, his behavior has only grown more juvenile. He feels more threatened by me at twenty-eight than he ever did at twelve. Hope's captor's insults are designed to belittle me. If that means he feels threatened, then I've made progress . . ." He trails off. "And that has nothing to do with finding your sister. I'm surprised you didn't cut me off a while back."

I shrug. "I decided to let you have it. In thanks for defending my maiden honor."

Ani snorts at that. She knows I'm really just letting Connolly talk to clear his head after Travis.

"You said you're new to this . . . whatever this is," I say. "Trading in cursed goods?"

"No, no. I mean, yes, I'm new to this particular business, but it goes much deeper than cursed goods. There are many ways to turn a profit from our talents."

"The gray market?" I say.

"Yes. There *is* a black one, but the gray market conducts an otherwise legal trade in magical goods and services. The *gray* comes from the fact that our powers give us an unfair advantage. One might say that you operate in this market yourself."

He pauses, as if waiting for an argument. He's right, though. My curse weaving gives me an advantage in the antique world. I'm not intentionally ripping anyone off, but I'd be the first to acknowledge that gray area.

When I don't comment, he says, "What you're doing now is small scale. It could be larger if you enlisted other curse weavers and expanded the operation, intentionally seeking out cursed objects across the country. The next step would be to involve others with magical talents, who would provide leads on cursed antiques."

"I don't think Kennedy is looking to go corporate with this," Ani says.

"That wasn't business advice." He changes lanes. "It could be if she wanted it. But I don't presume that what works for me works for everyone."

He glances in the mirror to meet Ani's gaze, and she gives a grudging nod.

He continues, "What I was doing was answering Kennedy's question with an example. That is how the gray market operates. For the last few years, I've been networking within it, mostly by offering my services as a luck worker."

"Working for *them*? Are you the same guy I spoke to this morning, who assured me, quite frostily, that he does not work for others?"

"I—"

"What was the wording? *I don't hire myself out like a common laborer.*"

"I . . . may have overstated the matter. Yes, I much prefer to work for myself, but here I must enter on the ground floor. This necklace auction is the first time I've acted on my own behalf. In other words, I'm a new player. That means I know some others, but I'm not embedded enough to know them well. I'd need help narrowing the field if you want to find out who has Hope. I'm not sure that's what you want, though—to find her rather than meet her captor's demands."

Before I can answer, Ani says, "We're meeting his demands. By having *you* back out of the auction."

Connolly lets out the softest sigh. "Again, it isn't that easy. I'm also not convinced Hope is the best one to uncurse the necklace. I don't think it's a lover's lament."

"Then what is it?" Ani asks.

I take over and explain as Connolly drives.

———

UNSTABLE IS the prettiest town in Massachusetts. Okay, I may be biased, but as we turn onto the main street—Bishop—my heart swells, and every muscle relaxes with the unmistakable relief of being home.

It's a postcard-perfect New England town, and everyone works very hard to keep it that way. We're too far from the ocean for fishing and too far from the forests for logging. The earth isn't great for crops, either. Our number-one industry is tourism.

Unstable staked its claim to fame at the beginning of the Victorian spiritualism craze. One of the first mediums to take her show on the road came from here. The town capitalized on that by welcoming other traveling psychics and mediums, who started adding Unstable as a pre-Boston tour event.

Soon mediums weren't just stopping by for a show; they were stopping here for good. When they tired of life on the road, they chose Unstable as their new home.

The old records show lots of blah-blah about ley lines, but the truth is, Unstable is just a very pretty place to live. It may be miles from the Atlantic Ocean, but it has several picturesque creeks, all feeding into a small lake. It lacks those huge swaths of quintessential New England forest, but the early settlers left plenty of trees standing, and every yard boasts majestic oaks or maples or elms. The earth isn't ideal for crops, but the rolling hills are perfect for livestock, and we're surrounded by grassy expanses dotted with cows and sheep.

It helped, too, that Unstable itself was so welcoming to those who "saw beyond the veil." No one wants to live anyplace they aren't wanted. In Unstable, that red carpet has been out for nearly two hundred years. It's still kept fresh and steam-cleaned. The only difference is that, as welcoming as Unstable is today, there isn't really room for new psychics and mediums looking to ply their trade. These are family businesses, like ours, priding themselves on having offered their services for generations.

The same goes for the nonparanormal trade that grew up to support the town. We have more B&Bs per capita than anyplace else in the state. Also more ice cream shops, candy stores and bakeries. There's some flux as tastes change—artisanal everything is huge now—but mostly current shops just adjust their focus to meet new demand.

Every one of those businesses—paranormal and otherwise—is in a building at least a hundred years old. Some have always been shops. Others are converted houses. A few—like ours—are residential homes that were built with a business entrance.

As we head down Bishop Street to the library, I sneak a glance at Connolly. I want him to be charmed by Unstable, and I'm afraid of seeing the opposite—that disdainful curl of his lip as I hear him talking about the tea caddy again.

Piece of kitschy trash . . .

Instead, he looks straight ahead, as if he doesn't notice anything worthy of either interest or scorn, and somehow that's more disappointing.

I direct him to the library, an adorable saltbox house near the east end of the business district. As we walk to the back entrance, Connolly says, "Jonathan went back to work today?"

After his best friend had been kidnapped?

He doesn't say that, but I still hear it.

"This isn't the city," I say. "He can't just call someone else in. There are three librarians. One is on leave. The other . . . can't be left in charge."

"A new hire?" he asks.

"Not exactly."

Ani opens the door first, pushing it for us before she hurries in. The smell of library wafts out, that sweet, slightly musky odor of old books. When Connolly starts to stride after my sister, I lift a hand to stop him.

"Give them a moment."

Ani makes a sharp left and heads for the community room, where Jonathan is waiting. I lead Connolly into the library proper. A white-haired woman hurries from behind the counter, her arms spread wide, the smell of Chanel No. 5 enveloping me in her hug.

"Miss Clara," I say. "So good to see you."

"And you, Kennedy." She puts me at arm's length for a good look. "You're growing so fast. Have you finished those Nancy Drew books? I have a few more. Also,"—she lowers her voice to a conspiratorial whisper—"I snuck in an order for those comics you like."

"Thank you, Miss Clara." I squeeze her hand. "I'll look at them later."

She sees Connolly and straightens, her gaze sliding over him, dark eyes radiating disapproval. "And who is this young man following you around?"

"He isn't following me," I say. "He's with me. We're going to talk to Jonathan in the community room."

"Ah." Her face smooths as she winks. "A secret project, huh? What is it this time? Another Memorial Day prank?" She pats my arm. "Just be careful with the fireworks, dear."

"Always. Jonathan and Ani make sure of it."

She chuckles. "They do keep you in line." Her gaze lifts to Connolly. "Are you going to introduce me, Kennedy?"

"Sorry. This is Aiden Connolly. Aiden, this is Miss Clara."

She looks him over again, her gaze softer now. "Aiden Connolly. A good Irish name for a good-looking Irish boy. *An bhfuil Gaeilge agat?*"

When Connolly looks at her blankly, she chuckles. "The answer is no, then. You don't speak Irish. You should. It's important to remember where we come from. The language, the stories, the traditions. Kennedy speaks Greek."

"I . . . didn't know that."

"I'll put together a little package of books for you."

I tense, ready for him to tell her not to bother, but he inclines his head with a murmur of genuine thanks. As we head toward the community room, he says, his voice low, "It's good of Jonathan to let her keep pretending to work here. Make her feel useful."

"He's not pretending. She *does* work here. She *is* useful. The memory lapses are sporadic, and everyone knows to just go with her flow. She can still do her job fine. She just can't be left to work alone."

"My mistake," he says. "I didn't intend any insult."

"I know. It's just . . . different here. Sometimes for the worse, but mostly for the better. In my opinion, at least. Depends on what you want out of life."

"Yet you moved to Boston."

"I did. It seemed . . ." I shrug it off. "Not important right now. Jonathan and Ani are right through there." I point at the door. "Time to talk."

CHAPTER SIXTEEN

ELLIE IS in the community room, confined to a makeshift bed, which will need to be washed later. As cool as *library cat* sounds, it's unfair to patrons with allergies. The only alternative is a hairless feline, and I've told Jonathan I could deliver that with a decent electric razor, but apparently, that would be "wrong."

Ellie and Connolly introduce themselves, which means glancing briefly at each other before settling into mutual ignoring. I get the same treatment from Ellie. Earlier, she acted as if she didn't need my goodbye, but now I get the cold shoulder, mingled with a generous dose of side-eye.

"You could cuddle on my lap," I say as I take a seat.

Her eyes narrow.

"Just a suggestion."

Jonathan picks up the bed and moves it to a chair between mine and Ani's.

"I don't think she wants that," I say.

"Oh, believe me, she does." He pats Ellie's head. "Better, right?"

The cat settles in and glares at me.

"*Constant* side-eye," I say. "Definitely better."

He chuckles. "That's her way of saying 'I love you, please don't ever leave me.'"

"Or 'Are you still here? I thought I ditched you for the nice guy.'" I turn away from the cat's accusing stare. "Moving right along. It's story time in a very appropriate setting. Jonathan, don't forget to do the voices and actions. I know you can."

"You go first," he says.

I don't need to do much to bring Jonathan up to speed. He'd been texting with Ani as cellular service resumed in Unstable. All I have to do is fill in the gaps.

Then Jonathan updates us on his morning. With Miss Clara on the desk and cell service restored, he's been able to pop in and out, investigating.

In Boston, unless we had proof of kidnapping, the police would be telling us to wait twenty-four hours before considering Hope a missing person. Here, they'd have opened a case right away. However, they'll also *not* open a case if we ask to handle it ourselves.

The police chief is Mrs. Salazar's niece, and if there's a queen bee in our psychic community, Mrs. Salazar is it. Her family has been here as long as ours. Do they have any actual psychic abilities? They believe so, and we don't argue. Even privately, we don't discount the possibility. That would be rude.

Several of the Salazars work in the paranormal trade. Most, though, have shifted into commerce and government, and locals especially appreciate the latter. Where else can you tell the police chief that your sister has been kidnapped by someone who wants her curse-weaving powers, but you're on top of it and don't need their help?

Why tell the police at all then? Professional and personal courtesy. The chief would be less than thrilled if she discovered we'd been asking questions about an unreported crime. This way, she's informed, and Jonathan can go about his investigation, which he has.

He's compiled a list of clues. Strangers in Unstable last night. Unrecognized cars on Bishop Street after dark. Also, black butterflies seen in our front garden, corpse candles spotted over the marsh and one psychic who dreamed of Hope wandering a dark wood, lost and alone, wearing a blue jacket.

All of these go onto the list with equal solemnity. Sure, we'll ignore everything after "unknown people and vehicles," but again, it'd be rude to leave off the rest. Even the stranger sightings likely have nothing to do with Ani and Hope's kidnapping. It might be midweek and not quite tourist season, but people still pass through Unstable, even late at night.

As for Ani and Hope's car, it was found just outside town, abandoned on what the kidnappers likely presumed was an abandoned road but is actually the favorite local dog-walking route. For now, we're leaving the car there in case we need evidence from it.

The other potential avenue of investigation is the woman who tried to hire my sisters. Connolly didn't recognize the description Ani provided. We're guessing she's with the kidnappers. We'll need to ask around and see who saw her that morning. It's a guarantee someone did.

In the end, though, none of us are certain how much we'll need any of this information, even the pieces that could lead us to Hope.

Are we going to search for her? While it seems obvious—my sister has been *kidnapped*—even Chief Salazar said that if we know what these people want, and we can give it to them, it might be wise to simply complete the transaction. No one wants to pay off kidnappers, but if the price is reasonable, that may be the victim's safest bet.

Is the price reasonable?

Hell, yeah. Connolly just needs to drop out of the auction. Yes, we're concerned that Hope might not be able to unweave this curse, but I can suggest to her captors that all three Bennett sisters take a shot and do their combined best.

"Have I been misled, then?" Connolly says when I suggest this. "I was under the impression that a failed unweaving is as dangerous as the curse itself, perhaps more so."

"That depends," Ani says. "Which is why we evaluate the curse first and weigh it against our skill level. Even Kennedy doesn't take chances."

"Even Kennedy," I say. "Wow. Thanks."

She glances over. "Shall we talk about *why* you don't take chances? Once burned, twice shy?"

"Literally burned," Jonathan murmurs. "I remember that."

"Hard for you to forget when it was *your* car she set on fire."

"He bought a cursed car," I say to Connolly.

"It was cheap," Jonathan says.

"Please tell me it was insured," Connolly says.

"It was. In the end, I came out ahead. The car was worth more than I paid."

"Because it was *cursed*," I say. "A lesson to both of us. I don't unweave spells above my skill level. You don't buy things that seem suspiciously cheap."

"No, I just don't buy them before checking with you guys." Jonathan looks at Connolly. "I'll also say, in Kennedy's defense, that it was my first car, so she was just a kid. Also, it was a really tough jinx. She'd have no problem with it now."

"Thank you," I say. "Back to the point, though, yes, we don't attempt overly difficult curses for fear of backlash. *Your* point was that this *is* a difficult one. Possibly beyond all our skill levels. That's why I'd suggest to Hope's captor that Ani and I get a look at it first. If it's too complex, we can warn him before he buys it."

"That's . . . not going to work," Connolly says.

"Because the seller won't let us see it? I'm sure we can find a way around that."

"I'm sure we can, too. Then, if it is too complex, you're just going to tell this man that none of the Bennetts can do it, so he should release Hope. Naturally, he'll take your word for it and let her go."

I peer at him. "Was that sarcasm? I think so, but it's hard to tell with you."

Before he can answer, I say, "Yes, you have a point. Let me turn that question over to you. What's our escape hatch there? It's the most famous curse in history. If it could be easily uncursed, a weaver would have done it by now."

"I wouldn't bet on that," Jonathan says. "It's been with regular humans for generations."

Connolly nods slowly. "I would agree. However, the necklace itself is thousands of years old. Surely, back when people believed in curses, weavers would have attempted it."

"On a limited scale," Jonathan says. "Without the internet—or even phone directories—it would have been hard to find real curse weavers. Which doesn't mean some haven't taken a shot at it. It's not going to be a run-of-the-mill curse."

I turn to Connolly. "What's your suggestion for a backup plan?"

"Isn't that obvious?" Ani says. "He's pointing out that our plan isn't foolproof and therefore we should let him buy the necklace and find another way to free Hope."

Connolly turns a cool gaze on her. "I was not going to say that. I raised a valid point that applies regardless of who gets the necklace. If Kennedy can't uncurse it for me, that hardly solves *my* problem."

"What *is* your problem?" I ask. "We're going to need to understand why this necklace is so important to you."

He doesn't answer.

Ani shoves back her chair, marches to the door and throws it open. "We don't need you, Aiden. All Kennedy has to do is admit you were listening in to the call, which means there's no way in hell you'd back out of the auction."

"I would ask you not to do that. In fact, I'd ask it very strongly."

"Is that a threat?" Ani says.

"No, it is not."

I cut in. "He means there's more than one way to keep him from bidding."

Jonathan swears under his breath and then nods.

Ani looks from him to me. "I don't understand."

"Whoever kidnapped Hope wants Aiden out of the picture," I say. "The easy way is for me to thwart his efforts. The hard way . . ."

I slice across my throat. Connolly gives me a look.

"What?" I say.

"You have definitely read too many crime novels," he says. "While we're here, we'll grab you some lighter reading material. Fantasy, perhaps. Or science fiction."

"Hey, plenty of killers in those, too. Assassins *everywhere*. It's awesome. Well, unless you're on their hit list."

Connolly shakes his head. "I am not on anyone's hit list. I'm not powerful enough for that."

"Don't worry. You'll get there."

"Thank you." He looks at Jonathan and Ani. "While I doubt my actual *life* is in danger, Hope's captor isn't going to shrug and say

'Oh, well' if Kennedy can't trick me out of the auction. He will take stronger measures to remove me. As strong as necessary, short of actual murder, and even that . . ."

Connolly drums his fingers on the table, notices what he's doing and pulls his hand back.

"My family has enemies," he says. "I don't think anyone would kill me, but"—a throat clearing—"I'd rather not find out what they *will* do. Consider that a confession. One I don't make easily. I'm at your mercy here, and it seems dangerous to pretend otherwise. I would ask you—very strongly—not to tell this man that I know he wants me out of the auction."

Ani looks at me, and Connolly tenses, as if we're silently debating his fate. We aren't. What we're asking each other is whether we believe he's in danger. The answer, I think, is that anyone capable of kidnapping isn't going to give up so easily.

"Let's take a break," I say. I nod at Ani and Jonathan. "You two talk. Plot. Check out our house for clues. Connolly? Ever had frozen custard?"

"Frozen . . . ?"

"Custard."

"No . . . But I'm not really hungry right now."

"Too bad. I am, and I need my first custard of the season. Coming or staying?"

He pushes back his chair. As we leave, Ani mouths, "We need answers."

We do. And I'm really hoping—with a frozen treat and a bit of privacy—I can get them.

CHAPTER SEVENTEEN

CONNOLLY WALKS out of the library and heads straight to his car.

"Uh . . ." I call after him. "Fleeing so soon?"

He frowns at me. "I thought we were going for ice cream."

"Custard, but yes, we are. It's within walking distance. Here, everything is within walking distance."

He pauses, and I swear I see that churning behind his eyes, as if he's trying to put the words *walking* and *distance* together in some way that makes sense in his world.

"We can drive if you want," I say. "But it's two hundred yards away. Also . . ." I nod toward Ellie, who's meandering through the gardens, as if she hasn't followed me out.

"Right. Yes. Of course. We'll walk."

He still pauses at his car door, looking through the tinted window and then patting his pockets. I think he's forgotten something, but he doesn't open the door or take anything from his suit jacket. I realize he's just mentally shifting into walking mode, figuring out what—if anything—he needs for the adventure.

I point at the blazing May sun and then pop on my sunglasses. "Might need these. You can probably also lose the jacket."

"Right."

He hesitates, and I bite back a laugh.

"Or you can leave it on," I say.

"No, no. It *is* getting warm."

He sheds the jacket and takes out his sunglasses. Earlier, I'd reflected that the men surrounding his car weren't federal law officers, despite their short hair and suits. That's what Connolly looks like, though, in his shades and tie. Or maybe not an actual agent as much as the TV version. Sculpted jaw, high cheekbones, lean build very nicely filling out his tailored shirt. The sun glints off his hair, making it more gold than red. Even the mud spatter on his shoes only adds to the image of the hard-working agent, nattily dressed despite tramping through the forest in search of clues.

He bends to check his reflection, pushing a stray lock of hair in place, the small flash of vanity oddly adorable. Also, in bending, he presents a very fine rear view, unhindered by his suit jacket.

He catches me looking, and his brows shoot over his shades.

"You've got a bit of dirt or something," I say. "Right here." I tap my hip.

"Ah." He brushes at the clean spot. "Thank you."

"Anytime. Ready?"

He nods, and we head onto the street, Ellie trotting along at a suitable distance. As we walk, I'm glad he grabbed his sunglasses. I'm sure it's easier on his eyes. Also, they look good. But mostly, I'm happy that I can't see his reaction to our surroundings.

It's turned into a gorgeous May day. A cherry tree drops petals like kisses blown in the wind. Magnolias perfume the air with a scent that always reminds me of great-aunt Dimitra. Every lawn is golf-course green, and whether it's a business or residence, flowers burst from gardens and overflow from pots. Every now and then, I catch the scent of fresh paint or fresh-cut grass. It doesn't matter if I walk through Boston parks every day—this is different. This is home at the most magical time of year, the town sparkling bright, ready for Memorial Day crowds.

Does Connolly see that sparkle? Does he smell the magnolias? Hear people greeting me as they spruce up yards and storefronts and gardens? Or is his gaze fixed down the road, searching for a sign that marks the end of our journey?

Or is it worse than that? Is he looking around and judging? Seeing past the pretty gardens and gorgeous architecture to the theme park beneath. Because that's what Unstable is, in its way.

It's not Salem—thank God. The only reference to that tragedy is in the names of our streets, honoring the dead. There are good people in Salem, who want a memorial to the horror of the witch trials, but there are too many who just want to profit off people's fascination with it. Here, we celebrate the paranormal and our fascination with *that*. A fascination with the possibility of magic in the world.

As we walk, we pass a dream therapist, a tarot reader and a numerologist. We also pass a B&B, a sandwich spot, a soap store, a candy shop—specializing in fudge, of course—and a little place where you can craft your own crystal bracelet. They're all services catering to tourists. Also all the sorts of places you might find in a theme park. I'm okay with that. I'm rather fond of theme parks, and there's an old-fashioned earnestness I love about this one. But what does Connolly see? I don't dare ask.

I already feel a bit foolish, wanting him to see the beauty of my town, like a girl with a new haircut, hoping a certain boy will notice. No, that analogy doesn't quite work. It's more like when I brought home college friends. I wanted them to like Unstable—and not judge me for liking it. I'm not sure why Connolly's opinion matters. It just feels as if it does.

We make it to the custard shop without a word exchanged. I almost jump when he speaks.

"I'll wait out here while you get your snack."

"You don't want one?" I say.

"I don't eat sweets."

"Don't eat sweets? Or don't *like* sweets?"

His hesitation is all I need. I tug him through the door, the bells jangling. Mrs. Madani emerges from the back, and thus begins the ten minutes of chitchat I'll endure if I step into any shop along this street.

I say *endure*. I mean *adore*. I love coming home and catching up with people I've known all my life. I try to cut this conversation short, being very aware of Connolly waiting, but he shows no sign of impatience, so I chatter away as I place my order. Connolly continues to protest that he really doesn't need anything until I threaten to get him an "everything" custard—every mix-in on the shelf. He orders a small salted caramel, and we head out back to the garden tables, where Ellie waits on the low wall.

"If you really don't want it, I'll eat it," I say as he stares into his bowl.

"No, I . . ." He lifts the spoon and nudges the custard, as if it might bare teeth. "It looks quite good."

"Looks good. Is good. Dig in."

He does . . . and finishes his before I'm halfway done mine.

"Not so bad, huh?" I say, arching my brows at his empty bowl.

Spots of color underscore the sunglass lenses. "It's . . . been a while since I've had sweets. I have a . . . tendency to overindulge."

I run a quick glance down his shirt. "Unless you're hiding it really well, I'm not seeing it."

"Because I know my weakness and steer clear."

I stop, midway through twisting to drop a spoonful for Ellie. "Like teetotal-ing sugar? That's some serious willpower. How long have you been doing that?"

He considers. "Twenty years."

"Since you were a *kid*?" I sputter.

"I started putting on some weight, and my mother excised sugar from my diet. I do have the occasional treat but . . ." He fingers the empty bowl, staring down as if hoping it might magically refill. Then he snaps upright. "Best not to tempt fate."

"Uh, look, I'm not going to comment on your mother's methods. Biting my tongue hard here."

His lips twitch. "I see that."

"But you're an adult, and something tells me you don't have a problem with self-control."

He lifts the bowl, displaying the spotless interior.

"Right," I say. "But that was a small. And you aren't rushing back in for seconds."

"Is that an option?"

His lips twitch again, and even with his sunglasses on, I feel the surge of warmth. It does something to my insides, and I quickly focus on my own now-melting custard.

"I'm just saying you seem like you can handle it," I say. "Which is none of my business anyway. Sorry."

His lips curve into a genuine smile, and when he tugs off his shades, that summer glow makes me scoop custard faster, and I stare into my cup as if it's a scrying bowl holding the secrets to my future.

"Don't apologize," he says. "You're very easy to talk to, and I don't mind a little easy conversation right now. Especially if it delays you reaching the real point of this excursion, which was getting me to explain why I can't drop out of the auction."

I lift my gaze to his. "That obvious, huh?"

"Well, either that or you just wanted to spend more time with me."

"I—"

He lifts his hand. "I'm teasing, Kennedy. Your sister has been kidnapped. You wanted to get me away from Ani and Jonathan in hopes I'll be more comfortable speaking to you alone."

"We do need to know, Aiden. In whatever detail—or lack of it— you can manage. Only one of us needs the story. We trust one another. If you'd rather speak to Ani or Jonathan . . ."

"No, I'd rather speak to you. I *will* ask for discretion, though. This . . ." He clears his throat and reaches for the sunglasses before thinking better of it and pushing them aside.

"The problem," he says, "is that even if I explain, I'm not sure you'll understand. Without standing in my shoes, you can't see the situation from my perspective."

"Just tell me what you can."

CHAPTER EIGHTEEN

I WOULD LOVE to say that Connolly launches straight into his story after that. He doesn't. He throws his empty bowl in the trash. Checks his phone while murmuring something vaguely apologetic. Double-checks his phone when there aren't any messages to stall him further. Attempts to pet Ellie. Gets scratched. Requires napkins to staunch the bleeding . . .

Five minutes later, he's looking at his hand, roughly bound in blood-soaked napkins. "Please tell me your cat has had her shots."

"I will . . . right after *you* tell *me* your damned story."

"I'm just—"

"Stalling," I say. "While my one sister is held captive and the other is already texting, wanting me to send you packing if you don't explain."

"The necklace isn't for me. That's why I said the money's not important. I need to win the auction and uncurse the necklace for a third party."

I lift a spoonful of melted custard and wave it at him. "Kinda sounds like being an employee. Oh, wait. *Service provider.* Isn't that what you called me?"

He doesn't answer. When Ellie rubs against his leg, he reaches down, but I snatch her away.

"Might I suggest there are better ways to escape this conversation than inviting bodily injury?"

I get a hard look for that, but he doesn't argue. I set Ellie down with the remains of my custard cup.

"Fine," he says. "I wouldn't say I'm working for this person, but that's splitting hairs. I'm uncomfortable with the situation."

"There's nothing wrong with working for others."

"Unless your parents run a Fortune 500 corporation, so no one believes your company is actually yours."

"They presume your insurance business is one of your parents' holdings. Like giving your kid a building set to keep him busy, encourage him to play independently, see what he can make with it."

He nods. "Which isn't the case at all. Even the initial loans didn't come from them." He fingers the sunglasses on the table. "I'm sorry. That sounded defensive."

"As someone who runs her own business, unconnected to the family one, I get it. I hear the whispers in the magical community. That I moved to Boston to get out from under my sisters' shadows. That I need to call them in for the tough jobs. Sometimes, I think . . ." I shake my head. "Sometimes, I *know* I got out to prove myself to the faceless nobodies whispering behind my back. Instead, I gave them more to whisper about."

"Yes," he says quietly. His gaze lifts to mine. "Exactly that."

"You have your own business," I say. "And I would love—*love*— to know how it operates with the luck working. Hell, I'd love to know more about luck working in general. But the point right now is that we're both ambitious young business owners. Those ambitions may mean taking on side jobs that add ladder rungs to levels we can't otherwise reach."

"Yes." He eases back, getting comfortable. "That's what I've done so far in the gray market. I have skills. Those skills get me places I otherwise couldn't enter—too young, too inexperienced, etcetera. But getting the necklace isn't a job. It's an obligation."

"You owe someone." I nod. "Drug debt or gambling?"

The horror on his face makes me laugh.

"I'm kidding," I say. "Though I believe you did mention cards before."

"I said I'm *good* at them. I haven't racked up a drug or gambling debt. It's my brother's." He hurries on. "Still not a drug or gambling debt. Or I hope not. Though . . ." He exhales and runs a hand through his hair.

"Your brother is a little wilder than you, I'm guessing."

"That bar is set low. Very low. Although, at the risk of bragging, I did skip an entire *day* of school in my senior year. Well, two classes. And one may have been study hall, but I was *not* studying. In fact, I had left the premises entirely."

"Was there a girl involved?"

His lips curve. "Possibly. So yes, that bar is low, and Rian jumps it. Vaults it, I should say. The debt is to someone in the magical black market. Rian bit off more than he could chew in a business endeavor, which he insists wasn't actually illegal but . . ."

Connolly pauses, and then adjusts his tie and eases back, and I see the curtains closing. He's decided he's too relaxed, too at ease, giving too much of himself away.

"All that is irrelevant," he says briskly. "Family business. The point is that Rian has gotten himself into a bind, and his debtor demands the necklace, and my parents expect me to get it."

"Ah . . ."

His eyes narrow, and he withdraws more, as if sensing mockery. It isn't mockery, though. It's comprehension. This is why he'd been so prickly about working for someone else. Ultimately, that "someone else" is his parents.

I don't say that. He doesn't want—or need—me analyzing him. It just helps my own understanding of what's going on. Aiden Connolly prides himself on his independence. He's distinguished himself apart from the family business, and when he does hire out his skills, it is to further his own advantage. He has complete control over his professional life . . . until his little brother screws up and his parents dump the debt at his feet. Then he's right back where he started, trapped in a dynamic he can't escape.

"I meant I understand," I say. "It's family business, like you said."

He relaxes. "Yes."

"Which is none of my business."

He squirms, gaze shifting. "Not to be rude, but yes. I have an obligation to my family. I must fulfill it."

"Which is no business of mine."

Now he hesitates, the slightest furrow of his brow, as if trying to figure out why I'm saying the same thing in a different way.

"Your business isn't my business," I say. "I'm sorry, Aiden. I completely understand family obligations. But *mine* is my sister and her safety. We're talking about her life versus your brother's debt. One of these things is worth more than the other. Maybe not to you, and I won't argue your perspective. Your family, though, is not my concern. Your obligation to them is not my concern."

"Of course. No, I didn't mean— I *wouldn't* imply that Rian's debt is worth more than Hope's safety. The problem is that Rian's debt *is* his safety. He's gotten mixed up with someone who doesn't take an IOU. I'm not saying his life is in danger, and I wouldn't ask you to risk your sister's life to keep my brother from whatever danger *he* faces. But I believe Hope is still in danger if I back out of this auction —the danger of being forced to unweave a notorious curse. Beyond that, I *can't* back out, Kennedy. It isn't an option."

"Why is getting the necklace *your* job? Your parents are the ones with power and connections."

"Rian got mixed up with this person because of me."

I frown. "You put them in contact?"

"Certainly not. Rian knows I'm making inroads in the gray market. My parents are pleased about that. I didn't do it to please them, but there you have it. They're happy. Just like with my business. I didn't launch it to please them. I don't work sixty hours a week to please them. But they are pleased."

Frustration laces his voice. He must hear it because he pulls back, his tone smoothing out as he adjusts his posture.

"My success led Rian to one-up me," he says. "That is our pattern, as siblings. Whatever I do . . ."

"He needs to do better." I soften my voice. "And he never does, does he?"

Connolly shakes his head. I understand that all too well. Ani's the one who brought home straight As, who glided from strength to strength with the effortless grace of a figure skater. I know now that's not true—she works her ass off and has plenty of self-doubt—but growing up, all I saw was Ani's success.

Mom and Dad never favored her, never held her up as an example, would never say "Why can't you be more like your sister?" Others did, though. Teachers. Coaches. Even classmates.

In Connolly's case, I highly doubt his brother had that parental support. Yet somehow, Rian's endless scrabble to overtake his brother becomes Connolly's fault. A mess Connolly has to clean up. His brother's keeper.

I decide I hate Connolly's parents. Sure, nothing I've heard so far makes them candidates for parents of the year, but still, I dislike leaping to judgments. He'd joked that he was genetically disposed to be an asshole. Now I realize he wasn't kidding.

Silence falls then. Ellie returns to wind around Connolly's ankles, purring, and I'm about to shoo her off, but he doesn't notice the cat. He's lost in thought. When she realizes he's not falling for it again, she hops onto my lap. I give her a couple ear-scratches and then let her cuddle and purr.

"Two days," Connolly says abruptly, making Ellie dig in her claws as she propels herself from my lap.

"Give me two days to work this out," Connolly says.

"Which only leaves two more days to find Hope before the auction."

He shakes his head. "I wouldn't ask you not to look for her. If she's found, then we hit Pause unless the situation changes and she's in danger. For now, we split our efforts. One prong is finding your sister. The other is resolving my issue. Give me two days to do that. Please."

It's reasonable. Very reasonable. So why don't I leap in to agree? For one very selfish reason. This is the point where we go our separate ways, and I was enjoying this. Enjoying getting to know him, and that is unforgivably selfish under the circumstances.

"My investigation will help your sister as well," he says when I don't answer fast enough. "One way for me to resolve *my* issue is to learn who has Hope so we can free her. I'm just asking for two days before you make any sudden moves."

"I'll need to check with Ani," I say. "But I don't see a problem with it. It's a good division of labor and resources."

"Agreed," he says. "Now, I believe the place to start is still Vanessa. She may not have your sister, but she's our best source of information." He rises. "If we leave now, we can be there before dinner."

The word *we?* rises to my lips. I swallow it fast. He'll hear it as a question, stop to reconsider and realize there's no good reason to bring me along. There is, though—at least for me. He's talking to people I can't otherwise contact, stepping into a world I know nothing about. For Hope's sake, I should be there, learning what I can and making sure Connolly doesn't do anything—even accidentally—to endanger her.

"Yes?" he says. "We can leave now?"

"Just as soon as I get Ellie back to my sister."

CHAPTER NINETEEN

ESCORTING Ellie is really just an excuse for me to get my thoughts in order—and see my sister—before we leave. Our house is a quarter-mile from the custard shop, and Ellie knows the way. It might have made more logical sense to drop her off *there* instead of with Ani at the library but . . .

Is it weird that I don't want to take Connolly home? It feels awkward, like being a kid again with a potential new friend. For me, bringing someone home is a huge step, inviting them into my private corner of the world.

I don't feel that way about my apartment in Boston. My family home, though, is the repository of my memories, the repository of me. I have to trust a new friend enough to pull back that curtain, and if the friendship never solidifies, I feel as if I've lost something. Maybe none of that makes sense. All I know is that I'm not ready to take Connolly across that threshold.

We talk to Ani and Jonathan. Then, as we're leaving the library, Connolly offers to let me drive. He has calls to make, and while he's fine with multitasking, he got the feeling earlier I'd rather he stuck to one or the other. I appreciate that. We've battled over this partic-ular patch of ground, resolved the issue and moved on with maximum efficiency and minimal conflict. Nice.

So I drive while he places calls. He lets Vanessa know he's coming and warns her that he's bringing a "colleague." He also speaks to his tech person about the signal device we found at the cabin. She says it was almost certainly working on an independent SIM card, probably pay-as-you-go. Following her instructions, he finds and removes the card, and we make a stop to overnight it. After that, he offers to drive, and I agree.

"Can I ask about your business?" I say when we're back on the highway. "Pure curiosity. You can tell me no if it's proprietary information. Or if you just don't feel like talking about it."

"You're giving me the opportunity to brag about how terribly clever I am, finding a different way to make money using my magical talent. I think you realize exactly how irresistible that is—as someone who has done the same thing."

I smile. "True enough. We don't get nearly enough chances to brag. So, insurance, huh?"

"Yes, and don't even pretend you find that part of it interesting. It's been many years since I made the mistake of presuming anyone found the art and science of insurance as captivating as I do. Do you know how long a blind date lasts after you wax rhapsodic about actuarial tables?"

"Twenty seconds?"

"Ten, actually. I believe I got as far as 'the fascinating thing about actuarial tables is—' before she excused herself to use the restroom and never returned."

"Her loss. She probably missed the most passionate defense of statistics she'll ever hear."

"She did. Which I'll spare *you*. What you're interested in is the fun part. How I can use luck to nudge those statistics to my advantage. But first, how much do you know about luck working?"

"It involves working with luck."

He makes a sound that might actually be a chuckle. "It does, oddly. The thing about luck is . . . Well, my gran calls it fairy dust."

The words barely leave his lips before he glances over. "And don't say it."

"Say what?"

"The L-word."

I grin at him. "Leprechaun? It *is* a type of fairy."

"I walked into that one. My gran's point is that it's the most ephemeral of the magical talents. When you weave a curse or cast a charm, you know exactly what the outcome will be. The luck worker must be more careful. We're taking this cloud of fairy dust and trying to direct it, rather than let it land where it may. There is, of course, a time and place for general luck, but most people want something specific."

"Like winning a game at the casino instead of scoring them a free drink."

"Precisely. Then there's the issue of balance as with any magical talent. Good luck must be balanced with bad, which unfortunately can't be directed. Just managed."

He changes lanes, shoulder checking first. "Most luck workers adjust their own good fortune, juggling it in ways that benefit them. That's what my parents do. Both being luck workers means they can operate in tandem, bolstering one another. Which is why I'm supposed to have joined the family business. To help with that."

"But you didn't. Is that a problem?"

"It would be if the corporation was in trouble. As it stands, my parents are quite happy to support me because they see my business as a future acquisition. That's what the Connollys do. They spot talent and innovation, wait for it to blossom into a successful company and then . . ."

"Make them an offer they can't refuse?"

"Yes."

"Except, in your case, they wouldn't buy the business from you. They'd bring you into the fold *with* your company. Pull it—and you —under their umbrella."

He glances over. "Are you quite certain you don't have a business degree?"

"Actually, I didn't finish my degree. Dropped out when my father died. But it was a history major and business minor."

"An unusual combination. But it also means you weren't completely unprepared to open an antique shop."

"Did it seem like I was?" I make a face. "Sorry, that was defensive."

"And my comment held an air of condescension. We'll both withdraw to our corners and get back on track." He checks his rearview mirror. "Luck working and insurance. That was the original question. How they work together. Any guesses?"

Before I can open my mouth, he says, "Was *that* patronizing?"

I smile. "Only if you insist that I guess. Or make me feel stupid for guessing wrong."

"Neither."

"Then I'll take a shot at it. You use luck to swing the odds in your favor. Like you would at cards, only on a bigger scale."

"Bigger in terms of numbers," he says. "The luck manipulations are generally small, which makes them easier to offset. Microdosing, if you will. Find high-risk, high-profit policies that would benefit from a little luck manipulation and balance them by negatively affecting low-risk, low-profit policies."

"You're the only one who's tried this?"

"No, just as I'm sure you aren't the only one who's tried buying cursed antiques for resale. You have an eye for quality, an engaging personality and solid curse-weaving skills. It's the combination that works. Same with me. I started this business in high school. Several luck workers have tried it since. They fail because they aren't statisticians with a genuine love for actuarial science. They also don't share my caution. I avoid risk by nature. I'm not exactly offering insurance on racehorses."

"You offer regular insurance. To regular people."

"Primarily, yes. Managing risk and reward in a way others, like my brother, would find stultifying. What he sees as slow and plodding, I see as . . ." One hand lifts in a graceful wave. "Crafting. Refining. The challenge for me is creative precision. I see luck working as building a quiet masterpiece, one subtle stroke at a time. While Rian is . . ."

"Throwing paint at the wall?"

"Yes." He wrinkles his nose. "That sounds dismissive, doesn't it? I don't mean it that way. Rian has his own style."

"Abstract art versus old master. I get it. I've been known to throw a bit of paint in curse weaving. It drives Ani nuts. She's like you, careful and precise. I want to . . ." I pat the dashboard. "It's like having a fancy car. I want to see what my weaving can do. Put it through its paces."

"Explore and create. You in your way. Me in mine."

I smile at him, and he glances over, that wave of warmth washing through me. Then his gaze flicks to the rearview mirror, and he frowns. I twist to look behind us. The car following is a convertible, driven by a woman my age, who seems to be shouting at us, until I realize she's just belting out a song.

I'm about to comment when I spot another vehicle—on our right and two cars back. A black SUV with dark-tinted windows. Just like the one Travis had been driving. That's what caught Connolly's attention.

"I need to make a call," Connolly says. "If you'll excuse the interruption."

"Certainly."

He puts on his earpiece and stabs the console display so fast I see nothing but flashed icons. Then, without preamble, he says, "I didn't complain about you sending Travis because you already know how I feel about it. Silence does not in any way imply acceptance."

Through his earpiece, I catch a woman's voice, her words as clipped as his own.

He continues, "If I opened this call with a proper greeting, you would again take that as proof I'm not upset about being followed. You wish me to act like a son? Then please remember that's what I am. Or, failing that, treat me like a business associate who has done nothing to earn your mistrust."

A response, short and to the point.

Connolly's voice cools to sub-Arctic temperatures. "That was a personal matter, intended to show you just how much I dislike being treated like a rebellious teen. If you insist on clinging to that as an excuse for surveilling your own sons, might I suggest I'm not the one you should be watching."

Another glance into the mirror, and as he does that, he sees me and gives a start, as if he'd forgotten he wasn't alone. When he speaks again, his voice is calm and even.

"I'm actively trying to help Rian," he says. "Having Travis tail me—"

She speaks, cutting him off.

Frustration twangs in Connolly's voice. "Travis or anyone else from your security division."

Another response.

"I'm being followed by a black Ford Expedition with custom-tinted windows, Mother. Are you honestly going to tell me that isn't yours?"

I twist to look back. The SUV is in the right lane and closing the gap fast. I squint, hoping to see through the windows, but I can barely distinguish outlines. Two people. That's all—

The SUV accelerates.

"Connolly . . ." I say. "Watch—"

The other vehicle jerks toward us.

"Aiden!" I shout.

The SUV slams our right rear bumper, the angle sending us straight into the concrete divider and then spinning back into traffic.

We're going to die.

It happens almost too fast for any thought to process, but some-how, that one does. Not a scream, but a horrified whisper.

We're going to die.

We ricochet off the divider and spin back into oncoming, steady, seventy-mile-an-hour traffic, and we are going to die, and I'm never going to see my sisters again or my cat, my damned cat and—

The car stops, tires spitting gravel. For a second, the world seems to stop, too, and I think I'm dead. I must be. There is no way we survived that without ending up in a heap of twisted metal. Yet we're on the shoulder, across three lanes of traffic, and we're fine. Cars honk, and tires still screech, a delayed reaction to the distur-bance. But we're sitting here, breathing hard, and we're fine.

We just shot across three lanes of solid traffic and missed every oncoming car? That's impossible.

No, not impossible. Just lucky. Very, very lucky.

I glance at Connolly. He's collapsed against the steering wheel. I grab my phone from the floor, thinking he's been injured. Out of the corner of his eye, he sees me, lifts a hand and croaks, "I'm fine."

When I hesitate, he says, "Really. Just . . . give me a moment."

Not an injury then—exertion from using his powers. A blast of luck, cast at a split-second's notice.

I can say curse weaving wipes me out, but this is the equivalent of lifting a car off a trapped child, and he's pale and shaking as he struggles for breath.

"I can drive," I say. "Get us off the road—"

He lifts one unsteady finger. Two heartbeats pass. Then he glances over his shoulder, fingers on the door handle, as if he's considering opening it.

"The shoulder's wide enough for you to get out," I say.

"Right now, it's probably best if I just slide over. And, yes, definitely best if I don't take the wheel until—"

A police siren bleep-bleeps before wailing to life.

Connolly exhales, his shoulders slumping.

"It's fine," I say. "Inconvenient, but fine."

I open my door as the police cruiser pulls in behind us. I'm climbing out when Connolly touches my leg.

"Can you talk to them? I'm not—"

"Please step out of the car," an officer says.

I close my door and turn to her. "Thanks for coming. We're fine, but my friend is winded and—"

She raps on Connolly's window as if I haven't spoken. "Sir? Step out of the vehicle."

He hesitates. Then he pushes the door . . . and it smacks into the officer, who stumbles back. Connolly scrambles out, hands raised.

"I'm sorry," he blurts. "The door slipped—"

"Step away from the car, and keep your hands up. We just had a report of a vehicle driving erratically and then veering into the center divider."

"What?" I say.

I replay her words. Someone called this in. Someone who managed to get police on the scene mere moments after the accident.

We've been set up.

I don't know if our attackers meant to cause a fatal accident, but they sure as hell weren't expecting us to walk away without a scratch.

Someone just tried to kill us. And frame Connolly for his own death.

"My license is in my wallet," Connolly says. "My right rear pocket. May I remove that?"

"Slowly."

Connolly reaches back with care, but the wallet sticks, and when he pulls, the movement somehow sends him staggering into the officer, who backpedals fast.

"Up against the car," she snaps. Then she turns to her partner, who's still in the cruiser. With a growl of frustration, she calls, "I could use a little help here!"

As her partner climbs out, Connolly snags my gaze with a look of wide-eyed desperation that I don't understand . . . and then I do.

This is why he hadn't wanted to step out onto the shoulder. Why he'd agreed I should drive. Why he'd asked me to speak to the officers.

Balance.

That's why the car door hit the officer. Why Connolly smacked into her as he pulled out his wallet.

This is the price he'll pay for that surge of good luck. A run of bad luck until he's set the balance straight again.

The officer tells her partner to grab the Breathalyzer. She thinks Connolly's drunk. Of course she does. The call said he'd been driving erratically. Now he's disheveled and clumsy. Clearly, *someone* had a three-martini lunch.

I look from Connolly to the Breathalyzer, my eyes asking a question I can't voice. He shakes his head. His bad luck can't make the device give a false positive. Yet as I try to think of a way out of this, the officer struggles with the machine, which isn't working right. The Breathalyzer won't condemn him . . . but his bad luck means it won't exonerate him, either.

"We haven't had anything to drink, Officer"—I read her tag —"Bradford. We just had the scare of our lives. An SUV struck our rear bumper. A black Expedition. It hit our corner like a pool cue lining up a shot. We went into the median and bounced off, and I thought we were doomed. Aiden managed to steer us out of it, but obviously, he's a little freaked out right now."

My explanation doesn't impress Bradford, but it does calm

Connolly, and the Breathalyzer finally works. It shows zero alcohol in his system.

"Fine," she says. "You weren't drinking, but we still had a report."

"I can't explain that," I say. "But if you look at the bumper, it's freshly scratched."

It's obvious Officer Bradford does not want to drop this. Oh, I'm sure she would have been reasonable . . . if Connolly hadn't smacked into her *twice*. She's actually being very good about it.

I consider appealing to her partner, but he looks on the far side of sixty, one of those guys who are already mentally practicing their retirement golf swing. He's perched on the cruiser hood with a takeout coffee.

When he lifts his cup to his lips, hot coffee streams out both sides, making him yelp. Bradford shoots him a look.

"Bad lid," he mumbles and adjusts it.

She turns back to Connolly as her partner lifts his coffee, and it spills again, this time soaking his shirt.

"Look, the guy's fine," he says, plucking at his drenched shirt. "He blew clean. He didn't hit anyone. It looks like the girl's right— they got clipped. Either we file a report or just let it go."

Bradford glares at her partner, but he's agitated and just wants to get back on the road. After a few warnings for Connolly, Bradford sends us on our way. I climb into the driver's seat, and we're off.

"Damn dribble cups, huh?" I say.

Connolly gives a dry chuckle. "That was you, was it? Nicely done."

"Nothing like what you pulled off. Our lucky break."

He runs a hand through his hair. "Yes, but I nearly got myself arrested for assaulting an officer."

"How are you doing?"

"Feeling about as lucky as a man walking under a ladder on Friday the thirteenth."

"Should I be concerned?"

"No. Just stay away from me when I'm opening doors, apparently." He glances at an exit sign. "To be safe, we should probably pull off. Take a walk. Buy a coffee. Let me trip over my own feet, scald my tongue, get it out of my system."

"What about scratch cards?" I ask.

He arches his brows.

"Buy a bunch of scratch-and-win cards. Work off your bad luck that way."

"Worth a try," he says. "Though I'd still suggest you maintain a three-foot distance for at least the next hour."

CHAPTER TWENTY

THE SCRATCH TICKETS don't work as well as I'd hoped. I suppose that'd be too easy. Connolly promises to keep it in mind for smaller balancing acts though he may be humoring me. As he'd said earlier, he can't direct the luck balance. The trick, it seems, is to just proceed with extreme caution and let the bad luck sift away, grain by grain.

After the scratch tickets, Connolly slips on the shop floor and, when picking himself up, manages to both bang his shin and fart—loudly and noxiously. I help him outside and leave him on the curb while I get the car. As he waits, a passing bird poops on his sleeve, and a car hits a puddle five feet away and still manages to splash him. At least it cleans off some of the bird shit.

Connolly has an extra shirt in his trunk, but we decide it's too soon in the bad-luck cycle for that. Instead, we hit a coffee shop. He goes into the bathroom to clean up . . . and breaks the faucet. So we sneak out and find another shop, where I bring him damp towels, and he cleans himself with moderate success. I buy us coffee while he sits at a table, touching nothing, not even his phone—which he insisted I confiscate until he's rebalanced. Apparently, he's had some experience with that.

At the frozen-custard shop, he'd chosen salted caramel, so I get him a caramel latte. I buy a cappuccino for myself and a brownie for us to share. At the table, I double-check the heat level of his latte—I'd asked for "kids' temperature"—and the integrity of the cup before passing it over. Then I started cutting his half of the brownie into small, unchokable chunks, earning me double takes and titters from surrounding tables.

"This is embarrassing," Connolly says.

I stop cutting. "Sorry. I should let you do this yourself. I just thought . . ." I wave at the knife. "I guess plastic is safe, though."

"I didn't mean that. Just . . ." He spreads his hands. "All this. It's like an anxiety-dream first date." He stops short and clears his throat. "Not that this is a date."

"You mean it feels like the anxiety-dream version of one. Where everything that can go wrong does."

He nods. "Yes. And I'm sorry for all this."

"Because you're getting shit on by birds for saving my *life*? I owe you a hundred cut-up brownies, Connolly."

"You wouldn't have been in danger if you weren't in my car."

"And we wouldn't have been in your car if we weren't trying to find my sister." I set down the knife and push the pieces toward him. "I think we're both feeling guilty here, and neither of us should. You didn't lose control of the car. I didn't grab the wheel and send us into the median. The fault lies with whoever tried to *kill* us."

"It wasn't my mother."

"Obviously."

He fusses with a tidbit of brownie before popping it into his mouth. "I know I haven't left the best impression of my family, and there are people who'd think she'd do something like that. I will not say she'd never do it to *anyone* but . . ."

"Not to her son. Like I said, obviously." I lean back and sip my cappuccino. "While I get the impression I wouldn't want her for a mother—"

I almost say "mother-in-law" before realizing how that could sound.

I continue, "But you don't strike me as the kind of guy who'd keep sending Mother's Day cards to Medea. I've refrained from commenting on anything you've said about them because they're your family. That's sacred ground."

"Thank you. It's clear you come from a very different sort of family, but yes, this is mine, and I am still part of it as difficult as that can be."

"So whoever tried to kill us either just happened to choose the same model of big-assed SUV. Or they wanted you to think it was your parents. Seeing a vehicle like theirs following you would be annoying, but not suspicious."

He chews another brownie scrap and recedes into thoughtful silence.

After a moment, I say, "Does this make sense?"

"That someone tried to kill us? No. We can argue that they might have just intended to give us a scare, but a massive SUV hitting a sedan at highway speeds? On a busy road? The chance of a fatal accident is always there."

"Either they intended to kill us or just didn't care if they did." I stir my drink and then look at him. "How much is this necklace worth?"

"As is? It's expected to sell for mid six figures. Remove the magic, and that could double. Remove only the misfortune curse and leave the youth and beauty part, and it'd fetch ten times that. But the value isn't the issue here. People will kill for much less. The issue is that we don't have the necklace. We are in no way assured of getting it. I'm one contender, and you're one potential curse weaver."

"If they even knew who was in the car with you." I stir again, my gaze on the foam as it melts into the coffee. "You must be the presumptive auction winner, then. You have your parents' backing with their money and influence. Someone expects you to win."

"But I *don't* have their backing. Not officially. I need to be the underdog, no threat to the big names. My parents agree, and they've quietly grumbled in the right ears about me getting involved with this."

"Someone knows the truth, though. That you're a serious contender."

"Am I?" He shakes his head. "I think I can be a serious threat, for my brother's sake. Right now, though? I don't see it, which means I don't see why anyone would bother trying to take me out of the game. Hopefully, Vanessa will have some insight for us."

"Tell me more about her while we finish this up. Then we need to get back on the road."

––––––

CONNOLLY ESTIMATES Vanessa Apsley's age at around forty though the question seems to confuse him. I explain it away with some nonsense about preparing to deal with someone of another generation, but the truth is that I'm just curious.

Earlier, Connolly said Vanessa is interested in "what he has to offer." Is it wrong that I read something salacious into that? Is it ageist even? That a presumably older woman could only want one thing from an attractive younger man? Connolly does have talent, obviously, so I'm clearly not giving Vanessa Apsley the credit or respect a woman of her stature deserves. And yet . . .

Call it a gut feeling. I'm sure Ms. Apsley recognizes Connolly's worth as an asset, but I get the feeling there's more to it, and when he struggles to picture her even enough to affix an estimated age, I feel bad for the woman. I also get a very definite picture of her myself—ordinary enough that she slides effortlessly into "middle-aged," a category covering anywhere from thirty-five to sixty.

That only matters in the sense that if she *is* interested in Connolly, I'll need to make sure she doesn't get the wrong impression about me. That could torpedo this meeting in the time it takes to say hello.

As for other details on Vanessa Apsley, those are as scant as his recollection of her person. He knows she has money. He knows she has power and influence. He knows she is a capital *M* major player in the magical gray market. She's cemented her reputation as a tough but fair dealer.

Connolly suspects Vanessa is one of the potential buyers for the necklace, though she hasn't committed herself. He's also certain she didn't kidnap Hope or try to run us off the road. Her reputation for nonviolence is unmatched.

Our goal then is to get information from Ms. Apsley without letting her know we're competition for the necklace. My sister is missing, and we think it has something to do with the Necklace of

Harmonia. I suggest we tell Vanessa that I've hired Connolly to help, that I knew him by reputation in the Boston magical community.

We're still discussing this an hour later, long after we're back on the highway. Connolly has put on his fresh shirt and he's driving again, his luck rebalanced.

"I don't mind pretending I'm working on your behalf," he says. "But she knows I don't like . . ."

"Hiring yourself out like a common laborer?"

"You're never letting me live that down, are you?"

"Have you . . . ever gotten the impression she . . . fancies you?"

His brows rocket up. "What?"

"I was just thinking, maybe, if you've had the sense she'd be . . . amenable to it, you could flirt with her."

"What?" His voice rises two octaves, as if I'd suggested using torture.

"Nothing misleading. Just a little . . . you know."

"I *don't* know. Well, yes, I do but . . . No. I— No."

"You sputter adorably."

I get a glare for that, and I throw up my hands. "It was just a suggestion. We need to find a way to pump her for information, and I thought—"

He chokes. "No. There will be no . . ."

"Pumping for information?" I glance over. "It's a figure of speech, Connolly. Get your mind out of the gutter."

"I'm not the one—"

"I said to flirt with her. *Mild* flirtation. Geez." I shake my head. "Very light, exploratory flirtation should be enough—"

"No."

I sigh. "I get the feeling you aren't properly committed to this mission, Connolly."

He looks over, sees my smile and relaxes. "I appreciate your creativity. But flirtation wouldn't work, even if it was remotely in my skill set. We're going to need to play this by ear. Follow my lead. All right?"

"All right."

CHAPTER TWENTY-ONE

WE REACH Vanessa Apsley's house. And by *house*, I mean mansion. Or maybe that's not the right word, either. *Estate* is better. We turn into the lane and have another half-mile drive. At first, I'm straining to see the house, but that only lasts as long as it takes to pass the high stone wall. Then my window's down, my head out of it like a happy hound dog.

"It's quite pretty, isn't it?" Connolly says.

"Quite—quite pretty?" I sputter. I wave my hand out the window. "It's the freaking garden of Eden, Connolly. Change of plans. Let me out here, and you can talk to the lady of the house. Take your time. Three or four hours should be enough."

The grounds are spectacular. Even that word falls short. It's like the most amazing botanical garden ever, everything in bloom despite the fact it's only midspring. Endless gardens that seem as if they just popped from the earth that way, like those despicable people who roll out of bed looking gorgeous. The art of one who can fling paint at the wall and come away with a masterpiece.

It's not just the flowers. In fact, for me, they're mere decorations on the cake. The cake—and the icing—is the rest of the landscaping. Graceful willows bending over babbling brooks. Pocket forests so lush and inviting that they're like something out of a fairy tale. A lily-dappled fish pond with an arching bridge. A waterside gazebo crying out for a glass of lemonade and a dog-eared novel.

"Do you garden?" Connolly says as we drive through this Eden.

"That only means I know the names of the plants. Ani inherited Dad's green thumb. You should see our yard. It's nothing like this, obviously, but I could spend all summer on our deck."

I push my head out a little farther to inhale the incredible scents.

"Careful," Connolly says. "There's a gate up ahead."

We already passed through one at the end of the drive. There's a second gate here, on a wrought-iron fence. Connolly talks into a speaker, and the gates open.

Beyond is what would, on another property, be the yard. At least an acre of it, filled with gardens, formal beds and winding paths and wooden benches and ivy-draped statuary.

The house itself is a surprise. After seeing the property, I expect a grand and imposing mansion. Instead, it's a single-story, low-slung and Italianate, hugging a front courtyard.

I'm so busy gaping that I don't realize Connolly has parked and left. The front door opens, and I twist to see a woman step out, her arms opening in welcome. Connolly strides over to greet her, and there is no doubt this is Vanessa Apsley . . . and also no doubt that I was very, very wrong about her.

I thought Connolly's lack of attention to her age meant he'd dismissed her as a generic older woman. Nope. It meant she was so far out of his league he'd never paused to consider her as anything but a business contact. That's no insult to Connolly. The blame here falls entirely on the shoulders of Ms. Apsley.

A few years ago, Hope went through a phase of devouring billionaire romances. Endless books about guys as rich as Croesus, with the body of Hercules, the face of Adonis and the creative talents of Apollo, all of whom fell madly in love with an everywoman main character. I used to tease her that guys like that don't actually exist. Vanessa Apsley is proof that the female equivalent does.

Connolly said she's divorced, but her fortune is her own. From this property, I'm putting her squarely in the multimillionaire category. As for her age, she could be anywhere from thirty-five to fifty. All I know is that she's so freaking gorgeous I can't help wondering whether she has the Necklace of Harmonia herself.

The house looks Italianate, and that'd be my guess for the woman herself. Mediterranean. Flawless olive skin. Waves of raven-black hair swept into a casual updo. The kind of bone structure that means she's probably even lovelier now than she'd been at twenty. Then there's her figure, which is so impossibly lush and perfect that a petty corner of my soul wants to credit plastic surgery and shapewear.

As I climb from the car, I'm not sure whether to fix myself up or just surrender to my car-rumpled frumpiness. Not that it matters—Ms. Apsley's attention is entirely on Aiden. As she holds him at arm's length, her gaze sweeps him up and down, telling me she *is* interested in more than his luck working. For a woman like this, Connolly might not be long-term relationship material, but he's worthy of a romp.

I'm about to slink back into the car when violet eyes turn my way. *Violet* eyes. Of course. Because a woman like this couldn't have normal-colored irises, could she?

Her gaze skates up and down me so fast my cheeks heat in humiliation. Then a smile teases her lips. With a clap on Connolly's arm, she heads my way, that smile growing.

"You're one of the Bennett girls, aren't you?" she says.

"Y-yes." I put out my hand. "Kennedy."

"The middle one."

She clasps my hand between hers, warmth and the faint perfume of bergamot enveloping me. Her voice holds traces of an accent I can't quite place. Italian, maybe? Definitely European.

Still holding my hand, she looks over at Connolly. "You think it's a joker's jinx, then."

Silence, as my heart thuds. She steps back and surveys us both.

"Think *what* is a joker's jinx?" I say slowly.

"The Necklace of Harmonia. That is what you're after, isn't it?"

"We . . . are aware of the auction," Connolly says.

She rolls her eyes. "Of course you are, dear boy. While the old-timers preen and posture, you're hoping to slide in and snatch the prize from under their noses. You've come to pick my brain under the guise of, what, a social visit? I hope you at least had a better story than that."

"We came to speak to you about a related matter."

"Are you going to pretend you aren't after the necklace?"

He meets her gaze. "Are you?"

"I asked you first."

"I wouldn't insult you by requesting information that would conflict with your business interests," he says. "I respect you too much for that."

"You mean you respect my ability to crush you under my heel."

"That, too." He nods toward the door. "May we step inside and discuss this?"

"*Are* you going after the necklace, Aiden?"

"Right now, I'm more concerned about obtaining information on other potential bidders because one of them kidnapped Kennedy's sisters."

She glances sharply at me. "What?"

"Her older sister is fine," Connolly continues. "The youngest is still being held to uncurse the necklace. I've promised to help Kennedy resolve that in return for *her* help with the necklace, which I do not particularly want, but I'm obligated to obtain in payment of a debt. If that obligation was waived *and* Kennedy's sister was freed, it would remove two buyers from the auction, which would help you . . . if you wanted it."

Well, that's definitely more than we planned to admit. I try to catch his eye, but he's studiously avoiding my gaze.

"Come inside," Ms. Apsley says. "I had dinner prepared, and I have a feeling it'll go cold by the time I get this entire story." She walks over to Connolly. "Which I will get, correct? The entire and true story?"

"As much of it as I'm able and willing to tell."

"Fair enough."

She extends a hand to me, takes one of us on each arm and heads for the door.

———

Vanessa's house—she's already said "call me Vanessa"—is as breathtaking as the grounds. Sumptuous is the word I'd use, a level of luxury that falls just short of decadent and is all the better for it.

The estate grounds had invited me to wander, to explore, to enjoy and unwind, and her house does the same. We pass at least three spots where I long to curl up with a book and at least four bookcases that I long to pillage for that very purpose. There's a window seat where the sun stretches over a pile of pillows. A chaise longue with a wicker side table begging to hold your cup of tea. A circular couch with deep cushions and an artfully crumpled angora blanket.

Every piece of furniture is perfect . . . and every piece would set me back several months' rent. I'd fallen into another misconception earlier, when Connolly said Vanessa was one of the top names in the gray market. I expected her to be well-off, but not as wealthy as those in the black market. Surely you can make more money dabbling in a criminal enterprise. Which is bullshit. Drug kingpins don't automatically have more money than CEOs. To expect that underestimates how much talent goes into a job. Clearly, Vanessa has that in spades, from both her business acumen and her magical ability.

As for her ability, it's dream shaping. It's a strange and rare power that I don't fully understand, and Connolly admitted he doesn't, either. We have a dream shaper in Unstable, but his family uses their powers for sleep manipulation, and they've lost any other skills through time and disuse. In short, he can grant sound sleep and banish nightmares, and that may sound like a small thing, but for someone with insomnia or PTSD, a good night's sleep is the stuff of, well, dreams. Maybe Vanessa has discovered a way to do that on a larger commercial scale.

Dinner is served by two young men who seem to have given up lucrative modeling careers to work for Vanessa. Not that she notices their physical attractions. It's as if they're just two more works of art decorating her home.

No, that isn't fair. She treats them as objects with genuine warmth and respect. They're neither pieces of furniture nor pieces of ass. Just young men who bring beauty to her home.

We eat in a proper Italian courtyard—an open-air room in the middle of the house. It's decorated with so much lush greenery, it's like dining al fresco in a tropical paradise.

The food is perfect for the setting, all plates of light bites with plenty of fish and vegetables, very Mediterranean. It's a meal made for talking over. Put a few choice items on your plate and nibble while chatting, then take a few more, and keep going into the night as wine and water glasses seem to refill themselves.

Connolly holds back unnecessary details while giving Vanessa a full picture of the situation. My sisters were kidnapped, and one was returned. The other is being held to unweave the necklace's curse. To secure her safe return, I'm supposed to pretend to work with Connolly and then flake out at the last moment. Connolly, however, can't agree to that because another buyer demands the necklace to repay his brother's debt.

I'd rather leave out the part where I'm only *pretending* to work for Connolly. That's admitting that I might double-cross Hope's captors. Yet it's also the supporting beam to this story. Otherwise, I should stay a million miles from him as competition for the necklace.

If Connolly trusts Vanessa with this, then I must, too.

"Who holds your brother's debt?" she asks when Connolly finishes.

He hesitates. "I'd rather not say."

"I noticed. Which is why I'm asking."

Connolly sips his wine.

Vanessa continues, "You're hoping I can help you find Hope Bennett's captor. Then you'll free her, which will also free you to fulfill your end of the bargain. However, even if we identify who has Hope, freeing her will be risky."

"Agreed," I say. "We can use the necklace either to free Hope or to relieve Rian's debt. These two things aren't equal. My sister is a hostage. Your brother is not, correct?"

"Our parents have him in a safe house in Europe."

"Then my sister's situation is the more urgent one. If Vanessa can help with your brother's case instead . . ." I peer at him. "Unless there's a reason you don't want that. Something you aren't telling me?"

"No." He meets my gaze so I can see the sincerity there. "The story is as I told it, and you have my word on that. I just don't feel free to"—he glances at Vanessa—"share information that isn't mine to share."

"I commend your familial loyalty, Aiden," she says. "But Kennedy is right. Freeing a debt is easier and safer than freeing a person. Whatever you tell me is private. You'll have noticed that my boys are timing their appearances perfectly. They stay in the kitchen until I signal for service. As much as I trust them, they shouldn't overhear your secrets. I didn't get where I am by treating my associates cavalierly."

"The person holding Rian's debt is Havoc."

"Havoc?"

"It's obviously an alias."

"I'm not remarking on the nom de guerre. My surprise reflects incredulity that your brother was fool enough to get involved with her. Apparently, you inherited his allotment of intelligence and common sense."

Connolly stiffens. "Rian and I are different, yes, but—"

"Oh, put your back down, Aiden. The point is that Havoc is trouble. An overly ambitious capo masquerading as a godfather."

I arch my brows.

She sighs. "Have you never seen mafia movies, child? A godfather is the head of a crime family. A capo is a lieutenant in charge of a unit of foot soldiers. Havoc worked in security for a good friend of mine. He had to let her go, and she decided to enter the game as an independent player, which has been nothing but headaches for everyone. Let's just say she lives up to her name."

"Can we pay off the debt another way?" I ask.

Vanessa shakes her head. "Unfortunately, no. Havoc cares about the necklace because *we* care about it. I may know ways to deal with that, though. If I decide there's something in this for me."

"The necklace."

She waves her hand. "I have no need of jewels."

She's right in a very literal sense. She isn't even wearing

earrings. There's little need to accessorize when no one's going to look beyond your personal beauty.

That does leave one question, though . . .

"Erin Concord," Connolly says, at a look from me.

Vanessa's brow furrows. "Hmm?"

"Someone set up an appointment with Kennedy. Someone named Erin Concord. I thought it might be you."

"Erin . . . Concord?"

"Erin for Eris," I say. "Goddess of discord. Concord as another name for—"

"Harmonia," she says, her face twisting in distaste. "That suggests you narrowly avoided a run-in with Havoc yourself. I've heard her use variations on that name."

"Eris, discord, havoc," I murmur. "Concord as an allusion to the necklace."

"Yes, Havoc tries very hard to be clever and usually fails."

"So Havoc tried to speak to me, possibly to hire me to uncurse the necklace once Aiden bought it."

"Someone also broke into Kennedy's shop," Connolly says.

"And did a whole lotta damage," I say, trying not to remember the scene.

Her violet eyes widen. "That *certainly* wasn't me. I've stayed out of the auction. Feel free to confirm that in any way you like."

"What do you want then?" I ask. "In return for your help."

"I haven't decided yet."

Connolly shakes his head. "We need a price up front."

She smiles. "Clever boy. Yes, never take a favor on loan. I meant that I'm not certain I *can* help, but I'll think on it, and if I can, you will know my price in the morning."

CHAPTER TWENTY-TWO

WE CONTINUE to eat and talk. Vanessa wants more information on Hope's captor—everything we can give her. The data will help her narrow the list of suspects, should she decide to help.

It's dark by the time the servers bring coffee and dessert trays. We're still picking at dinner and discussing the kidnapping. When we're ready to dive into dessert, Vanessa surveys the table and then excuses herself.

"All the more for us," I murmur after she's gone.

I pick up a plate of silver-dollar-sized tiramisu. When I hold it out, Connolly lifts his hand.

"None for me, thank you," he says.

"But it's tiramisu. Teeny-tiny, ninety-nine-percent guilt-free tiramisu. And there's zuppa inglese and galaktoboureko, too. Small enough to try some of each."

"They're all yours. I've had more sugar today than I've consumed in weeks."

"I can tell. You're chattering nonstop, running around, barely able to sit still. Clearly, you have a problem."

"That sounds like sarcasm."

"If there's any doubt, I'm not doing it right." I hold up the plate between us. "You do realize that you're actually reminding me of how many sweets I've had and suggesting I shouldn't have more, either."

"I said nothing of the sort."

"It's implied." I sigh and put the plate down. "I can take a hint. As delicious as these little treats look, if you have the willpower to resist, I should, too."

He raises a brow. "I thought you said they were guilt free." He takes a tiramisu. "Better?"

"If you only want one. Because ultimately, it's about you, and if you can look me in the eye and tell me you only want one—or none —then I'll stop harassing you. However, if you'd really like two, or even three, then I feel obligated to remind you that life is short and if the rest of dinner is any indication, these are going to be so worth it."

He takes one tiramisu and one galaktoboureko and puts them on his plate. "Better now?"

I wait until he takes a bite of the tiramisu. "Much."

"You are a terrible influence."

"No, I'm an excellent influence. I'm about to make your evening ten times better."

Shoes squeak, and we look up to see Vanessa standing in the doorway, one brow arched.

"Well, that was an interesting line to walk in on. Should I go out again?"

I smile and shake my head. "I was talking about dessert. Convincing Aiden to indulge."

"You're wasting your time. That's why I brought this." She lifts a plate of fruit. "Aiden doesn't eat . . ."

She stops as she sees the half-eaten mini tiramisu in his hand. "Well, well. I've been trying to tempt him for two years now, and I've made no headway at all." Her gaze rests on me. "Evidently, my sweets were not to his taste."

I shake my head. "I'm not sure what sweets Aiden actually does like. I haven't had time to bake him any, and I don't plan to. My sister has been kidnapped. I appreciate any help I can get in finding her, but I'm not offering cookies for the reward. Nor do I think he'd take them if I did."

Connolly frowns and then shakes his head, deciding to ignore my rambling in favor of polishing off the tiramisu.

Vanessa watches me for a moment, assessing. Then she says, "Understandable. However, if you did decide to bake for him, I wouldn't object. The boy is in desperate need of cookies, wherever they come from."

I choke at that. Connolly hands me a glass of water, still oblivious. Vanessa smiles, pulls out her chair, and sits.

"Tell me more about this issue with Havoc, Aiden."

———

By THE TIME we finish dinner, it's after ten. Vanessa needs to make some calls and check some files before giving us her answer in the morning. Until then, we are her guests.

I'd rather stay at a hotel. I don't know Vanessa well enough for a sleepover. But Connolly isn't fazed by it, and so again, I have to trust his judgment.

I thought I knew a lot about the magical world, being from a town and a family that accepts it as a fact of life. Yet when I talk about "the community," I mean a loose network of others with abilities. A social-support system. This corner of it is one I've only heard about in whisper and rumor and warning.

I'm out of my depth here and becoming more aware of that with each passing hour. Connolly is my bridge to that world, and I'm relying on him to provide safe passage. Is that wrong? Naive? Maybe. I only know that Hope is being held hostage in this part of our world, and I don't have anyone else to take me into it.

I'm not sure I could even make it to a hotel. I woke up at six this morning, worrying about my sisters. That seems like a week ago. Now I've eaten too much, had more wine than usual, and I'm afraid if I even lower my butt onto one of Vanessa's impossibly comfortable sofas, I'm not getting up again until morning.

I've also been abandoned by my hosts. Understandably. Vanessa is chasing answers for us, and Connolly has slipped off to clear his schedule for tomorrow. I'd already canceled this week's appointments—due to the break-in—and I'm trying very hard not to think about how long it might be until I can reopen.

What I haven't done is report the break-in to the police, which means I won't have paperwork for the insurance company. Connolly has assured me he'll look after all that . . . which only makes me worry even more that I'm relying on him too much.

My mood is off. Having Connolly disappear to tend to business only reminds me that I'm not in his league, career-wise. Ani would point out his background and the advantages it gives him. That feels like an excuse. Yet do I *want* to compete at his level? Live a life blinkered by work and ambition?

Here lies the core of my dissatisfaction these days. An inner drive to do more, be more, warring against a voice that says I'm doing just fine, that I was doing fine even before I left Unstable. Being home today only reminded me of how much I miss it. I left because I felt as if I should. I wanted my own business, and somehow that got tangled up with needing to move away from my family and . . .

Damn, I'm in a mood.

I pop off a text to Ani. We've been back-and-forthing all evening. She wants to be sure I'm safe, and I want to know whether they have any new leads. They don't.

I say good night to Ani and then send a text to Connolly before heading off to bed. I find my room ready. Not surprising. Vanessa strikes me as the sort who's always ready to throw open her door to guests.

My bedroom comes with an en-suite bath and a sunken tub that has me reconsidering my straight-to-bed plans. Yet as I picture myself sinking into that tub, I also see myself drifting to sleep and drowning. So, maybe not. Get to bed early. Rise early. Take a walk through the gardens and enjoy a hot bath before breakfast.

It isn't until I start to shrug off my jeans that I realize I don't have nightwear. Or clothing for tomorrow. Connolly has a bag in his trunk for emergency business trips, and I'd been in Unstable, where I could have grabbed supplies from home. I'm kicking myself for not doing that when I spot a nightgown folded on the dresser. As I lift it, a soft rap comes at the door.

"Yes?" I say, tugging my jeans back on.

"It's Aiden."

I hurry over and throw open the door. The hall lights are off, casting Connolly half into shadow.

"I thought I heard you in here," he says. "My business took longer than expected. Are you busy?"

"Just settling in."

A frown. "For the night?"

"I thought I'd turn in early. I texted you."

"Ah. I didn't see it. I will leave you to your evening, then."

It's only as he steps back that I see he holds a glass in each hand, wine shimmering in the half light.

"Oh," I say, gesturing at the wine as I think of something to say.

"You've probably had enough of this. I just thought if you were still up and wanted to talk . . . But you aren't, so . . ." He lowers the glasses to his side, out of sight. "I will see you in the morning."

"If you wanted to talk about something . . ."

"No, no. I just thought you might wish to discuss the situation."

Disappointment flutters through me. We've been talking about "the situation" all day, and more will only remind me that we aren't any closer to getting my sister back.

If he'd just wanted to talk, though? About . . . I don't know. Life? Thoughts? Random musings? Spend a bit of time unwinding and sipping that wine and talking about anything other than what's happening right now. I'm even tempted to ask about actuarial science.

Yet that feels like a dangerous path to go down, a dangerous thing to want.

"I don't have any questions," I say. "And I'm too tired to be coherent. I thought I'd get an early night and hike a bit before breakfast. I don't suppose you're the morning-walk type?"

"I could be." Something flickers over his face, and he straightens. "I mean that I should accompany you for safety. What time were you thinking?"

"Is six thirty too early?"

"I'm usually up by five. I'll meet you in the courtyard at six thirty."

We say our good nights, and he leaves. Once the door's shut, I stand there, lingering, and regretting for far too long. Then I snap out of it and return to that nightgown. It's more of a chemise, complete with short dressing gown. Both have tags still affixed to assure me they're brand new. I smile and shake my head. Now that's hospitality. Also, serious money, where you can have a drawer of new nightwear for unexpected guests.

Seeing that the chemise is new persuades me to wear it. It's also gorgeous, with silk that shimmers down around me as soft as a lover's kiss. Which is what it's designed for. Oh, it's comfortable, nothing like the polyester lingerie I've bought, shoved into a drawer and brought out only for those ten minutes of show before it's—thankfully—peeled off. This is what lingerie should be, the kind of chemise you could lounge in all evening, artfully hidden under the short dressing gown until it's time to retire for the evening with someone who will appreciate it.

One glance in the full-length mirror across the room, and I'm tempted to shoot boudoir selfies. Of course, then I'd need someone to send them to . . .

The chemise does look good, though. It's the perfect color, a rich maroon that sets off my skin tone. The perfect length, too, skating the tops of my thighs and showing off my legs. In the soft light, my hair—an unholy tangle from a long day—looks artfully mussed as it falls across my shoulders.

Such a waste.

I sigh, treat myself to a slather of decadent citrus-scented body lotion, and climb between sheets so luxuriant I want to sneak a look at the brand and set myself an aspirational goal. Instead, I sink onto a soft mattress and softer pillow, close my eyes and—

A soft tap sounds at the door. Exactly the same tap I'd heard when Connolly came by. I slide from bed and slip the dressing gown over my chemise.

As I cross the room, something seems . . . off. Not quite right. Not wrong, either. It's an odd sensation, lending a surreal quality to everything around me. Warm night air tickles past, raising delicious goose bumps and bringing the heady smell of roses.

I glance over to see the window is open, and although I don't remember opening it, the thought brings not even a twinge of concern, nor does that out-of-season scent. The breeze and the smell are delightful, and that is all that matters.

The moon hangs in a low crescent though I could have sworn it'd been fuller when we left the courtyard. Again, no concern, only the fleeting thought that it is the loveliest moon I've ever seen.

Carpet cushions each step, the pile as warm and comfortable as a pair of fuzzy socks. Hadn't it been hardwood before? No, I must have been thinking of another room.

I open the door to see Connolly standing there. Earlier, he'd been in half light, and he is again, and yet this time, it's different. Moonlight from my bedroom window somehow reaches him here, bathing him in the perfect mix of light and shadow. Shadowing angular cheekbones. Setting off a strong jaw. Making his eyes impossibly green and his hair glimmer red-gold even where it falls into shadow.

He's dressed in his button-down shirt from earlier, but it's open at the collar, the tie long gone, shirt sleeves rolled up over his forearms. His feet are bare, and somehow that odd detail sets something fluttering inside me.

"I . . ." he says, and then seems to stick there, searching for words, an excuse that explains returning to my door.

I know what will come next. He'll withdraw and straighten, maybe clear his throat. When he does exactly that, my insides flutter again, as if being able to predict his reactions means something, implies I know him better than I'd expect after only a day together.

"I thought I heard a noise," he says. "I wanted to be sure you were all right."

"I am. Sorry if I woke you."

"I wasn't sleeping." He steps closer. "Also, I'm lying. I didn't hear anything. I just wanted to say everything will be all right. After I walked away earlier, I realized I didn't say that. I know you're worried about your sister, and you're afraid I'll put my brother's debt above her life. I won't."

I look up into his face. He's right there now, as if somehow, I've moved closer, too, until I'm near enough to see the pulse at the base of his throat. Also, his shirt is unbuttoned. Completely undone when only the top button was open a moment ago. The shirt is open, the tails pushed back over his hips, giving me a glimpse of a muscled chest and firm stomach.

Okay, this makes no sense. Which means I'm dreaming, damn it.

Or am I?

Well, yes, clearly, I've fallen asleep, and this *is* a dream, but it feels real despite the fact that Connolly's shirt has miraculously unbuttoned itself.

Dream shaping.

Vanessa is a dream shaper.

However, if you did decide to bake for him, I wouldn't object. The boy is in desperate need of cookies, wherever they come from.

Oh, yes, Vanessa Apsley is the perfect host. Michelin-star dinner, decadent guest room, and now, a little sexy-dream nightcap.

A sexy dream for one?

She said *Connolly* was in need of "cookies." Not me.

I look up into those gorgeous eyes, warmer and softer than I've ever seen them. Yes, softer, and I know that's not always a sexy word, but for me, it's catnip.

Is this my dream version of Connolly? An idealized imagining? Or . . .

"Tell me a secret," I say.

His eyes dance, and he leans so close his breath tickles my upturned face. "A secret?"

"You want me to trust you. So tell me a secret. Doesn't need to be anything blackmail-worthy. Just . . . something I couldn't know if you didn't tell me."

"Ah. Let's see . . ." His lips lower to my ear, and he whispers. "I'm afraid of snakes."

"Snakes?"

His face moves over mine, one shoulder shrugging. "I had . . . an incident. It was traumatic. So, if we encounter any snakes on this adventure, you'll need to deal with them."

I look up at him, and I know some of this is fake. The lighting. The impossible green of his eyes. His shirt coming undone. But this *is* Connolly, asleep in another room, his dreams being nudged and manipulated by Vanessa.

A dream for two.

"Your turn," he murmurs. "Tell me a secret."

"I'm afraid . . ." The cool night breeze tickles my upper thighs, and I look down, blinking. "I'm afraid I don't know how I lost my robe."

He chuckles.

"No, seriously," I say. "I was wearing it, wasn't I?"

"Temporarily, and then it vanished."

"You noticed that?"

Another chuckle, this one edged with something that makes my pulse race. "I couldn't fail to notice. I just wasn't going to bring it up. That could make you self-conscious, which would be very rude of me."

"Well, I appreciate the consideration, especially given . . ." I blink at him. "You seem to have lost your shirt."

His shirt is completely gone now. He looks down, which gives me an excuse to ogle.

"Hmm," he says. "That's odd, isn't it?"

"It is."

"Well, having no idea where it went, as long as it doesn't offend you . . ."

"Not a bit. Does my lack of a robe offend you?"

Now he uses this as an excuse to give me a very slow once-over that turns into a twice-over, as if he has to be sure. Even when he speaks, his gaze is still fixed on the bottom of my hemline.

"Offended isn't the word I'd use," he says. His fingers touch the hemline. "This seems suitable coverage."

One fingertip grazes my thigh, and he withdraws fast enough for me to know it was accidental, but heat still darts through me. He toys with the hemline. Not lifting it. Not trying to get beneath it. Just sliding his fingers along the silk edge, and it's the sexiest damn thing imaginable, my whole body responding to a touch that isn't a touch at all.

There's an opening here. So many things I can say, just a bit of flirty teasing. Yes, the chemise is suitable coverage. Is he disappointed in that? Would he like it shorter?

Or I could lean into his fingers, give them permission to touch.

It's a dream.

Just a dream.

It's safe.

Is it?

Is it really?

Do we see where this leads and then, tomorrow, act as if nothing happened?

I look up at him. His gaze is still fixed on my hemline, as if transfixed by that silken fabric sliding over my thighs, but he's been staring too long, and I know he isn't seeing me anymore. He's thinking, just as I am. Deciding where to go next.

"I'm afraid of heights," I say.

His head jerks up, but he doesn't look startled, just smiles and says, "Are you? I'll need to remember that," and in his smile, I see relief. I feel relief, too, rippling through me as the moment passes.

It had been so tempting, but even if no harm came of it, I don't want to go there. Don't want to put that obstacle in our way. That's what it feels like it would have been. An obstacle to work around. The elephant in the room that we'd need to pretend we didn't see.

"Thank you," he says, those warm eyes still on me.

"For what?"

He leans on the wall, one sculpted arm braced up against it. "For making this easy for me."

For making it easy for him to walk away from this? For us both to walk away, without awkwardness or embarrassment? Maybe that's part of it, but after a moment, he says, "I can be difficult to get along with. I know that. Thank you for putting up with my bullshit."

"Oh, I'm not putting up with it. At all."

He laughs. A real, head-thrown-back laugh that melts something inside me. When he looks at me, his eyes dance. "I know. And I appreciate that. It's a welcome change." He takes a step back. "Good night, Kennedy."

Another step, and he's about to walk away when I say, "Aiden?"

He turns back to me.

"Thank you, too," I say. "For putting up with me panicking over my sisters. And for being . . . more."

His brows rise.

"More than you seemed," I say.

His lips curve, and he inclines his head, murmurs another good night, and we part. I withdraw into my bedroom, but stand there, watching him go, that very nice rear view made even better by the "missing" shirt.

He disappears into the darkness, and I sigh and lean against the doorframe.

Even in a sex dream, I still can't get laid.

I laugh under my breath and shake my head. It's for the best, and it was still a nice interlude, one that hints at . . . Well, I'm not going to think too hard about the possibilities it raises. We have siblings to save, and that will take all our attention.

Still, as I climb into bed, I may be smiling. I slide between the sheets, and I'm asleep in minutes.

CHAPTER TWENTY-THREE

WHEN A SOUND STARTLES ME AWAKE, I'm half hoping it's another knock at the door . . . and half hoping it isn't. No, I'm fully hoping it isn't. I want to leave that particular dream on its pitch-perfect endnote, with Connolly walking away but not *seeming* as if he was walking away. Deferring that which should be deferred.

I open my eyes, braced for another dream tap on the door. The room is silent, though. It's changed, too. The window is closed, and the moon's hidden behind cloud, casting everything into inky darkness.

The air smells different. Feels different. The gauzy unreality of the dream is gone. I catch the citrus scent of the lotion I'd slathered on, along with the faint smell of sweat, whispering that I probably should have had a bath after all.

A floorboard creaks, and I glance toward the hall.

Connolly? Woken from that sensual dream and wishing he hadn't left? Returning to see whether I feel the same? I can't picture that, though. More like he'd wake up and come to assure me that he meant nothing by it.

My stomach clenches at the thought.

Don't, okay, Aiden? Just don't. You enjoyed that tête-à-tête as much as I did, and we can pretend it didn't happen and move on. Set it aside. Don't make this awkward. Don't make it embarrassing. Please.

Yet after that creak, all goes silent again. Just the house settling and—

Another board creaks . . . right beside me.

I reach for the reading lamp over my bed. Only this isn't my bed, and there isn't a lamp there.

My phone. I'll grab my phone. It's plugged in right . . .

No, this *isn't* my room. I hadn't wanted to move things around searching for an outlet, so I'd plugged in my phone across the room.

I take a deep breath. Whatever I heard was the house settling. Everything's quiet now and—

The very distinct sound of a foot on a board, creaking it down and then releasing.

"Hello?" I say.

My voice quavers, and I'm about to try again, firmer, when I stop myself.

Yes, it sounded like a footstep, but that's what I was expecting. I've decided there's a person in my room, so I'm imagining I hear one.

Who would it be anyway? Connolly? Never. I can tease him about being an asshole, but there are many varieties, and he is a mile from the sort who thinks sneaking into a woman's bedroom is sexy. He's even further from the kind who'd slip into my bed whether I wanted it or not.

So who else is in the house? The staff is gone. That leaves only . . .

You didn't trust Vanessa.

Yes, but I only meant that I didn't know her well. If I'd *mis*trusted her, I'd have gotten to a hotel even if it meant walking there.

No one is actually in my room. I'm imagining—

The swish of fabric. Then a shadow shifts. A shadow shaped like a figure, there for one moment and then disappearing into darkness as it moves.

Moves in my direction.

I rocket up and blindly grab toward the nightstand. My hand hits something hard, a sharp edge smacking into my palm.

Too late, I picture the bedside lamp—on a huge solid base of marble. Pain explodes through my hand, but I reach to grab the lamp in both hands and—

A fist slams into my jaw. It's so fast, and so unexpected, that I fall back onto the pillow, blinking in shock.

I have never been hit. Never intentionally. A softball strike. A stray elbow. A wild flail. That's it, and the shock throws me more than the actual blow. My brain screams that this is as impossible as the crescent moon outside my window earlier. It's wrong, and therefore it's not happening. I'm dreaming. I must be.

A hand grabs me, and I smack it hard and scramble up, clawing toward the foot of the bed and then tumbling out. I hit the floor. The hardwood floor. Not a dream. Oh, God, this isn't a dream.

Fingers snag the chemise. I push up and run. I'm out the door and tearing down the hall, bare feet skidding on the hardwood. I reach the sitting room and—

Hands grab me again. I flail against them, but before I can get away, I'm whipped around. I see a figure. Then fingers close around my arm. I twist and find myself staring into irises the color of summer grass. A tumbled lock of red-gold hair. A hint of freckles under the eyes. That's all I can see, the hand gripping my upper arm so tight I can't move.

I know who it is. That face leaves no doubt.

My brain still rebels. Insists I'm seeing wrong. Having a nightmare.

Why are you so sure it's a dream? He isn't Ani. Isn't Jonathan. Isn't someone you've known for years. Aiden Connolly is a stranger.

His gaze locks mine. "Did you really believe me when I said I gave a damn about your sister?" He must sneer—I can't see his mouth, but the disdain comes through his voice, his eyes. "That I'd endanger my brother for some girl I don't know? Who are you, Kennedy? Who is she? Nobody. Little curse weavers performing in a sideshow."

The shock snaps then, and I start to fight. I don't care if this *is* a dream. Even in a nightmare, I'm not going to cower while Connolly insults me.

I rake my fingernails down his arm hard enough to slough skin.

He howls and slams me backward. I trip over an ottoman. Connolly comes at me.

I can barely see him in the darkness, but I can make out enough to fight. The problem is that I don't know *how* to fight. Never learned anything more than a bit of karate, useless here. It doesn't matter. I kick and claw and scream.

Get up. Get out.

One last kick with everything I have, and then I scramble the other way. When he grabs me, I lash back, elbowing him in the nose.

"Bitch!" he roars as blood streams.

Rivulets of blood run down his arm from the furrows my nails left. He grabs my wrist.

"Did you really think I was going to help you? You're going to help *me*, and you're going to help my brother. Because we matter. You don't."

"Kennedy? Kennedy!"

The hand on my wrist grips my shoulder instead. Grips it and shakes it, and my head jerks up. Connolly's there, his face only inches from mine.

"Kennedy," my name comes on a whoosh of relief. "Breathe, just breathe."

I scrabble backward, slapping his hands away when he reaches for me.

He raises his hands. "It's okay. You were having a nightmare. I heard you cry out."

"Stay away from me." My voice comes in a hoarse croak.

He flicks on a lamp. Light floods the sitting room. I'm on the sofa, my back pressed into it.

"You were sleeping, Kennedy," he says slowly. "I found you here. I don't know what you were imagining, but it wasn't real."

I creep along the sofa and gauge the distance to the door.

"I'm not blocking you," he says. "You can go anywhere you like. I made a mistake in my office. I'd never intentionally trap you."

"Stay away from me," I repeat.

He blinks, and something seems to dawn on him. "Was the nightmare about me?"

"Stay away."

"I am, but I swear I just got here now. I heard you scream, and I ran in here, and you were on the sofa, asleep and thrashing about."

He sounds like himself. That's an odd thing to think, but I realize he hadn't sounded like himself before. The voice, yes, but not the tone, not the word choices, not *his* way of speaking. Even the profanity wasn't anything I've heard him use.

Connolly rubs his hands over his face. I see him more clearly then. Dressed in an old fraternity T-shirt and sweatpants. When he lifts his face from his hands, it's clean, no blood oozing from his nose.

"Let me see your arms," I say.

He looks down at them in confusion.

"Lift them," I say. "Show me they aren't scratched."

He pushes the T-shirt sleeves to his shoulders and holds up his arms, rotating them so I can see they're unmarked.

"Okay," I say, nodding slowly as I realize he's telling the truth, and that realization sharpens to embarrassment. "Sorry. It was a very vivid dream."

"I could tell. Whatever you thought I did . . ." He looks at the sofa, and his fair skin pales, freckles popping.

"No," I say quickly. "Nothing like that."

My hand rises to my upper arm. Even awake, it feels tender.

"Kennedy . . ." Connolly says slowly. "Can you . . . step into the light please?"

I stand and move into the lamplight. He stares at me. Then he says, carefully, "May I come closer?"

I nod again, and he takes a step before stopping. He blinks. Then he moves back.

"I realize this won't help my case at all, but I think you need to look in the mirror. I'll stay out of your way."

He sidesteps and waves to a mirror on the wall. I walk to it. The first thing I see is the chemise. I think that's what he means—that I might want to throw something on. Then I step closer to the mirror and see dark marks on my upper arm.

They seem like shadows at first. When I lift my arm, though, I see the very distinct print of finger bruises and half moons where short nails dug in. I press one and wince.

"I did not do that," Connolly says. "I was in my bed, Kennedy. I was sleeping, and I thought I heard a sound. I got up and checked my phone—maybe I can prove that, show when it unlocked. Then you screamed, and I came running. I swear I didn't . . ." He swallows. "I didn't do that."

I stare at the bruises. Then I tilt my chin, looking for anything on my jaw. It seems fine . . . for now. "What did you see when you came into the room?"

"It was dark, so nothing at first. I could hear you, though. I ran to the sofa, where you were thrashing about."

"And then?"

"I grabbed your shoulder and shook you. I think I said your name. Then I realized it could be a seizure, and maybe I shouldn't shake you, but that's when you jumped up."

"That's what I experienced," I say. "Someone was gripping me by the wrist. Then you were shaking my shoulder. There wasn't a time gap between the two."

"I didn't— I *swear*, Kennedy, I did not—"

"I know. But it looked like you. Sounded like you. It was supposed to *be* you. I clawed my attacker's arm, though. I saw the gouges, the blood. I hit his nose, too, and made that bleed. You aren't hurt; therefore it wasn't you. I was dreaming."

His brow furrows. "You didn't give yourself those bruises."

"No, I didn't." I walk to the doorway. "Tell me more about dream shaping."

He stops. His eyes widen and then narrow, and the sudden fury in them makes me step back, but he's already turning, laser-beaming that look down the hall.

"We need to leave," he says. "Now."

"You think Vanessa—?"

"There's no one else here, and dream shaping *is* her power. I'd like to leave before she wakes."

"You think she's dangerous."

"I didn't think so, I don't know. But I think it's unwise for me to speak to her right now."

When he turns toward me, I instinctively backpedal and bash into a low table. He starts to reach out to catch me, but I duck his grasp. He backs off, his hands raised, anger and anguish warring in his eyes.

"I'm sorry," I say. "I just . . ."

"Completely understandable." He clips the words, his glare directed back down that hall. "No, I really don't think I should speak to her right now. Let's get our things."

CHAPTER TWENTY-FOUR

"I'D RATHER we didn't split up," Connolly says as we head down the hall. "I understand you won't want to come in my room, but I'd like us to stay within sight. It'll just take me a minute to get ready. I'm almost packed."

I nod and wait outside his open door. As for him being "almost packed," that's an understatement. His overnight bag sits on a chair, but otherwise, the room is spotless. He still looks around. Then he strides to a shadowy corner and plucks his dress shirt from a chair.

"So that's where it went," I say, trying for a smile.

He frowns at me, and it's clear he's only half paying attention. I should just drop the weak attempt at humor there, but I want to smooth this over.

He understands why I'm still skittish, and I'm grateful for that. It's yet another of those tiny things that say "this is a good man." This is someone I want to know better.

Some guys would get frustrated and remind me that the dream attacker wasn't really them. Connolly understands that what matters is the lingering fear, and he's respectful of that. But my suspicion still stings. I want to make him smile. Let him know that the nightmare doesn't taint the good part that came before it.

"From the dream," I say. "Your shirt disappeared."

He stiffens, and I realize he thinks I mean the nightmare.

"No, the one before that," I say quickly. "The first dream. The one Vanessa sent us."

I smile, but he isn't looking at me. He just stands there, staring down at that discarded shirt and . . .

Oh, shit.

"That . . . wasn't you, was it?" I say. "I mean, not actually you. Just a much nicer dream *with* you."

I realize how that sounds, and my cheeks heat.

I hurry on. "Nicer compared to the other one. It wasn't anything weird. Just you, uh . . ."

"Lost my shirt?"

My face scorches now, and I'm grateful for the dim lighting.

"Swimming," I blurt. "I don't even know if this place has a pool, but in my dream, we went swimming, and you misplaced your shirt and . . ." I clear my throat. "You have everything, so I should go get dressed."

I retreat fast. He follows and waits in my doorway while I disappear into the bathroom to change.

I rip off the chemise and pitch it into the corner. Last night, I'd thought how flattering and sexy it was, and how it was a shame no one saw me in it. Then Connolly did, and he appreciated the view just as much as I dreamed he might. Except, apparently, that's because I *had* dreamed it.

The way his gaze lingered on it. The way his fingers toyed with the hem, so irrationally sexy it still sends a shiver through me.

That hadn't been Connolly. Hadn't been a hint of what he might be like as a lover. It was entirely my fantasy version of what I'd want him to be like.

The worst is how damned sweet he'd been. Sweet and charming and chivalrous in the sexiest way, walking away with palpable regret. Our parting words, too, him thanking me for putting up with him, me thanking him for the same, a moment of precious understanding and acceptance.

Fake. All fake.

I'm yanking on my jeans when Connolly's voice sounds from the hall. It's quiet, his tone even, but there's a note that raises my hackles like that almost inaudible growl before a dog lunges.

"No, Vanessa," he says. "Stop right there. Please."

"I heard—"

"Turn around and go back to your room."

"Excuse me?" she says. "This is my house—"

"And we were your guests. We're leaving, and I'm going to ask you to wait elsewhere while we do that."

"Is Kennedy in—?"

A scuffle of feet, and then a shutting door, as if he's blocked her. "No, Vanessa. Please. I don't want to talk about this right now. Kennedy is upset—justifiably upset—and I want to get her out of here."

I leave the bathroom as I straighten my shirt.

From the hall, Vanessa sighs. Just sighs, deeply. "She's upset about the dream. All right. I admit I may have overstepped."

I grab the bedroom doorknob, but before I can even open it, Connolly's warning growl erupts into a snarl. "You may have *overstepped*? You terrified her."

"Terrified?"

I open the door to see they're halfway down the hall.

Vanessa spots me. "Kennedy. I'm sorry if the dream upset you. It was a test. I had to know if I could trust you."

"You tested a *guest* in your *home*?" Connolly says. "If you didn't trust her, you shouldn't have invited us to stay. And as for testing her by . . . by that . . . I have no idea how you thought *that* accomplished anything except terrifying her and driving a wedge between us."

"What? No. Well, yes, I suppose it could—" She waves her hands. "I think we're all overreacting a little here."

"Overreacting?" Connolly snarls the word. "You made Kennedy think I *attacked* her."

"Attack? No, there's some mistake—"

"Are you saying she's lying?"

"No, I—"

"Do you see those bruises on her arm? Apparently, I made those. Some nightmare version of me attacked Kennedy in her sleep. It was clearly a dream—I was in my own room and found her being attacked by an invisible force. Yet it was a dream that left actual marks. Are you telling me a dream shaper can't do that?"

"In a way, yes, but that isn't the dream I sent. At all."

"Is there another dream shaper hiding in your house? Someone who snuck past your security?"

"No, which means I need to figure out what happened here. Can we talk, please?"

"You are a dream shaper. Kennedy had a nightmare—a nightmare with real-life consequences—in your home, and you have admitted to sending her a nightmare to test her. Do I have all that right, Vanessa?"

"I didn't send a nightmare. I sent a dream about . . ." Vanessa looks from Connolly to me. "I think Kennedy would prefer I spoke to her about this in private."

"You are not speaking to her anywhere, private or not."

I make a noise.

Connolly catches my expression. Then he says, "I would prefer she didn't speak to you, but that's obviously her choice. But I would ask that it not take place in private."

Vanessa continues, "The dream I sent was one where she would . . . be in a situation in which she would feel at ease, her guard relaxed, and the . . . other person in that dream would begin a conversation that would allow me to determine how honest you were both being with your necklace story."

"How honest we were both . . ." Connolly begins. "You're saying I was the other person in the dream? You admit that you tricked her into thinking I was there—just like in her nightmare."

"The dream shaping went wrong," I say. "Aiden was supposed to talk to me and instead . . ."

I realize then why she'd wanted to speak about this in private. If that sexy dream had played out to the end, I would indeed have been relaxed, my guard lowered. She'd set up that fantasy dream to get to the pillow talk, where "fake Connolly" would initiate that conversation.

I swallow my embarrassment and say, "So Aiden was supposed to talk to me over . . . a moonlight swim or a glass of wine. A relaxed scenario. But the dream shaping went wrong. Things didn't play out the way you planned them, and the dream took a dark turn, preying on my own anxieties. I turned it into something else."

"I don't think that's possible," Vanessa says. "Yes, I only plant suggestions. For it to turn from what I had planned into a nightmare of attack, though? That's more than your fears reshaping my prompts. The fact it left physical marks also means the dream shaper used dark magic. I'm going to need to see what happened."

"See it?"

"I have a scrying bowl that allows me to replay shaped dreams. That's how I would have gotten the information. I would have fast-forwarded past any . . . unnecessary parts. I suggest you and I rewatch that together. Aiden? You may certainly stay nearby, but you don't need to be privy to Kennedy's nightmare."

He opens his mouth to protest, but I cut in with, "I agree." I meet his gaze. "Do you really want to watch yourself attacking me?"

He hesitates. His expression says no, but he doesn't want to leave me alone with Vanessa, either.

"*I'd* rather you didn't see it," I say. "It's bad enough remembering what happened. I don't want to rewatch it with you right beside me."

He nods slowly. "All right. I'll wait outside the door."

I'M NOT sure where Vanessa keeps her scrying bowl. We aren't allowed in there. She says she'll be back, disappears into the rear of the house and returns with a box, which she takes into the courtyard.

"You can fix yourself a coffee while you wait," she tells Connolly. "I have quite a selection. Try a few and see what you like."

She smiles as she says it, trying to ease the tension, but he meets her gaze with an impassive stare and only pulls a chair closer to the courtyard door.

"I'm going to need to close this," she says. "For Kennedy's privacy."

Connolly cuts his gaze to me. I nod, and he says, "I'll be right here, then."

Vanessa shuts the door. Moonlight fills the courtyard, but she still lights the candles and lanterns we'd extinguished after dinner. Then she takes a bowl from the wooden box. It's shaped like half of a clamshell. Or that's what I think until I get close and see that it's an actual half shell, just not the sort I'm used to seeing in New England. It's over a foot in length, and teardrop shaped. The inside is polished mother-of-pearl.

From the box, Vanessa also takes a pitcher. It's terra cotta and Greco-Roman, that classic black and clay coloring I've seen only in museums. There's a scene looping around it, but I can't make out more than figures. I think the pitcher must be empty from the way she carried it inside the box, but when she lifts it over the shell, water pours in until the shell is half-full. Then she waves her fingers above it and whispers a few words.

When she finishes, an image appears in the water. It's Connolly rapping on my door—the version of him I remember from the dream, the good one, where he's wearing his trousers and dress shirt, feet bare. Then I answer the door. There's no sound, but I see my mouth moving.

"How would you have heard any conversation?" I say. "It's like a silent film."

She taps her temple. "Not to me."

"This is normal for dream shapers? Being able to replay a shaped dream?"

She hesitates. "I wouldn't say 'normal.' High-level dream shapers can enter the dream themselves as a bystander." She wrinkles her nose. "That smacks of voyeurism. Yes, I know, you may feel this isn't much different, but I wouldn't have watched the whole thing. I'd have moved to the part I needed."

"Can we do that, please? There's nothing happening here."

She glances at the bowl and then flicks the water, and the figures move faster. "I see that," she murmurs. "I set up a perfectly good sexy encounter, and what do you two do? Talk, talk, talk some more . . ."

"Yes, well, apparently, even my imagination can't stretch far enough to picture him doing more."

She glances over, brows rising. "Your imagination?"

I wave at the bowl. "I'm working with your prompts, right? You send a fantasy Aiden to my room, and I take it from there. He did and said whatever I wanted. Well, what I wanted *and* could reasonably imagine him doing."

She stares at me. Then she laughs. "Oh no, it was actually Aiden. I see how that would be unclear, particularly given what happened later, but this part"—she waves at the bowl, where Connolly runs his fingers along the bottom of my chemise—"is all him."

"This is Aiden?"

"Also dreaming. That was the setup. Consider my role that of the set designer with a bit of director thrown in. I laid out the scene, and then I put you both into it, hoping it would lead where it should, prodded by your magically shortening nightgown and his inexplicably lost shirt."

She glares at the shell as Connolly heads back to his room. "Where it should lead—with normal hot-blooded young people— *isn't* to talking. Nor to a sweet parting." She flicks the water, and the image stills like a paused video.

"That's him," I say slowly. "The real Aiden. Dreaming the same dream."

"Of course."

"Lying *bastard*," I say.

Her brows shoot up. "Did he claim he wasn't there at all?"

"Yes," I grumble. "I made some comment about his missing shirt, and he pretended to have no idea what I was talking about, which was insanely embarrassing. He lied."

"He did." She unpauses the replay with a tap of her finger. "I could say that, given what happened afterward, he may have thought it best to remove himself completely, and I'm sure that's part of it but . . ."

I keep grumbling. There's no real venom behind it, though. She's right—given the fake-Connolly attack, he might not want to admit he'd been in my dreams at all.

She continues, "You figured it out, and he didn't. He thought this little encounter was his dream, and his alone, and when he realized otherwise, you caught him off guard."

"So he lied. Lied and embarrassed me to save himself any embarrassment."

"Oh, I'm sure you'll find a way to repay him. For now, though . . ."

She waves at the shell, where I'm back in bed, sleeping. Then I seem to wake up, inside another dream, the one with the intruder. When I tense, Vanessa says, "Would you like to step away while I watch this?"

"I . . ." I take a deep breath. "I didn't fight, okay? Not until the end. He hit me, and I just froze."

"All right."

"Just . . . don't . . ." Another deep breath. "I always thought that if something like that happened, I'd fight. But I just . . . I've never been hit. I couldn't believe it was happening."

"You're asking me not to judge you."

I nod.

There's silence. When she speaks, her words are hard. "Where did women get the idea that there's something wrong with them if they don't fight when a man hits them? If they're paralyzed with shock and disbelief? If they take time to react? Or if they decide not to react—that it's best to just wait it out?"

"Every movie where a woman gets attacked, and the audience dismisses her if she doesn't fight back."

"It's not just movies. It's every judge and defense attorney and jury member who wonders why she didn't fight. Unless she kills him. Then they wonder why she fought so hard." She meets my eyes. "Whatever you did here was the right thing, Kennedy. I'm just very, very sorry."

She glances at the screen, where not-Connolly has me by the upper arms. She smacks the water, hard enough to make half of it spill over the sides, and the picture disappears.

"That wasn't me," she says. "That wasn't you, either—not your mistrust of Aiden reshaping my dream prompts into a nightmare."

She starts the replay again and fast-forwards to a point where I'm smiling at Connolly. "See this? The image quality is perfect."

I nod.

She fast-forwards to another point, where I'm running from not-

Connolly. I see the difference. Both segments were in half darkness, but the first one is crystal clear, the second clouded and shadowed, figures blurring and wavering.

"This one is being dream shaped," she says. "Not by me, though. It's like a feed picking up an external signal. Mine comes through clear. The other doesn't."

"The other being sent by a second dream shaper?"

Her fingers tap the water, stopping and then dismissing the replay. "I would say yes, but that seems implausible. Or perhaps I simply have too high an opinion of my security and my reputation. No one got into this house last night. Could they get on the grounds, though? Close enough to your room to send their own dream and interfere with mine? The interfering part is harder to believe, though again, that may be my ego speaking."

She sits and thinks for a moment. "My dream, though, had been canceled by your actions. Yours and Aiden's."

"Please note that the fact I'm not complaining about this doesn't mean I'm not seriously pissed off. And weirded out. And a whole lot of other things."

Those violet eyes rise to mine. "Hmm?"

"You orchestrated *sex*, Vanessa. Between two parties who were not in a mental state to give their consent. I know it wasn't real sex. But still . . ."

She shakes her head. "I didn't orchestrate anything. As I said, I simply set events in motion. I gave the push. You two failed to follow through in the correct direction."

"It was the correct direction for *us*."

"So you say. Oh, don't give me that look. This is why I wouldn't shape more than the setting. Whatever happens between you must be your choice."

I pull out a chair. "While we've detoured to address concerns, I have one with you pushing Aiden in my direction. You hinted at it last night. But unless I'm sorely mistaken, you'd have been quite happy if he knocked on *your* door last night. Which makes me question you sending him to mine."

"Only because you're young and terribly American, with terribly American sensibilities."

I arch a brow.

"Yes," she says. "I find Aiden attractive. I would have happily taken him to my bed. For a night. Or a weekend. Even several weekends. But as fond as I am of attractive men—and sex with attractive men—I'm even more fond of matchmaking. Aiden is comfortable with you, and for him, that's rare. You make an adorable couple."

"Right now we're—"

"Yes, yes, busy saving hapless siblings. I understand that. Which is why last night's push was about more than any matchmaking. I wanted to confirm your stories before I allowed you into my confidences."

"As for this . . ." She glances at the bowl. "My dream shaping ended when Aiden left and you returned to bed. That gave another dream shaper an opening. We'll need to check the security cameras."

She rises.

I stay seated. "First, if I'm going to stay, I have to understand what's going on. You said you need to trust us. With what?"

She's silent for a moment. Then she calls, "Aiden? Come in, please. Time for a chat."

CHAPTER TWENTY-FIVE

VANESSA LIED when she said she didn't want the Necklace of Harmonia. That's no surprise. I'd planned to spend my morning walk with Connolly discussing the possibility that she'd use our information to scoop the necklace from under our noses.

So why test our trustworthiness? Why not just send us on our way with a "Sorry, can't help"?

Why the secrecy at all? She's a major player in this market. Won't it be assumed she wants the necklace? Wouldn't it seem odd if she claimed she didn't?

We don't get answers for the last part. Oh, she skates around with excuses. Everyone knows she isn't keen on jewelry, so she'd planned to stay out of the fray, and then hop in and outbid them.

What about the first part then? Why not just send us off? She knows we aren't going to back out of the auction. We can't with what's at stake.

Here's where we do get an answer. She expects both of us to back out of the auction and help *her* get the necklace. But first, she'll help us free Hope and Rian. Once they're safe, then we'll repay the debt.

As for *how* we'll help her, I figured she'd want me to uncurse the necklace. She doesn't. In fact, she doesn't want it uncursed at all.

"You're going to accept the curse?" I say. "Take it on yourself? Eternal misfortune in return for eternal beauty? I . . . don't know if you've seen a mirror lately, but I don't think you're going to ever have a problem with that last bit. Is it the youth you want?"

"I'm not taking on the curse. I'm destroying the necklace."

I glance at Connolly, who frowns.

"I could try to uncurse it for you," I say. "I mean, if it's beyond my skill, then I'd appreciate not being forced to do it, but I could try. At least then you'd have the necklace, which is both gorgeous and valuable."

"I don't want to own it. I don't want to sell it. I want it to not exist."

Connolly and I exchange a look.

"Is that a problem?" she says. "Does it matter what I do with it as long as your siblings are safe?"

We both admit that it doesn't matter.

"Then let's leave it at that," she says. "I will not need Kennedy's curse-weaving skills."

"Then what *are* we doing for you?" I say. "Besides Aiden bowing out of the auction?"

"You two are going to be my ticket in. I've told the other contenders I don't want the necklace. That means I need a back door. Everyone knows I'm fond of Aiden. So they will understand if I've agreed to help him in return for access to his skills."

I choke on a snort.

"*Luck-working* skills," she says, with a mock glare at me as Connolly furrows his brow, oblivious. "However, if they do think something else?" She shrugs. "Better they believe I'm pursuing *that* than the necklace."

"Kennedy and I will discuss your proposal," Connolly says.

She looks at him. "I'm offering to get your brother out from under his debt and Kennedy's sister away from a kidnapper. In return, I want nothing more than for you to pretend I'm helping you win the auction. I'm not sure what there is to discuss."

"Whether we trust you." He pauses. "I don't suppose you know of a way we can test that. A dream sequence perhaps?"

Vanessa looks affronted, as if she can't believe he's still bringing that up. It was an entire hour ago. Ancient history.

"All right," she says finally. "You and Kennedy can take some time to discuss it. But first, allow me to sweeten the pot. There's a showing tonight. I can get you in."

"A showing of the necklace?"

"Yes. A private party. Black tie. The Hill-Cabots are sparing no expense to woo the buyers."

Connolly frowns. "When did the invitations go out?"

Silence.

I look at him. "Apparently, you aren't on the guest list."

"I'll try not to take that personally," he murmurs.

"They decided you weren't worthy. That's the definition of personal."

He meets my grin with a sour look. "Thank you."

"You're welcome." I look at Vanessa. "That's it, though, right? They're the lions fighting over a kill. To them, Aiden is only a circling jackal, hoping to snatch a bite."

"Circling jackal," he murmurs. "You aren't salving my ego at all here, Kennedy."

"Does it need salving?"

His lips twitch. "No, it does not. And you're right. This is where I wanted to be. My ego might prefer that I was considered a serious threat. My business sense knows this is better."

"It is," Vanessa says.

"So why is Aiden being targeted if he's not taken seriously as a contender?"

"That's the question, isn't it?" she murmurs.

"Kennedy and I will discuss your proposal." He turns toward the door. "I don't suppose I could get the coffee now?"

She sighs, flutters her hands and heads indoors.

———

I HAVE NEVER WANTED to be rich. Oh, sure, I'd take a quarter-million-dollar inheritance from some long-forgotten stranger I helped with an uncursing. I'd stick it into the bank and never again have my gut seize up when I see a bill in my inbox. That's my idea of heaven. Actually "wealthy," though? In the way Connolly grew up? I can't see that it would make my life significantly better.

I don't understand the appeal of high fashion or flashy jewels. My crowd only wears designer clothes when they can get a bargain and then tell everyone how little they paid for them. They buy fake jewelry and happily admit it's fake. If I bought a car like Connolly's, my friends would only be impressed if I told them I got it at auction for a fraction of retail and then spent fifty bucks cleaning that dead-thing smell from inside.

So no, I've never seen the appeal of buckets of money . . . until I walked into Vanessa's house and realized if I *did* have obscene amounts of cash, this is what I would spend it on. Indulgent luxury. Soft beds and sunken tubs. Plush furniture and candle-lit court-yards. Also, food. Not quantities of food, but quality and variety, a cornucopia at my fingertips.

Vanessa doesn't bring Connolly a brewed cup of coffee and a carton of flavored creamer. She returns with a breakfast spread. Two pots of fresh-ground coffee, both single origin, one African and one South American. Cream. Three kinds of sugar, none of them in little packets. Steamed milk. Cocoa. Cinnamon. A plate of homemade pastries. A platter of fruit with everything from strawberries to mangos to pomegranates.

It's two in the morning, and Vanessa slides all this on the table as if it was waiting in the kitchen, her breakfast prepared by last night's staff. Imagine waking up to that every morning. Yep, I might not have batted an eye at Connolly's car or custom suits, but this? I would totally take this.

Connolly gets halfway through his first cup of coffee before he speaks. While I don't tease him about the pastries, he still takes one of the miniature muffins and a small plate of fruit. I make myself a coffee with steamed milk and a sprinkle of cocoa and then take a square of banana loaf and fruit. As wonderful as the spread looks, it *is* the middle of the night, and we had a huge dinner.

Once Connolly's had his coffee, we start talking, and we don't stop for the next hour.

Neither of us jumps at the chance to work with Vanessa. Her offer seems too good to be true, and so we presume it is. There must be a catch, even if her reputation suggests she's trustworthy.

We analyze our chances of doing this without her. They aren't good. We have only the barest information on Hope's captors. Sightings of cars and strangers in Unstable, which are useless until we have a suspect. A mechanically altered voice on a phone. A man talking to a blindfolded Ani in the back of a van. A SIM card, which Connolly's tech contact will have this morning, but even she doesn't expect to get anything from it.

We need to go to the party. Listen to voices. Study the main players. Then there's the necklace, the guest of honor. I want to get close to it. See whether I'd be able to uncurse it if it came to that.

We decide to make a counteroffer. We'd like Vanessa to take us to that black-tie event before we agree to anything. Afterward, the three of us will assess the real chances of rescuing Hope and lifting Rian's debt before the auction. If Vanessa thinks she can do it—and we believe her—we'll proceed.

"I want to apologize to you, as well," Connolly says, before we call Vanessa back in.

I tense.

"Not about the nightmare." He refreshes his coffee. "Yes, I do feel the compulsion to apologize for that, which I understand is awkward because you realize it wasn't me."

"I do. One hundred percent. If we have to speak about it, I'd rather we referred to my 'attacker.' Any resemblance to you is no different than a costume."

"I appreciate that." He sips his coffee. "What I want to apologize for, though, is that night in my office. I don't think I ever properly acknowledged that what I did was wrong."

"Blocking me from leaving? You did apologize. We're good."

He shakes his head. "I mean the test. I knew you were upset over it, but I dismissed your concerns as overreacting. I needed to test you, and therefore tricking you was acceptable."

His gaze lifts to mine. "When Vanessa said she'd sent a dream to test you, I was furious. You came to her in good faith, and instead of treating you like a fellow professional, she resorted to trickery and subterfuge to test you. It was disrespectful."

I nod and tap a little more cocoa on my coffee.

"That's what I did," he says. "I didn't see it that way. I do now. If you were an employee who'd given me reason to distrust you, a test would be warranted. But you weren't. If I wanted to test you, I should have said so. Told you I had a curse-weaving job and asked for proof of your abilities, and then it would have been your choice to agree or walk away. I thought I was being clever. I wasn't."

I nod, accepting his apology. We sip a little more coffee in silence. Then Connolly rises and says, "I'll ask Vanessa to join us."

———

VANESSA AGREES TO OUR TERMS. Connolly gives his word that we will deal fairly with her. We won't use her to gain access to the party and then run off with any information we gather there. I don't think she's worried about that. Connolly may have entered this auction expecting to be treated like a serious contender, but he's getting a clear lesson in the truth. Like when Hope's captor needled me about my skills—a reminder that, to the greater magical world, specializing in the joker's jinx makes me, well, a bit of a joke.

Connolly isn't a joke. He brings the power of his family name and, while he's new in this game, his reputation is solid. He thought that bought him a seat at the head table. It only got him through the door. I look around Vanessa's place, and I know we're both seriously out of our league here. Having Vanessa vouch for Connolly will be critical.

The party is tonight in New York, and we have nothing to wear. Naturally, Connolly has suitable attire at his condo in Boston, and I have suitable attire in an alternate universe where I'm Princess Kennedy, heir to the throne of some tiny European country.

While Connolly could drive to Boston and back in time, we both opt for a formal-wear rental shop. As much as I'd love to pop back home—if only to see Ani—Unstable is on the other side of Boston, which makes the trip out of the question.

All that preparation will come later. First, Vanessa shows us the security video. Vanessa had already checked it while we talked, and she'd found the breach. The video shows just the occasional glimpse of a shadowy figure coming over the fence and avoiding all motion detectors on the way to my window. Someone who knew her security system and where I'd be sleeping as her guest. That, apparently, narrows it down to pretty much everyone in the inner circle of bidders. Not exactly helpful.

Next, we need sleep. The coffee sustained me enough to get through two hours of talking and negotiating and planning. Then I'm exhausted, my entire body dreaming of that incredible bed I barely got to sleep in. Of course, thinking about sleep reminds me *why* I'm so tired.

Vanessa promises me a sound and uninterrupted sleep. For a dream shaper, that's no idle boast. Of course, granting sleep must be balanced with sleep deprivation, but Vanessa assures me she has backup mechanisms. I suppose that's easy enough to do. For everyone in need of sleep, there's someone needing a night without it.

We part ways and head off to bed, and I'm asleep before dawn's first light.

CHAPTER TWENTY-SIX

THE PROBLEM with a disrupted sleep is that it doesn't matter that Vanessa granted me an excellent makeup slumber, my day is thrown off. I'm in bed until nearly noon, which I haven't done since I was a teenager. When I get up, there's no one around, just a note telling me to help myself to food. I do that, snacking on the leftover breakfast trays.

Connolly's bedroom door was closed when I passed, so I presume he's sleeping. Vanessa's note says she's stepped out to run errands, which seems like a thing Vanessa would hire people to do, so I'm guessing it's work, not picking up dry cleaning and groceries.

I decide to take my brunch onto the back patio. I know there is one—I saw it the day before. But do you think I can find it now? For a house that didn't seem large, it's a lot bigger than it looked. I'm considering just going out the front when a warm breeze wafts through a doorway and whispers that I've found the elusive patio.

I follow the breeze. Through the doorway, I see an airy room with French doors opened to that patio. I'm stepping through when a woman's voice wafts out.

"—this was not the plan."

Those words stop me in my tracks. I back up and peek through. It's not Vanessa—the words have a faint brogue, rather than a European lilt—and there isn't anyone else in the house as far as I know.

I lean to see a wicker table and chair set. On the table is a laptop, opened to a video chat. Connolly sits in the chair, his back to me. While the woman's accent suggests she's Irish, I don't presume anything until I see her face better. Then there's no doubt who she is. Marion Connolly. Connolly's mother.

She's dark haired, but otherwise, the resemblance is unmistakable, from the light freckles across high cheekbones to the green eyes. There's a look on her face I've come to recognize on her son's —the annoyed impatience of having to speak to someone who isn't playing the role they've been assigned.

"The plan—" she's saying.

"I am well aware of the plan, Mother. I devised it."

I should back out. Leave them to their private conversation. Yet given what they're saying, I can't. My gut might trust Connolly, but my brain is another matter, and my brain says that I need to be sure their "plan" matches the version I've been given.

"The plan," Marion Connolly continues, as if her son hasn't spoken, "was for you to hire one of the Bennett girls. Preferably the oldest. While my sources say the youngest shows promise, the oldest has proven herself. She is steady and reliable. That middle girl—"

"—is my choice. Kennedy has always been my choice."

"We agreed—"

"We agreed that I would hire one of the Bennetts. I decided on Kennedy. Knowing you would question that, I tested her skills. They are excellent."

"I'm sure they are."

At her tone, he stiffens. "Whatever you are implying—"

"I'm implying that there's a reason she skipped off to Boston. Small-town life wasn't for her. My sources say she's the wild sister, flighty and reckless. There's an appeal to that for a man like you."

"A man like me?" Connolly seems to be speaking through gritted teeth. "Do I even want to know what that means?"

"It's a classic setup. The steady, successful young man and the manic fairy girl."

"Manic *pixie* girl. I am well aware of the trope, Mother, and that is not Kennedy. Nor am I the moon-eyed boy in that scenario. I'm a grown man, capable of making decisions that have nothing to do with a pretty face or a charming demeanor."

"You find her charming. And pretty."

"Because she is both, and if that's meant to make me stammer denials, may I say again that I am a grown man. I can recognize that a young woman is attractive while knowing—unequivocally—that it did not affect my decision to work with her."

"Work *with* her? She's supposed to be working *for* you, Aiden. The plan was for you to hire a Bennett girl, buy this necklace, uncurse it and pay off your brother's debts. Instead, you're chasing this girl's sister."

"Because she's been kidnapped."

"Which is not our concern. Apparently, though, it's the concern of a boy—oh, sorry, a *man*—who wants to impress a girl."

I walk through the doorway. "That is not what Aiden's doing."

Connolly jumps and puts his hand on the laptop lid, as if to close it.

"Sorry," I say. "I didn't mean to interrupt. I was looking for the back door when I overheard that last bit. I'll leave in a second." I turn to the screen. "Aiden isn't trying to impress me. He's trying to pay off his brother's damn debt, which is somehow his responsibility. Aiden and I are trying to work out a solution that resolves both our problems. If we can't do that, then we part ways. He's been very clear on that. If saving my sister interferes with helping his brother, then we'll find ourselves on opposite sides."

Icicles drip from Marion's voice. "I was having a conversation with my son, Ms. Bennett."

"Too bad. Being the object of that conversation, I felt compelled to defend myself. Your plan was to hire a Bennett 'girl.' Great. But then two of those 'girls' were kidnapped just as Aiden was trying to hire the third. Do you really expect me to go along with his plan now? Get the necklace for him even if it costs my sister her life? Hope's kidnapping *is* your concern if you want a Bennett's help. You sure as hell can't hire Hope. Or Ani, who wants nothing to do with your family. So you're stuck with the . . . what was it? Manic pixie Bennett?"

I look at Connolly. "Pixies. Fairies. You guys have some kind of fixation with the little folk. It's almost as if—"

"Don't." He doesn't smile, but the strain in his face eases.

"I'm just saying . . ."

He shakes his head and turns to the screen. "This conversation is over, Mother. I was merely updating you, which I now regret."

"I really didn't mean to interrupt," I say. "I'll retreat now. Just one more thing." I turn to Marion. "You might not have the Bennett you wanted, but if this works out—if Hope is freed—you'll have *all* the Bennetts working together to uncurse that necklace. None of us gives a damn about the thing. You can have it. But if Aiden can help me rescue Hope, then we all owe him. We'll repay that debt."

I don't say that if Vanessa ends Rian's debt, no unweaving will be necessary. I suspect Connolly hasn't told his mother that part.

I lift my coffee and plate. "I'll take this outside and let you talk."

"I'll join you," Connolly says. "We're done here." He turns to the screen. "If you would like an update in the morning, I will call you."

I step back into the hall so I don't hear her reply. When Connolly comes looking for me, I meet him with a cup of fresh coffee.

"Thank you," he says. "I'm sorry you needed to endure that." He pauses. "How much did you hear?"

"The pixie part, obviously. And the part about you wanting to impress me."

He winces. "Right. Well, that's embarrassing."

"Nah," I say as we head toward the patio. "We're young. We're single. Everyone figures we're just trying to get laid."

He chuckles. "It would be easier if I were twice your age."

"Hell, no. They'd say the same thing. It'd just be creepier."

"True." He pushes the open French doors wider. "Are we sitting or walking?"

"One and then the other. We still have a couple of hours, and I fully intend to get a hike through these grounds." I glance at him. "Which you don't need to join me for. I know it's not your thing."

"I will survive. And I have a feeling we'll both require a bit of calm before tonight."

I'M WALKING with Connolly when Hope's captor calls. I've been expecting this. Time for a check-in. Also time to check on *my* progress. I tell him I'm working for Connolly.

"Yes, I know," he says.

"Word travels fast," I say.

The obvious question is *how* he knows, but he isn't going to answer that. Even by admitting he's heard the news, he's giving me a clue. He has a connection to one of the very limited number of people who know I'm working for Connolly.

"We got an invitation to the event tonight," I say. "You might have mentioned that. If you want the necklace uncursed, Hope and I will need time with it before we uncurse it."

"You aren't uncursing it, Miss Bennett. Your sister is. If that was a hint for me to bring her to the gala, it was clumsily done. She will have all the time she needs with it once I've procured the piece."

So you're going to the event? I know better than to ask that. He'll deny it . . . or change his mind about going. He's implied he'll be there, and that's enough.

I want more hints. Little things he might let slip if we continue speaking. Figures of speech and tonal patterns that a voice manipulator won't disguise. Yet the longer I keep him talking, the more likely he is to realize what I'm doing. Better for him to think I've cast my die and I'm doing as he asks.

"I'll still make sure I get a good look at it," I say. "I'm supposed to be uncursing it for Connolly so he'll expect me to take an active interest. May I at least report my findings to Hope? I can write them down if you're concerned."

"I'm not."

Because you're already listening in when I talk to her. And, after my last conversation with Hope, you've dismissed us as a couple of silly "girls" who'll do as we're asked.

"May I speak to her now?" I ask.

"You may. Five minutes."

Connolly has been walking beside me, listening in and silently assessing. At that, he motions that he'll go on ahead and give us privacy.

I get my five minutes alone with Hope. Well, relatively alone.

We're still careful. She slips in a few reminiscences to tell me she really is fine. That's what I need. It's all I get, too.

After our call, I need to start getting ready for this evening. I've set aside enough time to use the sunken tub though I'm not really in the mood to enjoy it.

Hope's captor will be at the event tonight. I'm supposed to be on his side, doing his bidding. What if he finds out the truth?

All I need to do is play my role as Connolly's hired curse weaver. Do that, while not letting Hope's captor know I'm looking for him. That second part will be tougher, but I can pull this off. I need to.

———

CONNOLLY DRIVES the three of us to New York. When we stop for gas, he goes inside to grab a coffee, his caffeine level having apparently dropped to critical levels if he's accepting gas-station swill. Once he's gone, Vanessa explains the plan—Connolly will drop us off at a dress-rental shop and then meet us outside the event.

"So you're renting a dress, too?" I ask.

Her brows arch in genuine horror.

"That's a no," I murmur. "Sorry. If you're not, though, you don't need to hang out with me. You know Aiden better, and he might appreciate a second opinion on his tux."

"If you think Aiden requires anyone's help selecting his clothing, you may need glasses. The man has impeccable fashion sense."

I look out to where Connolly is half-visible through the store window. He's wearing what I presume would be his idea of "casual clothes." Dark linen trousers and a gunmetal-gray shirt rolled up his forearms.

"His taste is very . . . monochromatic," I say.

She sighs. "He's working with a palette that suits his coloring. It's flattering, isn't it?"

"Sure. I guess."

"It's very flattering. And do you know why? Because it isn't the color that matters. It's the style and the fabric and the cut, which is perfection."

"If you say so."

"The man could have stepped out of a men's fashion magazine, Kennedy. Are you honestly telling me you haven't noticed?"

I shrug. "He's hot. I've noticed that. The clothing, though? I'm thinking he'd look good in old jeans. Really worn, comfy, form-fitting jeans. And a Henley."

She shudders. "Well, at least you didn't say plaid."

"Ooh, yes! A plaid flannel shirt. Rolled up like he's wearing it now. Old jeans. Maybe work boots. I have a thing for work boots."

"And, apparently, for lumberjacks."

I lean back in my seat. "I dated a lumberjack once. Well, forestry service, but close enough. Now *he* knew how to dress. An entire closet of plaid flannel. Of course, then plaid flannel came back in style, and everyone mistook him for a hipster. He decided, hey, maybe I should just roll with it. Grow my beard. Wear a bun. Drink microbrews. Start ironically listening to country music. That's when I dumped him. The hipster stuff was bad enough, but once you start consuming popular media just to mock it, I'm out."

"On that we agree though I'd have been out as soon as the hipster phase began."

"Nothing wrong with a little lifestyle experimentation. But yep, it went beyond experiment and into full-blown lifestyle." I watch Connolly as he comes back, coffee in hand. "He does dress well, doesn't he?"

"You seriously did not notice until now?"

I shrug. "Guess it's a good thing you're coming shopping with me instead."

"Apparently."

———

WHEN WE'D DECIDED to rent our formal wear, I'd breathed a sigh of relief. I could afford that.

My first thought on entering the shop? I cannot afford this.

I don't know how much the rentals are. I don't want to find out, or I'll embarrass Vanessa by squawking "Do you know how many discount dresses I can buy for that?"

I balked the moment Connolly dropped us off and I saw where

we were heading. That's when Vanessa assured me that I wasn't footing this bill. Pride made me want to refuse, but before I could, she reminded me that I was going as her guest. I think that meant I shouldn't need to pay, but what I heard was that my outfit would reflect on her, and I couldn't show up in a fifty-dollar rental . . . if such a thing is even possible to find in Manhattan.

I'm going to think of it as a uniform, as if I'd been hired to serve champagne. With that in mind, I settle into a chair as Vanessa speaks to the staff. We've been there less than five minutes before the owner sweeps in and insists on serving Vanessa himself. I could chalk that up to the fact she's drop-dead gorgeous, but it takes the guy five whole minutes to look above her neckline, and that's not because he's admiring her perfect figure. His gaze devours her outfit instead. Apparently, Connolly isn't the only one with fashion sense, and even Vanessa's "driving to New York" dress is enough to tell him she's someone he wants to look after personally.

When Vanessa introduces me, I don't miss the disappointment in his appraising look. Still, he says, "Your sister, I presume?"

Vanessa favors him with a regal smile. "You flatter me."

"No," I murmur. "Pretty sure I'm the flattered one."

She turns that smile on me, my voice having apparently been louder than I thought. "This is my young friend, Kennedy," she says. "I'm taking her to a black-tie affair this evening with another young friend." She winks at the owner. "I'm playing matchmaker."

The owner and the two assistants all chuckle obligingly.

"Matchmaker and fairy godmother," she says. "I want this to be a night to remember, and I'm hoping you can help me with that."

"I believe we can."

CHAPTER TWENTY-SEVEN

I CAN'T DO THIS. I don't know what in God's name made me think I could. Sure, Vanessa said "black-tie affair," but I've been to those. Pull the nicest dress from my closet—maybe even splurge on a new one—and I'm all set. Black-tie just means the guys wear tuxes and the women wear cocktail dresses, and everyone drinks bubbly and has fun playing fancy dress-up.

This isn't playing. This is what those events aspired to. Saying I've been to a black-tie gala is like saying I've been to fancy afternoon teas because I put on tea parties as a kid.

Vanessa called us a car for the trip to the gala. Not a taxi. A hired car, which isn't a limo, because as I'm quickly realizing, that would be gauche. That's the sort of thing people like me do for prom and bachelorette parties and then joke about how posh we are. The truly posh wouldn't be caught dead in a stretch limo. Even fancy SUVs are for security staff. We arrive in what could be the twin of Connolly's car, driven by a guy in a suit who very unobtrusively opens our doors.

"Should I tip him?" I whisper to Vanessa.

Her look answers, and my cheeks heat.

"It's included in the car hire," she murmurs. "But thank you for thinking of it."

The man is gone before I have time to double-check the back seat for my phone—which I'm apparently clutching in one hand. I slide it into the tiny bag Vanessa had produced from her suitcase. The suitcase that miraculously appeared at the hotel room where we'd gotten ready.

After renting my dress, Vanessa had insisted on alterations, and we'd retreated to a hotel a quarter-mile away, where her suitcase waited along with someone to do our hair and makeup. My dress had arrived by courier.

The dress is definitely the most elegant thing I've ever worn. It's floor length with a full skirt, maroon and black in a watercolor abstract floral pattern. Sleeveless with one shoulder completely bare. Sexy and dignified, all in one package.

My hair has been swept over that bare shoulder, curled into waves and partially pinned with a vintage comb Vanessa brought. The rented heels are flattering, but not sky high. As for my makeup, let's just say I want to take photos, so many photos, some of them blown up for my bathroom mirror in the vague hope I might be able to recreate the flawless look. My nails—fingers and toes—are manicured and painted a soft iridescent pink like the inside of a shell.

In short, I feel gorgeous. The whole experience had indeed been very fairy godmother. I'd loved it. Reveled in the pampering and primping. Right up until now, as we arrive at the event.

I'm not sure what I expected. It'd be a small affair, obviously. Vanessa expected only a half-dozen invitees plus guests and security. Then we arrive, and I discover where it's being held.

There'd been a time, as a child, when I'd dreamed of being a museum curator. When I dreamed of working *here*—the place that inspired my love of antiques and history.

The Cabot Museum of Greco-Roman Antiquities.

Where I'll see Josephine Hill-Cabot's cursed Greco-Roman necklace.

I hadn't made the connection, and when I realize where we're going, I feel stupid. Then I see the line of cars and the steady stream of black-tie guests.

"I thought it was a small gathering," I say as we stand on the sidewalk, watching the parade of designer finery.

"They've obviously combined it with another event. Likely a

fundraiser. We'll have exclusive access to a smaller gathering inside."

Exclusive access. To the inner circle. At a gala where I don't belong in the *outer* circle.

Earlier, I'd mused that I'd think of my dress as a uniform. I should have infiltrated as serving staff. I'd be at home there, making a few extra bucks, serving champagne and then retreating to the wings with my fellow staff, where we'd alternate between swooning over a gorgeous dress, bitching about demanding guests and snarking about how many homeless people could dine on the wasted food.

Connolly's car pulls up. Or it looks like his, but so do a dozen others. The driver's door opens, and I catch a flash of red-gold hair, and I grin, feeling like the girl sitting alone at a table when her date arrives.

Then he steps out of the car and hands his keys to the valet, and my despair rushes back tenfold.

Vanessa has joked about playing fairy godmother. This, then, is my true Cinderella moment. Yes, yes, Connolly is my business partner, and I can't entertain thoughts beyond that. Yet in this scenario, he plays the role of Prince Charming, and I would be a bald-faced liar if I said I hadn't twirled in front of the mirror and envisioned his reaction to my transformation.

The story of Cinderella is a fantasy of privilege. All it takes is a little fairy dust—or a proper stylist and unlimited funds—to transform the drudge into a princess. What the story leaves out is how Cinderella would have felt walking into that ball. Or it tells us she felt incredible, floating on air. That's a lie. This is how she really felt, seeing her prince. Struck by the horrible realization that all the stylists in the world can't transform her into someone who fits into his universe.

Connolly belongs in this scene. When he climbs from the car, when he speaks to the valet, when he strides toward the sidewalk, it's with the same nonchalance I would feel hopping out of a taxi at a friend's BBQ. I'm freaking out at the thought of going through those doors, and to him, it's just another party.

If he attracts any attention, it's only admiring glances from women . . . and a few guys. Vanessa mentioned Connolly's fashion sense, and now that she's called my attention to it, I feel blind for missing it. The guy is wearing a rented tux. It should sag here, bunch there, something about it seeming not quite right, even to my untrained eye. Yet I don't see the slightest imperfection.

Vanessa talked about style and fit and fabric, but all I know is he looks amazing. He strides past guys who looked fine a moment ago, and I suddenly see the imperfections in *their* attire—pants a little long, shoes not quite the right shade, coat a little tight in the shoulders, royal blue bowtie that doesn't flatter a skin tone.

They look stylish and at ease. Connolly somehow looks *more* stylish, *more* at ease.

Before I can finish processing that, he's in front of us.

"Sorry to have kept you both waiting," he says. "I mistimed traffic."

That's it. Nothing about my dress. Nothing about how I look.

I chide myself. This isn't a date. If he thought I looked nice, he assimilated that a hundred feet away. Still, it's just one more lead weight tossed onto my mood.

"You look nice," I say.

He glances down, as if he's forgotten what he's wearing. "Ah. Yes. Well, not many choices when it comes to tuxes. Makes things easy." A pause. A long pause. Then, "Oh, and, of course, you look, well, lovely. That's a very, er, lovely dress. Now, shall we—"

"Is there a back-up plan?" I blurt. "Maybe I can sneak in and steal a server's outfit instead."

Connolly frowns at me.

"I just . . ." I begin. "I think this will work better if you two are guests, and I join the staff."

Connolly studies me and then turns to Vanessa. "May we have a moment?"

"Of course," she says.

Connolly puts his fingertips against my back and leads me to the lawn, where we can tuck into a shadow.

"You do look lovely," he says. "I'm sorry if I bungled that."

"No, it's not—"

"You told me I looked nice, and my awkward response seemed

forced and insincere. I realized I should have complimented you first, and so I stumbled over a response."

"Aiden, no. You aren't obligated to say anything about how I look. I just . . . I don't fit here. That's obvious."

His frown is genuine, which helps lift my spirits.

"I'm not fishing for compliments," I say. "It isn't the dress or the shoes or my hairdo. Vanessa looked after all that. What she can't fix is the fact that I'm a million miles out of my depth here. I'm going to screw it up. Use the wrong fork or whatever."

"It's finger food. There won't be forks."

"Then I'll be the dolt who asks for one." I exhale and meet his gaze. "I don't belong here, Aiden. I know it. You know it. Everyone here is going to know it."

I expect a quick blanket denial, which will only make this conversation more awkward. Instead, he considers and then says, "When we were in Unstable, how did I seem?"

"Seem?"

"Relaxed? At ease? Before we got the custard, that is."

"Unstable isn't your kind of place. I was mostly thinking about how you must see it, our little provincial town. Terribly quaint. Which is code for backward and boring."

"I wasn't thinking that at all. However, I wasn't relaxed, either, because all I could think was that I didn't fit in. I was glad we left my car behind the library. While it's just another vehicle in Boston, it seemed showy and ostentatious in Unstable. I felt the same. As if I'd walked into a country fair wearing a bespoke suit. Yet even if I'd been wearing jeans, I think I'd have felt as if everyone knew I didn't belong."

He glances at the museum. "That's how you feel here. Except no one's going to notice if you eat the canapés wrong or even ask for a fork. They're too busy with their own concerns. Looking for networking opportunities. Flirting with someone else's wife. Wondering when they can get out of their tight shoes. If they notice you at all, it will be as an attractive young woman they might like to get to know better."

I must make a face because his eyes warm.

"Don't worry," he says. "I will stay close enough to protect you. Unless you'd rather I didn't."

"Please do."

"Then . . ." He offers his arm. "May I?"

I hesitate and then smile, take his arm, and we head back to Vanessa.

———

THAT ISN'T the end of the discussion. It could be—I've had my mini-meltdown, and I won't trouble Connolly with any more of my fears. Yet while he doesn't dwell on it, he doesn't presume my chin-up forward motion means I'm feeling fine and confident. He whispers and murmurs asides as we return to Vanessa and as the three of us go in. Words of advice and encouragement.

Just keep looking forward.

Watch the step here.

Vanessa will check us in—we'll just talk over here.

Pretend it's just the two of us if that helps.

You really do look lovely. Maroon suits you.

We'll do a few rounds of the main party before heading to ours.

If you need anything, just let me know.

None of it feels patronizing, and I've come to realize that when I feel patronized by him, it isn't his intention. Oh, it's certainly not always me being overly sensitive. But the more I'm with him, the less of that I get as he relaxes.

What seemed condescending had been mostly awkwardness. Now, as he guides me through those first few minutes, I see only kindness and consideration, two of the last things I'd have expected from the guy who walked into my showroom two days ago.

People say I'm kind, but in my case, it comes easily and naturally. I like people, and I treat everyone the way I want to be treated. That's how I was raised. I'm naturally outgoing and open. Connolly is neither. And he definitely wasn't raised to treat others with respect. Sure, if they "outrank" him, then they get respect because he wants something from them. I suspect he'd been raised to treat those "under" him much differently. Yet there is an innate kindness that his upbringing couldn't quite stamp out. It's a shy kindness, slipping out only when he's comfortable and confident that it won't be mistaken for weakness.

As he warned, we don't head straight into the inner party. Following Vanessa's lead, we tour the main room. I try very hard not to pause at every exhibit. It doesn't matter than I've seen them a dozen times—I want to stop and admire, which would make me stand out in a room where people are treating ancient statues as mere decoration.

As we circle the room, I discover the piece of advice Connolly left out. That key piece that makes all the difference. I don't need to worry about what people will think because as long as I'm with Vanessa, they won't notice me.

My ego is somewhat cushioned by the fact that they don't notice Connolly, either. Vanessa walks through a room and draws every eye. Connolly and I get to relax and enjoy the tranquility of the shadow she casts.

It's like something out of a movie, really, with well-bred ladies and gentlemen whispering in an undulating wave of, *Who is she?* as we pass. The guesses follow. Hollywood mostly, possibly modeling, but the money is on "actor." These people might not have seen a movie in decades, but clearly Vanessa is some major Hollywood star. As soon as they decide that, they try picking apart her styling. The exact fate I feared falls onto Vanessa as they decide she isn't "one of them." Beautiful, to be sure. Unearthly beautiful. But that which makes her so striking also proves she doesn't belong here. Her face is her passport into this party rather than breeding or brains.

The problem, of course, is that when they try to find fault, they can't, and I have to hold back a snicker at those whispers. Half-started insults they can't finish. That dress is . . . Her shoes aren't quite . . . She's very clearly . . .

We hear it all on that walk through the party. And Vanessa's expression never changes. She scans the party, gaze traveling over faces. More than once it pauses on a handsome man. Yet it never lingers long. She admires and moves on. As for the whispers, it's as if they're spoken in a frequency she can no longer hear.

We pause in a quiet spot. One snarky whisper reaches us, some woman saying she should ask for the name of Vanessa's plastic surgeon. When her companion replies that Vanessa probably didn't pay in cash, I start to wheel just to let her know we heard, but Vanessa catches my arm.

A man on our other side sees Vanessa holding my arm and leans in to whisper something to another man. They both snicker like teenage boys.

"The well-bred aren't that well-bred, are they?" I mutter. "It's like a school dance."

"Shall we give them something to talk about?"

She makes a move to tug me closer, and I acquiesce with a smile. Then she glances at Connolly.

"Come over here, Aiden, and we'll really get tongues wagging."

He frowns, pulling his attention back from wherever it had wandered.

She puts out her arm, motioning for him to take it. "We're trying to make people talk. Play along. It's fun."

He realizes what she means, and his cheeks redden.

"Perfect," she says. "Nothing says 'naughty conversation' like a blushing man." She leans toward him. "Pretend I'm saying something truly scandalous. Or sliding my fingers along your thigh."

His cheeks flame brighter.

"Excellent," she says.

"Don't tease him," I say. "That's my job."

Her brows waggle. "Is it now?"

"It is." I lean over toward Connolly and stage whisper. "Is that a rainbow over your head, or are you just happy to see me?"

He relaxes and gives a soft laugh, shaking his head.

"I'm missing something, aren't I," Vanessa says.

"Yes," Connolly says. "And we aren't telling you what it is. Now, I was looking for a server to get us a drink, but may I instead suggest we cut this part of the evening short and continue to the main event? We must be fashionably late by now."

"We are," Vanessa says.

"Then lead the way."

CHAPTER TWENTY-EIGHT

I'VE SEEN this scene in movies. We'll go to a curtain or a roped-off entrance, where the uninvited are subtly jockeying for admission. *What do you mean I'm not on the list?* It doesn't matter that they have no idea what the other party is for—it's private, and that means they want in.

There is no curtain. No roped-off hall. Vanessa finds a security guard and murmurs something to him, and he snaps to attention. "Follow me, please," and he's off, walking briskly toward a side hall. A few heads turn as we pass. Several people even fall in behind us. Then they see where we're going. To the restrooms.

We lose our entourage there. Once they're gone, the guard directs us to a corridor past the restrooms.

"The Edith Cabot Memorial Room," he says. "Would you like me to escort you?"

"No, we can take it from here," Connolly says. "Thank you."

I don't recognize the name of the room. It's been a few years since my last visit, and I presume it's new. It isn't. As soon as we continue down the hall, though, I know exactly where we're going.

"Oh!" I say. "The treasure room!"

Connolly glances over. "You've been to this museum?"

"Enough times to know my way around blindfolded. I've never been in the 'Edith Cabot Memorial Room,' though. Never knew what it was called. It's just always been the treasure room, a.k.a. 'the door I could never sneak through.'"

His brows arch.

I shrug. "There's nothing as tempting as an unmarked, locked door in a museum. Clearly, it's where the treasure is kept. I used to sneak here from the restroom, hoping to find it unlocked. It never was."

"Well," Vanessa says. "Tonight it *is* unlocked. And it contains treasure."

I grin. I can't help it. Connolly smiles over, and I take his arm again. As we walk, a woman slips out from a door marked Staff and converses with Vanessa, confirming our invitations. Then she melts back into her hideaway, and we are free to continue.

The Edith Cabot Memorial Room is at the end of the hall. While the door is open, the dim lighting makes it impossible to see anything beyond. I expect a murmur of voices, a tinkle of glasses and laughter, but all is silent.

I'm wondering whether we're the first to arrive when we draw close enough for me to make out shadowy figures. A few more steps, and the figures coalesce into people.

I expect the "inner-circle event" to be a scaled-down version of the main one. People in evening wear milling about as servers circulate with champagne and appetizers—sorry, *canapés*. Instead, it looks like . . . well, it looks like a pub, and not a very lively one at that.

It's a small room. Glass display boxes mark it as a museum, but they're widely spaced, decorations rather than attractions. A temporary bar consumes a quarter of the space. A few people sit. A few stand. The rest . . . well, there is no *rest*. A rough scan counts maybe ten heads, and that includes the bartender.

Two people catch my attention even before we reach the door. They're the type of people you notice, even when they're making no effort to draw attention to themselves.

The man at one end of the bar is an arresting figure, if only for his size. Even sitting, he's as tall as the woman tending bar, with shoulders twice as wide as hers. "Built like a bull" is the phrase that comes to mind. He's shed his jacket, rolled up his sleeves and has one massive muscled forearm resting on the bar. Maybe in his forties. Dark wavy hair. Dark beard. Handsome, in a brooding way.

The other man is a ginger. Which would always catch my eye, but in this case, a flash of red-gold hair has me doing a double take, thinking it might be Connolly's brother. On second glance, there's not much resemblance to Connolly beyond the hair, and even that is lighter on the man, more of a blond that gleams red in the candlelight.

What really caught my eye wasn't his hair but his pose. There's a stone divan in the corner. I'm pretty sure it's an artifact. Also pretty sure it hasn't been left out for seating. Yet the man isn't just perched on it. He's fully reclined, one leg lazily over the edge, looking for all the world like a wealthy Roman lounging in his courtyard.

He even has the attendant maiden crouching at his side, offering him a drink. I think it's a server until I notice her dress, which is at least as fancy as mine. She's in her thirties with sculpted arms and an athlete's lean body and wears her blond hair swept up off a pale neck draped with jewels. It's a strong look, yet she's on one knee, holding out a champagne flute for the reclining man and chattering away like a teenage girl. He's ignoring her completely. Even has his eyes closed, and I wonder whether he's asleep until he lifts one hand and waves her away as if she were a serving girl at his Roman bacchanalia.

I can understand her interest. He's good-looking. *Really* good-looking. Maybe forty, well built, with a classically handsome, knife-cut face.

The moment we reach the doorway, the man's eyes snap open, like a hound catching a scent. He sits up so fast that his elbow strikes the proffered flute, spilling it onto the kneeling woman. He doesn't even notice. The only thing he sees in that moment is Vanessa, and he's on his feet in a blink, a smile lighting his face into something incandescent.

At the same moment he spots Vanessa, so does the big man at the bar. His is a very different kind of stare, something hard and almost possessive. He starts to rise, stops and downs his drink instead, pushing it forward for a refill. As the ginger-blond man passes behind him, his head jerks that way, eyes narrowing. He looks between Vanessa and the other man and then snaps his fingers for his drink, attention back on the bartender.

"I knew you couldn't stay away," the ginger-blond man says as he approaches. He pulls Vanessa into a half embrace, and she air-kisses his cheek.

"Marius," she says. "I'd like you to meet my guests."

Marius Archer. Arms dealer.

When Vanessa had been speculating on who might attend, she'd mentioned Marius Archer. Oh, Vanessa had smoothed over the edges on that one—*he's in the military technology business.* And maybe the guy doesn't actually sell weapons themselves, but yeah, mentally, he's been "Marius Archer, the arms dealer" to me. The problem is that I'd already assigned that name to the guy at the bar, if only subconsciously, and it takes a moment to shift it to the handsome ginger-blond in front of me.

Marius turns our way. His gaze lands on Connolly first, and there's a flash of something almost like pleased recognition, quickly doused with, "I know you, don't I? Conlin, is it? No, O'Connell?"

"Connolly. Aiden Connolly. We've met. Multiple times."

"Right. Of course. The Connolly boy. Luck worker. Good to see you again, Aiden."

Marius turns to me, and his smile widens. When he says, "I definitely haven't met you," it could come with a leer or a creepy grin, but it's light, off-hand flattery, like the appraising glance that accompanies it.

"Kennedy Bennett," I say.

"Bennett?" His blue eyes spark. "One of *the* Bennetts, I presume. It is lovely to meet you, Ms. Bennett. I presume you're here to help Vanessa procure an object she has very clearly, very definitively said she does not want." He looks at Vanessa and lifts a brow.

"I *don't* want the necklace," she says. "Aiden does. His invitation, though, seemed to get lost in the mail."

"Most did, I think. The Hill-Cabots have a very precise idea of who does and who does not qualify for their attention." He looks at Connolly. "Your parents should have said they were fronting you. That'd have gotten you an invitation."

"He has one now," Vanessa says. "And I have the opportunity to wear a pretty frock and spend an evening among friends without having to jump into the feeding frenzy for that accursed necklace."

A look passes through Marius's eyes. Then he finds a blazing smile and says, "Well, it'll all be over soon enough, Vess."

"The necklace isn't here yet, is it?" I say, scanning the exhibit boxes.

"Oh, no. That will be a very special presentation, full of pomp and circumstance."

"Will they let the curse weavers near it?" I say. "That always helps. I'm presuming there are curse weavers here besides me."

"Mmm, her, I believe?" He nods toward a gray-haired woman who is alone in a corner and pretending she's busy checking phone messages, as if she hasn't been abandoned by her host.

Marius scans the room, and his gaze lands on a blond hanging off an older man. "And possibly her, though if you ask me, I'm thinking she's . . ."

"Paid companionship?"

He laughs. It's a bark of a laugh, sudden and surprised. "Yes, that's one way to put it, I suppose. The nicest way."

"You didn't bring a curse weaver yourself?"

"If I win the auction, I'll decide what to do with it at that point. No sense putting the cart in front of the horse."

Could that mean he already has a curse weaver? Hope? I'd used *paid companionship* to see how he reacted. He didn't, and nothing in his demeanor or his word choice or his tone reminds me of the guy on the phone.

Vanessa rests her fingertips on his arm and murmurs. "As lovely as it is to see you, Marius, I'm afraid I need to . . . pay my respects. Before the tension grows any tighter."

"Hmm." Marius glances over his shoulder at the big man, who's studiously working on his drink. "Would you like me to take your guests around? Perform the necessary introductions?"

"Thank you for offering, but . . ." She glances at him. "I think perhaps it's a good time to take some air. It's a bit stuffy in here, and you won't want to miss the unveiling."

A look passes between them. Marius forces a smile. "All right, then. I'll step outside and see you all later."

He leaves, and Vanessa assures us she'll be back to perform introductions in a few moments. As she heads toward the man at the bar, Connolly leads me deeper into the room.

"Her ex," he murmurs.

"Which *one*?"

"Both."

I try not to gape at Vanessa and the man at the bar, but I can't resist a peek. She's beside him, leaning in, and he's ignoring her.

"Ex-husbands, I'm guessing?" I say.

Connolly pauses. "I don't like to gossip, but in business, it helps to understand the competition, including their interpersonal dynamics."

"And there are definitely dynamics at play here."

He nods. "Hector is her ex-husband. Marius is an ex-lover. She gets along very well with Marius, as you saw. Hector . . . is another story."

"I see that," I say.

Vanessa's talking to Hector as he looks straight ahead. When Vanessa starts to leave, Hector grabs her wrist. I tense. Connolly puts a hand on my arm.

"Better not," he murmurs. "That's why she asked Marius to leave. Her relationship with Hector is fractious, but she prefers to handle it herself."

Even as Connolly speaks, Vanessa is peeling the man's massive fingers from her forearm. He grunts and takes his hand back and then says something, and they fall into conversation, his gaze on her now.

"Hector," I murmur. "That'd be Hector Voden. Construction, right? He owns the Voden Group."

While I'd pictured him as the arms dealer, this fits, too. As Vanessa's ex-husband, though? No. Marius certainly fits as a former lover. But this guy at the bar, bristling with hostility and contempt for everything around him? Married to charming, vibrant Vanessa?

"He must have been a very different guy when he was younger," I murmur.

"Presumably. Now, may I get you a drink?"

CHAPTER TWENTY-NINE

I WANT to say I'll go to the bar with Connolly, but that'll seem as if I want to eavesdrop on Vanessa and Hector. Which I do . . . to hear Hector's voice and see whether he could be Hope's captor. Vanessa will make sure we are properly introduced, though, so I let Connolly head to the opposite end of the bar with an order for something bubbly.

The problem with such a small party is that it's hard to people-watch without staring. Even harder when people-watching—and listening—is what I'm here for. These are the major players. I want to put names to faces. All I have so far are Marius and Hector, whom Connolly said are at the top of the food chain, along with Vanessa. There are a few others, but without more data, I need to wait for introductions.

The one I really want to meet is Havoc. She holds Rian Connolly's debt. Is there a chance she also holds my sister? Playing it both ways? Or screwing over the Connollys?

Hmm, seems I had to get that necklace myself. Now you really *owe me.*

I scan the attendees, looking for someone who fits Vanessa's description of "a capo who thinks herself a godfather." Self-important and chafing at being kept out of the upper echelons.

That's when the woman who'd been kneeling beside Marius sets her sights on Connolly. As he's turning from the bar, drinks in hand, she lays her fingers on his arm, stopping him.

"Aiden Connolly, I believe." Her voice wafts to me. "You look so much like your brother."

I freeze. Connolly murmurs something I don't hear. The woman laughs, a tinkling sound as her fingers glide down Connolly's arm and over the back of his hand. He stiffens. There's a look in his eyes I know well. I've seen it in every girl cornered by a guy at a bar.

I start toward them. Connolly doesn't notice me. He's listening to the woman as her fingers slide from his hand to the champagne flute he's holding. When she tries to tug it away, he gives a tight-lipped, very un-Connolly smile and nods toward me.

"I can certainly get you a drink if you'd like," he says. "This one's for my . . ." He finishes that sentence with a nod toward me, and I'm impressed by how smooth that is, leaving the last word to her interpretation.

"Hey," I say. "That looks delicious. What is it?"

"Kir royale. Champagne and crème de cassis."

"Mmm." I take the flute in my left hand and extend my right. "I don't believe we've met."

"Kennedy, this is Havoc. Havoc, Kennedy."

"Pleased to meet you, Ms . . . Ms. Havoc?"

"Just Havoc," she says.

Vanessa appears and envelops the younger woman in an embrace. "Havoc, how lovely it is to see you."

There's no snark in Vanessa's voice, but Havoc stiffens and disengages fast.

Before anyone can speak, Vanessa takes my arm. "If you don't mind, Havoc, I promised to properly introduce my guests about the room. We should do that before the necklace arrives. After that, no one will have eyes for anything else."

"Your guests?" Havoc's gaze cuts from Vanessa to Connolly. "I thought you didn't want the necklace."

"I don't, which is why they are my guests. Aiden is planning to bid, but he wasn't invited. I was invited, and I'm *not* planning to bid. It worked out perfectly."

"Then why's she here?" Havoc jerks her chin at me.

"Because she's a curse weaver." Vanessa speaks in measured

tones. "And the necklace is cursed. Presumably, Aiden wants it uncursed."

Havoc glowers. "Obviously. I just mean why is she *here*."

"To look at the necklace," I say. "It'll help me prepare."

She sniffs. "I would think a decent curse weaver wouldn't need that."

"No," I say evenly. "A decent curse weaver knows to take every opportunity to familiarize herself with a curse. Particularly such an infamous one."

"So you're saying it might be too much for you."

Vanessa tugs my arm and inserts herself between us. "It may be too much for anyone, Havoc. That's the point. The more homework Kennedy can do, the better prepared she'll be. Now, if you'll excuse us . . ."

"Take Kennedy around please," Connolly says. "I need to speak to Havoc."

Vanessa nods and leads me off. Once we're out of earshot, I say, "I feel as if I've made an enemy without even trying."

"Havoc is the sort of woman who considers herself 'not like other girls.' She prefers to associate with men."

I make a face.

"My sentiments exactly," she murmurs. "As for her reaction, you're with Aiden, and that's a problem."

"She likes him."

Her lips purse as we stop in a quiet spot. "No offense to Aiden, but this is about me. We have . . . history. She knows I've taken an interest in Aiden. She's not sure whether I want him as a lover, an employee or a business contact. She's covering her bases."

I glance back to where Connolly is talking to Havoc, and she's standing far too close, her face tilted up to his as if they're having a very private conversation.

"Several months ago," Vanessa continues, "Havoc and I were at the same party, as we often are, unfortunately. I was talking to Marius and several others, and Aiden's name came up. Luck workers are always valuable assets. I was saying I thought he was worth cultivating. He has obvious talent. He's confident and self-assured, but not a braggart or a grandstander. He's intelligent, but never needs to be the smartest man in the room. Polite and respectful, but no fawning sycophant. He's an excellent luck worker, who reflects well on anyone who employs him. A week later, I hear through the grapevine that Havoc has hired his brother."

"She wanted her own Connolly luck worker."

"Perhaps, but I'm more concerned that she saw Rian—who seems a bit of a wild card—as a way to Aiden. It didn't take long for her to snare Rian in a debt he couldn't repay. And then, oh look, there's this necklace she'll accept in exchange. A necklace Aiden could get."

"Forcing Aiden to jump through hoops isn't exactly the way to get his attention."

"Havoc wouldn't see that. She's a doer, not a thinker. A better criminal than criminal mastermind."

"You said she used to work for someone higher up."

Vanessa nods toward a figure coming through a doorway.

"Marius," I say. "I saw her trying to get his attention earlier."

"Hmm." She glances around. "Now, where shall we begin these introductions? How about over here . . ."

WE MAKE THE ROUNDS. I pay the most attention to voices but also to attitudes. Do they know who I am? Why I'm here? Do they treat me like Hope's captor did? Do their word choices invoke him? The cadence of their speech?

Connolly joins us partway through, which helps. He can double-check my interpretations of attitude and voice.

It's maybe a half hour later when we finally approach the last potential buyer. The guy at the bar. Vanessa's ex. Hector Voden.

"Aiden could handle this," I say to Vanessa. "You don't need to speak to him again."

She waves her fingers. "It's fine. We've been divorced longer than we were together. We'll never get on, but it's not as if we did when we were married, either." A tight smile. "When you travel in the same circles as your ex, you develop a veneer of civility."

Before I can argue, she's sweeping us toward Hector.

"Saving the most important introduction for last," she says. "May I introduce Hector Voden. Hector, I'd like to introduce my guests for the evening."

Hector turns. His gaze slides up me and then down Connolly. There's nothing lascivious about it. Nothing flattering, either.

"I see you haven't lost your taste for pretty young things," Hector says, returning to his drink.

"Now, now. These are business associates. I believe you know—"

"The Connolly boy," he says. "One of them anyway. This would be the prissy one."

"Moving right along, this young lady is . . ."

"One of the Bennett girls. To uncurse the necklace that you insist you don't want." He peers at me. "Please don't tell me you're the middle sister."

"Yes, I'm Kenn—"

He snorts and looks at Vanessa. "This is why you'll never play at the top, Vanessa. What made you pick her? I could say it's that weakness for pretty young things, but from what I hear, she's not even the prettiest. Let me guess, she's the only one who'd accept your offer."

He looks at me. "Is that right, Miss Bennett? Your sisters turned Vanessa down?" His gaze shifts to Connolly. "Or did you do the hiring, boy? Had to scrape the bottom of the Bennett barrel?"

"Well, this was fun," Vanessa said. "You are as charming as ever, Hector. We will leave you to the companionship of that glass and avail ourselves of the buffet."

He mutters something as we leave. I'm sure it's not a compliment.

As we walk to the food, I glance at Connolly. Alarm bells had rung nonstop during that conversation. Hector's dismissive attitude. His sneering tone. Calling Connolly prissy. Dismissing my skills. Referring to me as *Miss* Bennett. Saying I wasn't the prettiest sister . . . as if he's seen the one who is.

At my look, Connolly nods. It's not just me, then.

Vanessa murmurs. "Was I right? That was the most important introduction of the evening?"

"It was," I say.

"Yes," Connolly says. "It definitely was."

She sighs. "That's what I was afraid of."

CHAPTER THIRTY

THAT SHOULD FIX EVERYTHING, right? Hector has Hope, so all we need to do is . . . What, exactly? He won't be keeping her at home. Wherever he does have her, she's well guarded.

Do we call the cops and report him as her kidnapper? That'd only make things worse. Confront him and demand her return? Yeah, this isn't a guy who quails at threats.

Vanessa murmurs that she'll handle this. We'll talk more later, but she promises to get Hope back for us, and knowing who has her, she's convinced she can do it.

The main thing now is to not react. Hector feels secure in sniping against Connolly and belittling me without fear that I'll realize he's the man on the other end of that phone. Either he presumes I won't figure it out or he just doesn't give a damn. Like I said, it doesn't really matter if we know it's him. I have my orders, and I'm obviously carrying them out.

I'm assembling a small plate from the buffet while trying to figure out what's what. Connolly leans over and whispers, "Any allergies?"

I shake my head. Then he starts very discreetly making recommendations. I'm picking up a shrimp puff when his gaze cuts left. I follow it to a white-haired man in a tux with a dark-haired woman on his arm. The guy must be in his seventies; the woman isn't much older than me. They've just appeared through the back entrance.

"The Hill-Cabots," Connolly whispers. "Josephine's son, George, and his wife, Brianne."

"Wife? Oh my God, she's been cursed by the necklace!" I hiss.

He glances over, and then his lips twitch as he realizes I'm joking.

"That, dear Kennedy, is the curse of wealthy men, forever destined to remarry increasingly younger women."

"Curse, huh?"

He lifts one shoulder. "Depending on how you look at it. My father would disagree. He always jokes he's the only one of his cronies still with his first wife . . . because she's too scary to divorce."

"That's actually not funny."

"No," he says, lifting a canapé to his lips. "It is not. Tell my father, though, and he'll only insist you lack a sense of humor."

He glances toward the couple, who stand there, their linked hands lifted like actors coming out for an encore. They've paused, waiting for everyone to note their arrival. Everyone has noted it . . . and gone back to whatever they were doing.

Connolly points toward a tray of pastries. "Those look quite good."

"Is no one even going to acknowledge that the *Hill-Cabots* walked into the room?"

"Didn't you see me glance over?" He selects a pastry for his plate. "I said I come by my arrogance naturally. So do most people here—and the rest are following their lead." He nods toward the couple, still awkwardly poised. "They have money and breeding. Just not quite the right breeding for this crowd."

"No magical powers."

He lifts a plate of tiny tidbits for me. I take one.

"This is the true source of my parents' arrogance," he says. "They travel in monied circles, but those circles lack the little extra they have. It makes them feel superior. When you feel superior, you act superior. When you act superior, people recognize your superiority, which means . . ." He shrugs. "There's no incentive to change. The self-fulfilling prophecy has been neatly self-fulfilled."

While the Hill-Cabots try to figure out their next move, Hector swivels from his spot at the bar and grunts. "Well, get on with it."

The couple blinks at him.

"Do you have the necklace?" he says. "That's what we're all here for. You could have saved yourself a shitload of money by skipping all this"—he waves around the room—"and wheeling the damn thing out an hour ago."

I hate to say it, but he has a point. The champagne is lovely. The canapés are lovely. The chance to play fancy dress-up is lovely. But we just want to see the necklace.

A wave of Mr. Hill-Cabot's hand, and two tuxedoed security guards wheel out a box covered with a black-velvet cloth. The men pushing it wear white gloves, making them look like magicians about to whisk off the cloth and release a pair of doves.

Hector's sigh ripples through the room as I swallow a snicker.

"And you call me dramatic," I whisper to Connolly.

He wrinkles his nose. "I expected they'd have better taste."

"I'm sure they do. This performance is for us. The fools willing to buy a cursed necklace."

His lips twitch. "Touché."

One of the gloved guards reaches for the cloth.

"Stop," Hector says. "We'll do that. You can leave now."

Mr. Hill-Cabot clears his throat. "We'd prefer our guards stayed—"

"I mean all of you. You, the sideshow magicians, and your granddaughter."

Mrs. Hill-Cabot squeaks as her husband harrumphs and corrects him, which only has Hector shrugging and saying, "It's your money" to more protests and a wave of soft laughter that ripples through the room.

This is the problem with guys like Hector. When their snark is directed at deserving targets, it's hard not to laugh, even when you really don't want to.

"I think what Hector is saying," Marius says, stepping forward, "is that we'll be more comfortable examining the necklace on our own. Your guards can certainly stay outside the doors and prevent us from leaving until you're in possession of the necklace again. We can just better . . . fully appreciate its . . . unique qualities without oversight."

He glances at Mr. Hill-Cabot, and a look passes between them, one that says Marius knows the old man realizes there's something wrong with the necklace—and he's pretending otherwise. If he wants to maintain that charade, he's going to need to leave the room.

If he wants to come clean, though? Admit he realizes he's selling tainted goods? Admit that the people in this room aren't regular folks who just want to examine its fine workmanship?

Mr. Hill-Cabot could do that. Step out of his tidy life and into a stranger, darker place where the world isn't quite what he thought it was. All he has to do is say that he knows why we need to see the necklace in private.

The old man clears his throat. "All right. We will return in thirty minutes. Until then, I must insist that no one leaves the room."

Chin up, Mr. Hill-Cabot turns to leave. As he goes, Vanessa glides over and whispers something. Mr. Hill-Cabot nods stiffly, and she heads for the door with them after a wave our way, telling us she's going out.

Marius notices and starts forward, as if to join her. A lift of her fingers, and he hesitates, and then, with an abrupt nod, walks to us instead.

"Is everything all right?" I ask.

He murmurs something I don't quite catch, vague words of assurance, even as his troubled gaze follows Vanessa. Then he nudges me.

"Go on, and get in there," he says. "Everyone may seem very polite, but once that cloth is off, they'll be piranha smelling blood."

Connolly puts a hand against my back and escorts me forward. The box sits on its pedestal, still covered. Gazes flit from Marius to Hector. If there was any doubt who the top dogs are here, that dispels it.

Marius catches Havoc's eye and waves for her to do the honors. She preens as she strides forward, all gazes on her. I'm sure she sees this as a mark of honor. It's not. It's the boss sending an underling to do the work while he freshens his drink.

Havoc doesn't stand on ceremony. She walks up and whisks off the cover, and the guests surge forward as one body.

Marius lifts a hand, and everyone freezes. For a moment, I wonder whether this is some magical power I've never heard of. Then I realize it *is* power. The power to make people stop in their tracks with only a laconic raised hand.

"I know everyone wants to take a look, and everyone will have that chance," Marius says. "First, though, Ms. Bennett."

I glance around, as if there's another Ms. Bennett here.

Marius continues, "As a curse weaver from the esteemed Bennett clan, she should get a first look."

Connolly starts to propel me forward as someone says, "What? I have a curse weaver, too." A bald man waves at the gray-haired woman that Marius pointed out earlier, and I struggle to recall names.

"Yes, but you are not me," Marius says. "I'm taking first dibs. Unless . . ." He turns to Hector. "Would you like to have a look?"

I swear the whole room truly does freeze then, every breath held.

"Seen it," Hector says.

"You don't want to admire the craftsmanship?"

A sound from deep in the crowd. A gasp? A titter? I can't tell, and I feel as if I'm missing a joke, but when I glance at Connolly, he lifts a shoulder, saying he doesn't get it, either.

"Nope," Hector says as he raises his glass to his lips. "Looks fine from here."

"The Bennett girl isn't *your* curse weaver, Marius," the bald man says. "She's his, isn't she?" A dismissive wave at Connolly.

"She is Vanessa's guest, and since Vess stepped out, I'm asking in her place and claiming the right to let Kennedy examine it first. Also, I'm curious to know what a weaver thinks." He looks at the bald man. "Or we can bicker about this until our thirty minutes are up. Your choice."

The bald man grumbles but falls silent. Marius motions me forward. He also waves for the other curse weaver to approach though he warns her back before she can get close.

Connolly stays with me, his hand against my back as if I need the guidance. No one interferes, and we both approach the necklace.

In life, it's more beautiful than any photograph could capture. Thousands of years old, yet it gleams as if the gold has just been cast.

I've seen snakes on necklaces before. They're usually shaped like rope, forming a solid choker. This one is fine threads interwoven into a light chain that looks like snake scales. Two snakes, one down each side. At the bottom, their mouths open around a garnet. A carved garnet, depicting something I can't make out. When I bend to squint at it in the dim light, Connolly whispers, "A loom. It shows a loom."

I'd never heard that the gem was carved though I know it was a popular practice at the time. A loom symbolized women's work. While it's kind of like giving a modern woman a jewel engraved with a vacuum, it would have been appropriate for a bride. A symbol of her new household. Here, though, it has a second meaning. Weaving. Curse weaving.

I shudder. Such an exquisite piece of jewelry, with a curse sharper than . . . well, sharper than a serpent's tooth. I wonder whether that's symbolic, too. The serpents delivering a curse in their jaws. Beauty with a core of pure venom.

"May I . . . ?" I move my finger toward the glass case and look first at Marius and then at Hector. It takes effort to do the latter. I want to ignore him, but I can't afford the insult. Play this as if I don't know he has my sister locked up somewhere.

"Of course," Marius says. "If it's safe to touch, please do so. We'd love to hear your thoughts."

Hector grunts what I take as agreement.

"It should be safe to touch," I say. "It's taking possession of it—wearing it—that's the problem. I'll wear gloves, but I think . . ."

I trail off. I'm blathering. Thinking aloud, my anxiety pulsing for everyone to hear. I can ignore the insults about my specialty, but deep inside, there's always the little girl who wants to prove herself. This is my chance, and I'm afraid of blowing it.

I take a deep breath, put on my gloves and reach very slowly toward the necklace.

"Oh, come on," a voice says. "Enough with the drama."

I glance over to see, with some surprise, that it comes from the other curse weaver.

"It isn't drama," I say. "I'm listening for the curse, letting it speak to me."

"Who are you again?" Marius murmurs to the woman, and his voice might be soft, but it carries like a whip, the woman jerking.

The woman blinks, and pity darts through me.

She straightens. "Lesley-Ann Morrison."

"Never heard of you," Marius says.

I squirm and hope it doesn't show on my face. I know Lesley-Ann by reputation. It is . . . not a good reputation.

There's a hierarchy in curse weaving. Many practice it quietly and efficiently and earn the respect of their peers for their discretion. The way the Bennetts do it is not discreet, and so the fact that we are still respected is, as Yiayia always said, our highest badge of honor. We are respected *despite* openly plying our trade.

The Morrisons . . . Well, the Morrisons are a prime example of the other kind of curse weaver who markets their abilities. A lot of sound and fury, signifying very little innate talent.

No one interferes again as my fingers stretch toward the necklace. I close my eyes and open my mind, and the sibilant whispers snake out, slowly coalescing into words.

Liar, liar—

I jerk back, blinking. The words aren't right. The tone isn't either. There's a malevolence there I don't expect. Yes, the Necklace of Harmonia carries a terrible curse, but it's either an ex-hex or a joker's jinx, directed at one specific target. That malevolence sounds like—

I give my head a shake and start to reach out again. As I do, an inner warning bell sounds.

I ease back and reconsider.

"Really?" Lesley-Ann says. "Look, little girl, you might come from a family of famous weavers, but unless I'm mistaken, your own specialty is the joker's jinx. You're—"

"—the curse weaver I hired to do this job," Connolly cuts in.

"Marius might not know who you are, Ms. Morrison, but I do, and you didn't even make my long list."

"Who the hell are *you*?"

I don't glance up as I eye the necklace, but I can feel Connolly's cool stare crossing the room.

"If you don't know the answer to that," he says, "then might I suggest you're traveling in the wrong circles?"

A few snorts of appreciative laughter. Connolly gains points with that, even from those who also don't know who he is. Whispers follow the laughs as that gap is filled in.

Nicely done, Connolly. Nicely done.

He might be pushing his own agenda, but it gives me time to refocus on the necklace.

I reach toward it, eyes closed, following the tendrils of weaving, opening myself to those whispers.

Ugly whispers.

No, don't judge. Just assimilate. Listen. Learn.

Liar, liar, pants on fire—

I jerk back harder now, blinking fast. The *liar, liar* may have sounded anachronistic, but this definitely is. No ancient Greek would start a curse with a modern schoolyard chant.

Ancient Greek.

That's what I noticed before. Yes, the curse is in Greek, as expected. But it's as modern as that taunting phrase.

A shadow moves over me, and I glance up to see Connolly studying me.

"Something's wrong?" he mouths.

I nod but say nothing. I close my eyes and reach out again, even more careful now.

Liar, liar, pants on fire.
Open your mouth,
See what transpires.

Misanthrope's malice. That's what the nasty edge on that whisper meant. Someone's cast a malice on the necklace. Which means I really don't want to touch it. I do want to listen again, though, to be sure, because this makes no sense.

I reach out, as close as I dare while Connolly bends for a closer look.

Liar, liar—

Connolly straightens abruptly and snatches my hands back. "Don't. It's a fake."

CHAPTER THIRTY-ONE

THE CROWD RUMBLES its disapproval as Connolly says, "The necklace is a fake. Look at the gem."

"Speaking of drama," someone murmurs.

Connolly wheels on the unseen speaker. "This is not the correct necklace. It's a forgery. The carving technique is modern, and the loom isn't quite right."

"Isn't *quite* right?" someone else says.

"I've studied every photograph ever taken of the necklace," Connolly says. "This isn't it."

"That's it, boy," Hector says from the bar. "I can tell from here."

"No, it's not." Connolly turns to him. "It's a very good forgery, but it isn't the Necklace of Harmonia."

"Go have a closer look, Hector," Marius says. "You can clear this up. You are, after all, the expert."

The crowd shifts, all eyes on the pair. Hector lifts his glass.

"Get off your ass," Marius says, advancing on him, "and check the damned necklace."

Hector turns in his chair. Then he rises, and murmurs ripple through the crowd. Hector looked big sitting down, but when he stands, it's like watching a giant unfold itself.

Hector towers over Marius, who isn't a small man. Menace crackles from both men, raising the hairs on my neck.

"Aiden's right," I interject, finally finding my voice. "This isn't the right necklace. The curse is wrong. That's why I was taking so long. Confirming what I was hearing and trying to figure out why it wasn't right. Because it's a forgery. I don't know enough to recognize the craftsmanship, but I definitely recognize a modern curse."

"Bullshit."

Heads turn to follow the voice. The bald man who hired Lesley-Ann strides forward.

"It's a trick," he says. "They're working together. They've already admitted that. He says it's a fake necklace. She says it's a fake curse. And we all bow to their superior wisdom and let them take the 'forgery' away." He fixes us with a look. "You're children, playing children's games, which work very well, I'm sure, with other children. I don't know how you got an invitation—"

"Vanessa," someone says.

"Who conveniently isn't here to witness her guests misbehaving."

"Hector?" Marius says. "Resolve this for us. Please. Just check the damned necklace and confirm it's Harmonia's." When the big man stays rooted to the spot, Marius throws up his hands. "Pretend someone else is asking. Better yet, let's go with self-interest. You want this necklace like everyone else here. You'd like to be sure it's the right one, wouldn't you?"

As the two face off, the bald man waves at Lesley-Ann. "You get in there and check, then. Tell us this girl is full of shit."

Lesley-Ann walks up to the necklace and reaches for it with bare fingers. I jump. I may also squeak. I yank off my gloves and thrust them out, but she only gives me an eye roll, brimming with disdain.

"Malice," I blurt. "It's a misanthrope's malice."

That makes her stop.

I exhale. "Take the gloves. Go slow."

She takes the gloves. Then, gaze locked with mine, she holds them out . . . and drops them. When I lunge to stop her, Connolly yanks me back. I glare at him, but he shakes his head, wordlessly telling me that if she insists on doing this, I can't take the risk along with her.

It's not a risk, though. It's a certainty. This is a misanthrope's malice. It will latch onto *anyone* who touches it.

"Don't," I say. "Please—"

She lifts the amulet and turns a sneer on me. "Whoops."

"Don't lie," I say. "Whatever you do, don't tell a lie."

Her brows knit. "What are you prattling on about, girl?"

"You hear it, don't you? Or see it? However you interpret curses, you can read this one. And you know Greek, right?"

"Of course I know Greek," she snaps . . . and the hem of her dress bursts into flame.

Liar, liar, pants on fire.

Lesley-Ann shrieks. Connolly moves, as if to help her, but instead he shoves me farther away.

"Everyone get back!" he shouts. Then to her. "Drop and roll!"

She's batting the flames. They're small, but they won't stay extinguished.

"Don't touch her," I say. "It's a misanthrope's malice. You'll catch it if you touch her."

"It doesn't work like that," Lesley-Ann snaps. "Someone *help* me. You won't catch it."

"Stop lying," I say. "That's only making it—"

Her mouth opens, as if to snap at me again. Instead, her eyes bug, and her throat starts to spasm. Someone leaps in to help her as she begins to choke, and I want to warn them back, but she's choking. She needs help.

That's when I remember the second part of the curse.

Open your mouth,

See what transpires.

Lesley-Ann doubles over and retches, and something tumbles out of her mouth. *Things* tumble out of her mouth. Tiny, wriggling *things.*

A man yelps. A woman screams. She's spewed up the tiny things, and they're on the floor, writhing—

Snakes. It's baby snakes.

Connolly shoves me with both hands, propelling me across the room. A man shrieks, and I glance back to see his trousers aflame. It's the guy who tried to help Lesley-Ann. Then another man bellows. He's waving an arm, snakes hanging from his fingers, tiny fangs sunk in.

"Are they poisonous?" someone screeches. "Tell me they aren't poisonous."

I skid to a halt. Connolly tries to push me onward, but I shrug him off and run back, ignoring his shouts. When I'm close enough to see a snake in the dim lighting, I can make out the hourglass-shaped marks on its back and the yellow tip on its tail.

"Copperheads," I shout. "They're baby copperheads."

Someone screams. "Poison! They're poisonous!"

"No!" I shout. "Well, yes, they're venomous, but they won't kill you. These are babies."

"Which makes them even more dangerous," someone says.

"No, that's a myth. Well, yes, they haven't learned venom control yet but—"

Hands grab me. I catch a flash of red-gold hair and turn to shove Connolly off again, but it's Marius, with Connolly right beside him.

"I need to—" I begin.

Marius's chuckle cuts me off. "I'm sure everyone appreciates the herpetology lesson, Kennedy, but how about we get you two out of here now that we've established no one is going to die in horrible agony."

"They still need medical attention," I say. "I should—"

"No," both Marius and Connolly say in unison.

"You should not," Marius says as he strong-arms me toward the back door.

"Agreed," Connolly says. "You tried to warn Lesley-Ann. You tried to warn everyone."

"But the curse—"

"If I'm correct about malice hexes, it will run its course quickly and be done. Uncursing it wouldn't significantly help the situation, yes?"

"Well, yes, but—"

"If the situation isn't lethal and the curse will unweave itself, then we need to get out of here. They're going to blame us."

"What?" I squawk. "We're the ones who warned them. They can't blame us."

"Can," Marius says. "Will. That's a curse, and you're a curse weaver."

"But—"

I wrench from his grip. Both men grab for me, but I duck their hands and twist to look back at the chaos. Snakes writhe over the floor. Fire sparks everywhere. Screams fill the air as people bang on the locked main door.

I want to rush back in and do something. Connolly and Marius are right, though. There's nothing I can do except try to keep people calm, and that isn't ever going to work. They're panicked. That's the real "curse" here. Not the snakes or the fire, but the panic they induce, the fear and terror of people trapped in a room with venomous snakes and flaring fire.

Connolly takes my arm. "You can't help, Kennedy. They'll be fine."

Marius pushes me toward the back entrance. He shoves it open, and we stumble into the hall.

I turn to Marius. "Where's Vanessa?"

"That's what I'm about to find out. Are you guys okay?"

We say that we are, and he disappears back into the main room. We make it three running steps down the hall before two guards leap from a side room.

"Stop!" one says. "No one's allowed to leave."

"Screaming?" I say. "You do hear that, right? The screams of terror?"

He pauses, and I want to smack him. Then I realize I can barely hear the screams myself. They're drifting through the open door, but that's all. The room must be soundproofed for parties.

"Snakes," I say. "There are snakes."

The guard's face screws up. "What?"

"So many snakes. Baby copperheads. There must have been a nest. Which is weird because copperheads aren't native—"

Connolly's elbow to my ribs suggests this may not be essential information. "There are snakes. Poisonous—"

"Venomous," I correct, and then catch his look. "Sorry." I look at the guards. "There are snakes. Also, fire."

One guard frowns. The other shakes his head. "Look, Miss, maybe there's a snake—one snake—but if there was a fire, we'd hear the alarm."

"They're tiny fires. Tiny snakes. Big chaos." I wave toward the room. "You really need to do something about that."

"Hey!" a voice bellows, echoing down the hall. "Where do you two think you're going?"

We turn to see Hector, his huge form nearly filling the hall as he stomps toward us. One foot drags slightly, as if he's been injured in the melee.

"There!" I say, pointing at Hector. "Talk to him. He's in charge."

I grab Connolly, and we take off down the hall, both the guards and Hector shouting after us.

"Those guards didn't have guns, right?" Connolly says.

"It's a museum."

"Just checking."

Ahead, a door marked Exit calls to us. As footfalls thunder behind us, we burst into a sprint. I make it there first. I hit the push bar, expecting to trigger an alarm. The door swings open . . . and smacks a guy in a tux.

"This is *not* an exit," I hiss as I grab Connolly, dragging him behind me through yet another hall, this one crowded with partygoers. "False advertising."

"You can sue them later."

Apparently, we've looped back to the restroom hall, and people have ingested enough champagne to be lining up. Laughter and chatter sound to my left, so I run right. Ahead, another Exit sign blinks.

I'm halfway there when Connolly steers me into a side hall. Just at that moment, a voice says, "Did a young couple just come through here?"

Connolly nudges me along the short hall to another door marked Exit. I push this one open . . .

Darkness. Not the darkness of a parking lot, though. It's an exhibit, dimly illuminated with floor lighting.

"Also *not* an emergency exit," I whisper as we go through.

"More fodder for your lawsuit."

"I'm not suing. I am sending a very strongly worded letter, as a long-term patron of this establishment. This is a clear safety violation."

As I talk, he's prodding me along. Then he stops, lets out a yelp and stumbles, staggering as he smacks at his trousers.

"Fire?" I say. "Did you catch—?"

Something slithers from his pant leg. I dive and grab the little guy, gripping him carefully.

"Lose something?" I say, holding it out to Connolly.

Connolly's arms windmill as he flails away. That's when I remember the "dream" from the night before. The one where he'd told me a secret. The one he claimed was my dream alone.

"You aren't afraid of snakes, are you?" I say, eyes widening in mock innocence. I purse my lips. "Wait. Do I recall something about a childhood incident?"

When he doesn't reply, I hold out the baby snake, and it hisses on cue, showing off its adorable tiny fangs. Connolly tries to retreat, only to smack into the wall.

"Answer the question, Connolly," I say. "Or I swear, it goes back in your pants."

"Yes," he says quickly. "Yes, we were on a family trip to India, and I found a cobra in my bedroom."

"Huh. Weird how I knew that."

I hold out the snake again.

"We really don't have time for this, Kennedy," he says.

"Three words. Keep it simple. *I was there.*"

He hesitates. The snake hisses.

"I was there," he says.

"And you lied."

"I—"

"The lying liar lied."

"Yes, but—"

"No time for explanations." I tip the snake into a nearby vase. "Come on, lying liar. We've got about five seconds before—"

The door opens, light flooding the exhibit. We both drop. We crouch there, shoulder to shoulder, gazes trained toward the door, which is hidden behind an exhibit display.

The door stays open. Voices drift in.

"Someone said they went in here," one says.

"Who? The guy who was so wasted he could barely stand?"

Hector's voice reverberates through the room, thick with scorn. "Failed the IQ test for the NYPD, didn't you?"

The other man responds, his voice crackling with outrage. "I chose to be a security guard, sir."

"Good call. Now, how about you take the word of the sober woman who said they went out the next door instead of the idiot who can't hold his liquor."

I exhale as the door closes, the men retreating. Then I settle in on the floor and whisper, "We'll give it a few minutes and then take the other way out."

Connolly doesn't seem to answer, but when I squint over in the darkness, he's shaking his head. "We need to move now."

"Hector just saved our asses."

Silence. Real silence now, heavy with words unsaid.

My cheeks heat. "He didn't, did he? I'm being naive."

"Not naive. Trusting. Which I find refreshing."

I manage a weak smile. "Thank you. Right now, though, I need a little jaded paranoia."

"That's what you have me for. Now, the problem will be finding the actual exit."

"This exhibit connects to the main hall and the temporary exhibition room. We should get to that, which will take us to the back hall. That definitely has an exit door."

"Ah, right, you know your way around. I forgot that."

"Easy to forget when I can't find a damn exit. In my defense, I've never tried leaving through an emergency door. That would be wrong. Sneaking into a locked exhibit? Acceptable. Setting off alarms? No."

A soft chuckle. "All right, then. Let's proceed to the temporary exhibition room. You can lead."

CHAPTER THIRTY-TWO

WE MAKE our way through the L-shaped pottery exhibit. We're turning the corner into the base of that L, which ends in two doors—one leading back into the main area and the other to the temporary exhibit. From the sounds of it, the snakes and fire haven't reached the general party, but I still suspect no one is going to let us walk out. After all, we might have the real necklace.

I want to say that's fine. We don't have it, so let security frisk us and search my bag. Again, though, that's me being naive, and this time I recognize it before I say anything. If this were a regular event with a regular stolen necklace, I'd trust the guards to check us and set us free. But there are other forces at work here. Magical forces plus criminal ones.

Someone switched out the necklace, and Connolly and I make excellent scapegoats. Sure, we're the ones who spotted the forgery, but that could be part of the setup. I've read enough crime novels to see that coming a mile away.

Wait! This is the wrong necklace. Now, in the ensuing confusion, I will sneak out with the real one, mwah-ha-ha!

We've barely stepped around the corner when the door behind us creaks open. We both drop to the floor. The door opens, light flooding in, and then it shuts, and flashlights click on.

"They're in here," Hector whispers. "Now move fast before those idiot guards figure it out."

His lowered voice suggests we weren't supposed to hear that. His idea of a whisper, though, is my normal speaking voice, and it bounces back to us easily.

I glance at Connolly. He motions for us to creep toward the doors. We do that, crouched down, and get two feet before Hector speaks.

"Miss Bennett and Mr. Connolly. I know you are in here, and I know you took the necklace. I also know you two children aren't the masterminds behind this. Convenient that Vanessa slipped out right before you examined it. I'm guessing she has the necklace and is long gone, escaped before the chaos."

Heavy steps thud into the room with the faint drag of his injured foot. We use the sound to cross the room, stopping when Hector does.

"My wife can be very . . . persuasive. I'm sure you've realized by now that her abilities go far beyond dream shaping. She has seduced you, and I don't mean she's taken you to her bed. Maybe she did, and maybe she didn't. Her greater power is the ability to seduce without even batting her lashes. Believe me, I spent a very long time entranced by Vanessa's charms."

More thumps. A whisper I don't catch, presumably from one of his men.

"What I am saying," Hector continues, "is that I don't blame you for getting caught up in this. You are truly children, in over your heads, and it is my wife's fault. All you need to do is come out and speak to me. Tell me the truth."

We're nearly at the door. One lunge, and we'd be there. But we're listening. We're both listening in spite of ourselves.

"I have something you want," he says. "Something you were supposed to buy with that necklace. Yes? You know what I'm talking about. I won't say more because I suspect you haven't shared that particular secret with your new partner. The problem is that if Vanessa has the necklace, she's not giving it to you. I'm sure she promised to help with your . . . sibling issue, but now that she has the necklace, all bets are off. My wife might be endlessly charming, but she's as sharp-toothed as those vipers. Beautiful and deadly and amoral, as you are about to discover."

"Sir," one of the men whispers. "Listen."

They're still in the other part of the room, and we haven't moved, so whatever Hector's man hears, it isn't us. As they go silent, the sound they've noticed travels to us. It's a soft rustling.

It's not us. It's nowhere near us. It's back in the other half of the room, where we . . .

Where we'd been.

I grin as I realize what we're hearing. Then I creep to the door, ignoring Connolly's sharp look of worry. I motion that I'm not leaving yet. I'm waiting for something. Something I know is . . .

"Hands up!" a voice barks . . . in the other part of the room.

There's no answer except a curse and then a crash as a two-thousand-year-old vase smashes to the floor, freeing the baby copperhead I dropped inside it. I'm happy about its escape—I'd been trying to figure out how to come back and free it—but I'm far less happy about the destruction of a priceless Greek artifact.

Still, it's the distraction I was waiting for, and I yank open the door and shove Connolly through.

We get five steps into the temporary exhibit before my eyes adjust enough for me to look around.

"It's the exhibit on Alexandria!" I whisper. "I've been wanting to see this. I got an e-mail about it, and I meant to make plans to come—"

"And you can do so after we get out of here," Connolly says, pulling me through the displays.

"But as long as we're here . . ."

He turns to look at me.

"Kidding," I say. "Geez, you really do take me for a ditz, don't you?"

"No, I take you for a creature of limitless unpredictability and dauntless intrepidity. I would not put it past you to sneak in a quick tour while fleeing evil henchmen, and I mean that in the best possible way. Now come on."

"I really am coming back," I whisper. "Did you know that there were supposedly a thousand curse scrolls in the Great Library of Alexandria? Some theorize that they were rescued along with—"

"I would love to hear this," Connolly says as he continues steering me toward the exit. "Tomorrow. Over breakfast."

"I'll hold you to that, you know. But in return, you can tell me all about the marvels of actuarial science."

A soft chuckle. "Careful. I might take you seriously."

"You can. I'm interested."

He hesitates for a second, and in the dim light, I feel his gaze on me, but I can't see his expression. Then he snaps out of it and murmurs something I don't catch.

We're at the exit door in a few more running strides. We pause there, listening. Silence from the room we left though I'm sure they're still there, searching.

I ease open the door. We get through just as the other door opens. I'm about to shove our door shut, but Connolly keeps hold of it, very carefully and quietly letting it shut. It's almost closed when Hector calls back to one of his men, his voice booming.

"Forget this bullshit," he says. "I'll take it up with my wife. Lars? Get back to the hotel and check on our guest. Make sure Vanessa didn't do an end run around me and stage a jailbreak."

Connolly and I look at each other. Then we take off.

———

WE DON'T RUN out the nearest exit. We have a new goal to pursue— Hector's henchman, Lars, who has just been dispatched to check on Hope. Hector launched a homing pigeon to show the way to my sister, and we are following that bird.

Now, one might think that at a black-tie fundraiser, all unalarmed exits would be sealed to prevent people from sneaking in. I say so to Connolly, and his look reminds me just how little I understand this world.

Yes, if this were an invitation-only event—like our smaller gala— people might try to sneak in. But the larger gala is a fundraiser, meaning if you don't have the funds, you're sure as hell not going to risk the humiliation of being discovered sneaking in.

Which is all to say that the exit doors aren't going to be guarded. Or they wouldn't be if there weren't fire and snakes and a stolen necklace. Luckily, I'm familiar enough with this building to know an exit that may have been overlooked—the one used by school groups. Sure enough, it opens and doesn't set off any alarms.

Once out, we need to find Lars. I hadn't seen him at the party—presumably, he'd been stashed in some henchman closet. That isn't a problem. Outside, we swing around to overhear Hector at the front door, where he is, well, hectoring the guards who are under orders not to let anyone leave right now. All we need to do is wait out of sight until Hector's man has been patted down and allowed to leave. Then we follow.

We're expecting Lars to retrieve his car from the valet. As he's waiting, we'll run to the parking lot, get Connolly's car—he has another key—and track the guard from there. Which shows how little we both understand evil henchmen. Having your car in the valet lot would be really inconvenient if you needed to make a quick getaway.

We follow Lars to a lot a block away. When he heads in to fetch his car, Connolly flags down a passing taxi. He's opening the door for me just as Lars's sedan appears. It veers onto the road without stopping at the curb.

"Follow that car!" Connolly says to the taxi driver.

"Did you just say . . . ?" I begin.

His cheeks heat. "Er . . ."

"You did, and I'm totally swooning."

He smiles as he shakes his head. "Get in. You follow him while I retrieve my car and catch up."

"Ooh. Adventurous *and* practical. I think I'm in love."

"We'll plan the wedding later. Now go."

———

I CAN JOKE ABOUT SWOONING, but honestly, I'm impressed as hell. It takes guts to tell a taxi driver, "Follow that car!" with a straight face. To actually have them do it, instead of laughing you out of the vehicle? Then having the quick wits to realize the best course of action is to split up and fetch your own vehicle rather than both hop into the taxi? It truly is swoon-worthy.

Connolly and I stay in touch by phone. The driver does his job admirably. It isn't exactly a high-speed chase. In Manhattan, following a car just means trailing it from backed-up traffic light to backed-up traffic light. Here's where Connolly's driving skill comes in handy, that ability to swing between perfect gentleman and inconsiderate asshole. He must channel the latter for this one because, within ten minutes, he's coming up behind us.

"I'm going to switch cars," I say. "Can I pay before you pull over?"

"I don't think—" the driver begins.

A horn tap, and Connolly is beside our passenger window. He pulls down his visor, plucks out a bill and presses a hundred to the window.

"Hey, I keep emergency money in my visor, too," I say to the driver. "Only mine's a tenner."

"You and me both, lady," he says, shaking his head.

I put down the window, reach out and grab the money, which is actually a trickier maneuver than it seems in the movies.

I hand the bill to the driver. "Keep the change."

"Now I suppose you want me to pull up on his other side so you can jump across moving vehicles."

"Could you? That'd be kinda awesome."

He smiles and shakes his head. "If your idea of awesome is spending the rest of your date in the morgue."

"It could be. Except for the being dead part. I'll switch cars at the next red light."

We do that. As I'm leaving, the driver calls, "Enjoy the rest of your date with Mr. Bond!" and I flash him a thumbs-up. I'm barely in the car before the light changes and Connolly's on the move in hot pursuit of Lars. Well, slow pursuit, but it works. Connolly's careful to stay a few car lengths back or in another lane, trusting me to keep an eye on the henchman.

After twenty minutes—or about five Manhattan blocks—Lars pulls into a parking garage. It's a private one, so we can't follow, but there's a public one across the road. While traffic is still crazy at this time of night, the garage isn't full—the nearby buildings are all offices, except for a boutique hotel that's under renovation. Before Connolly parks, he lets me out.

I start jogging. Then I stop and take off my heels so I can run quietly.

Lars drove into a narrow garage under a building, and it must be for that hotel under renovation, because it's nearly empty. I need to hide behind a bin to watch. I'm peeking out when I see the decal on the bin.

Voden Construction.

Lars walks to a door, flicks his security card and goes inside. I see the door closing and, with it, our chances of getting in. I dart over as fast as I can and wedge my purse between the door and the frame. By the time Connolly catches up, I've replaced my purse with steel from the scattered debris.

"It's Hector's company," I whisper as we go in.

He nods, and the lack of surprise tells me he already noticed a sign—he's just not taking this detective moment from me. I appreciate that.

Knowing little about construction, I'm not sure what you'd call this. A renovation? A reconstruction? Basically, it looks as if they're redoing an old office building as a luxury boutique hotel. All I know is that they're stripping its soul. They've torn up gorgeous floorboards, rich with the patina of age. The original wood-paneled walls? Shredded. The intricate brass fixtures? Heaps of scrap metal and broken glass that make my antique-shop-owner heart weep.

This floor of the hotel is in shambles, but footsteps sound overhead. We take the stairs up to find a level near completion. The hall is still ripped up, but an open door shows what will be a very modern, high-end hotel suite. That matches what Hope described.

My sister is here.

I started this evening hoping to get a clue about who might be holding her captive. Instead, not only did I solve that mystery, but I found *her*. We hadn't discussed this possibility because it seemed beyond our reach. Yet here we are, with Hope in this very building. An empty building, only one henchman between us and my little sister.

Connolly's nudge snaps me from my thoughts. Then I realize

he's prodding me toward an open doorway. Lars's footsteps have stopped, and we don't want to smack right into him. We step into the room to listen.

Lars has paused around the next corner. Opening a door?

No, not *a* door. The door to my sister.

Tears spring to my eyes, and I glance away, but Connolly catches the movement.

"Everything okay?" he whispers as Lars begins talking, obviously making a call, his voice too low to hear.

I nod. "Just . . . it's happening so fast. She's here, isn't she? Hope's here, and we're going to—"

I press my hand to my mouth. "Sorry. I'm just . . ."

"Your hair looks lovely like that."

I look up sharply, frowning. "What?"

"Your hair. It looks lovely."

I stifle a laugh. "It did look lovely, an hour ago. Took an hour to get it pinned up and curled just so, and I don't want to imagine what it looks like now."

"Better. It was fine before. This is better."

He takes out his phone, snaps a shot and then shows me. It's as bad as I'd expect after fleeing venomous snakes, crawling across museum floors and walking through construction zones. Half my hair has escaped the updo, and the curls are now frizzy exclamation points around my face. Then there's the dust and dirt and cobwebs.

I press my hand to my mouth to keep from laughing. "Thank you for the cleverly crafted distraction."

"And thank you for the adorable photograph, commemorating our adventure." He pockets his phone and takes out something else. "You left this in my car."

It's my derringer. Seeing it, I break into a grin.

"Now trade it for your shoes," he says. "I can carry those."

I shake my head. "I've got them."

He puts out a hand. "And leave me defenseless?"

I pass them over, and he wields the heel like a dagger, making me stifle another laugh.

"Thank you," I say. "You really are something, Aiden Connolly. Something completely unexpected."

"The good kind of unexpected?"

"The best kind." My cheeks heat, and I'm thankful for the near-dark.

"So the wedding is still on? My mother will be delighted."

I choke back a laugh. "I doubt *delighted* is the word. Now, let's get out there before Lars finishes his call."

Connolly lays a hand on my arm. "He didn't have a gun earlier, but he could have taken one from his car. Be very careful."

"I will."

CHAPTER THIRTY-THREE

WE EASE INTO THE HALL. Lars is still on the phone, and there's nothing to hear even once we reach the corner. It's just yeah and no and grunts from his end. Then, between the noises, I catch the distinct sound of a card gliding through a card reader. He's opening the door.

Opening the door while on the phone, distracted.

I don't think. Well, yes, I do. I think, *He's opening the door to my sister while distracted on the phone!* Hesitate, and I'll lose my chance. My personality favors leaping over looking, and this is where I need that recklessness. I zip around the corner and out of Connolly's reach before he can grab me back.

As I dash, there's a frisson in the air. A crackle that seems oddly familiar. A scene flashes. The car skidding, an electricity that felt like fear. Only it wasn't fear. It was luck.

Connolly casts his luck my way, and Lars doesn't notice movement out of the corner of his eye. That's all I need. Then I'm out of his sightline and creeping along the shadows, covering the five feet until I'm at his back.

I almost forget to check Lars for a gun. When I lift mine, though, it triggers Connolly's warning. I glance down. The guy left his tux jacket in the car, and I don't see a gun in his hand or a holster. I lift mine and press it into his back. Lars freezes. Then he spins, grabbing for me, but I'm already out of the way, ducking to the side, gun raised. He sees the gun and pauses. His eyes narrow.

"That's not a real—"

Connolly grabs him from behind, his arm going around the man's neck and yanking him off his feet. Lars stumbles but wrenches free. I'm about to jump in—no idea what I'll actually do, but I'll do something—when Connolly punches him. A luck frisson comes again, a little late, or that's what I think. I'm wrong. The luck boost wasn't to help his punch, which is perfect. It's the next bit, where Lars staggers and Connolly hits him again and he falls to the floor, unconscious.

"Nice," I say.

He flexes his hands and manages a wry smile. "I had a boost."

"Only in the 'knocked unconscious' part. That *requires* luck." I turn to the door and inhale, and when I reach out, my fingers are shaking.

"You've got this," Connolly murmurs.

I nod. When I take the doorknob, he says, "You go on. I'll be out here."

"No, come in. Please."

He shakes his head. "Better to leave my temporarily unlucky self out here. If you need me, I'll be looking for banana peels to slip on."

I smile. Then I'm inside the room. It's the sitting area part, lit by the ambient glow of lighting I can't see and don't care to find. All I want is the door, which will lead to my sister. I find it in a sweep. It's closed, and I'm glad to see that. Lars had clearly been coming inside, and the thought of him watching Hope sleep fires a rage that tempts me to go out and give him a kick for good measure. I can only hope that Hector was keeping his men on a short leash and they did nothing more than peek inside to confirm that Hope was still here.

I turn the knob and push the door open an inch. Then I listen. Nothing. My heart pounds, and I shove it and—

And there's Hope, sound asleep in bed. There's no light in here beyond what's coming from the doorway, but I can see her dark hair on the pillow. The covers rise and fall with her breathing. I slip over to her side of the bed. She's facing the other way, and I blow a breath over her hair.

"Hopeless," I whisper. "Wakey-wakey."

She flips over with a groan and—

It's a guy, maybe my age, with dark hair falling into green eyes. He blinks, and then his handsome face stretches into a sleepy grin.

"Well, hello there," he says. "Now this is what I call hospitality. So much better than a mint on my pillow."

I stumble back, gun rising.

His grin only grows. "A hot girl in a slinky dress with a gun? Someone definitely has a dream shaper on staff. Please tell me you also brought handcuffs."

A commotion from the sitting room. Connolly charges through the doorway. Well, he tries to charge, but the luck-balancing has him staggering and stumbling through. I back up until I'm against him, my gun still aimed on the stranger as Connolly's arm goes protectively around me.

The guy sighs. "And she's with my brother. Of course she is." He jabs a finger at the ceiling. "I thought you people didn't believe in torture." He thumps back onto the bed. "Can we restart this dream and leave my brother out of it? Thanks!"

Connolly strides toward the bed. "Rian?"

The guy looks from Connolly to me as I flick on a light. "Not a dream, I take it?"

"If it were, I wouldn't be covered in dirt and cobwebs," I say.

Rian grins. "In mine, you totally would. You'd be coming to rescue me, having fought your way past legions of minions. There were legions, right?"

"One. But Aiden took him out."

"Of course he did," Rian murmurs. "Because Aiden is amazing and does everything amazingly, including rescuing his screw-up brother. Also, he does it in a tux with a hot chick in tow."

"Kennedy is not *in tow*," Connolly says. "Nor is she a *chick*."

"See? I can't even get away with casual misogyny around him."

I turn to Connolly. "Can you look after him? I need to find Hope."

He hesitates, and in that hesitation, my heart sinks.

"You think Hector meant he had your brother," I say. "Not Hope."

Still no response, because the answer isn't the one I want. I'm madly reviewing what we heard. That Hector had something we wanted, something we were going to get by doing what he wanted. A sibling issue. It totally fit if he had Hope.

It also fits if he had Rian. Or it would . . . if Connolly wasn't buying the necklace to repay his brother's debt to Havoc. If he was buying it to regain his *brother*. From *Hector*.

"You lied," I whisper, looking at Connolly. "This wasn't about a debt. You knew what Hector meant."

His eyes widen. "What? No. I had no idea—"

"You lied."

"Whoa!" Rian says, swinging out of bed. "I don't know who you are, but if my brother lied, it was to get me out of here. Which he did. Or he will once we actually leave."

I spin . . . to see that Rian is naked. My hands fly to my eyes, and I backpedal, hitting Connolly, who tries to grab me, but stumbles, and somehow, not only do I end up on the floor, but he's on top of me.

"I'd say that's a sweet move, Aiden," Rian says. "But I'm guessing it's a luck balance, 'cause you're never that smooth."

"I didn't lie to you, Kennedy," Connolly says, his face over mine. "I swear it on my car."

"Your car?" Rian sputters. "You turn not-smooth into an art form, big brother."

Connolly ignores him. "I still don't know what's going on here. I thought what you did—that your sister was here."

"Wait," Rian says. "This is an accidental rescue?"

"Are you dressed yet?" Connolly calls over to him.

"Why? Afraid of the competition?"

"You do realize we're on the floor because she recoiled in horror, right?"

Rian laughs. "Ouch, nice one. Yeah, I'm putting on my shorts."

Connolly rises and helps me up. I let him but don't speak. I'm not sure what's going on here, and I'm not fleeing the room, but that's the most he can hope for at the moment. I want to believe him too much to do it lightly.

Connolly turns to his brother, who is, as advertised, in his underwear. I won't comment on that because it feels weird to say Connolly's brother is hot. Okay, I guess I just said it. Still, while I may be biased, he's not as good-looking as Connolly. I see the resemblance in the face and definitely the eyes. Rian's taller, broader and dark haired. What I care about right now, though, is that he's not my sister.

"I'm not here to rescue you, Rian," Connolly says, "because you aren't actually here. You're in Europe, lying low, while we repay your debt, which is to Havoc, not Hector Voden."

"Huh. Is that what Mom said?"

"Can we discuss this somewhere that isn't the villain's lair?" I say. "Or maybe I can let you two work it out while I search, in case my sister is here?"

"There aren't any other hostages," Rian says. "Believe me. I've been rapping on pipes and shouting when my guards leave. There haven't even been construction workers."

Connolly says, "The three of us will still conduct a brief survey of the finished rooms to be sure."

"Thank you," I say.

We start for the door. Connolly looks back at his brother. "Clothing, perhaps?"

Rian grins. "Up to your friend there. Does she really want me covering up?"

"*She* doesn't care," I say. "Since *she* will be busy checking rooms. You, however, may care if you get splinters where you don't want splinters."

"That part's covered."

"Not well."

Rian's grin grows. "You noticed."

"Trying very hard not to."

"But your gaze is irresistibly drawn—"

"—to the door. Where I am now heading. In hopes of finding my sister."

Connolly starts to follow me out, stumbles and crashes into me.

I turn to him. "Since some of that bad luck should be mine, can you transfer it?"

He shoos me toward the door.

"Take his hand," Rian calls after us. "You can transfer some of it that way."

Connolly pulls his hands in. "But you are not going to because you need all your own luck if there's any chance your sister is here. Now go."

———

MY SISTER IS NOT HERE. We do a very quick sweep, staying in sight of one another. Most of the rooms are under construction. We find two habitable ones with no sign of actual habitation. Then we regroup and head for the stairs. We reach the first level when Connolly's arms shoot out to hold us back. He tilts his head, considering.

"Yes," a voice calls. "There is someone in this hall. Someone who has been waiting far longer than he should have needed to wait."

Hector throws open the stairwell door and fills the space. "You aren't very good at this, are you?"

"Where's my sister?" I say.

His look answers the question that my gut already has. Still, I have to push.

"My sister. The one who specializes in the lover's lament—the curse that's apparently on the Necklace of Harmonia."

His face purples. "Lover's lament?" He roars the words, making us all shrink back. "Who calls it that?"

"Everyone," Rian says. "It makes sense, right? Aphrodite screwed around with Ares, so Hephaestus cursed her. He was upset and—"

"It is *not* a lover's lament." Hector spits the words. "I do *not* have your sister. I have this idiot, courtesy of Havoc, who owed me a favor and repaid it thus."

"So when Havoc demanded the necklace to repay Rian's debt," I say, "she was actually getting it for you?"

"I have multiple courses of action in play. Many irons in a very large fire."

"Because you *really* want that necklace."

"A moot point now as I do not have it. My wife does. That's where you come in. At the museum, I realized even if we caught you, I might have difficulty getting you out of there. Better to bring you here."

In other words, this was a trap. I don't say that. Neither does Connolly. We won't give him the satisfaction of gloating over how easily we fell into it.

"What do you want, Hector?" Connolly says.

"It's Mr. Voden to you."

"All right. Mr. Voden, then."

Rian grumbles under his breath. He wouldn't have given Hector the satisfaction. I'm not sure I could have done it, either, at least not as smoothly and sarcasm-free as Connolly. But it's the right move, and Connolly's ego is healthy enough that he doesn't need to get into a pissing match with the guy blocking our escape route.

"I want that damned necklace," Hector says. "My wife has it. I want it."

"And we're supposed to get it for you," I say.

He snorts. "I wouldn't ask you to get my mail from the post box. You'd drop it in a puddle halfway back. All I want is confirmation—and proof—that my wife has it."

"You're going to hold me captive until they come through," Rian says.

"No, they can take you. You're not worth the upkeep."

Rian opens his mouth to protest, but an elbow to the ribs stops him.

Hector continues, "I believe I've proven my point. I obtained your brother easily, Mr. Connolly, and he was in no danger of escaping. Nor were you in any danger of finding him until I let you do so. I'm not going to threaten you. You already realize that if you fail me, you won't like the consequences."

Mwah-ha-ha.

Even as I think that, I tell myself to be careful here. It'd be easy to dismiss Hector as a textbook villain. He is a figure of power in this world, one that operates just far enough outside the normal one that it doesn't need to abide by any rules.

Hector turns to Connolly. "You're ambitious, boy. It vibrates off you. The fact you chose to work with my wife shows a distinct lack of discernment, but you wouldn't be the first who fell for her charms. I don't have any charms. Just brute power. She could have ignored me earlier. She didn't dare. They all make sure to pay their respects when I am in the room. If you want into this game, the person you need to impress is me."

I want to laugh. Is Hector actually dangling future employment in front of Connolly? After kidnapping his brother?

He is, and he sees nothing wrong with that. In his world, this is just business.

As for Connolly, he's a raw asset, a student ripe for learning. Put in a little effort, and he will be very valuable. But at the heart of it, this isn't about Connolly. It's about Vanessa and Hector. She sees promise in Connolly, and Hector wants to take it from her.

Hector is sending Connolly on a mission to test him. Letting him take Rian to prove he wouldn't be a tyrannical boss. He's wooing an asset to hurt his ex-wife. Nothing more.

Hector has dismissed me as he's dismissed Rian. We don't have what it takes, and that isn't just about power—it's about drive and ambition, too. Connolly is the one who can, ultimately, be useful. And who can be used.

CHAPTER THIRTY-FOUR

WE DON'T SPEAK on the way to the car. Rian is checking his phone and wallet, which Hector returned. Connolly has his deep-in-thought face on, and I probably have mine on, too. Hector doesn't have Hope. I want to kick myself for jumping to that conclusion so fast, but the more I think about it, the more I'm convinced someone wanted us to think he did. If that guy on the phone wasn't Hector, he sure as hell was doing a fine impersonation of him. That can't be a coincidence. We've been led on a wild-goose chase.

Now we're being led on another.

Does Vanessa have the necklace? I can see how it might look that way. She brought us. We identified it as a fake while she was already out of the room—with the real necklace. Fire and snakes and panic ensure her clean getaway.

And yet . . .

I remember the look on her face when she'd excused herself before the necklace was uncovered, and no matter how much I analyze that mental image, I don't see deceit. She'd been upset. Which doesn't make much sense, but it also isn't the face she'd pull on as an excuse to leave. She's said she isn't interested in the necklace. Why not just go with that? *Oh, that thing? I'll just step outside for some air while you all make fools of yourselves over it.*

So much of this doesn't make sense. It seems to until I dig deeper. Then I come up with explanations for why people are behaving as they are, when the truth is that I feel as if I'm watching a foreign movie with the subtitles off and telling myself I understand what's going on. I don't. There's more here, and I'm not getting it. Connolly and I are skimming the surface as everyone else swims below us, pursuing goals we can't see for reasons we can't fathom.

When we reach the car, Rian says, "Any chance I can get an update here? On what's going on?"

Connolly snaps out of it with a sharp shake of his head. "Yes, of course. We need to talk. First, is Hector telling the truth? Your debt was to Havoc, but she sold it to him?"

Rian shrugs, hands spread. "I guess so? I wasn't exactly part of that conversation. I was taken from outside my apartment last week. Havoc said she was tired of waiting for me to pay her back, and I was her guest until my debt was repaid. Her goons stashed me in an empty room first, and then moved me to that hotel. I thought it was because our parents convinced them to put me in better quarters. Apparently not."

"How were you treated?"

Another shrug. "Well enough for a captive, I guess. Bored out of my skull. Binge-watching TV is awesome . . . for about twelve hours. I tried talking to my guards, but they figured it was a trick. Otherwise, it was like being quarantined at the Holiday Inn. Not exactly five-star food and guest services. Decent enough, though. I figured, as long as it kept being decent, that meant Mom and Dad were playing ball. I knew they'd pay the ransom. They were just stalling to teach me a lesson."

"No one was stalling," Connolly says. "Your captor demanded something other than money. I was working on that."

"*You* were working on it?" Rian sputters. "Mom and Dad offloaded this on *you*? Outsourced this inconsequential task that wasn't worth their time?"

"I think it was more complicated than that," Connolly murmurs in a practiced tone that suggests he's accustomed to smoothing over their parents' bad behavior to keep Rian from being hurt. Who does that for Connolly? No one, I bet.

"They didn't even tell you I'd been kidnapped," Rian says.

"I . . . presume that was for my own good. So I'd proceed with a clear head."

"Right. I'm pretty sure I could be strung over a vat of boiling oil, and you'd still proceed with a clear head."

When Connolly opens his mouth, Rian claps him on the shoulder. "That sounded pissy. I just meant you don't get rattled easily. They should have told. Our parents are assholes."

Connolly's mouth opens again, but again Rian cuts him short with a shoulder squeeze. I remember how quick Connolly had been to admit his parents *were* assholes. But there's a difference between saying it to me and saying it to the guy who shares those parents.

"You can defend their honor later," Rian says. "Let's stop jabbering and get going. I want to hear this full story."

———

I offer to explain the situation while Connolly drives. Or I can drive, and he can explain. That makes Rian laugh.

"Good luck with that," he says. "No one drives Aiden's car but Aiden."

"Er, right," I say. "So I'll tell the story then?"

"Please," Connolly says.

"Whoa, what? Seriously? You're letting someone else explain something?" Rian looks at me. "When we were little, people used to think I was mute because Aiden did the talking. All the talking."

Connolly unlocks the car. "Please explain what 'people' you mean and under what circumstances." When Rian doesn't, Connolly says, "Adults in dire need of explanation. Like when a softball went through their window. Or someone kept their daughter out all night."

"You were better at talking to grown-ups," Rian says.

"Better at cleaning up after—" Connolly cuts himself off. "Climb in. Rian? Can you take the back seat, please?"

"Actually," I say, "is it okay if I sit back there, too? Easier than twisting around to talk."

"Did you hear that, Aiden? Your friend wants to sit in the back seat with me." He waggles his brows. "I think I'm making an impression."

"I'm *sure* you are," Connolly says, and I sputter a laugh as we get into the car.

"Seat belt on," Connolly says. "And keep your hands to yourself."

"What if she doesn't want me to? Or what if she's the one touching me?"

"If she touches you, I'll expect a scream of pain to follow."

"Be still my heart." He glances at me. "I'm still hoping for those handcuffs."

"I'm thinking a gag might be more appropriate," I say. "Now hush up and listen. I have a story to tell you."

———

CONNOLLY HAS A TEXT FROM VANESSA. It's not the first. While we'd been fleeing the museum, she'd evidently texted to ask if we were okay. Connolly said we were, not mentioning the fact we'd been huddled behind an exhibit at the time. Then she texted while we were in pursuit of Hector's henchman, asking if we needed a place to stay the night. Nope, we were good. Connolly had still refrained from saying anything about the fact we were kinda busy. Nor had he mentioned the texts to me. Both of these suggest he'd been mulling over the possibility Vanessa was complicit long before Hector claimed so.

Her third text says she's heading to Marius's and asks us to join her. She needs to speak to us in private.

That one Connolly passes to me.

"It could be a trap," I say. "It probably is."

"Yes."

"So we're going?"

"Hell, yeah," Rian says. "This Vanessa chick probably has your sister. She's in on it with this Marius guy. If you don't go, you miss your chance. I know where we can pick up a couple guns. There's this guy in Brooklyn—"

"No," Connolly and I say in unison.

"Fine, skip the guns. I can get us some mace. Or smoke grenades."

"He's kidding, right?" I say to Connolly.

"I wish," Connolly murmurs. "No, Rian. While I hate the idea of stepping into yet another trap, it does seem the most efficient step. Our defense is that we know it may be a trap. We'll be ready. And by *we*, I mean Kennedy and me. You are going to a hotel."

A pause. A long one. Then Rian says, "You hate me, don't you? Take me out of one hotel room, dangle adventure in front of my nose and then stash me in another hotel room."

"It will be a nicer one. Five star. I was thinking the Empire. If we hurry, the bar might still be open."

Silence. "What's that supposed to mean?"

Connolly sighs. "That you've had a very difficult week, and I know you're fond of the bar at the Empire. Have a drink, make a new friend."

"Get wasted. Get laid. That's my life, right? Oh, and getting into trouble that you need to fix."

Connolly's hands tighten on the steering wheel. "Right now, I would not turn down a drink myself. I'm sorry if you found that offensive, Rian. You were complaining about being stashed in a hotel room, and I was giving you options. As for the stashing part, that's not an insult, either. Bringing you along means explaining you to Vanessa and Marius."

"Aiden's right," I say. "If we tell the truth, they'll know something's up with Hector. Weave a web of lies, and we'll get tangled in it."

"Then bring me along and let me stay outside. Backup in case of emergency."

Connolly hesitates.

"Or do you think I can't handle that?" Rian says. "That I'll screw it up like I screwed up that job for Havoc? I didn't screw it up, by the way. I don't know what Mom and Dad told you, but Havoc pulled the rug out from under me. Then she could claim I owed her, which puts the Connollys in her debt."

"My concern isn't that you can't handle it, Rian. It's that I think you've been through enough."

"That's for me to judge. Otherwise, you're saying I can't handle it."

I clamp my jaw shut. I can't interfere. Maybe Connolly *doesn't* trust Rian to pull it off. Or maybe he doesn't trust Rian to judge his own post-trauma mental health. He can't say either, though, without offending Rian. Yet there's nothing to stop Rian from hopping into a cab and saying "Follow that car" after Connolly drops him off.

"All right," Connolly says. "You can come along, but you are staying outside any security perimeter. Understood?"

"Understood."

CHAPTER THIRTY-FIVE

MARIUS LIVES JUST outside New York City. Here's where property value comes into play. Vanessa's place is midway between Boston and New York, but off the beaten track, in an area that has little to recommend it besides the fact it's only two hours to either city. Marius lives within enviably easy commuting distance, so while his property is a fraction of the size, I bet the land is worth more.

His house is what I'd expected from Vanessa's. Two-story, white brick, palatial design complete with columns. Like Vanessa's estate, it's gated, but in Marius's case, it's an eight-foot metal fence with security cameras, another clear message.

We drop Rian off before we're in camera range.

We don't get a chance to announce ourselves. The gates roll open as we approach. It's a circular drive, and we stop at the top of it. As we get out, I inhale the distinct smell of horses and glance over to see a distant barn. There's a pool around the other side with markers for swimming laps. I can also see what looks like a range with targets. Archery? Marksmanship? Either way, it tells me to be careful around Marius. He might seem laid-back, but he deals in war, and I suspect it's more than just a random career choice.

The door opens before we get there. Marius steps out. The tux is gone, replaced with jeans and a T-shirt. His feet are bare, and he has a beer in hand. It's a very different look, one that I suspect is more to his natural taste, like this estate with all its toys for active living.

"I feel overdressed," I say as we climb the stairs.

He laughs. "I'd say to make yourself comfortable, but that could sound suggestive. I got out of that monkey suit the first chance I had. Feel free to kick off your shoes and lose the tie and jacket."

We step inside, and I remove my heels. Connolly keeps his shoes and tie on but does let Marius take his jacket.

"Head on into the living room," Marius says with a wave down a side hall. "I'll give Vess a shout."

"She isn't here?" I say.

His voice drifts back as he takes Connolly's jacket away. "We split up after the party fiasco. She's changing back at her hotel. I said I'd call when you got here."

I glance at Connolly. He has his phone out, and he's texting. A moment later, he nods, confirming that Vanessa replied. Nothing suspicious, then.

We head in the direction Marius indicated. It takes us down a hall and then opens into a cavernous room with several seating areas, as if it'd originally been for large-scale entertaining, and he's tried to make more of a comfortable setup. I don't see which seating arrangement he'd been using, and I'm about to let Connolly choose one when I see the statues. Gorgeous Greco-Roman statues in each corner, which of course require closer examination.

"His own private museum," Connolly muses as I approach one.

"Right? No wonder he hasn't made this into multiple rooms. These statues would overwhelm a smaller space."

"That one looks familiar," he says.

I nod. *Crouching Venus.* The original is in the British Museum. This must be a reproduction, but a contemporaneous one—from the same time period. She's gorgeous, isn't she?"

It's my favorite Aphrodite. Usually, she's depicted standing and naked, as if on display. Here, she's crouched and covering herself with one arm while she looks over her shoulder, as if some unwanted intruder approaches. The upright nude statues speak to pride. *Witness me, I am beauty incarnate.* This one resonates with me more. Some see modesty in her pose and expression. I see exasperation and annoyance.

Stop looking at me. Stop chasing me. I am more than what you see.

"I forgot to ask what you'd like to drink," Marius calls from the next room. "Beer? Wine? Spirits?"

"Beer is fine," I say.

"I'll take . . . a whiskey," Connolly says.

A chuckle from the hall as Marius peeks around the corner. "Scotch, I'm guessing."

"If you have it."

"Oh, I have it. I have it all."

When Marius is gone, I move to the statue in the corner nearest Aphrodite. As I approach it, my breath catches. Another one I know well.

It's a young man, sitting on a chair. There's a length of fabric wound around one arm and over one thigh, but he's otherwise naked, showing off a perfectly muscled body. It's the expression that gets me as it always does with this statue. His head is slightly tilted, looking away from the viewer, lost in his thoughts. The pose is casual, one foot resting on a helmet, his hands on the hilt of a sheathed sword. A shield leans against his leg.

"Another god?" Connolly says.

"You don't recognize him?"

He shakes his head.

I reach out to touch it and stop myself. "That's because he's usually shown older. Bearded. Look at the objects with him. Sword. Shield. Helmet . . ."

"A warrior? God of . . ." He frowns. "Ares?"

I smile. "God of war. He looks different here, doesn't he?" I nod at the *Crouching Venus*. "Neither is what we expect. They're more nuanced portrayals. Deeper. More . . ."

More human.

I don't finish the thought. My brain has already raced ahead, seizing something in these statues and running with it. Running to a place that makes me almost laugh, and then stop. Stop and think.

No, that isn't . . .

That can't . . .

I wheel on Connolly so fast he startles. "Hector was limping tonight. I thought he hurt his foot in the chaos."

Connolly shakes his head. "No, he has a limp."

"A twisted foot," I murmur.

I just stare at the two statues and remember all the little things tonight that didn't quite make sense. The undercurrents running through the gala. Hector and Vanessa. Marius and Vanessa. Hector and Marius. The last nudges hardest as I remember Marius when the necklace came out and then when Connolly declared it a forgery.

You don't want to admire the craftsmanship?

Go have a closer look, Hector. You can clear this up. You are, after all, the expert.

Get off your ass, and check the damned necklace.

"Kennedy?" Connolly says. "You're thinking something."

When I hesitate, he leans in, breath warm on the top of my head. "If it's a theory, you can share it."

"However crazy it sounds?"

He nods. "I know I've made you feel . . . patronized. I hope you've come to understand that I don't mean that. However wild the theory, I'd like to hear it."

I still hold back. It really is wild. Crazy. Preposterous, even. He can say he won't judge me for it, but he presumes my theory is just slightly off-the-wall. Not this.

Yet it fits. It all fits. The only alternate explanation I can come up with is that we're the audience for a very elaborate performance. Which makes no sense. We're a couple of twenty-something nobodies to these people. There's nothing to be gained by such a setup.

Which means . . .

Oh, hell. I have no idea what it means. The only thing I can do is share it. A leap of faith in Connolly and how far we've come.

I tell him my theory. He blinks. That's it. A blink that says he must have misheard. He looks from the statue to me.

"Did I mention the crazy?" I say. "Forget I said anything, okay?"

I start to turn away. He reaches for my arm, but I've moved, and his fingers land on my hip instead. They rest there lightly as he leans toward me.

"Tell me more," he says. "Give me data. My mind isn't like yours. You've seen clues I haven't. Share those. Please."

I do. As I talk, he doesn't react. I think that's my answer. He isn't making the same connections. He's right. Our brains work differently. I have the wild imagination, and sometimes that helps, my "outside the box" thinking. He's the analyst. I've provided the data, and he's processed it and found my theory flawed.

"How do you want to . . . ?" he says and cuts his gaze toward the hall.

It takes me a moment to realize he's saying my theory is sound. That, as crazy as it seems, the explanation works. Before I can react, Marius comes in, carrying a tray of bottles and glasses.

"I brought Macallan and Ardbeg for Aiden to choose from," he says. "I prefer the Ardbeg, but Vess says it's too peaty."

He notices the statue we're admiring and nods but says nothing, just sets the tray on a table.

"*Ludovisi Ares*," I say, gesturing to the nearest statue.

That makes his eyes light up. "It is."

"It's missing Eros, though." I nod at the statue's leg. "That was a later addition, I believe. From the Renaissance-era restoration."

"It was. A rather ridiculous one, too. Who looks at that statue and says, you know what it really needs? Cupid."

"Eros is Ares's son."

He rolls his eyes. "No, Eros is like that long-lost nephew they shove into long-running TV shows. You know what will spice this up? A cute kid."

I gesture from Aphrodite to Ares. "I like your choices."

"Do you?"

I nod. "They're unique representations. Nuanced. Like real people."

He wrinkles his nose and waves at *Ludovisi Ares*. "Not sure I'd call that *nuanced*. It's an idealized version. A boudoir shot, all hazy lighting and filters. But statues are always that way, and I like this one best."

He hands me my beer and a glass. When I wave off the glass, he grins and takes it back.

"Not sure I agree on the idealization part," I say. "They're gods, right? They should be perfect specimens."

"Depends on your view of gods. You're supposedly descended from them, right? You from the *arae*." He nods at Connolly. "You from Fortuna. How do you reconcile that? Having gods in your family tree?"

I shrug. "My grandmother would say that it depends—like you said—on your view of gods. A mortal with powers could be mistaken for one. That works for the *arae*—a group, rather than individuals. When it comes to the actual named gods, though? The issue is time."

His brows rise.

"Imagine one mortal woman has power, maybe a lot of it," I say. "People revere her as a god. But are they still going to be doing that a thousand years after she dies? Two thousand? On a large scale, especially in prehistory, you'd need more. Godhood would need to be conferred by the greatest power of all: immortality."

"Reasonable," he says and then opens his beer. "Not gods residing on Mount Olympus then, but humans with gifts, one of which is immortality."

"Yes."

He sips his beer. Just sips it. He's waiting for me to go on. That's all I'm getting. All the steps are mine. All the heavy lifting is mine. If I don't have the guts to make this leap—if my ego can't risk the humiliation of a mistake—well, then I don't deserve answers.

I look from the statue to Marius, trying to mentally find the bridge. My natural inclination leans toward humor. A joke. A clever quip. I'm grasping for one when Connolly, who has been silent until now, speaks.

"Someone set up an appointment with Kennedy," he says, "under the name Erin Concord. Erin for Eris, another name for Discord. Concord as another name for Harmonia. Alluding to the necklace with a little clever name play. I think you all have an affinity for that—plays on names."

Connolly nods toward the statue. "Mars, also known as Ares." A nod toward the other statue. "Venus, also known as Aphrodite.

Hephaestus, also known as Vulcan. Marius Archer. Vanessa Apsley. Hector Voden."

Marius throws back his head and laughs, the sound echoing in the giant room. Then he looks at us, still grinning. "Well, that took long enough." He lifts his beer. "Bring your drinks, and let's chat."

CHAPTER THIRTY-SIX

WE SETTLE into the seating area by the fireplace. I take the love seat and Connolly sits beside me, close enough that our hips touch. I could read something into that, but I understand it's protection. He's staying close, presenting a united front in case of trouble. After all, we did just unmask the god of war. Even if he is chilling in jeans and bare feet, drinking an IPA.

It does make sense. The clues were all there, not the least being that he's an actual freaking arms dealer. Well, military technology, but it's the theater of war, and that is his stage.

Still . . .

I begin. "I think we can be forgiven for not jumping to the conclusion that the people we're hanging out with are actual Greek gods."

Marius makes a face.

"Fine," I say. "Not gods. Still the actual beings whose names and deeds we know two thousand years after the fall of Rome."

"I'd be careful with the 'deeds' part. Think of mythology as classical tabloid stories and take them all with a boulder-sized grain of salt. Lacking actual celebrities in the ancient world, people pushed immortals into that gap. Who's sleeping with whom? Who's . . . well, mostly who's sleeping with whom. Or who's raping whom." His lip curls. "Like the one about me raping a vestal virgin and fathering the twins who founded Rome. Did not happen." He pauses. "Well, the twins, yes. And the vestal virgin. But it was consensual. Like I said, celebrity status. Some vestal virgins figured banging a *god* was a loophole to their vow of chastity."

"So you and Vanessa . . . ?" I say.

"We were on a break. It's been over three thousand years. There have been a lot of breaks. Like the latest one. But . . ." He fingers the label on his beer. "I need to tell you a few things about Vess before she gets here."

"Is she actually coming?" I say.

He nods. "I did ask her to invite you here, and then I suggested she had plenty of time to change first. Before she arrives, you need to understand about the necklace and about Hector. She won't want to talk about them, or if she does, she'll gloss them over." He gives a very-Vanessa dismissive wave. "Oh, it was nothing. The past is the past. It's all fine now."

"It's not fine," I say.

His lips tighten, and he glances to the side, looking so much like his statue that chills run up my arms.

"No, it's not fine. It's never been fine. That's what I was—" He straightens. "More on that in a minute. What do you know about the Hephaestus and Aphrodite myth? How they got together?"

"Hera was caught in a magical trap. Hephaestus knew how to free her and demanded Aphrodite in payment. Zeus happily agreed because it kept the gods from fighting over her. Not only was she the most beautiful woman in the world, but well, she was one of the few goddesses who wasn't a blood relative."

He chuckles. "True enough."

"So Hector really is your brother. Zeus is your father. Hera's your mother."

"Et cetera, et cetera. Yep. There are other immortals, but we were the one family that reliably bred them. Vess was the daughter of an old immortal, who brought her to my father for fostering when she was twelve. I was a couple of years younger than her, so we became friends, and I was definitely not part of the potential bridegroom pack—I was only fourteen when she married. As for the myth, yes, my mother got caught in a magical trap, which I suspect Hector devised himself so he could demand Vess. He wanted her. She did not want him."

Marius's gaze travels to the other statue, Venus covering herself as she looks over her shoulder at an unwanted intruder. "She was sixteen. Handed over as payment for services rendered. That was hardly unusual at the time. Hell, it was hardly unusual until the last century. Vess did what most women of her time did. Accepted her lot and tried to make the best of it. Put that in a story today, and she'd seem weak. Vess may be much older and wiser than she was then, but one thing she never was? Weak. Or stupid. That's always the story, though, isn't it? The gorgeous, empty-headed goddess of love. Like the handsome, dumb-as-dirt god of war. No wonder we ended up together. We can just sit and admire one another and never be expected to make actual conversation."

He shakes his head. "The point is that Vess was *not* weak or stupid. She knew there was nothing to be gained by fighting the marriage. The problem was that Hector didn't want Vess the woman. He wanted Vess the thing. The object. The prize. The most beautiful woman in the world was his, and he sure as hell didn't want to have to *talk* to her, much less treat her like an actual person. She was the ultimate trophy wife. A trophy to be kept in a very tiny box and brought out for display. These days, people see control for what it is: abuse. Back then?" He shrugs. "The older immortals told Vess she should be happy. Hector didn't beat her. He put her on a pedestal. He protected her. What more could she want?"

"Freedom. Agency."

He smiles, warmth setting his face aglow. "Agency. Exactly. So eventually she took it, which included . . ." He points at himself. "The biggest so-called cuckolding in history."

He shakes his head and sips his beer. "In the modern world, she'd have left Hector the moment she decided she wanted to be with me. That wasn't an option. Hector was her husband. Zeus was her foster father. They *owned* her. So we started our affair as discreetly as possible but . . ." He shrugs. "We were young, and the young are never as discreet as they think they are. You know the story, I presume?"

"Hephaestus put a golden net over the marriage bed, which

caught Ares and Aphrodite, and he then brought in all the gods to witness it."

"I sure as hell never slept with Vess in Hector's bed. And there was no magical net. Just my greedy bastard of a brother who wanted to humiliate his wife while demanding back what he paid for her. He found out where we had our love nest and brought witnesses. Then he demanded I repay the marriage price to her adoptive father, who is also our father."

"That's not complicated at all."

"Tell me about it. According to the myth, I defaulted. I didn't. I paid every last drachma—happily, because it meant Vess would have her freedom. Hector's the one who defaulted. Took the money and refused to let her go. Said if she ever left him, he'd kill me, which meant she'd never leave him."

"He still calls her his wife," I say.

His jaw tenses. "A technicality. One can't obtain a modern divorce when one can't prove a marriage. They've been apart for over a millennium, and she still isn't free of him. Wherever she moves, whatever circles she travels in, whatever business she does, he's right behind her, elbowing his way in. Whole damned world to live in, and he's two hours from her doorstep."

I could say Marius lives even closer, too, but that's different. While they may not be together, I get the feeling they're never really apart, either, and that's by choice. A romantic might prefer to imagine a love so deep that a couple stays together for eternity, but this seems more real. Friendship is what truly lasts. I see that sort of love in the way he talks about her, in the anger he's struggling to tamp down when he discusses her past.

As for Hector, that absolutely isn't love. It's obsession. Not active stalker-peeping-in-her-windows obsession, but a more insidious kind. She and Marius move to New England, make a home for themselves, start a business network, and Hector sees both a business opportunity and a chance to remind them they'll never be free of him. I'm sure some people would ask why Vanessa doesn't just move on again—the same people who'd ask an abused woman why she doesn't leave the city where her ex lives, leave the firm where he works, leave her friends and her family and her job and let him have the satisfaction of driving her out. The question is particularly moot when I suspect Hector would just do it all over again. She has learned to live with him. Learned to be civil to him and enjoy her life despite having him in it.

"On to the necklace," he says. "That's the part you really need to understand."

"Why she had to leave the room at the party," I say. "Why she won't be around it."

He looks at his beer, then puts it aside, pours an inch of Scotch into a glass and downs half.

"Time . . . is different for us," he says. "It passes differently, perhaps because we have so much of it. Some of our children are immortal. Most are not. Vess and I have seen our children grow old and die, our grandchildren grow old and die, great-grandchildren, too. I say *our* children. The myths say that, too. We consider them ours because . . ."

He finishes the drink. "Vess was still Hector's wife, and for a very long time, he expected everything that comes with that. To my shame, I never thought much of it in the early days. You've seen how Vess is. That airy dismissal. This was the same. Sex was just another wifely chore like managing his household. She loved me, not him. I actually congratulated myself for being so forward-thinking, understanding her situation and not being jealous. I often wonder whether that's the one thing she can't quite forgive me for."

He eyes the bottle but then sets down his glass with a decisive clink. "She was his wife. That meant she could not refuse him sex. So when I talk about *our* children, that's because he refused to recognize any of Vess's children as his, even when some very clearly were. I happily claimed them and parented them with her."

"Including Harmonia."

"Especially Harmonia." His eyes light. "She was almost certainly not mine, but I didn't care. Hector rejected her, and I embraced her. Our first child. An immortal, no less. She would always be ours." His gaze drops. "She *should* always have been ours."

"Hector cursed her. With the necklace."

He nods. "And fools that we were, we thought he was actually acknowledging her as his own. The necklace was supposed to grant eternal youth, beauty, health and success. Harmonia already had most of that, but she appreciated the gesture. She married happily, and we had her and her husband for centuries. But to us, that's a blink in time."

"What happened?" I ask softly.

"Death happened. In the myth, Harmonia and Cadmus turn into snakes because the necklace depicts two snakes. The snakes actually symbolize us. Vess and myself. The jewel is Harmonia—our jewel. The loom represents time. A limited amount of time for our daughter. The curse grants things she already had at the cost of great misfortune, and for an immortal, death is the greatest misfortune of all."

"Even death after a long and happy life?"

His gaze lifts to mine. "The misfortune was for Vess. Harmonia was her first child. The one who loved her unconditionally. The bright joy of her life. Gone."

"I'm sorry."

"No, *I'm* sorry. Sorry I didn't destroy the damned thing before it ever touched our daughter. That I didn't find a way to destroy it after that so Vess wouldn't have had to live knowing it was out there, cursing innocent women. But now, finally—"

He stops short and rises. "That can wait. This can't. I have something for you." He hesitates. "First, two things. One, please don't treat Vess any differently now that you know who she is. It's an open secret in our corner of the world. It's not as if anyone's going to publicly out us, and it cements our power base. But for Vess, it's different. Being the so-called god of war brings me added clout, added respect. The goddess of love and beauty, though?" He glances at the statue of Venus crouching. "It diminishes what she is."

"I wouldn't do that," I say.

"Thank you. The second thing?" He takes a deep breath. "I have a lot of explaining to do, which I will. Just bear that in mind when you see . . ."

He waves vaguely toward a dark hall.

"All right," I say. "Building the suspense, I see."

He glances at Connolly. "You can wait here, please, Aiden. This is for Kennedy."

"Perhaps," Connolly says, rising. "But I'm not staying here while you take her out of my sight. That's a matter of safety."

Marius hesitates. Then he nods. "All right. Come along, then."

CHAPTER THIRTY-SEVEN

As WE WALK, Connolly is on high alert. I glance over to see him noting windows with small nods of approval. When I catch his eye, though, he only reaches to briefly squeeze my hand. Telling me he doesn't expect a trap; he's just being careful.

He was quiet as I talked to Marius. Listening and assimilating but also wary. Bad enough we're alone, at night, in the house of a powerful arms dealer with unknown powers. The fact Marius is also a three-thousand-year-old immortal? It doesn't matter how laid-back Marius seems, how hospitable he's been. He can afford to be all that. We are mere mortals, no threat to him.

Connolly is also letting me focus on what's ahead rather than what to do if this goes sideways. What could Marius possibly want to show *me*? Specifically me.

We're walking down a hall of doorways in a rear main-floor wing. Marius pauses at a door and holds the knob.

He turns to me. "Just remember that I will explain. And I will make it up to you. Both of you."

At my look of complete confusion, he waves. "Go on. Aiden and I will wait here."

Connolly opens his mouth to argue.

"She's fine," Marius says. "Let her have this moment."

Again, Connolly starts to say something. Then he stops. His face darkens, mouth setting in a firm line as his glare locks on

Marius. Then he says, stiffly, "Yes, you should go in alone, Kennedy. And yes"—another glare at Marius—"he will make it up to you."

"What is—?" I begin.

"Just go inside," Marius says, swinging open the door.

He reaches through and flicks on a light. When I step into the room, he closes the door most of the way behind me. I stand there, looking around. It's a sitting area that seems to be for guests, with an entertainment system and a bookcase, a sofa and a recliner, a little private spot to rest. I'm not surprised then to open the adjoining door and see a bedroom.

From the light coming in behind me, I can see that the bed is unmade, and that makes me jump back. There's no one in the bed, though. There's another door, an open one into a darkened bathroom.

An empty bedroom with a breeze blowing through the open window.

What am I supposed to see in here?

My gut whispers that I should know the answer. This looks familiar, doesn't it? Like the rooms where Rian was kept. A nicer and more opulent version.

I know the answer. I really do, but I still turn, searching for proof. It's on the nightstand. A nearly finished novel, propped open under a lamp. A book cover I recognize.

I said I'd like a copy of that book you recommended, the one based on a Russian fairy tale.

I grab the novel, and then I turn, looking from side to side. I race into the bathroom, just in case I've missed something. I haven't. It's empty.

Book in hand, I charge from the rooms, yanking open the outer door to find Marius and Connolly still there, Marius grinning, Connolly's expression as dark as when I left him.

"You bastard," I say to Marius. "You're the one who kidnapped my sister."

I lunge toward him. He steps back, hands up.

"You're angry," he says. "I understand that."

"No, I don't think you do."

"Perhaps not, but we'll discuss it. I can explain, and whether you accept that or not, I will make it up to both of you."

"Make it up . . ." I sputter. I shake my head sharply. "This is a threat. Or, as you probably call it, a negotiation. You've shown me that you have Hope, and now you want something in return."

"What?" Connolly says. He wheels on Marius. "I thought you were returning Hope to her sister."

Connolly had figured it out before I did. That moment when his gaze had chilled and darkened, when he'd agreed not to come in the room with me. He'd figured out what was in there. *Who* was in there. What Marius had done.

"No," Marius says. "Hope's there. She must be in the bathroom."

"She's not."

He throws up his hands. "There's no other place for her to go."

I remember that cool breeze wafting through. "She escaped out the window."

"The windows have been boarded over," Marius says as I run back inside. "She's in the bathroom. She must be."

I barely hear him. I'm running into the bedroom. The window is definitely open, night air billowing the curtains. I race over and—

There is no window. Just an empty hole in the wall. I lean through to see a pane of glass and boards on the ground.

I wheel to Connolly as he comes up behind me. "She escaped. She figured out how to remove the window and the boards."

Connolly leans out and shines his cell phone light over the debris.

"Right?" I say. "She escaped."

He glances at me. He says nothing. He doesn't want to because his response won't be what I want to hear. It's the last thing I want to hear.

Marius is already on his phone, his words staccato gunfire, the words all but lost behind the pounding in my ears. I catch only a few.

Perimeter. Cameras. Move.

"No," I say, grabbing for his phone. "She's escaped, and you are not sending your goons after her."

He lifts the phone from my reach. "I don't have *goons*, Kennedy.

Not since I fired Havoc. I have security. And your sister didn't escape. That glass has been cut out. The boards have been pried from the outside. If you're going to tell me that someone rescued her, then I will certainly call off my team. Otherwise . . ."

Otherwise . . .

I do not want to think about *otherwise*.

"Did Vanessa know?" I say as I hurry to the bathroom, double-checking there. "Or Rian. He's outside. Maybe he . . ."

Maybe he what? Used X-ray vision to see my sister in a locked room? Found a pry bar and glass cutter conveniently lying around the yard?

"Vess had no idea I took Hope," Marius says between orders to his security team.

"I'll call Rian," Connolly says, and I'm about to comment when something jangles in the room, like an old-fashioned phone.

We all freeze. The sound comes again, muffled. Connolly is there first, striding to the bed. He flips up a pillow to reveal a tablet.

I'm at his side as he lifts it, and he hesitates only a second before passing it over. The screen lights up with a passcode prompt.

I turn to Marius. "Is this Hope's?"

He shakes his head. "I offered her one, but she was fine with books and a game console."

I stare down at the code. Then I enter the last one I remember Hope using. It fails.

"Don't keep trying or you'll lock it up permanently," Marius says. "I have people who can crack it. Looks like an off-brand model."

He's right. It isn't a brand I recognize, and there's a button for a hint on the password. I press it.

Is your name Kennedy Bennett? If not, put me down.

"Hope must have snuck the tablet in," Connolly says.

Marius shakes his head. "My people used a metal detector."

"Well, then," I say. "One of your *people* had a problem with you kidnapping someone, and they snuck her a tablet."

"No. My staff aren't monsters, but they trust me implicitly. I needed to trust them as well—trust they wouldn't do anything to a twenty-year-old girl. Only two people had contact with Hope, and both have been with me a very long time."

When my phone buzzes, I jump. I take it out to see a text with six numbers. I snatch back the tablet and punch them in. It unlocks to a wallpaper of Hope sleeping. I know what this is now. I know, and rage boils up in me at that photo, my little sister curled up in bed, sleeping soundly.

The picture changes. It's Hope, wide-eyed over a gag. My rage erupts, and I jab the screen, hitting and swiping and trying to make it do something, anything. Marius reaches out to take it but then hesitates and wisely withdraws his hand.

Hope is gagged and bound to a chair, but her expression has changed. It's hard now, impassive, and she's so still that only the flickering shadows tell me this is a video. She's being taped, and she knows it, and while there's terror in her eyes, she's stone-faced, not giving them anything. I love her for that. I love her for a million things, but seeing this, my heart swells even as it breaks. She's so scared and alone, but she's not giving her captor the satisfaction of seeing it.

A figure walks into view, seen only from the back. It wears a black robe, and seeing that, every horror movie slams into my brain. The figure turns, and all I see is a pale chin under the shadow of the hood. Then gloved hands rise and flick back the hood, and Marius starts to swear. He starts, and he doesn't stop, a snarled spew of profanity that barely penetrates my own rage.

On the screen is a face I saw only hours ago. A woman's face, smiling with smug superiority.

Havoc.

She shrugs off the robe, and I realize that was just another bit of theatrics. As if this is a game. As if my sister—bound and gagged beside her—is just stage setting in her performance.

Because she is.

The reality of that hits me in the gut, stealing my breath. I see Havoc's gloating face, and I see the smirk of someone who has put one over on her enemies.

This isn't about Hope. Not about me, either. We're just stage setting. Props.

"Kennedy," she says. "Nice to see you again. Is Ares with you?" Her eyes widen in mock-horror. "Whoops! I mean Marius. I didn't give anything away, did I, *sir*? Are you there? I'm sure you are. Swearing up a storm, I bet. Don't bother. I can't hear you, *sir*. For once, you need to listen to me. Painful, isn't it? You thought you were being so clever, and I swooped in and scooped the prizes from under your nose. Both the prizes."

She reaches into her pocket and pulls out a silk bag. From it, she takes the Necklace of Harmonia.

"There's a reason the Greeks named two gods of war," she says. "Athene is the smart one. God of strategy. You're the god of brute strength and dumb luck. But that was never enough. You had to be clever. You always need to prove you're clever. Except you aren't."

Havoc's gaze sweeps the screen. "Is she there, too? Mighty Aphrodite?" Another lip curl. "All this is for her, isn't it? Everything is always for her. That's what happens when you're the goddess of love and beauty. Even the mighty god of war stumbles around like a schoolboy trying to catch your eye."

Havoc dangles the necklace. "May I guess your plan? You kidnapped this girl to unhex the necklace. Then you'd present it to Aphrodite. The cursed necklace, defanged at last, in memory of your dear, sweet Harmonia."

Venom drips from every word, and I glance at Marius, but he's staring at the screen, his jaw tight, eyes blazing.

"Do you know the problem with gods? Even I—a fellow immortal—am beneath your notice because I lack your precious powers. The whole lot of you is forever fixated on one another. Aphrodite trying to prove she's over Harmonia's death. Prove to you that she's healed and prove to Hephaestus that he can't hurt her anymore. You know she's lying, and so you're fixated on healing that wound by getting her this necklace. And Hephaestus? Three thousand years later, and he's still determined to keep this necklace in the world, punishing Aphrodite by hexing new women. You three are forever locked in ancient history, and the rest of us, as always, are mere ants, scurrying about your feet."

She steps toward the camera. "You're all so easily duped when you're focused on one another. I could do whatever I wanted. First, the Connolly boys. Your star progeny."

I glance quickly at Connolly, but he only frowns and then shakes it off, as if clearly Havoc has misused the word.

"Hephaestus was only too eager to get his hands on that bit of leverage. Then you still make your play, grabbing a curse weaver and setting her sister on the task of taking young Connolly out of the game." Havoc pauses. "You're asking how I know this. You have a leak, sir. I'd say to plug it, but I've already done that. You'll find Carson in your stable."

Marius tenses, color draining from his face.

"You and Hephaestus assembled your teams. I did try to wreak a bit of havoc there. Can't help myself, really. A mishap on the highway. A nightmare under a dream shaper's roof. It should have sent the Connolly boy and the Bennett girl running. Seems they aren't that bright. As for the younger brother, don't worry, I have him again."

She walks across the room, and there's Rian, slumped on the floor.

Connolly blinks hard and jabs buttons on his phone.

"He's fine," Havoc continues. "Just sleeping very soundly. He really is your kin, Ares. As big a fool as you. His brother springs him from captivity and what does he do? Sees a pretty girl, bound and gagged, and leaps in to save her. A simple trap for a simple boy."

Her gaze flicks to Hope and then back to the camera. "Kennedy? I presume you're still there. I'm sure all this doesn't make much sense to you. I'm also sure that Marius has made you quite the generous offer to help him uncurse the necklace. Did he offer to release your sister? Probably. But now the person you need to deal with is me."

A pause, as if she's giving that time to sink in.

"The same goes for you, Aiden," she continues. "Forget Marius and Vanessa and Hector. Their petty squabbles don't concern you anymore. I have what concerns you." She points to Rian and then Hope.

Havoc lifts the necklace. "I want the curse removed. Only the curse. The blessing must remain. I already have a buyer lined up. A Saudi who knows just enough about the magical world to understand what I'm offering. For it, he's willing to pay me enough that I never need to bend a knee to those damned Olympians again."

She hoists the necklace. "So here's the deal. I have one luck worker and one curse weaver. They have the right bloodlines, but they're young. I want guarantees. Kennedy? You'll bring your other sister. Aiden? You'll join them. That puts together a nice curse-breaking quintet."

Her gaze lifts to meet the camera dead on. "You're thinking you can double-cross me. I know you are. So I'll be adding an incentive for removing the curse."

She walks over to Hope, lifts the necklace over her head and then lowers it . . . and clasps it around her neck. Hope's eyes bug in horror. And the screen goes blank.

CHAPTER THIRTY-EIGHT

"I NEED TO CHECK THE STABLES," Marius murmurs as he slips from the room. He stops and adds, "We'll get this fixed. I promise we will."

Connolly's on his phone, madly texting and then calling his brother. "He texted just a few minutes ago. It must not have actually been him. I should have called. I—"

Silence as he cuts himself off midword. I barely hear any of it. I'm still staring down at the tablet. The screen is black, but that last image stays imprinted on my retinas.

"I'm sorry," Connolly says, his voice moving closer. "I'm rattling on about my brother, while your sister . . ."

He doesn't finish. We both know the rest. Putting that necklace around Hope's neck was no mere symbolic gesture.

It transferred the curse.

"I'm sorry," he says. "I should have said something. Your sister . . ." He clears his throat. "I'm sorry."

I shake my head. "Rian has been kidnapped. Right after you got him free. That's your concern as it should be."

"*All* of it is my concern," he says, his fingers brushing my elbow. "This is *our* concern. Your sister and my brother, and . . ."

"The curse," I whisper. "If we can't lift it . . ."

If we can't lift it, my sister is cursed to endless misfortune. To eternal beauty and youth, yes, but will she want that? No. There are thousands—millions—of people who might, but my sister would not, even without the curse that dooms her to misfortune. She's had enough of that already, both parents dead by her eighteenth birthday.

I look around, suddenly lost.

"Call Ani," he murmurs.

I give a start, as if he's read my thoughts. Then I nod. I take out my phone and stare at it.

"Would it be easier if I told her?" he asks.

Easier, yes. Proper? No. I shake my head.

"Would you like me to leave the room?" he says.

I hesitate. When I shake my head again, he says, "You don't need to be polite, Kennedy. I understand this is a private moment. I'm only offering to stay if it would help."

"It would. I-I'm not sure—I'm not sure I can do this. I might . . . I might need you to take over." A thought hits, and I inhale sharply. "You should call your parents. Let them know."

"Let them know what?" Bitterness drips from his voice. "That my brother is *still* held captive? Hardly new information to them, considering they—"

He bites that off. "Sorry, you don't need that."

I reach over to squeeze his hand. "I'm hoping they lied about his situation to protect you and help him. But being totally selfish here, if you don't need to tell them about the change in circumstance right away, I would appreciate a little moral support during this call."

"Then you have it."

———

THAT CALL. That terrible call. I would say it's harder than any I've ever made, but that'd be a lie. I have a father who died in a car accident and a mother who died of cancer. I have made horrible calls and received even worse ones. This is still one of the toughest. I must tell Ani that I was in the same house as our sister—having a beer, chatting with the owner—while our sister slept under the same roof.

Of course, I had no idea she was here. I'd have torn the place apart if I did. My guilt comes from feeling as if I should have known. Should have walked through that door and sensed her here. Should have found some way to get more information from Hope on our calls so I'd recognize the setting.

I say all that to Ani. I can't help it. This is my big sister, and I am a sinner at confession, blurting every possible misdeed. Connolly shakes his head and gestures and mouths rationalizations I can't hear.

I do hear my sister's rationalizations, of course.

"Hope couldn't take the risk of saying more during your calls, K."

"I know, but—"

"Even if she could, how would you possibly recognize the house from the description of her room?"

"I know, but—"

"You dropped everything to find us. You've teamed up with a stranger to find Hope. I don't want to even know what risks you've taken to help her, but I know you have. You have done everything you could. The fault, clearly, lies with the person who kidnapped her. This Marius wanted to make amends by returning her? Great. An hour earlier, and we'd have had her, and what the hell did he stall for anyway?"

I don't answer that one. Why did Marius stall? He didn't. He'd delayed his reveal to answer my questions, which bounces the guilt-ball back into my court.

I haven't told Ani that our sister was kidnapped by Ares, god of war. That's a different conversation. To give it the space it needs would suck that space from Hope's situation. That is our focus. The rest will come when Ani and I have had time to digest what happened to Hope.

"You did everything you could, K," she says.

"I don't feel like I did."

"I know," she says softly. "I know."

Ani doesn't sit still as I talk. It might be the middle of the night, and she'd been asleep when I called, but she's up now, packing her bag.

"You need to tell Jonathan," I say. "Bring him with you."

She hesitates.

"Seriously? Are you considering taking off to handle this without telling him?"

"I don't want to presume. He has work, and he's done so much already. I'd love to have him along, but I don't want him to lose his job, taking more time off."

"That won't happen, and you know it. If wanting him with you isn't enough, then remember that you'll need him to help drive while you and I talk. Also, we need his research. *Hope* needs it."

She pauses. A knock comes through the phone. Then, "Ani? Is something wrong?"

"He was sleeping downstairs?" I say. "Of course he was. You were kidnapped—he's not leaving you alone."

Outside our door, heels click through a distant hall.

"Marius?" Vanessa calls.

Connolly and I look at each other.

"May I take this?" he mouths.

I nod, and then continue talking to Ani while he goes to meet Vanessa.

———

WHEN I END my call a few minutes later, Vanessa enters, as if she'd been just outside the door. I glance over her shoulder for Connolly, but she shakes her head.

"Aiden is helping Marius," she says. "He found one of his employees in the barn. Dead. I understand the man betrayed him, but it is still . . . difficult. They're handling the body."

She comes inside and closes the door. Then she motions to the sofa. "May we?"

I nod. This isn't what I imagined. I told Marius I wouldn't treat Vanessa any differently, and I meant that, but with everything that just happened, I'm not myself, and I'm painfully aware that my distraction and silence might seem as if I'm seeing her with new eyes. Seeing her through a different lens, one she doesn't want.

"Marius explained," I say awkwardly as we sit. "That's all . . ." I wave my hands. "That's all fine. Sorry. I'm just not myself right now. It isn't you."

"You've just discovered that Marius kidnapped your sister, and now she's been taken again and also cursed. I don't expect you to be thinking about me at all, Kennedy."

I nod.

"He wants to explain," she says. "But I don't think you'll want to talk to him right now."

I nod again.

She continues, "The short version is that yes, he tried to hire Hope and then did something incredibly stupid when he couldn't. As for his deal with you, by that point Havoc had given Rian to Hector, and Marius knew it—Hector had taunted him with it. To foil Hector's plans to get the necklace, he inserted you with Aiden."

"So Hector would believe he had a curse worker—I was working with Aiden, who was trying to free Rian. Except, if I was only pretending to work with Aiden, that left Hector's team without a curse worker."

"Also, I believe, it was to keep someone worse—like Havoc— from hiring you, but that's no excuse. He did many, many stupid things. And now, moments after recognizing that, I'm going to do something incredibly selfish. First, we will fix this. I am at your disposal, as is Marius. He owes you, obviously but . . ."

She inhales. "Here is the selfish part. I'm going to ask you to accept his help, however furious you are with him. I'm also going to ask you . . . No, I was going to ask you not to judge him too harshly, but that goes too far. Judge him as you will. I just want to say that . . ."

She flutters her hands and leans back with a sigh. "There is no right way to say this. No way that won't seem like me defending a man I love because that is exactly what I'm doing. No one in the world is more important to me than Marius, and whether we share a roof or not, a bed or not, it doesn't change that. He did something incredibly thoughtless here."

I choke on a snort. I can't help it.

"Yes," she says. "Thoughtless seems like a ridiculous word under the circumstances, but that's exactly what it was. His crime is lack of consideration. He'll tell you that he did everything he could to make your sister comfortable, and that will mean nothing to you because he *kidnapped* her. It just . . ."

"Doesn't mean the same to him because we're mortal?"

"Doesn't mean the same to *us* because we're *immortal*. You and your sister were a means to an end. He wouldn't hurt either of you. He was moving pieces on a chessboard. You were pawns. Then he met you, and he realized he *was* hurting people. You can be as furious as you want with him. That's understandable, and no one will deny you that right, least of all Marius. Just, whatever you decide, don't turn down his help."

I want to. I want to storm out of here. Work with my sister's kidnapper? Never. But that would be cutting off my nose to spite my face. If he can help, then he does owe me, and I'm going to need all the help I can get.

———

MARIUS IS SUBDUED when I see him again, and I'm sure it's partly the awkwardness of being my sister's kidnapper, but it's also from what he found in the stable. As loyal as the man had been to his boss, he'd also been loyal to his former *under*boss, and that would be Havoc. He'd been with Marius for centuries, and despite the man's betrayal, Marius is grieving.

We get a crash course in immortality from Vanessa. Broad strokes only. It's a power like any other. A very limited power that they pass along to only some of their descendants.

Vanessa, Marius, Hector and the other surviving "Olympians" have other powers. That's what made them revered as gods. The dead employee had been a more recent immortal—a descendant of Marius—with no other powers. Immortal, it seems, does not mean invulnerable.

The "lesser immortals"—my term, not theirs—tend to align themselves with the Olympians. Working for the Olympians makes their lives easier. Josephine Hill-Cabot's eternal youth and beauty forced her to retreat from the world. The Olympians—and others like them—have carved out their own world within ours, populated with lesser immortals and mortals with magical abilities, those who've been brought into the fold, which I guess now includes us.

There's a whole lot more there to understand, and any other time I'd be like the kid at the front of class, waving my hand and bouncing in my seat, desperate for all the answers. That will come. My mind is absorbed with Hope's situation, and all I want is information that will help me free her.

Vanessa's crash course in immortality isn't meant to help us understand Marius's grief over the dead man. It's to help us understand Havoc.

"She's immortal," I say. "But without power."

We've moved into a smaller sitting room, and I'm on one loveseat with Connolly, while Marius and Vanessa sit together on another.

Marius takes a deep breath. "Her real name is Eris."

"Eris?" Connolly says. "Discord?"

"She prefers Havoc," Vanessa murmurs, with an unreadable look.

"But isn't Eris supposed to be . . ." I look at Marius. "She's your daughter."

As he nods, I look between him and Vanessa. Even before Marius shakes his head, I know the answer to my unasked question.

"Vess isn't her mother," Marius says. "We were on a break."

"So many breaks," Vanessa says, and they share a quarter smile.

"Yes, so many breaks," he says. "And many children resulting from them, particularly for me. That's the problem with being an immortal millennia before reliable birth control. The myths make it sound like we were banging everything in sight. When you live for thousands of years, though, a few dozen affairs is hardly outrageous. In our case, it wasn't even affairs as much as flings and one-night stands while we were on our breaks. Havoc was the result of a one-night stand and a lot of wine."

Vanessa rolls her eyes.

"What?" Marius says. "You know what Denny's bashes are like. You and I had just had a fight, and you'd taken off to Macedonia. So I drank. Way too much. And I was . . ."

"Vulnerable to the designs of an ambitious woman?"

He makes a face but doesn't argue.

Vanessa looks at us. "Havoc's mother was mortal. A minor princess who wanted more. Having the child of a god was her way of achieving it. She came from a kingdom of warmongers—sorry, proud warriors—and so she targeted the god of war. Havoc was the result and . . ." She glances at Marius, who nods that she can continue.

"We can make this lighthearted," she says. "A romp between the god of war and an ambitious princess. There was a myth about it, which didn't survive. The cunning woman plying the foolish and heartbroken god with wine until she got what she wanted. Along comes a child, and the seductress turns into a harpy, demanding marriage and mansions and whatever else he can provide. Such a lark, ha-ha. There are many stories like that, and what they all ignore is that a child was involved. A child born to two strangers—a father who wants nothing to do with the mother, and a mother for whom the child is only a tool to further her own ambitions."

A moment of silence, as if for Eris, the child who became Havoc.

Vanessa continues. "Havoc's mother wasn't merely ambitious and driven. I would understand that. She was . . ." A glance at Marius, and then she lowers her voice as she murmurs, "Monstrous."

He nods, gaze averted.

"When she realized Havoc wouldn't win her a god for a husband, she took it out on the child. Marius stepped in and negotiated to take custody. He raised her for a few years with the help of his sisters and me. It . . . did not work out."

"Havoc is her mother's daughter," Marius says. "To me, she was nothing but sunshine and light. To the women in my life—both her aunts and Vess—she was cruel and dangerous. We thought we could rechannel her aggression. She was my daughter, too, after all. We'd rein in her mother's influence with love and a soldier's discipline. We sent her to Hippolyte."

"Queen of the Amazons," I say. "And another of your daughters, right?"

"Our daughter," he says, nodding at Vanessa, and they share a smile. "The myths misname her mother."

Vanessa rolls her eyes. "Because no one could believe the goddess of love and beauty could bear such a warrior."

"Hippolyte is ours," Marius says. "She is the best of both of us. Just as Harmonia was in a very different way. One a sweet and giving child, the other a fierce and wise warrior. We asked Hippolyte to raise Havoc among the Amazons. She did her best, but when Havoc reached adulthood, it became apparent that she was a danger to her sister warriors. She respected no one. Obeyed no one."

Vanessa clears her throat, and the look that crosses Marius's face is an exhaustion and a frustration so deep that, for a moment, he is an old man, bowed by the weight of responsibility and miscalculations.

"There's an exception, isn't there?" I say. "Her father."

Vanessa nods. "The one person she cares about. The one person whose opinion she values."

I remember the party, when we'd walked in, Havoc kneeling beside that divan, talking to Marius. Talking to him. Offering him champagne. And him lying there, eyes shut, as if she didn't exist.

Remembering that, my expression must render judgment because Vanessa leaps in.

"Marius has given her what she wants for centuries, for *millennia*. He gave her the attention she needed. Made her his lieutenant. Took responsibility for her. He has been her guardian since Hippolyte returned her."

"It's fine," Marius says. "I accept resp—"

"You *always* accept responsibility." Her words come sharp. "She was an adult. An adult immortal, and you still looked after her, and I respected the hell out of that, Marius, even when it drove me mad with frustration." She looks at us. "We have nearly a dozen immortal children. No matter how we raised them, no two are the same. There are those, like Hippolyte, who awe us, and we can scarcely believe she's ours. There are those, like Harmonia, who delight us, and we are honored to have them in our lives. There are a few who frustrate us, but it is the loving frustration of doting parents. There are also a couple, though . . ."

A pained glance at Marius. "There are a couple we have lost, not through death but through the eventual realization that we cannot parent them forever. That we did our best, but we cannot be responsible for them forever."

"Havoc is one of those," I say.

"I only wish—" She stops short. "Sorry, that's bitterness talking. Havoc doesn't consider herself *ours*. I would have happily been a mother to her, but she'd rather die a thousand painful deaths. Havoc, though, is the one we kept close for as long as we could. Eventually . . ."

"I fired her," Marius says.

"Fired her?" Vanessa snorts. "You set her up in business on her own. Convinced her it was time to fly the nest while giving her everything she needed."

"She felt fired."

"That's her problem." Vanessa looks at us. "Things hit a tipping point. Marius and I separated because of her. I couldn't take it anymore. He did everything he could to ease her leaving, and she acted like an abandoned child. So he did the only thing he could."

"Last year, I told her I didn't want her as part of my life until she treated everyone in it—Vess, my siblings, our other children—with respect."

"You saw Marius ignoring her at the party," Vanessa says. "That seemed cruel. It was calculated strategy. Hundreds of years of his attention didn't help, so he's withdrawn it."

I look at her. "Basically, you're telling us that my sister has been cursed by a bratty immortal throwing a tantrum because Daddy's giving her the silent treatment?"

"I'm sure there's more to it—" Marius begins.

"Yes," Vanessa says, meeting my gaze. "There are side benefits to her scheme. Hurting me. Insinuating herself with Hector. Even owning Harmonia's necklace would be a triumph to her—she hated her sister almost as much as she hates me. And then there's the pure joy of wreaking havoc. That's what she is—Havoc, goddess of chaos. Mostly, though, it's a tantrum, and your siblings have been pulled into it."

"I'll fix this," Marius says. "I'll—"

"What?" Vanessa says. "Give her a hug? Buy her a pony?" She rubs her temples and makes a face. "I apologize. That's three millennia of evil-stepmother frustration talking." She looks at us. "If a reconciliation would fix this—even just long enough to get your sister and brother back—we'd do it. But Havoc won't fall for it. She might accept my head on a pike, but I'd rather try a few less fatal options first."

"Then let's talk."

CHAPTER THIRTY-NINE

ANI IS STILL another hour out, and I haven't told her what's happening here. I'm struggling to find the words. Or maybe struggling to find a way to explain the inexplicable. To tell her that we're caught in a power play between immortals.

In some ways, it'd be easier to do in an e-mail where I can lay everything out and not have her cut me off halfway to administer drug tests. But I communicate better in person.

Postponing that conversation also means more time to get a better handle on everything that's happened. When Ani does arrive, we need to hit the ground running. Havoc has already sent her timeline. The uncursing will be later today at a location to be revealed.

It turns out that Havoc knows her family well, as one would expect after thousands of years. She was right about why Marius wanted the necklace. It was a gift for Vanessa. That necklace killed their daughter. Its continued existence in the world—and the victims it leaves in its wake—remind her of Harmonia's fate and her own guilt.

I see nothing wrong with her falling for Marius while trapped in a loveless, abusive marriage. The blame for this necklace lies squarely on the guy who made it. Hector wanted to hurt her, and so he has, for millennia. When the necklace surfaced, Marius was willing to move mountains to free Vanessa from the "curse" of its existence.

Vanessa—having no idea what Marius intended—wanted the Necklace of Harmonia for the same reason: to get it out of the world. Only she wasn't going to bother with the uncursing. Destruction was her only goal.

After speaking to Vanessa and Marius, Connolly and I find the kitchen and put together breakfast to give them time alone. This is their shared grief, as parents, and two thousand years hasn't dimmed that pain. Their daughter was punished for their supposed sin. I didn't think it was possible to hate Hector more. I was wrong. However "monstrous" Havoc might be, it's obvious that Vanessa and Marius had experienced that level of cruelty long before she came along.

Connolly and I are still fussing in the kitchen when they call us back in. Enough grieving. Time to move forward.

Step one is sorting it all out. Who did what?

Marius sent the woman who tried to hire my sisters. He was also the guy on the phone, where he'd intentionally channeled Hector. Setting me on my task was half about pushing the wealthy Connolly family off the board and half about keeping me from being hired by other potential buyers.

Havoc sent the guys who tried to run us off the road. If that stunt had killed us? Oh, well. We were mortal, so we'd die soon enough anyway.

Tracking Connolly's car meant Havoc knew he'd gone to see Vanessa. Vanessa's security system had been installed by Marius, and while he'd kept Havoc out of that, she obviously got the specs from his employee and sent a dream shaper to scare me off.

As for my appointment with Erin Concord, it seems obvious that was Havoc. But neither Marius nor Vanessa is entirely certain it was. It could have been her, or it could have been someone pointing the finger at her, should we ever figure out the rest.

That leaves one thing unexplained.

"Who trashed Kennedy's shop?" Connolly says.

"Still not me," Vanessa says.

Marius frowns. "Trashed her shop?"

When Vanessa explains, he says, "It sounds like Hector. That's certainly his style. A bully's warning, telling you not to get involved. Yet I don't see a connection between him and you. He doesn't want the necklace uncursed. His joy comes from seeing it out there, hurting people. Hurting Vess."

"Presumably it was Havoc, then," I say, "raising havoc."

They exchange a look. Then Vanessa says, "Havoc and Hector may share some traits in common—he is her uncle, after all—but they each have their own style of villainy. Hector is a brute. For him, it's all about control. A modern therapist might blame his twisted leg. His own father did that to him, and while it's a minor impediment, Hector always felt lesser than his siblings. Not as clever as Athene. Not as popular as Apollo. Not as charismatic as Dionysus. Not as powerful as Ares. Not as athletic as Artemis. Not as quick witted as Hermes. Hephaestus always ran at the back of the pack."

"And then he couldn't *run* at all," Marius says. "He has a talent—an incredible one. He is the master smith, the creator of wondrous things. But even in that . . ." He shrugs. "A modern shrink would see a need to control. He creates, and he destroys. So he'd absolutely destroy your shop to send a message. Havoc, though, has a different brain. Single-minded ambition and single-minded cruelty."

"She's fixated on Daddy," Vanessa says, "impressing him and pushing away everyone else in his life. If you get in her way, she'll mow you down. But destroying your shop just because she can?" She shakes her head. "That isn't Havoc."

"Which doesn't mean she isn't responsible," Marius says. "But she would, as Vess said, have mowed through to get to a goal. Is there anything in your shop she might have wanted?"

Connolly and I exchange a look.

"There's a tea caddy," he says.

Their brows rise.

"Cursed tea caddy," I say, and I explain.

"So yes," I say as I finish. "We definitely wondered whether the tea caddy was the cause of the trashing. We also wondered whether the guy who brought it was testing me. But when you dig down, it's . . ."

I wave my hands. "It's like I have two jigsaw pieces, and I see enough similarity that I want to connect them, but they don't fit and I'm left deciding they must belong to separate puzzles."

Connolly nods. "A stranger demands Kennedy's curse-working right at the time we're preparing for the auction. A joker's jinx, which could be a test for the auction. The man mentions her sisters and claims they sent him, which means he knows something about the magical world. But then he abandons the box and never contacts Kennedy again. Also, it's a very minor jinx on a very ordinary box, hardly a test at all."

Marius and Vanessa sit in silence, obviously thinking it through.

"I don't like coincidences," Marius says.

"Neither do I," Vanessa murmurs.

"Would you like to see the box?" I say. "It's in Aiden's trunk."

"Absolutely," Vanessa says. "Bring it in, please."

———

WE'RE HEADING outside when Ani texts to say she's approaching the gates. Marius opens them and then stays inside with Vanessa. Connolly stands a few feet away, offering silent support as I approach Jonathan's car.

Ani and Jonathan climb out. I'm in Ani's embrace in two seconds flat. She hugs me, and I take a moment to enjoy her mothering, making sure I'm okay, assuring me we'll fix this. Then I tell them who they're about to meet: Ares and Aphrodite.

When I finish, Ani says, carefully, "What have you had to eat since you've been here, K?"

I glance at Connolly. "Called it."

"You did."

"I haven't been drugged," I say.

Another furtive look toward the house. "Just get in the car, Kennedy. Please. Whatever these people have told you—"

"Called that, too."

Connolly murmurs. "You did." He walks over. "Kennedy said you'd think she'd been drugged and try to whisk her away." He stops beside me. "Everything Kennedy says is true, even if I'm having trouble wrapping my head around it myself. It's preposterous. But when matched with the evidence . . ." He shrugs.

"Great," Ani says. "You've both been drugged. Get in the car, you two, and we'll figure out a detox."

When we don't move, she looks at Jonathan. "Help me out here."

He says nothing, just stands there, frowning slightly, lost in thought.

"Jonathan?" she says.

"I'd like more information," he says.

"You're not—" she sputters. "You aren't actually buying this?"

He turns a look on her. A deceptively bland look I know well.

Ani flushes. "Okay, that *was* insulting. Sorry. I'm just . . . Gods? Really?"

"Immortals," he says. "And one could say the same about you. Curse weaving? Really?"

Jonathan shades his eyes, looking around the property. Then he motions us toward a crumbling stone wall where a few chairs have been set in the shade. He's suggesting we settle in for a chat, which implies we're going to discuss this rather than flee the premises. When Ani glances back at the car, he says, "Right. Ellie. I should let her out."

"You brought my cat?" I say.

"I didn't know how long we'd be gone," he says.

I shake my head. "No wonder she likes you best."

"After another car ride, I don't think she likes anyone."

He hands me the carrier, and I take it to the chairs. I open it on the ground and then hop onto the low wall. Ellie glares at me.

"Oh, sorry," I say. "Did you want this spot? Plenty of room for us both."

She settles on the grass and begins cleaning a paw.

Connolly walks over and looks at the wall.

"Yes, it's dirty," I say. "Also crumbling. A picturesque perch, but definitely not clothing friendly."

"Then it's a good thing this tux is rented." He turns and boosts himself up gracefully. "I really should change into my clothing from yesterday."

"Same," I say.

"Ani packed you a bag of clothing," Jonathan says as he sits on a chair.

"Because *you* mentioned it," Ani says to him.

"Because you were understandably distracted." He turns to us. "Back to the discussion of gods. Or, I suppose, immortals. Hasn't that always been your family history? Not descended from immortals per se, but from people with magical powers who were revered as deities? Powers they passed on through their bloodline? Yes, no one theorized those original magic users could still be around, but the basic idea follows. You said Venus—Vanessa—has the power of dream shaping. The old stories credit other sources for that ability, but that doesn't preclude her from being the original. What about Marius? What's his power?"

I hesitate. I'm pretty sure I know the answer to this, from Havoc's "villain reveals all" speech.

First, the Connolly boys. Your star progeny.

You're the god of brute strength and dumb luck, Ares.

She'd mocked Marius about battle luck. There's the physical resemblance, too, the one that made me first wonder whether Marius could be Rian. It would also explain Vanessa's interest in Connolly, consciously wanting to watch out for her lover's descendants. But also as a potential lover because he subconsciously reminded her of Marius himself.

Connolly clearly hasn't figured this out, and I'm not going to tell him now. It derails the conversation and hardly matters in the moment.

I make a noncommittal noise, and Jonathan continues, "We can get to that later."

"Just as long as we aren't descended from Hector," I say with a shudder. I glance at Connolly. "And now that I say that, he's the most likely suspect, isn't he? For being a curse weaver. He made the necklace. He's the craftsman."

"If he *is* the first curse weaver, it has nothing to do with you," Connolly says. "We can't choose our families." A quirk of a smile. "As I remind myself almost daily."

"Right," I say. "Moving along, then. Whether you believe they're immortal or not, Ani, that doesn't change the fact that Havoc has Hope and Rian, and she has the necklace. There's still a cursed necklace that needs uncursing. If we do that, we get our siblings back."

"If we fail, our sister stays cursed," Ani says.

"Trying not to think about that. Except as further incentive to get this right."

"So we've been pulled into a family squabble, essentially. One would think they'd have worked it out after a few millennia."

Jonathan shrugs. "Or it just gets worse. There are grudges in my extended family that have gone on for generations. People do crazy things out of old pain and pride."

"For Hector, it's pride," Connolly says. "His wife—a mere woman—continues to show him up by flourishing without his care and protection. He won her. Ergo, she belongs to him, and if he can't have her, he's going to make her life miserable."

"An obsessed stalker," I mutter.

"I can imagine he'd *love* hearing himself described that way," Connolly murmurs.

"Remember how he blew up when we suggested the curse was a lover's lament?"

"The only thing hurt is his pride," Ani mutters. "He's a controlling, abusive asshole."

I nod. "And Vanessa's options are to stand firm and be civil to her abuser or let him keep her on the run, keep her hiding."

"I *really* hate this Hector guy."

"Yep, Havoc's a bitch, but she's a child throwing a tantrum. Hector was the real villain here. He's out of the picture, though. It's Havoc we need to deal with."

"Goddess of chaos and discord," Jonathan says.

"Should be no problem, right?" I say. "She's bound to act rationally."

Ani starts to respond. Then her gaze cuts to the side, and she does a double take. I follow her gaze to see Vanessa on the front porch, shielding her eyes against the dawn sun.

"Holy shit," Ani murmurs.

Jonathan squints over and blinks. "Uh, goddess of beauty, I'm guessing?"

"Right?" I say. "I always pictured Aphrodite as a thin twenty-year-old blonde, but this makes more sense."

Marius appears behind Vanessa and says something to her. She nods and calls, "How's it going?"

"Fine!" I shout back.

"I think Aiden must be due for his second coffee," she calls. "If you'd care to bring your sister and her friend in to chat."

"Coffee with the gods," Jonathan murmurs. "Dare I hope for pastries, too?"

"The best pastries," I say.

"After all, they are gods," Jonathan says.

"Nah, just rich. Really rich. That's what happens when you have three thousand years to build a stock portfolio." I glance at Connolly. "Let's grab the tea caddy and head in."

CHAPTER FORTY

THE FIRST FEW minutes are awkward. Like introducing superheroes at a cocktail party where they're dressed as their alter ego. Everyone knows who they are, but we're going to pretend otherwise.

After those few minutes of initial awkwardness, Ani turns to Marius and says, "I don't care who you are or how sorry you are, you did a shitty thing, and I'm not sure you can ever make it up to us."

He dips his chin. "Understood."

"You should have just told us when you sent that woman to hire us. I'm not saying we'd have taken the job, but we're professionals who deserve to be treated with respect."

"I see that now."

"And you didn't before?"

Vanessa starts to answer but stops herself. Beside her, Marius fidgets and then straightens and meets Ani's gaze. "No, I did not. I was too focused on my goal, and I convinced myself that if I treated Hope well and reimbursed her handsomely, it was fine. It was not at all fine."

"You never wanted me, did you?"

"I would have happily hired you both, but when it came to kidnapping, I thought only taking Hope somehow made it better. When I discovered they took you as well—unable to get just Hope—I ordered them to leave you in that open shack."

"I'd have rather you kept me kidnapped. Then I'd have been with my sister."

"Understood. I do owe you both. In my haste to get this necklace out of the world, I forgot how to be human for a while."

Ani considers and then nods abruptly. Marius motions for me to bring the tea caddy. The others leave us to it while they talk. We're setting up the tea caddy when Ellie meows at the window. Marius's brows shoot up.

"Sorry," I say. "I brought a cat. Well, Jonathan did, but she's mine. I'll just leave her outside."

"Better not," he says. "I have dogs, and they'll be let out soon."

I open my mouth and then shut it. His brows rise again.

"I was biting back a joke about letting loose the dogs of war," I say.

He smiles. "Apt enough. They were in the kennel while you guys were outside, but my stable hand will be freeing them. You won't want your cat out then."

"True. You're probably attached to your dogs."

He laughs. "I am. And to be honest, your cat might be able to inflict some damage on them right now." His expression turns serious. "They were drugged. I had them in the kennel last night so they wouldn't bother you when you arrived. I should have let them out after that. Things might have been different if . . ." A sharp shake of his head. "No, if I did, I might have lost them. They're woozy but fine. Which is more than I can say for . . ."

He waves it off. "Enough of that. Go let your kitty in. That'll give the dogs some fun later, smelling a cat in their house."

I open the door for Ellie, and she struts in like she owns the place . . . and then smells the canine residents, hisses and shoots under the nearest chair. I shake my head and return my attention to the tea caddy, which we've set up on a table. Both my unweaving kit and Ani's wait nearby.

The others join us, Jonathan and Vanessa deep in conversation. Seeing the tea caddy, Vanessa stops short.

"Dear Lord," she says. "That is a travesty."

"I was just thinking how cute it was," Marius says. "A kitty caddy."

"No," Vanessa says as she sets down her coffee. "Just no."

"Sorry, I'm with Marius on this one," I say. "But you and Aiden can shudder together over it. What'd you call it, Connolly? A kitschy piece of trash?"

Marius sputters. "It's Victorian rosewood. Whatever you think of the design—which I maintain is cute—it's hardly trash."

"Right?" I say. "It's a quality antique. The real artistry, though, is the curse. That's why I was loath to remove it. It's an expert weaving."

Ani's brows rise as she looks from me to the box and back.

"Don't give me that look," I say. "A jinx can be fine art."

"Not questioning that. Just . . . Well, it's an odd canvas for a master, isn't it? Cursing a cat tea caddy with a cat-hair jinx? It's a little . . ."

"Kitschy?" I turn to the others. "Specializing in the joker's jinx requires a certain personality, which is why our mom and Yiayia got me hooked on jinxes. It's part innate talent and part personality match. A jinx specialist—even a master of the art—is going to have an off-kilter sense of humor and a taste for, yes, kitsch."

"But the fact it's an expert jinx means something, doesn't it?" Jonathan says. "It's a rare specialty, usually avoided by serious weavers. No offense, K."

"None taken. Your point, however, *is* taken. So I'll ask Ani for a second opinion."

I step back from the table and wave Ani up. Our methods in weaving, as in most things, are different. I'm attuned to the music, those whispered threads to be followed and untangled. I remember talking about that when I was young and new to curse weaving. I figured it was the same for everyone. Like the process of riding a bike. Ani had just stared at me.

Music? What music? It's a problem. Like a mathematical equation.

Mom and Yiayia explained that different weavers experience curses in different ways. Ani didn't actually see numbers, but it *felt* like working out a math problem. I don't hear real music—it just feels that way. And for Hope, it's like opening a book, a story leaping off the pages.

Different curse experiences mean different uncursing methods. I listen and absorb and mentally follow strains of music like threads in a tapestry. Ani leans over the box, staring at it. Then her gloved hands open the lid and turn the box over and poke and prod.

Finally, she sets it down and turns to me, looking slightly dazed. "That is . . ." She blinks and rubs her wrist over her eyes. "Unexpected."

"Am I right then? It's a doctoral class in curse weaving."

She nods. "I'm not sure I've even encountered anything quite like it. Certainly not in a jinx."

"No offense, K," I murmur.

"You know what I mean. And I hope you also know what I mean when I say this isn't like any jinx I've encountered. You're good. *Really* good. But this is . . ."

"I'm a decent journeyman. This is the work of a master. Way beyond my skill."

"Beyond your unweaving skill?" Connolly cuts in, sounding puzzled.

He's been quiet until now. He does that, I've realized. Receding into the background to observe and assimilate. The guy I met that first morning seemed like the sort who'd always be in the middle of any room, making his opinions known. That *can* be Connolly when it suits him. And this is him, too, when he's acknowledging he's not the professional in this sphere.

I shake my head. "I can unweave it easily enough. It's . . . hard to explain. Weaving curses is like building a house of Lego. You can jam the pieces into a log cabin shape, or you can recreate the Taj Mahal. Both are just as easy to break down. In that case, though, everyone would see the difference. This is . . ."

"Like keeping your ledgers neat—tidy handwriting, color-coded headings, annotated categories," Ani says. "It doesn't affect the figures, but another accountant would see and appreciate the difference."

"Ultimately," I say, "it means nothing for the uncursing. We're just admiring the work. We might not agree on the caddy itself, but we can agree on that."

"It does mean something, though," Connolly says. "Who has the skill to weave a jinx like that? When I was asking after a jinx specialist, your name was the only one that kept popping up."

"That's flattering," I say. "It'd be more flattering if it wasn't such a limited field of expertise. My guess is that we aren't dealing with an expert in jinxes. It's an expert curse weaver overall. I can weave any curse. I'm just best at jinxes. Anyway, enough speculation on that. Whoever sent this may have hired an expert weaver. Or they may have bought it already jinxed, meaning whoever wove it is long dead."

I glance at the others. "Okay, glove up and take a look. We're trying to find clues on the box unconnected to the weaving. Secret hatches. Coded messages. Whatever."

Vanessa goes first. Then Connolly, Jonathan and Marius. Each takes their time. This is a puzzle, after all, and everyone here has the curiosity and the ego to want to be the one who solves it. Marius has laid out a tiny screwdriver—the sort used to repair eyeglasses—to let us carefully poke and pry without damaging the caddy. We spend a half hour at it, only to conclude that the tea caddy is just a tea caddy. Cursed, yes, but otherwise unremarkable.

It's time to tackle that one remarkable thing.

I pull on gloves. "I really hate doing this. Feels like smashing a priceless vase."

"I could unweave it," Ani says. "If you'd prefer."

"I'd prefer not to unweave it at all. But since this caddy seems significant and we can't find any other clues, it seems someone wanted it uncursed."

I take out my kit. As Connolly has pointed out, I don't always need it. I can weave—and unweave—minor curses without it. That impressed him, but it hardly makes me a supercharged weaver. Ani has argued it makes me a reckless one. The kit is for our safety. It contains herbs and charms to protect us against a backfire.

Ani always uses her kit, even for the simplest curses. It's easily done, so why not protect yourself? Yet there are times when you don't have your kit and really need to cast a minor curse—like jinxing a police officer's coffee cup into a dribble glass. Ani sees the kit as a bike helmet, always essential. I see it as training wheels, and

I want to learn to operate without it. That means learning precision and care, the opposite of recklessness.

Whatever our philosophies, this isn't the time to practice my parachute-free weaving. I arrange the herbs and charms in a protective circle around the tea caddy. Then I adjust the desk lamp Marius supplied. Finally, I examine the caddy, as if it's the first time I've done this, running my gloved hands over it.

When the first notes of the curse slide toward me, I close my eyes and focus on them. This is always tricky. My brain insists I've already done this and wants to leap ahead to the unweaving. I'm impatient by nature, and this feels like studying a textbook page after I've already memorized it. I have to remind myself that curses are indeed more like music, open to interpretation, each listening a new discovery. I must hear this melody again, unhindered by my memory of it.

There are lessons to be learned here. Take my time and appreciate the work of a master. Follow the tune, unweave the threads. Find the dangling end. There it is, tucked under another thread. Tease it out and—

The end catches. It's the tiniest catch, one that I wouldn't have even noticed if I weren't so focused. After all, it's a minor curse. I could unweave it with all the skill of a five-year-old ripping open birthday presents. Yet I'm feeling my way with care, and when that tug catches, just a little, I pause.

The world contracts to this curse. I don't hear the others shifting and breathing. I don't even feel the tea caddy under my gloved hands. It's just me and that thread, and I swear it takes shape in front of my eyes, a tiny golden thread that seems so innocent and shiny, only to rear back and flash fangs.

Trouble.

"No," the curse seems to whisper. "There's nothing wrong here. Just pretty golden threads, tied so masterfully. A simple curse, expertly woven. There's beauty in simplicity, isn't there? No need to look deeper."

I snort under my breath. A sound behind me, and I turn to see Connolly rocking forward, Ani's sharp glance warning him not to disturb me. His eyes meet mine, and they're troubled. Concerned.

"There's something odd here," I say. "Let me try again." Now Ani's the one rocking forward, and I raise a gloved hand. "I'll be careful."

I lay my hands on the caddy and close my eyes again. I don't rush the process. Now I have reason for patience. The curse reappears, those pretty golden threads, the loose end dangling so innocently.

Nothing odd here. Come give me a tug.

I touch the thread. Then I take it gingerly and—

That resistance again. It's slight, and I know I could pull through. I also know I shouldn't. Instead, I work other threads, nudging them aside. There's something in this artful tangle. Something hidden—

And there it is.

"Tricky bastard," I whisper. "Almost got me, didn't you?"

"Kennedy?" Connolly says.

I turn to them. "There's a hidden curse. Like a grenade. If I tried to uncurse the outer one, I'd have triggered a bigger curse."

"Then leave it," Ani says. "I don't want you getting hurt, and this has nothing to do with Hope."

"We don't know that. I'll be careful, but I want a closer look."

Her mouth opens to argue, but a glance from Jonathan stops her. I tune that out and return to the curse. Ani's right—this almost certainly has nothing to do with Hope or the necklace. In speculating otherwise, I'm defending simple curiosity. But I can't help it. This curse gets more interesting by the second, and it's not as if we're under a time crunch.

I nudge back those golden threads from the hard wire below. Then I start in on that one, urging it to play its own tune. The outer jinx drowns it out. Like a two-person pickpocket team, one distracting my attention while the other lifts my wallet.

No matter how hard I focus, I can't tease out that second melody. I ask Ani to try, and she does, but she isn't able to even see the hidden curse.

"I'm no good at jinxes," she says. "I can pick up the cat-hair one, but that's it."

There's only one thing to do, then. And I do it fast before anyone can stop me. Whip off a glove and touch the caddy barehanded. Both Ani and Connolly surge forward, but it's too late. My fingers are pressed skin to wood.

The threads dazzle now, the music crystal clear. When I push past the outer jinx, the inner curse starts a whispering song.

"Oh," I murmur. "You cheeky little devil."

I ignore the shifting of the others behind me, their movements betraying their impatience. This is a song for two, a melody for my ears only, and I must give it my undivided attention. When I finally pull back, I'm grinning.

"You've solved it?" Vanessa asks.

"Nope. But I know what it is. Gambler's gambit."

Connolly frowns. "Gambler's . . ."

"Gambit. An opening chess play. Put your pawns in danger in hopes of gaining the advantage."

"I know what a gambit is. I just haven't heard of that sort of curse."

"It's related to the jinx," I say. "Kissing cousins. The gambit is much rarer because it requires serious skill. It's a weaver's game. A challenge."

His brows crease. "For the owner of the object?"

"No, it's a challenge—usually a friendly one—to another weaver. I said the inner curse was like a grenade. That's not quite accurate. The inner curse is the gambit. I have two choices. I can unweave the cat-hair jinx, and the tea caddy will be fine. Or I can gamble and try unweaving the inner curse for a bigger reward."

"Which is?" Connolly says.

I shrug. "No idea. That's the gamble."

"And if you fail?"

"Then the original jinx stays on permanently, and the inner one locks—it can't be unwoven to win the prize. The question is whether I bother trying for the gambit or just play it safe and remove the cat-hair jinx. In this case, it's not really a question at all. The curse is a minor one. I don't risk much if it stays on. So it's a friendly challenge, first to see whether I notice the gambit and then whether I can unweave it."

"It *was* a test then," Jonathan says. "Someone else, presumably interested in the necklace, was testing your skill."

"Meaning it's pointless now, isn't it?" Ani says. "Interesting, and I'm intrigued myself, but we're far past the point of caring who else wanted the necklace. We just need to uncurse it."

"I'm going to work on this," I say. "You guys can go discuss the plan for tonight."

"Is there a plan?" Jonathan says. "Besides trying to uncurse the necklace? I don't see that there's much else to strategize about. Havoc put the necklace on Hope, but she's not going to leave it there. If she did, we'd try to take Hope and run. She'll keep them separate. Rescue Hope, and she'll be stuck with the curse. Even then, I don't think there's much point fleeing with Hope. Havoc isn't going to keep her if you fail to uncurse the necklace."

"Is that what we expect?" Ani says, glancing at Marius and Vanessa. "If we fail with the necklace, she'll turn over Hope and . . ." A look Connolly's way.

"Rian," he says. "Havoc doesn't seem to be threatening to kill them if we fail. But I'm not sure she's thought that one through."

"She hasn't thought anything through," Vanessa says. "That's the problem dealing with Havoc. She's making this up as she goes."

"Presumably," Marius says, "if you can't uncurse the necklace, she'll return your siblings, but Hope will stay cursed."

Vanessa shakes her head. "There will be more. She'll realize she hasn't thought this through and come up with another threat. But Jonathan is right. At this point, I don't see backup plans. The goal is to uncurse the necklace. That's Havoc's goal, and with Hope cursed, it's also yours. The only potential 'plan' is to be prepared for an unweaving."

"I'm prepared," I say. "Well, as much as I can be. I could use some sleep. And I'll want to ask more questions about the necklace. But right now, I'd like to work on this. It'll help me as much as anything."

"A distraction," Vanessa says. "All right, then. We'll leave you to it so we aren't hanging over your shoulder."

"I'd like to stay," Connolly says. "If that's all right. I'll be quiet."

Ani starts to say she'll stay, too, but I shake my head.

"It isn't dangerous," I say. "And I know you think I'm wasting my time. I can focus better if you're doing something *you* feel is helpful."

She hesitates and then nods, and a few moments later, they're gone, leaving me with Connolly and the curse.

CHAPTER FORTY-ONE

CONNOLLY and I are alone in the room with the tea caddy. Once everyone's gone, he says, "I can leave if it will bother you, but I think it's best if someone's here. For your protection."

"It really is fine," I say. "Either way. You can stay, but please don't feel obligated."

"I don't."

"All right," I say. "Then I'll put you to use. Distract me."

His brows rise.

"Clear my head," I say. "The curse is still ping-ponging around in there, and I'd like to reexamine it with an open mind."

He nods. "Right. Well, I . . ."

He looks around, clearly searching for a topic of conversation. When his gaze goes to the window, the dark cloud of weather-related commentary threatens, and I jump into the gap.

"Have you spoken to your parents?" I say.

"You mean telling them that I rescued my brother . . . and lost him again three hours later? Yes, I did."

"You didn't lose him. He was kidnapped."

"I rescued him from a kidnapping, only to have him kidnapped by someone else? Ah, yes, *that's* better."

"Rian isn't a child, Connolly. He's an adult. A responsible—well, an adult anyway. He's what, my age?"

"Twenty-four."

"An adult, who did not want to be stashed in a hotel room, and you respected that. Ultimately, the only person responsible for Rian being kidnapped is the person who kidnapped him. If your parents don't see that, then I hope you've reminded them that they didn't even tell you he'd been kidnapped in the first place. Did they explain themselves?"

"Their explanation is that they were handling it as they saw fit, and as my parents, they don't need to explain themselves."

"Seriously? *That's* what they're going with? 'Because we're the parents, that's why.'"

"This isn't helping you clear your mind and relax, is it?"

"I don't need the relaxing part. Just the mental palate cleanser. This did it. Thank you." I give myself a shake. Then I look at him. "How are you doing? Not about your parents—that's none of my business. Otherwise, though?"

"Angry with myself for not insisting Rian go to that hotel. But, as you say, he's an adult. I just . . ." He shrugs. "I didn't push because he made me feel I was being unreasonable."

"Just don't say 'I told you so' when you see him again. As the reckless younger sister of an uber-responsible sibling, I can guarantee he's already feeling the sting of that. Just like he felt the sting of you rescuing him."

Connolly nods. "I'll remember that. And how are *you* doing?"

"Feeling like an idiot for being in the same *house* as Hope while she was being re-kidnapped."

"Marius wasn't on our radar as a suspect." He pauses. "I haven't asked you how you're doing with that. Being here. If it bothers you, we'll leave."

"It bothers me that it doesn't bother me as much as it should if that makes sense. I liked him. I'm furious, and I still need to sort out what I feel, but for now, it's like I'm stuck at 'I like him.' Which is uncomfortable."

"Uncomfortable but useful. He regrets what he did, and he's committed to helping us. I've only had minimal contact with him before this, but yes, he was on my short list of people I wanted to cultivate. Now that I know what he's capable of?" He shrugs. "I'm uncomfortable with it, and at the same time, recognize that my discomfort may mean I'm not cut out to play on this level. When he called me a sanctimonious prick, I was more offended at the sanctimonious part. But he's not wrong."

"One, that wasn't really Marius. It was Marius channeling Hector. Two, there's nothing wrong with having a higher ethical standard. At least, not in my book. Not in Marius's books, either, I'll bet. Hector would be another matter. But it helps if we can still work with Marius right now."

"Your sister seems all right with it. At least for now. As a matter of practicality."

"Ani is always practical." I look back at the tea caddy. "Okay, I've had my mental break. I need to get to this before Ani bursts in to remind me that this is a wholly *impractical* way to spend my time."

"It might not be."

I smile at him. "Thank you. I'll put a time limit on it, though. One hour to solve this puzzle. Now, do you want to passively observe or would you like the chatty-Kennedy running monologue?"

"I would definitely take the monologue if you don't mind."

"Not at all."

———

IT'S BEEN FORTY-FIVE MINUTES, and I can hear the mental timer running down. At first, it was fun, prodding at the gambit while explaining the process to Connolly. I've uncursed objects with my family, of course, but that's like making a cake with fellow bakers—you don't talk about it; you just do it. So sharing it with an interested observer is kind of awesome. It grew steadily less awesome when I couldn't wow him by solving the damned puzzle.

It *is* a puzzle. At least a riddle. Not solving it takes this from a fun shared—and show-off-y—encounter to potentially ego-shattering humiliation. Like the time I invited all my friends to my softball playoffs . . . and got benched for goofing off.

The curse on Connolly's mirror was a standard one. We have hundreds, like bakers and their books of recipes. But a true weaver can go beyond the book and create her own. That's what the tea caddy jinx is—there's obviously no "standard" curse for putting pet hair in hot drinks. The curse itself, though, is straightforward and unambiguous.

The gambit is different. Oh, it happily held up its name tag. *Hello, I'm Gambler's Gambit!* But that was just the introduction. Now I need the actual gambit—the riddle to unlock the prize. That isn't so easy.

First, it's in ancient Greek. Naturally. I say *naturally* with a generous dose of sarcasm. Yes, that's the language used to curse the Necklace of Harmonia, but considering the time period, it was the equivalent of me weaving a curse in modern English. This, though, is a modern curse in ancient Greek, which is the equivalent of doing a sermon in Latin. It's unnecessarily elitist—saying that if you lack a certain background or education, you don't deserve to understand it. Pure theatrics, and while I know curse weavers who still use it, I totally reverse-snob them by writing *them* off as pretentious hacks.

So I'm a little disappointed to discover that this master of the craft went for ancient Greek. In this case, though, I'll grant them an exception and say it's probably intended as part of the puzzle.

Yet even knowing ancient Greek, I still can't solve it.

In English, the gambit isn't nearly as pretty and poetic as in its native tongue, but it roughly translates to:

My second secret is for the wise drunkard, who treats his morning-after woes with the enemy of my first. Return what I've lost, and all shall be won.

"You're quite certain of the translation?" Connolly says.

My narrow-eyed look answers for me.

His reply is drowned out by Ellie, who has been meowing at the door for the last ten minutes. Meowing, I should point out, on both sides of it. When she started, we let her in . . . and she promptly meowed from our side, wanting out. Let her out . . . and she wants back in. The issue, of course, is the closed door, which is an affront to all feline sensibilities.

I stomp over and open it a few inches. "There. Is that better?"

She looks from me to the door and sniffs, as if to say I'm really no fun at all.

I return to Connolly. "Yes, I know the curse doesn't make sense. I get the part about the wise drunk. The weaver is referring to a hangover cure. But 'with the enemy of my first' seems like a mistranslation. It's not. I'm sure of that. First *what*, though? First secret? The wise drunkard treats his hangover with the enemy of my first secret?"

Ellie hops up on the table and eyes the tea caddy.

"This is why that door was shut," I say as I go to scoop her off. Then I stop. "The first secret. The jinx. The tea caddy puts cat hair in tea. What's one supposed cure for hangovers? The hair of the dog that bit you. The cat being the enemy of the dog."

"Okay . . ."

"So the second secret is for the wise drunkard, who treats his hangover with the hair of the dog that bit him."

"Okay . . ."

"Obviously, we solve the riddle with booze. Just douse the caddy in cheap vodka and set it on fire."

His brows shoot up.

I sigh. "Really, Connolly? I'm kidding. Though at this point, turning this thing into a big ole bonfire is mighty tempting. As for what the riddle means, the answer, I believe, is 'not a damn thing.' It's misdirection. Like those stupid math problems your friends share on social media where you spend ten minutes dutifully calculating the answer, only to discover it's a trick question."

His blank look tells me his friends don't do that. Or, more likely, he doesn't spend nearly as much time social-media surfing as I do.

"It's a trick question," I say. "Misdirection. Which I fell for. It's the second line that counts. *Return what I've lost, and all shall be won.*"

I walk to Connolly and bend to Ellie, who's rubbing against his pant legs, her purr getting louder the longer she's ignored. I nudge her aside, retrieve my prize from his trouser cuffs and stand, waving it. As he frowns, I walk back to the caddy, open the top and dangle the cat hair over it.

"Return what I've lost," I say. "Yes?"

His eyes light up. "Ah. Yes."

"Feel free to tell me I'm wrong," I say. "I only get one shot at this."

"No, you are correct. The caddy gives out cat hair. That's what it loses. Put it back in and 'all shall be won'—you'll earn the prize."

"Okay. Let's do this, then." I take a deep breath and carefully place the cat hair in the tea caddy.

It shimmers, and I blink. "Um, Aiden? Am I hallucinating?"

He comes over, looks inside. "Not if you're seeing that hair turn into some kind of worm."

The wormlike hair shoots to the corner of the box and then wriggles into the crack. It disappears, and there's a pop, and the bottom springs open.

"We did check for a false bottom, right?" I say.

"We did, but apparently, our tools don't detect magical trapdoors."

He reaches in and lifts the false bottom. There's no compartment under it. Just the actual bottom, with a folded piece of paper.

He takes out the note. When he starts to unfold it, I grab his hand.

"That's locked," I say.

His brows rise.

"It's letterlocked," I say. "See the way it's folded? A very old form of encryption. If you unfold it wrong, you risk destroying the contents."

He frowns. "Destroying the letter by unfolding it?"

I wave off his incredulity while taking the letter. "Just trust me. Call the others in here. I'm going to need Jonathan's help."

CHAPTER FORTY-TWO

I LEARNED about letterlocking as a kid. One of those bits of trivia that history buffs stumble over and then dive down the rabbit hole. Twelve-year-old me had been fascinated by the idea of protecting a written letter with something even cooler than invisible ink. Hell, forget twelve-year-old me. Twenty-five-year-old me still thinks it's awesome.

I'd originally studied letterlocking to keep Hope from reading my notes to Jimmy Woo, who lived down the road. There'd been nothing in those notes that I wouldn't have sent a female friend, but Hope was absolutely convinced otherwise. She was seven, and I was twelve, and with that came all the "Kennedy and Jimmy sitting in a tree" chants a younger sibling can sing. While she claimed she wanted to read my notes for "proof," I think my romance-loving sis was just hopeful.

So I locked down my letters with actual letter locks. It's an old way of cutting and folding correspondence so, if it gets into the wrong hands, it'll self-destruct. Well, no, though that'd be cool. Instead, letterlocking predates envelopes. Envelopes hide letters from prying eyes. They also show if the messenger has opened it, by breaking the seal. Before that, you were basically handing your note to someone and trusting them not to read it and, sorry, but here's where my curiosity would win over my ethics every time.

A simple letter lock is just a way of folding and then sealing the letter to keep it from being easily read. But there's another level, one where the adhesive and the folds are done in such a way that tearing the letter open will damage the contents. The most difficult —and most secure—method is the dagger-trap. That's what's on this one.

I need Jonathan because, back in my letter-locking days, he'd been my accomplice. We share a fascination for this kind of arcana, and so when I'd wanted to learn more and practice, I'd gone to him for help. Even at fourteen, he'd been a budding researcher.

Now when I bring the others in, Jonathan has only to look at the folded sheet to smile.

"Is that a dagger-trap?" he says.

"Seems so. Take a look."

Ani nods. "That's one of those things you and Jonathan used to play with as kids."

"Kennedy was a kid," he says. "I was a responsible young adult helping a child with a valid research project."

"She was sending love notes to one of the neighbor boys."

"Not love notes," I say. "That was the point. Hope wouldn't believe they were just regular letters, so she kept intercepting them."

Connolly frowns. "Why not just text each other?"

"We were twelve."

To his blank look, I say, "You totally had a cell phone by twelve, didn't you? And your own laptop, tablet, Xbox . . ."

"No Xbox. My parents didn't believe in video games. But we needed the other devices for school. They were part of the supply list."

"Yeah, the rest of us had pencils and colored markers on our supply list, Connolly. And while Jimmy and I could have e-mailed, the letters were retro-fun."

"Retro," Vanessa murmurs. "To describe a method of communication that only faded in the past decade."

"Would you prefer antique? Outdated? Quaintly old-fashioned?" I lift the letter. "Hey, you guys were around when people did stuff like this, right?"

"We were around when they were writing on stone tablets," Marius says.

"He's joking," Vanessa cuts in.

"Uh, no, people were—"

"Fine. They did still occasionally write important decrees and such on stone."

"Wait!" I say. "The Rosetta stone. That's a decree. You could have translated it, right?"

"Sure," Marius says. "I remember when they first found it. Athene wrote to Napoleon, offering to translate. She never heard back. So she got hold of one of the etchings and actually sent the full translation—ancient Greek, Demotic and hieroglyphs—to the British Museum. Someone there sent her a reply, basically suggesting she stick to needlework and music and find herself a good husband. That went over well."

Vanessa snorts. "It doesn't help that she used her actual name. Not many girls in Georgian England named Athene."

"Yes," Marius says. "The rest of us have modernized our names, sometimes more than once. Athene insists on sticking to hers. Though, in her defense, it's not as uncommon as it once was."

"If she'd used a *male* name, she might have gotten a better response from the museum," Vanessa says. "That's what I suggested. But no, it had to be a woman's name so she could make a point."

"My sister likes to make points," Marius says. "Mostly so she has the right to fume and rage about it for the next few centuries. If you ever meet her, just casually mention the Rosetta stone. It's kinda fun. As for that letter lock, yes, I used them, back when I ran a network of spies for . . ." He waves a hand. "That hardly matters. The point is that, yes, I'm familiar with these."

"And perhaps familiar with the person who sent this one?" Connolly says.

Marius and Vanessa exchange a look.

"You already have your suspicions, don't you?" I say. "From the gambler's gambit."

"We . . . may know who sent it," Marius says. "And, yes, the letter lock seems to confirm that suspicion, but we are"—another look to Vanessa—"not at liberty to say more. I could open that for you, but I believe you're supposed to do it."

"Part of the test."

"Yes. If it is who we suspect, they will want you solving that yourself, and we shouldn't interfere."

"Well, then, let's get to it," I say. "I'm going to guess that the *test* is the fact that I recognized what it is and know how to get the information needed to open it. An open-book quiz. Since I doubt, other than you, Marius, no one alive today has memorized the steps to opening these."

"Even I would need help," he says. "So, yes, feel free to look it up."

I do, and Jonathan and I set about opening it with Ani reading instructions. It really is mostly a matter of knowing what this is and how to avoid triggering anything that'll damage the note. Well, damage key parts of it, that is. Like I said, it's not as if the paper will burst into flame. Or so I hope.

Opening a dagger-trapped letter is much easier than creating one. The letter has been pleated and then secured at multiple levels with "daggers" cut from the page itself and threaded through the paper and then sealed with wax. Once folded, it's further locked with thin wire also threaded through the letter. One hasty pull and the wax will tear the words from the page.

When I'm finally done, I unfold the page.

"Is that . . . ?" Connolly begins as I smooth the paper. "A greeting card?"

It is. Not the sort you buy in a store, but the sort I vaguely recall from my childhood, where you'd create it online, print it, fold it and then send it snail mail, saving yourself from the outrageous racket that is the greeting-card industry. It looks quaint and cheap now, especially when produced on a monochrome printer. But it is definitely a card.

"Congratulations to a fan-tab-ulous granddaughter on her graduation day!" I read. There's a picture of a teenage girl reclining on pillows, texting with her friends, earbud wires snaking from her ears. It's exactly the sort of cringey card one might get from a grandparent who proves just how out of touch they are by trying to prove they aren't.

I open the card.

"Greetings from the first planet from the sun," I read. "Best of luck with your college application. Live long and prosper." I pause. "There's a phone number, too." I close the card, look at it and then open it and reread it to myself.

"I'm going to refrain from saying I don't get it," I murmur.

"Well, I'll say it then," Ani says. "Either that's meant for someone else, or it's a joke."

"Kind of a joke, I think?" I say. "But one for me. Someone gave me the tea caddy. Opening it could be a kind of 'graduation.' I passed the test. The phone number must be a method of contact. As for live long and prosper, it sounds familiar . . ."

"Star Trek," Marius and Jonathan say in unison. At a nod from Marius, Jonathan continues. "It's from the original series. Spock's catchphrase." He puts out a hand, separating his fingers between the third and fourth. "Live long and prosper."

"Right!" I say. "We watched the movies. Okay, so we have a *Star Trek* reference plus a planetary one. There must be a link. The first planet from the sun is Mercury. Does Mercury play any role in science fiction? It's usually Mars." I smile and glance at Marius. "You get all the Martians . . ." I stop.

"Planets," I say. "Mars. Venus. Mercury. The god Mercury. Hermes. Trickster of the Olympian Pantheon. Greetings from the first planet from the sun. Greetings from Mercury."

CHAPTER FORTY-THREE

I LOOK at Vanessa and Marius. "That was your guess, right? It's from Marius's brother, Mercury."

Marius's mouth opens, and I see denial coming. "Okay, not your brother, but still Mercury."

"Still Mercury, yes. Not my brother, but my sibling."

"Oh. Mercury is your *sister*."

"She calls herself my sister and uses feminine pronouns, but she is what we would have called androgynous. Today, gender fluid is the more correct term."

Jonathan nods. "Most trickster gods are said to have the power of shapeshifting, and they're often gender fluid."

"That's Mercy," Marius says. "Always has been. And yes, we suspected the tea caddy was from her."

"Is there any connection to the necklace?" I say. "Is Mercy a potential buyer?"

"Not a buyer. As for a connection, yes. The curse is Mercy's work."

"The curse on the tea . . ." I glance up sharply. "Wait, you mean Mercury cursed the Necklace of Harmonia?"

"She says—" Vanessa begins.

"Yes," Marius says. "The simple answer—the only one that matters—is yes. Mercy wove the curse for Hector."

"May I speak?" Vanessa says. "Or are you going to interrupt me again?"

Marius shifts. "I just . . ."

"You don't want to make excuses for her. Don't want to listen to her excuses, of which she has many. But in this case, I think it's important." She looks at me. "Mercy says Hector claimed the necklace was for me. A punishment for my infidelity. Mercy owed him a debt, so she couldn't refuse. She tried to trick him by weaving a curse that wouldn't affect me. Except it wasn't for me. It was for Harmonia. So I don't blame Mercy. I blame Hector."

"Either way," Ani says. "Mercury can unweave it."

"No," Vanessa says. "It was woven in payment of a debt. To unweave it reneges on the debt. I don't know if that applies to curse weavers in general, but it does with Mercy. Hector is her brother. She owed him a debt. He demanded the curse, and so she could not refuse nor can she unweave it."

"Mercy *is* a curse weaver, though," I say. I tap the front of the card, where it says granddaughter. "That's what this means. Not actual granddaughter, but there wasn't room for the hundred *greats* before granddaughter."

"It isn't that distant a relationship," Vanessa says. "A few greats, perhaps."

Ani shakes her head. "My mother's family has been curse weavers for centuries."

"They've *claimed* to be curse weavers," Vanessa says. "And perhaps they were, from another source. We aren't the only immortals in the world. Either way, your family isn't originally from Mercy's bloodline. She wondered what would happen if she inserted herself in there, either bolstering an existing ability or giving that ability to those who already claimed it. Go back a few generations in your history and you'll likely find a great-great-grandmother who mysteriously vanished after giving her husband a few kids. Those children were likely the ones who truly cemented the Bennett name as curse weavers."

"So we're not descended from the *arae*?"

"The *arae* are an obscure bit of lore arising from some of Mercy's antics. That's the way mortals deal with the unknown. They make up stories. Immortals with magical powers become gods. Humans with magical powers are said to be descended from ancient races or minor gods because I suppose saying they were descended from *actual* gods seemed like hubris."

"Except gods aren't actually gods," Marius says. "So no real hubris there. Mortals with powers are descended from immortals with powers."

I nod. "Curse weavers—Greco-Roman ones at least—come from Mercury."

"And Fortuna?" Connolly asks, almost hesitantly. "She was a god. She's an immortal?"

"There is no Fortuna," Vanessa says. "No one I've ever met. Though there is a race of luck workers in Ireland. Little people who grant wishes and find pots of gold. I believe you're descended from —" She breaks off with a laugh. "Seeing your expression, I can't even finish that. I figured out what Kennedy was teasing you about and couldn't resist. Although Athene has long speculated that part of the leprechaun lore arises from red-haired luck workers, descended from your actual progenitor."

"Which would be me," Marius says.

"You?" Connolly says.

Marius quirks a smile. "Yes, sorry. I'm sure this Fortuna, whomever she might be, would have been much cooler."

"No. That's just . . . It's unexpected. That's all." Connolly pauses. "Havoc did mention about battle luck."

Marius makes a face. "Yes, that's an old and tired jab. One of Hector's, originally. Battles are won through skill and luck. Skill is strategy. Athene is our family scholar—and damned fine with a sword—so she became the god of battle strategy. That left me as god of brute strength and dumb luck. My power actually *is* luck so . . ." He shrugs.

"No one wins a battle by luck alone," Vanessa says. "It requires careful and planned use of that luck. That's Marius's specialty. Strategic luck."

Marius smiles at her. "From what I gather, Aiden is well versed in the strategic use of luck, so while I appreciate the defense of my honor, I trust he doesn't need it. So yes, Aiden, you get your luck from me, through both sides of your family." He pauses. "And if that sounds vaguely incestuous, remember how many generations you're dealing with. Go back far enough, and any two people likely have common ancestors. The Connollys have actively sought out fellow luck workers—both descended from me and others—as marriage partners. That's strengthened your innate talent."

"Havoc said something about your favorite progeny," I say.

Marius looks uncomfortable. "We all have . . . families of descendants we pay more close attention to. Ones who have accomplished things that bring them to our attention, and it is, if this doesn't sound too odd, like having a favorite sport team. We follow your progress with interest."

"Is that why Havoc took an interest in Rian?" I say. "Why she double-crossed him? To piss you off?"

"Most likely. However, when Hector demanded him as debt payment—also to needle me, no doubt—she handed him over because by then she had her eye on a bigger prize."

"The necklace."

He nods.

So the Connollys are favorites of yours, and the Bennetts are favorites of Mercy's?"

"They are."

"Does that make us special?" I say. "Please tell me it makes us special."

"I believe it does," Vanessa says.

"Yes!" I fist pump. "Suck it, Lacey Moore, in fifth grade, who told me I wasn't anything special."

"You've been holding onto that grudge a long time, haven't you?" Jonathan says.

"Only because she told me in fifth grade, sixth, seventh . . . Oh, and then when we went to high school, she told Jimmy Woo when he wanted to ask me to the freshman dance. 'Why Kennedy? She's nothing special.' Suck it, Lacey."

"Jimmy Woo?" Ani says. "The guy you just said you *weren't* sending love notes to?"

"Not when we were twelve. By fifteen, though? He was hot. I totally would have gone to the dance with him, if it wasn't for

Lacey. Well, and the fact that I was already going with someone else."

Ani shakes her head. "Moving right along."

"I'm special," I say. "Let's just savor this for a moment." I take a deep breath. "Okay, moving on."

Vanessa glances at Marius. "Definitely Mercy's child."

"That doesn't sound like a compliment," I say.

"I adore Mercy," Vanessa says. "When I don't want to throttle her."

"Sounds familiar," Ani murmurs.

"Is that why I'm the one who got this?" I say, waving at the tea caddy. "I can joke about being special, but Ani and Hope are her progeny, too."

"I don't want to speak for Mercy," Vanessa says. "But she has a soft spot for both the Bennetts and for jinxers. That is, after all, her own specialty. To our eternal dismay."

"Wait. The actual *god* of curse weaving specializes in the joker's jinx?"

"Not a god," Marius murmurs. "But yes. My sister is very fond of a good prank. Overly fond, one might say."

"*Every*one *does* say," Vanessa says.

"So for anyone who has ever mocked me for specializing in the jinx?" I say. "Suck it." I glance at Vanessa. "Wait. Hector mocked me for that . . . and he knows what his sister's specialty is."

"Yes, he does. And now that Mercy has revealed herself and I can discuss her without breaking any confidences, I can warn you to stay well away from my ex. That's a general tip for anyone, but you in particular. He has little love for most of his siblings, but Mercy is his particular nemesis."

I lift the greeting card. "Okay, all that was very illuminating, but back to the card. We've figured out most of it. I'm guessing the 'live long and prosper' is just a closing with a pop-culture twist."

"That would be typical Mercy," Vanessa says.

"Best of luck with your college application," I read. "Okay, so figuring out her gambit and letter lock means I graduated. The college admission is, I'm guessing, the necklace curse."

"She's wishing you luck?" Ani says. "How about some actual *help*."

"Can she give that?" I say. "A clue? A nudge in the right direction?"

Marius and Vanessa look at each other. Marius shrugs.

"We aren't sure," Vanessa says. "We'd ask, but with Mercy, one doesn't get a cell-phone number. She just pops up on your doorstep and stays for a month."

"We can contact her, but it's the technological equivalent of smoke signals," Marius says. "It would take days to get a response."

"You have a number there, don't you?" Connolly says.

"Duh, right." I wave the card.

I take out my phone. The line rings twice and then connects.

"You've reached the DARC Helpline. If you suspect a family member or friend is the victim of domestic abuse, we can help. Please listen to the following options—"

I hang up.

"I think I got the number wrong," I say.

I compare my outgoing call list to the number on the card. It matches. I dial again with it on speaker as Jonathan takes the card to look it over.

The same message comes on. I listen through to the list of options, which are exactly what I'd expect. Then I hang up.

"Wait," Connolly says. "Try pressing the option to speak to someone. Ask for Mercy. It must be a fake answering service. In poor taste, but . . ."

Vanessa shakes her head. "Mercy wouldn't do that. She might love her pranks, but she would never fake a domestic violence hotline."

"It's real," Jonathan says, holding up his phone. "I reverse searched using the number. It brings up the Domestic Abuse Resource Center. That line is specifically for friends and relatives of victims."

I shake my head. "There must be a typo on the card. Or the number was changed. Or . . ." I shrug. "I got nothing. Anyone else?"

No one has any other ideas. While I'd hate to think I've missed a chance to connect with the person who wove the necklace curse, I don't see any other option.

Mercy has reached out with a test. I passed it, and ultimately, I only got a "good luck!" that suggests, if I prove myself and uncurse the necklace, I'll actually get to meet her. Nice, but, as Ani says, we'd rather have had some actual help.

"I need to balance after unweaving that," I say as I take out my eight ball.

"Is that . . . ?" Marius begins.

"A curse bomb?" Ani says. "Yes, it is. I would suggest we all clear the room while she does this."

I roll my eyes but wave them out and then set to work.

CHAPTER FORTY-FOUR

VANESSA ISN'T COMING to the uncursing . . . and she's furious about it. This isn't Havoc's demand. It's Marius's request. A strong request. They argue about it. We go outside to give them privacy, and even on the back deck, we can still hear them arguing. Or we hear Vanessa. She pauses every now and then, presumably when he has something to say, but we don't hear it.

In the myths, Mars and Ares are depicted as one might expect of the god of war. As Marius pointed out, his aspect of war is brute strength, the strategy belonging to Athene. The Greeks valued strategy and therefore valued her more, with Ares characterized as either a thick-headed brute or a quick-tempered braggart. In the Iliad, he switches sides like a hyperactive child until Athene gets so fed up that she sics a hero on him. Injured, Ares cries and runs home to Zeus, who is thoroughly disgusted. I'm really going to need to ask Marius what he did to piss off Homer.

The truth is much different. I might seem like the last person who should judge, considering I didn't even put him on the list of suspects for my sister's kidnapping. But having spent more time with him, I realize he's very capable of that. It was a chess move, deliberate and considered. What I can't imagine is him blustering or raging, and certainly not fleeing a battlefield to run to Daddy. There are aspects of Marius where I see Connolly as I suspect Vanessa did. Oh, on the surface, they seem very different. Connolly is, as others have pointed out, a wee bit uptight. Marius exudes chill. What they share, though, is an innate steadiness.

That doesn't seem like a sexy quality. Steady, stable, centered . . . terms better used for a good horse than a good man. It's something I lack, though. My first-grade report card said the teacher "appreciated the mercurial energy" I brought to class. Ironic, now that I can claim Mercury as an ancestor. I appreciate steadiness, though. Unflappability. That's what Connolly has been. Unflappable in the face of all this. People like that are usually compared to rocks: *He's my rock, my anchor.* Yet rocks don't move. They are inertia embodied. Connolly and Marius are more like water. Moving steadily forward, calm and relentless.

In the end, it's not Vanessa's volcanic fury that wins this argument. Her flame is doused by Marius's water. She rages and argues; he listens and reasons. Ultimately, she stays behind of her own volition, however reluctantly.

We're preparing to leave when Vanessa takes me aside. The others are all busy, and no one notices us slip off for a walk around the grounds.

The dogs are roaming, and Vanessa introduces them. They're mastiffs, not surprising given the age and origin of the breed—Caesar took an early form of mastiff when he invaded Britain. These two are as big as ponies and as well trained as dogs that size need to be. Vanessa introduces me in Greek, which I presume tells them I'm not to be rent limb from limb. They sniff me. I pat them—after receiving the necessary permission—and then off they go, gamboling like puppies across the acres of lawn.

"I'm very uncomfortable with what I'm about to ask you," Vanessa says. "It's unfair, presuming on too short an acquaintance. I don't dare ask Aiden because it could put him at odds with you, which is unfair to you both. I'm asking you because I have seen how strong your bond with your sisters is, and so I know you would never place any obligation to me over their safety."

"True. Sorry."

"Don't be. That's as it should be. I don't want to deal with anyone who'd value a 'god' above their family. People show their true selves when my favor is the prize. It isn't about me. It's about what they can get from me."

We arrive at the stables. The horses are out, a gorgeous trio who all trot over to bask in Vanessa's affection, and as she pats them, her face glows. They are genuinely pleased to see her. Yes, hoping for a pat or a treat but, like the dogs, happy just to say hello. More than she can say for most people, I realize.

She continues as she strokes the nose of a roan mare. "Marius is right that I shouldn't be at the uncursing. My powers are of no help, and my presence will only make Havoc worse. I am the usurper of Marius's affections."

"Her father's affections."

She pauses and then says, "That's where I'd like you to forget what you know. Forget she is his daughter. That's the problem. Marius and I have always been doting parents. It doesn't matter whether we're a child's biological parents or not—we have shaped ourselves into a family for them. We adore our brood, even when they exasperate us or disappoint us. When they go astray, we blame ourselves. We've clearly failed. Even if we logically know that isn't the case—that a child received as much of our love and attention as the others—in our hearts, we feel failure."

"That's the case with Havoc."

She nods. "I wonder what I could have done differently. So does Marius. We can each see that the other did nothing wrong. We can say so with vehemence and frustration. It doesn't matter. There is something wrong with Havoc. Fundamentally wrong and unfixable. Marius finally acknowledged that when he nudged her from the nest, and this is his punishment. He wants that necklace, and she will keep it from him because he wants it for me. When you go to that uncursing, she will torment him. Taunt him. And she will bargain. Here is where I need your help."

I say nothing, just pat one of the horses as I listen.

"I don't need that necklace back," she says. "I would love to destroy it but not at the expense of saddling Marius with Havoc again. That is what she'll demand. Give her back her job. Let her live here, above the stables, again. I'm asking you to forestall that negotiation.

Insist on the unweaving first. Then, once the curse is off and your sister is free, tell Marius that I said the uncursing was enough. I don't care where the necklace ends up as long as it doesn't hurt anyone else. He'll still want to destroy it—as a symbolic gesture—but I don't need that."

"Just get it uncursed," I say.

"Yes, and do whatever you can to keep him from making a deal he'll regret. If your sister's life is somehow at stake—or Connolly's brother's—then you must protect them, naturally, but be aware that negotiation is her true goal. Thwart her if you can. Would you do that for me?"

"Make sure the bitch who cursed my sister doesn't get what she wants?" I smile. "Happily."

———

HAVOC GIVES US AN ADDRESS . . . and when we reach it, she gives us another one. Then another, bringing us steadily closer to her actual location.

"Is this supposed to be a security measure?" I say. "Avoid giving us the location so we can't bring reinforcements? Or arrive and ambush her early?"

Marius—who has been grumbling since the first redirection—makes a noise suspiciously like a growl. "It's needless complication, that's what it is. She could easily select a location where we can't sneak up. As for bringing reinforcements, it only requires a text and GPS coordinates once we arrive."

"Didn't Vanessa say Havoc was your head of security?"

"She carries out orders very well. Strategy is not her strong suit."

"Unless the goal is chaos. Pissing you off while living up to her name."

More grumbling. We reach the location. We've brought two cars —Marius and I are in Connolly's while Ani went with Jonathan in his. Marius had an SUV big enough to take us all, but we want our own vehicles in case we need to make a getaway.

When Marius sees the final location, he's slightly mollified. She's chosen a farmhouse surrounded by fields. An adequate strategic choice. We'd be thwarted if we'd planned any kind of onslaught, but we haven't, so this is fine.

Havoc—flanked by two guards—meets us in the driveway.

"Who's that?" Havoc says, gesturing at Jonathan.

"Our librarian," I say.

She gives me a sour look. "Does this really seem like the time for jokes?"

"Ever seen *Buffy*? Jonathan is our Giles. Velma, if you prefer *Scooby-Doo*. The research guy. Every magical-crime-busting gang needs one."

Her eyes narrow. "I don't care who he is. He isn't invited."

"Maybe not, but he's here to help. You do want that necklace uncursed. That isn't just a ruse to get something you really want, right?"

"Kennedy is correct," Marius cuts in. "Jonathan provides valuable resources, and they need all the support they can get to uncurse this necklace. Ask to see his ID. Run a background check. Pat him down. Wand him. Do whatever you need to assure yourself he isn't a threat."

"Threat?" She sniffs. "He's mortal. I can smell him rotting just like the rest of them." She turns to her guards. "Search them. Confiscate their phones. Bring them inside."

———

I WALK through that door behind Ani, who then tugs me up beside her, looping her arm through mine. Connolly's straining to see into the house, just like Ani. Looking for our siblings, listening for their voices. All is quiet, though.

The guards lead us into a large room. The living room, I'd presume, but the house has been stripped of all furniture, and it's just a big and empty room with boarded-up windows. One door is also boarded, the wood so fresh I can smell it. Removing all possible exits except the entrance, which the guards promptly flank.

We walk in and—

Marius stops so abruptly his shoes squeak. He turns on Havoc. "What the hell is he doing here?"

I know who it is without looking. Hector stands in the corner, leaning against the wall, a cane in one hand. He has the same expression of bored annoyance he wore to the museum gala, but as his gaze shoots toward the door, there's a malicious gleam in his eye. That gleam fades when Havoc's guards shut the door behind us.

"She's not here," Marius says.

There's a pinprick of disappointment before Hector finds his sneer. "So that's what you get for your grand gesture? You try to win the necklace so you can present it at the feet of your goddess, only to have her kick you in the face." He snorts. "You don't give up, do you? You'll never see her for the ungrateful bitch she is."

Marius stiffens at the *ungrateful bitch* part, but it's only a flash of anger before he finds his calm and a winsome smile.

"Nah," he says. "Yes, that was my plan, and Vess isn't thrilled that I kidnapped the Bennett girl to do it, but she knows my heart is in the right place. Relationships aren't about putting the other person on a pedestal . . . or in a pretty cage. They're about making an effort to understand what the other needs and providing it where possible. Whatever mistakes I make, Vess always knows where she stands with me, and I know where I stand with her. Venus and Mars, planets that sometimes have the entire earth between them, but are always within each other's sight." He glances at Hector. "Then there are those who aren't even in the same solar system."

Hector's face darkens. Havoc walks between them. "And as much fun as it is to watch you two spar, today there's a new pretty bauble for you to fight over."

Havoc takes a pouch from her jacket's inside pocket, and she slides the necklace out onto one gloved hand. "Shall I start the bidding at one million? I know you can both afford it." She turns to Marius. "Unless you'd like to offer something other than money. I hear there's an opening in your company. I always liked Carson's job better than my old one."

Damn, that didn't take long.

"Whoa, what?" I say. "An auction? I thought we were here for an unweaving."

"First, the auction. Then the unweaving . . . if Marius wins it. Hector likes the necklace just the way it is."

"No, no, no," I say. "You've cursed my sister. You did that so we'd be forced to fix the necklace for you."

Havoc hesitates. Marius and Vanessa were right. Havoc acts without thinking through her strategy. She put the necklace on Hope for extra drama. Then she realized how much more fun she could have pitting her father and uncle against each other.

"Kennedy is correct," Connolly says. "According to the video, you cursed Hope as an incentive for the Bennett sisters to provide the unweaving. I presume Hector won't want the necklace if the curse is removed."

"That presumes they *can* uncurse it," Havoc says as she recovers. "Which I very much doubt. Fine, the auction is for the final product. Marius? Just remember that the girl's situation is your fault. You kidnapped her. Perhaps you want to consider offering me Carson's job? I—"

"Hector?" I cut in. "You've been set up. You see that, right? You're only here to put the screws to Marius. Now you're being asked to bid on the necklace, not knowing what condition it'll be in a few hours from now. Havoc expects you to pay the same price for it, cursed or uncursed. Is that what you signed up for?"

"There's an easy fix," Connolly says. "The necklace should be auctioned off after the Bennetts attempt to remove the curse. That way, all parties understand what they are getting."

"I'll bid afterward," Hector says. "I want to know what I'm getting. These children aren't going to be able to uncurse it, but it'll be fun to watch them try."

That's settled, then. Havoc doesn't see the trap I've set. If we do uncurse the necklace, then Hope is free. I can tell Marius what Vanessa said—that she only needs the curse removed. Marius won't need to bargain with Havoc to get the necklace itself.

"Now bring out our sister," Ani says. "We'll need her help."

"She's already seen it," Havoc says. "It's beyond her skill level."

"What?" I say. "No, the deal was that we'd all try—"

"And she has."

"That may be," Connolly says. "But my brother's luck weaving could also help—"

"Nope. You've got the best luck weaver of all there." Havoc nods at Marius. "You don't need your brother. And you girls don't need your sister—unweaving isn't a group effort. Your siblings stay hidden until you've done this."

Which is ridiculous. Hope has been cursed—we aren't going to grab her and run. This is the problem dealing with irrational people. You can't reason with them. We try. We all try, even Marius, until Hector finally says, "How about I just buy that damned necklace and skip the bullshit? You're walking on thin ice with me already, Havoc, and that's a dangerous place to be."

"Fine," she says, turning to us. "Is that what you want? I sell the necklace to Hector? Leave your poor sister cursed forever? Because you can be damned sure he isn't ever going to uncurse it."

This isn't right. It's not right at all, and I don't know whether we're being tricked or Havoc is just throwing her weight around.

Push harder, though, and Havoc will do what it seems Havoc does best. Make rash and reckless decisions. She'll forget her ultimate goal—getting back to her father's side—and just sell Hector the necklace to punish Marius out of pure spite.

Ani asks Havoc for a table, and she's nice enough about it that Havoc sends a guard to fetch one. What he finds looks like the sort of thing homeowners leave behind when they move—a rickety occasional table. Ani has a piece of velvet in her kit to set the necklace on, my sister being so much more particular about these things than I am. With our gloves in place, we arrange the necklace on the cloth and prepare to begin.

CHAPTER FORTY-FIVE

I'D ADMIRED the copy of the necklace at the gala. I don't do the same for the real one. Yes, I can see the difference, excellent workmanship raised to grand-master level. But the craftsman is the asshole sneering at us from across the room.

This necklace is ugly and twisted, a mockery of a lover's gift. All I want is to get the damned curse off it and see Hector's face when I do.

Ani and I lay out the necklace. Then we stand on either side of the table, gloved fingers on it, and we focus independently, each reading—

"Oh!" Ani says, jerking back before I've even sunk into listening mode.

"It bites, doesn't it?" Havoc says, with a smug smile. "That's what your sister said. Like the jaws of a trap snapping shut. Feel free to give up now."

Ani glares at her. "It startled me, that's all."

I motion that I'm going to move away and let Ani take the floor, undistracted. She barely notices—she's already targeted her laser-beam focus back on the necklace. I go and stand by Connolly. His hand brushes mine and then squeezes, and even that brief touch feels like a grounding wire for my sparking fear. I squeeze his hand back, and then we stand there, close enough that the backs of our hands touch.

Ani keeps at it for about ten minutes, her expression impenetrable. Finally, she steps back with a frustrated growl.

"I've never encountered anything like this," she says to me. "I can *feel* the curse there, but when I get close, it's as if someone wipes the board clean and flings chalk dust in my eyes. Poisoned chalk dust." She makes a face. "That sounds silly. I don't know how else to describe it."

I turn to Havoc. "We need to speak to Hope. It will help to know what she experienced."

"That's what she said. So I came prepared." She takes a piece of paper from her pocket. "She said to tell you that it was 'like one of Kennedy's invisible ink tricks.' She saw the curse, but then 'the words disappeared,' and she got 'some kind of psychic shock.'"

"Yes," Ani murmurs. "That's it. A psychic shock."

"She said that the person who kidnapped her—Marius—thought it was a lover's lament, but it's not. She couldn't tell what it was, but she knew it wasn't that."

"Of course it's not," Hector says to Marius. "If you thought I ever loved that bitch—"

"You didn't," Marius says, his voice soft but cutting through the room. "That was the problem."

Hector bristles and grumbles, but we've already turned our attention back to the necklace.

"My turn to take a shot," I say. "At least I know what to expect." I turn a hard look on Havoc. "Which helps."

She sniffs. "Nothing will help you, little girl. I don't know why anyone thinks it *can* be uncursed. It is the work of a master. The ultimate master."

"Mercury," I say. "We know."

She deflates a little, only to come back with, "Well, give it a try. This should be fun."

As I step forward, Connolly touches my arm. "Is there anything I can do? Bolster your luck?"

I shake my head. "At this point, luck doesn't have anything to do with it. Either I hear the curse, or I don't. I'll need the luck when I'm unweaving it."

Connolly glances at Marius, who nods, confirming.

"Is there anything I can do, then?" he says.

"Clear the room so I can focus?" I say with a half smile.

"Not a chance, girl," Hector says. "We aren't walking away so you can pull some trick."

"You mean you're not doing anything that'll make this easier for me," I shoot back.

"How about noise-canceling headphones?" Connolly says. "I have a pair in my— No, you hear curses, right? That might interfere."

"It won't. If you could get them, that would be great."

Havoc sighs but sends a guard with Connolly. He returns with a pair of headphones. I tug them in place, turn on the noise-cancel, and the room's sound deadens.

"Whoa," I say. "These are so much better than mine."

Connolly says something I can't hear. I lift one earpiece.

"I said if you pull this off, they're yours."

"I wouldn't take your headphones, Connolly. You can buy me a new pair."

His lips twitch. "Get my brother out of this, and my family will owe you far more than a pair of headphones."

"Nah, that's enough. Just headphones and your eternal gratitude."

His eyes warm as his smile grows. "It's a deal. Now hold up your end of the bargain."

"I intend to."

That's bravado, of course, but it helps, a surge of false confidence that my brain mistakes for the real thing. Headphones in place, I position the table between me and the wall with everyone else hidden behind me. When Havoc tries to get in my line of vision, Connolly motions her back. Her mouth sets, but after a look toward Marius, she steps away. I smile once for Connolly and again for Ani and Jonathan. Then I turn to the necklace and shut out the world.

Ani and Hope described seeing the curse hovering there, a mirage that vanished when they homed in on it. I get silence. Peaceful silence. I run a gloved finger over the necklace with my eyes shut, and then it comes, the barest whisper, as tantalizing as a half-heard secret.

I love the secrets of strangers. If I see girls leaning together to whisper on the bus, I turn off my music to eavesdrop. I can't help it. I'd respect their privacy if I knew them, but the secrets of strangers are delicious and, arguably, harmless. When this curse whispers, I want to strain toward it. Then I remember Ani and Hope's experience, and I stop myself.

I stop, and I wait, and I regroup. Then I put out my feelers again. When the whisper comes, I don't try to hear what's being said. I block out words and focus on the notes, the music, the envelope surrounding those words. That lets me draw close enough to hear a tangle of melodies. A knot. A puzzle. Like the dagger letter. Rip it open, and I'll destroy the contents.

I mentally unweave the tangle, and when I do, the tune evaporates, leaving only words.

What am I?

I'm so focused on the tune that the words seem incidental, as if someone in the room has asked, and I answer without thinking.

"Jinx," I whisper. "Joker's jinx."

As soon as the words leave my mouth, horror fills me. I spoke too soon. Didn't think it through. Even if it is a jinx, those words would have meant nothing to Mercury millennia ago, when she wove this curse.

Yes.

I open my eyes, certain that word must have come from someone else. But no one seems to have spoken, and the headphones mean I couldn't have heard them even if they did.

Then I realize something else. The words are in English.

I should panic then. I should think this necklace is another fake. Except it's not, and my gut knows that, and my instinct says this is magic, deep magic, the likes of which I've never encountered.

Who am I for?

Now I do hesitate. I clear my throat.

"You were created for Hephaestus, who said he wanted to give you to Aphrodite, but he gave you to Harmonia instead."

A very complete answer. I believe they call that "hedging your bets." Try again.

I glance over at Ani. Her brows lift in question.

I want to tell her what's happening. To ask her if she's ever encountered such a thing.

Magic. Deep, impossibly deep magic.

"Is this Mercury?" I say. "Mercy?"

There's a shuffle in the room, and I catch Connolly's frown, but I shake my head and turn away.

Please restrict your responses to the options offered. Thank you!

"Can you offer me more options?" I say.

This necklace provides a limited range of interactive ability. Please restrict your responses to the options offered. Thank you!

"In other words, yes, this is Mercury, but no, you can't help."

Allow me to repeat the question. And consider carefully before you respond. Who am I for?

"You were intended for Aphrodite."

Intended. Yes! Such a lovely, flexible word. It does not, however, answer the question. The necklace was for Aphrodite. And the curse? Consider carefully with all the information available to you. Feel free to ask a friend to help. Be aware, though, that only the weaver knows the true intended victim.

"Wanna be my friend?" I say.

I swear the voice chuckles.

The weaver cannot provide the answer you require. It is beyond her abilities.

"In other words, I need to make an educated guess."

Preferably very educated. This SAT contains only a single question.

SAT. College entrance. That's what she'd joked about in her card. An image of the card flashes back. First planet from the sun.

Then there are those who aren't even in the same solar system.

I'm not sure why that line from Marius pops into my head. He'd been needling Hector, because Hephaestus—or Vulcan—didn't get a planet.

Vulcan.

I open my eyes and spin to face Jonathan as I lower the headphones. "Star Trek."

"Uh-huh," he says carefully.

"Spock is a Vulcan, right? That's his race."

He nods, still careful, as if struggling to make a connection.

I continue. "Live long and prosper. Spock might say that, but it's a Vulcan greeting. It represents his race. Which is named after . . ." I nod toward Hector.

Jonathan lights up now as he sees where the question comes from. "Yes. There are two main fan theories on the origin of that. One is that it was named after a disproven planet believed to orbit between Mercury and the Sun. The other is that it's named after"—a furtive glance Hector's way—"the god. Either way, since the disproven planet is named after the god, so is the race." He pauses. "That's more than you needed to know, isn't it?"

"Nope, it all helps. Thank you." I pull the headphones back on to think.

So that line in Mercury's card referred to Vulcan. To Hephaestus. To Hector. Is this my answer?

One thing gives me pause. That damned phone number. If everything in the card had a meaning, then why the hell did Mercury include the phone number for . . .

Friends and family of victims of domestic abuse.

A helpline for those who want to help friends or family suffering at the hands of an abuser.

"Hephaestus," I say aloud. "Vulcan. Hector. Whatever you call him, that's who you meant to curse. Except—since the necklace wasn't for Aphrodite—it didn't work."

I expect some kind of game show reaction—a buzzer or a bell. Instead, there is the softest breath of a sigh, one of relief, and then the curse opens in a way I've never experienced.

Voices wash over me. Hector demanding the necklace. He wants a curse hidden beneath blessings. Give Vanessa the gift of eternal youth and beauty, more than she already has, but conceal a curse within, one that will strike any man who dares love her. Yet Mercy tweaks the curse. It will strike those who *pretend* to love the necklace's recipient. False lovers. Hector himself.

Yet the necklace is for Harmonia. Cursing Marius would be the petty act of a jealous man, and Hector refuses to be the jealous husband. Cursing Harmonia's husband—and destroying Harmonia's happiness—is a worse blow for both Vanessa and Marius.

Except Mercy's curse was intended for a *false* lover. So how did that affect Cadmus? How did it kill Harmonia?

The story of Cadmus and Harmonia doesn't fit. Miscalculate, and I can't unweave the curse.

I back out from the weaving, remove the headphones and turn to Marius. "Did Cadmus love Harmonia?"

When Marius blinks at the question, I add, "That's the myth. That they were deeply in love and lived long and happily together, dying in old age and then becoming snakes."

"Yes," he says. "All true except the snakes. It was absolutely a love match."

"What's wrong, K?" Jonathan asks.

"I need to understand the curse to unweave it. I think I do, but the Harmonia part isn't fitting. According to what Mercy is telling me, she actually cursed Hector."

"What Mercury is *telling* you?" Hector says. "That's a necklace, girl, not a cellular telephone."

I ignore him and keep my attention on Marius. "Hector didn't ask Mercy to curse Vanessa. He asked her to curse whoever loved the wearer of the necklace. Mercy figured he meant you. Except the necklace went to Harmonia."

"So Hector cursed Cadmus?"

"That was the intention. Instead, Mercy cursed *false* lovers of those who wear the necklace. Which, if the necklace went to Vanessa, would have been Hector."

Hector snaps. "What kind of nonsense is this, girl?"

Ani clears her throat. "Harmonia's story has never fit, has it? In the myths, Harmonia chose to join him in death." She glances at Jonathan, who nods. Then she says to Marius, "Was Cadmus immortal?"

"Semi-immortal, which means a very long life, but yes, he eventually died."

"Is it possible . . . ?" Ani asks uncomfortably. "Is it possible she *chose* to die with him? That the necklace had nothing to do with it?"

Marius rubs his face, and when he speaks, his words are steeped in exhaustion. "Yes. I've always wondered that. But Vanessa . . ."

"It's easier to blame a curse," Ani says softly.

"Blame *me*, you mean," Hector huffs. "Vanessa blamed me for Harmonia's death, when I had nothing to do with it."

"Not for lack of trying," I shoot back. "You tried to ruin her life. Whether you succeeded or not is irrelevant."

I look at the others. "Remove Harmonia, and it works for the others who owned the necklace. False lovers were punished with misfortune."

Jonathan and Connolly—who've researched the necklace the most—both agree.

"All right then," I say. "I'm ready to uncurse the necklace."

"And I'm ready to buy it," Hector says.

CHAPTER FORTY-SIX

EVERYONE TURNS TO HECTOR. He's looking squarely at Havoc.

"I want you on my team," he says. "Not just head of my security division, but a seat on the board. I will recognize you, officially, as my niece."

Her blink of shock says Uncle Hector has never given her so much as a birthday card.

"That's what you are, Havoc," he says, his voice a gentle rumble. "I never liked the way your father treated you. Or your aunts. You deserved better. This old feud between myself and my brother, though, meant I was never allowed a place in your life."

"You lying son-of—" Marius begins.

Hector raises his voice. "Recognition as my niece. Head of my security division with a seat on the board at Voden Construction. We'll work out compensation later, but the job will come with a half-million-dollar signing bonus."

"Huh," Ani says. She frowns at Havoc. "Are you sure Hope said it *wasn't* a lover's lament. Because someone sure sounds like a man scorned."

Hector wheels on her, and Marius slides between them with a murmured, "Leave the mortals out of it, Hector."

"Well," Havoc says, "that's quite the offer, Uncle. How about you, Father? What's your counteroffer?"

I tense, mind spinning for a way to intercede.

"None," Marius says. "Hector's making you an excellent offer. I'd take it."

She turns to stare at him. "You're giving up the necklace? He won't uncurse it. You know that, right?"

Marius shrugs. "We'll survive. Take his offer. The only thing I ask for is the Bennett girl and the Connolly boy."

"Fine, I'll have them released—"

"Brought here," he says. "Before you complete your transaction with Hector."

Hector waves dismissively. "Bring the mortals. Get this over with."

Silence. Absolute silence.

"You don't have Hope, do you, Eris?" Marius says. "Not anymore."

"What?" Ani pivots between Marius and Havoc.

"I know my daughter very well," Marius says. "Normally, she'd have Hope and Rian here, to taunt us with. Reminding us what's at stake. So why aren't they available even by remote video?"

"Because I don't trust—" Havoc begins.

"You've secured this room because you expected to have Hope and Rian here. They've escaped, and you've blustered to cover that."

Havoc lifts her chin. "I changed my plans. That's all."

"Then get them on the phone."

Marius doesn't give her time to even answer. He turns to one of the guards.

"I've seen you before," he says.

The man straightens. "Yes, sir."

"And you know who I am?"

More straightening. "Yes, sir."

"Where are the captives?"

"They've escaped, sir," he says, without a moment's hesitation, and if it were possible to feel sympathy for Havoc, I'd feel it here. Marius doesn't need to offer anything—no reward, no threat. The god of war asks a question, and Havoc's man almost trips over himself betraying her to answer.

Or is there more at work here? Luck? Some other kind of magic?

The dead employee—Carson—had obviously betrayed Marius. Was that because Havoc blackmailed him? Or because, after centuries together, the allure of working for a "god" had worn off and he'd accepted a payout? Whatever the reason, this man obviously feels very differently.

"They escaped when we were moving them into the car," the man says. "The girl used some kind of charm on her guards, and they got away."

"Some kind of charm?" Ani says. "That'd be the curse you idiots put on her. You made her even more beautiful than she already was . . . and then put a couple of straight guys in charge of her. My sister isn't stupid."

Marius laughs under his breath. "No, she is not. The hostages are gone, and presumably, that's why Havoc confiscated our cell phones —so Hope and Rian couldn't contact their siblings once they found a phone. All right, then. Havoc? You've lied to us. Broken an oath. That means I have the right to insist this uncursing proceed. If the necklace cannot be uncursed, you may sell it to Hector."

Havoc glances at Hector, who doesn't react. "And if it can?"

"Then you may sell it to me for a half-million dollars or sell it on the open market, whichever you prefer. But having misrepresented a deal to a fellow immortal, you owe me an attempted uncursing." He looks at me. "You'll still do it? Even with Hope and Rian free?"

I nod. "Definitely. My sister is still cursed. And I know this is what—" I stop myself before I say that this is what Vanessa wants. No need to remind Hector of that.

Marius meets my gaze, and it's as if he's read my thoughts and seconded them. Get this done. Now. Before anything else goes wrong.

Connolly doesn't ask whether he can help, but his glance my way voices the question.

"I'm going to get a start," I say to Connolly. "When I reach the heart of it, I'll take that luck boost if you can give it."

"I can absolutely give it," he says.

"As can I," Marius adds.

I nod my thanks. This time, when I step up to the necklace, I don't need false confidence. I've solved the puzzle. Mercy couldn't tell me exactly what she'd done, but now that I've figured it out, the music surges, as if I'd been in a symphony hall wearing the best earplugs on the market. In solving the puzzle, I've unstopped my ears, and the music is glorious as the melodies weave together.

The songs of beauty and eternal youth rise up. We've debated whether they were blessing or curse, but Mercy's intention sings through. With the necklace intended for Vanessa, those "curses" were digs at Hector. His wife was already blessed. If she shone a little brighter, that would only hurt him more.

If I remember the real victims of this curse—the women, like Josephine Hill-Cabot who suffered the curse of eternal youth and the pain of false lovers—that only bolsters my determination to kill this snake that Hector unleashed. I blame him. Not Vanessa. Not Marius. Not Mercy, who couldn't avoid her debt and tried to help her brother and his lover. I blame Hector.

The key to the puzzle is Hector. Mercy wanted to punish him for his mistreatment of Vanessa, and now I will. I'll kill this thing he created. Stop at least one torture he can inflict on her.

I reach the heart of the jinx and begin to unweave the strands. Beauty, youth, misfortune . . . Beauty is first, and the easiest to untangle. Tease it out and cast it away. Next, youth. That one's trickier, but I get it undone and there, at the bottom, lies the true curse. Misfortune to befall a false lover. It lies there, still and quiet, but it is a resting snake with deadly fangs, and I know better than to dive in.

This is where I back out and ask for help.

"Can you confirm, Ani?" I say. "Be sure I've removed the first two curses."

She nods, and when she approaches the necklace, she hesitates and then shakes that off, shoring up her resolve. She's been "bitten" by this curse already and instinctively doesn't want to get near it, but she forces herself to relax and soon sinks into the trance state of unweaving. When she comes out of it, she's smiling, and in the glow of that, I'm a child again, quivering in the joy of having impressed my sister.

"You did it, K," she says, grinning at me. "It's cracked open like a walnut shell. Not even a twinge of trouble. Well, except for that final curse, which is a nasty one."

"But the others are gone?"

"Completely gone. The remaining jinx *is* amazing work. A beautiful and terrible thing."

"Agreed. I hated to undo the tea caddy, but I'll happily zap this one as much as I admire the craft." I glance at Connolly and Marius. "This is where I'll need all the luck I can get."

"Maybe I should give it a shot," Ani says. "You've done enough. I might not specialize in the jinx, but I can unweave them."

"And steal my thunder?" I say.

"I wasn't—"

"I know," I say, moving over to give her a one-armed hug. "It's dangerous, and you're thinking of me." I pause. "And of Hope in case I mess it up."

"First part, yes. Second part, no." She meets my gaze. "I wasn't thinking that at all, Kennedy. You can do this. I'd just rather you didn't take the risk."

"I'll be fine. If anything goes wrong, I'll back out. This is for Hope. Either I'll get it right, or I won't do it at all."

I return to my place. I don't glance at Connolly or Marius. I trust they'll know when and how to help, and I won't micromanage them. My entire focus needs to be on this curse.

Hope is safe. She's escaped with Rian, and by now, they'll be someplace secure. I just need to finish setting her free.

A little voice whispers that might not be enough. Sometimes uncursing an object doesn't uncurse the people who've caught it any more than finding a vaccine will cure those already suffering from the disease. Most times, though, an unweaving is both vaccine and cure. That's what I need to focus on. Don't fret about the thing I cannot control—concentrate on the one I can.

I slide into my trance state, and the music swells around me.

Before, the melody had been a siren's call. *You want to be beautiful, don't you? You want to be young forever. Take me. Put me around your neck. Win my blessing.* But those sweet whispers are gone now, and somehow, the necklace is all the more seductive for it.

Wear me, and punish false lovers. Woe betide anyone who pretends to cherish you.

There's an odd appeal to that, one I didn't see until now. Slide this necklace around my neck, and I am guaranteed true love.

Which is a lie. An insidious and ugly lie. The necklace won't tell me a true lover from a false one. It'll only punish the false, and if I've fallen for that person—married him—I would suffer, too, as did so many who wore this necklace.

This is where Mercy misjudged in her eagerness to punish Hector. Hurt him, and she'd have hurt the woman trapped in a marriage with him. Mercy's heart had been in the right place, but she'd been reckless, overeager to help Vanessa.

Yes.

The word wafts up on a whisper of grief and melancholy that takes me by surprise. Mercy isn't here. Whatever magic allowed her to communicate with me snapped when I solved the puzzle. But this is still her, an echo of regret.

Vanessa joked that I reminded her of Mercy. Maybe so, but here is where I feel the most kinship with her. That burning desire to help . . . only to dive in too fast. I don't feel that now, though. Instead, I'm surrounded by steadying forces—Ani, Jonathan, Connolly, Marius. Tethers holding me down as I unweave this curse.

I start slowly, tentatively. When something shimmers around me, a frisson of undefinable awareness, it gives me pause until I recognize it as luck. Just the barest tingle of it, holding back until I need more.

I let that luck wash over me, and I mentally tap the herbs of protection, calling on them. Then I touch a loose end on the curse and follow it, unweaving—

The necklace bursts into flame.

A flash fire leaps from it, scorching my fingers and flaring up into my face as I stagger back.

My eyes fly open to see the necklace itself isn't on fire. It's the velvet under it, igniting impossibly fast.

I stagger back as the flames shoot up. Ani grabs me. There's a low roar and then an explosion as the table combusts in a whoosh of flame and smoke.

Ani yelps, and I wheel to see her blouse aflame. I lunge toward her, but Jonathan's already there, tackling her to the floor and rolling out the fire.

Another scream, this one from Havoc. An oath from Marius. I can't see them through the smoke. It billows around us. Smoke and fire. That's all my shocked brain can process. *Everything* seems to be on fire. The drapes. The carpet. Even the walls, fire rolling up them in waves.

"Out," Marius shouts. "Everyone out."

My mind still can't quite comprehend what I'm seeing. It's too fast. Too sudden. Too *complete*. As if the room had been kindling doused in kerosene, the fire like lava spewed from a . . .

From a volcano.

In that chaos, I manage to see Hector. He's standing in the one corner of the room that isn't burning. And he's smiling. A malicious, ugly little smile.

Something hits me. It's Connolly, grabbing me with both hands.

"Kennedy!" Ani shouts.

"I have her!" Connolly yells back.

Everything is fire and smoke and chaos. People as dark shapes running for the exit. The room in flames. Connolly hauling me—

"The necklace," I shout, that one thought piercing my shock. I spin out of his grasp. I hear him curse, but I'm already diving for the smoldering pile of ash that had been the table. Within it, the necklace burns bright as the sun. I reach for it, fingers clasping the necklace.

Pain sears through me as the red-hot metal burns my hand even through my glove. I don't let go, though. I can't. If we leave, Hector will take the necklace, and we'll never see it again. I can't see him anymore, but I know he's here, gloating over having foiled my unweaving.

He will not have foiled it. I won't let him.

Connolly whips what is definitely a handkerchief from his pocket and tries to take the necklace, but I pull it away before he touches it. Then I bundle it into the handkerchief and pass it back.

"I'll take care of it," he says. "I'll give it back."

I meet his gaze, our eyes watering with the smoke. "I know."

I grab his hand with my uninjured one, and we run for the doorway. Outside, Ani yells, "Kennedy? Has anyone seen Kennedy?"

"Coming!" I try to shout, but smoke and heat sear my throat, and I only cough the word.

Connolly's hand tightens on mine, and when I stumble, my lungs scorching, he scoops me up, ignoring my protests. He charges through the open doorway.

"Well, isn't that sweet," a voice rumbles. "Such chivalry."

It's Hector, standing in the next room. Smoke swirls around him, never touching, leaving him clear-eyed and calm.

When Connolly barrels past, Hector doesn't stop him. Steps aside even . . . and we see the exit engulfed in flames. Connolly spins with me still in his arms, and I point at another doorway, this one leading into an untouched room. At a lazy wave of Hector's arm, fire fills it. Outside, Ani's screaming for me, but they can't get to us.

"There's a cost to passing," Hector says. "I think you know what it is."

"She uncursed the necklace," Connolly says. "If you want the empty shell, it's back in there."

As he speaks, he bumps me with his hip. His hip pocket. Where he put the necklace. He adjusts his grip on me, leaving me in his arms . . . which also covers me as I slide out the necklace and clutch the bundle in my hand.

Hector's speaking. He's saying he heard me scream, knows I grabbed the necklace, knows I wouldn't bother if it was uncursed. His voice is calm, unhurried. After all, we're the ones coughing and sputtering as we inhale deadly smoke. If we want to stall, that's our prerogative.

Connolly does exactly that, arguing while I work on the unweaving. I touch the necklace with my finger. A warning voice screams that I don't have my protective herbs, but I can't worry about that.

I hear the curse. I see where I left off. I continue unraveling—

Connolly coughs, and it's not a little hack, it's a doubling-over wheezing cough that tells me he's inhaled too much smoke. I struggle to get down, but he only grips me harder.

Faster. Must work faster.

Faster is dangerous.

I don't have a choice.

I unweave as fast as I can. I'm almost there when Connolly staggers. He takes a balancing step and trips. It's then that I remember his earlier luck working. The backlash. I'd forgotten all about that. Quickly, I grasp his hand, hoping to transfer some of that bad luck to me, but Connolly collapses, and as I twist and grab for him, the necklace falls. Hector lets out a rumbling chuckle of triumph.

Connolly is lying on his back, unconscious, possibly dying from smoke inhalation, and that bastard only sees his necklace.

My hand slams down on the necklace. My bare hand. My skin touches the gold, and my entire body convulses, as if with an electric shock, as the curse passes into me.

I grip the necklace, hard as I can, and I don't even need to focus —that bare-skin touch lets me hear the music right away. The curse holds on by a thread, and I rip it away, no time for caution.

The music stops.

The necklace is uncursed.

Hector grabs my collar and hoists me into the air. I twist and whip the necklace toward the door.

"It's outside!" I shout to the others. "Someone get it!"

Hector drops me and lumbers toward the door. At a wave of his hand, the flames dissipate. I don't see what happens. I don't need to. The way is open, and Connolly needs to get outside. *Now.*

I grab him under the arms. I've hauled him halfway to the door when Jonathan and Ani charge through. Jonathan takes over, and Ani catches me before I collapse, my lungs giving way in a fit of coughing.

Outside, Marius and Hector face off, the necklace on the ground between them. There's no sign of Havoc or her guards. There's a hose and a dropped bucket, as if Ani, Jonathan and Marius had found water and been preparing our rescue.

I brush off Ani and let myself collapse to all fours, gulping clean air until I can manage a raspy, "It's uncursed. I finished it. Just let him have it."

Hector turns my way, not seeming to have heard me. Marius swoops in, grabbing the necklace. I don't see what happens then—

I'm crawling to Connolly, who's flat on his back, unconscious. Jonathan is rescue breathing into Connolly's mouth. When I reach them, there's nothing I can do. Jonathan has this. He's the expert. I can only watch and pray—

I stop short and turn to see Marius backing away from Hector, who's advancing on him.

"Marius!" I shout.

He doesn't seem to hear me.

"Ares!"

His head whips my way. Hector charges. Marius feints.

"We need a little luck!" I shout. Then I glance at Connolly. "A lot of luck. Please!"

Marius sees Connolly as if for the first time. He yanks the necklace from his pocket and whips it as far as he can. Hector lurches after it, and Marius runs to us.

"Keep going," Marius says to Jonathan. "I can provide luck, but not miracles."

While Jonathan continues the rescue breathing, Marius closes his eyes, and every muscle in his body seems to quiver with exertion. There's a wave of energy, so strong the air audibly crackles.

Nothing happens.

Connolly lies motionless, his face as still and pale as marble.

Then he coughs.

I scramble to Connolly and help him sit up. I kneel beside him, supporting him, and whispering that we did it—we uncursed the necklace, and we're fine. We're all fine.

That is a lie. A lie he needs. A lie I need, because the truth is that when the curse broke, I felt nothing. The weight of it still lies in my chest. It's a small thing, though, compared to this: Connolly is alive.

"Sir?" a voice says.

We turn to see the guard who'd betrayed Havoc.

"I . . . I thought you might want these." He lowers a bag of cell phones to the ground and backs up, bowing and then dropping to one knee, and there is something chilling in the gesture. It's an offering. Placating an angry god.

Marius's lip curls in obvious distaste. This isn't what he wants, this obeisance. It might serve him well right now, but he'd rather the man just returned the phones as one person helping another, doing the right thing.

An imperious wave from Marius sends the man tripping over himself to back away as Marius picks up the bag. He passes out our phones. Immediately, my screen lights up with missed messages. I hit the one I want, a voicemail from an unknown number. A voice crackles from my phone, high and sweet.

"Hey, it's Hope! Guess what? Rian and I got away. We're fine, just hanging out in a coffee shop. Give us a shout when you get this!"

Tears fill my eyes. Then I turn to Connolly, lift the phone and replay the message and watch his face light up.

CHAPTER FORTY-SEVEN

A HALF HOUR LATER, we're in the downtown core of some small city whose name I've already forgotten. All that matters is that my sister is here, chilling in a coffee shop with Connolly's brother.

There's a no-stopping lane in front of the shop. While Jonathan finds a proper parking spot, Connolly pulls in there and hits his emergency flashers. It's like the gas station all over again, and I'm out before the vehicle has come to a complete stop. This time, I don't have a moment of worry that my sister isn't here. I can see her at a table in the front window, sipping some frozen concoction and laughing at something Rian's saying. Then she sees me, and she flies from the table. Rian motions that they'll come outside, and I'm bouncing on my toes when that door opens. Hope doesn't make it two steps before I've caught her up in a bear hug.

"Is that smoke?" she says, nose wrinkling. "What'd you do, fall into a campfire again?"

"Are those seriously your first words, Hopeless? You were kidnapped. Twice."

She shrugs. "It was no big deal. The first time I was treated like a princess. A little less princess-worthy in round two, but a few bats of my lashes and I was out, thanks to that beauty curse."

"Hey, it was more than a few bats of your lashes," Rian says. "That took serious acting skills."

She smiles at him. "And a bit of luck."

He shrugs. "You had it under control. And then there was that punch." He looks at me. "Your sister is awesome."

Hope glows, and when she looks at Rian, I may detect an eyelash bat or two. Great. My sister is crushing on her captivity-mate.

"So what's with the fire damage?" Hope says.

"They escaped a burning building," Ani says as she walks over with Jonathan. "And still found time to grab that necklace and uncurse your ass, little sister."

Hope throws herself into Ani's arms. We stand outside that shop and talk until we've gotten enough side-eye from passersby that Connolly suggests we continue the conversations elsewhere. Vanessa has offered her place for a rest stop before we journey home. We agree that's wise and pile into cars.

So Hope is fine. In the end, she saved herself, and she'll be flying high on that for a long time. Her curses are gone, too. All of them. Youth and beauty, which she didn't need, and the rest of it, too. When I unwove the curse, it unwrapped its tendrils from my sister, and that's what counts.

As for me?

Well, I don't need to worry about balancing after uncursing the necklace. The curse isn't gone. I no longer feel the lump of the curse curled in my gut, but that only means the snake has burrowed in, becoming part of me. I'm cursed. I felt it enter. I did not feel it leave. Hope and Ani can see it in me, and Ani has vowed to find a way to uproot it, but I know that won't happen. The necklace is uncursed, and there's nothing more to be done.

I've already joked that it's like the ultimate guardian for my heart—no one unworthy may enter. It's more than that. I feel the truth of the curse in my soul. Yes, woe to those who pretend to love me, but it's more all-encompassing than that. If I fall for the wrong person, someone who can't love me back, we'll both suffer.

My sister is fine, though. Connolly is alive and well. Rian is fine. Marius even has the necklace—Hector threw it down in a fit of rage when he sensed that the curse was gone. So we all came out of this as unscathed as we could have hoped.

The rest? That little part that isn't perfect? I'll deal with it. I'll have to.

———

It's been three days since I got more than a few hours' sleep, and I barely manage to shed my smoke-steeped clothing before I tumble into Vanessa's spare bed. A half hour later, I'm awake and lying there, listening to Ellie and Hope's soft snores beside me. I give it another ten minutes, but my body has acquired the exact minimum amount of rest it needed, and my brain says there'll be time to sleep after all this is over. Time when I'll be alone in my apartment with Ellie, thinking of all the things I wish I could have said when I had the chance.

I slip out and find the clothing I arrived in two days ago, somehow washed and folded and waiting for me, along with a tray holding every toiletry a guest could want. I make quick use of it, including the tiny pot of under-eye concealer—thank-you, Vanessa!

As I step from the guest wing, voices waft from the courtyard's open door, and I glance through to see Ani and Jonathan deep in conversation. I finger-wave, but they don't notice me. When they're talking like that, the rest of the world falls away. I remember how many times I'd watched them with envy. That's what I wanted with a guy. Not surface conversation, skating over topics of vaguely shared interest, always aware of potential judgment, always trying to make a good impression without revealing too much.

I have that idealized level of comfort with my family and with female friends, but never with a guy—even in friendship there always seems to be an unspoken barrier. I caught glimpses of that possibility with Connolly. Perhaps mirages shimmering with misguided hope. Or maybe a glimmer of something real.

I leave Ani and Jonathan, and I cover a few more steps before I hear another couple in conversation. I pass a doorway to see Vanessa and Marius on the divan. He's reclining just like when I first saw him. This time, though, there's none of that bored insouciance. He's on his back with his head on Vanessa's lap, and they're as rapt in each other as Ani and Jonathan. Their conversation is more relaxed, though, words intertwining like melodies.

Will getting the necklace end their "break"? I have no idea, and I'm not sure it matters. Whatever their sleeping arrangements, they *are* a couple, in all the best ways. Marius didn't want the necklace to win her back. He wanted it because she needed it.

I continue on without stopping. I'm looking for someone else, and I don't want to get sidetracked. When I'd been stumbling toward the bedroom earlier, Connolly had said something about needing to speak to his parents, that I'd find him in the study if I couldn't sleep. I should have taken that as a hint that he wanted to talk, but I'd been too exhausted.

Kind of like our first night here, when he'd showed up with wine, hoping to talk. Talk about the situation, he'd said, and in my disappointment, I'd withdrawn. I regret that now. Connolly hadn't showed up at my bedroom door to discuss a situation we'd discussed to death already. He'd simply wanted to spend more time together, and he hadn't known how to say so. If I'd doubted that, the dream Vanessa "sent" us proves it. That was the real Aiden Connolly, the one stifled under restraint and formality.

When I reach the study door, though, I can hear him still talking to his parents. I interrupted that once; I won't do it again.

I'll make him a coffee. Dig up a treat for the side—I'd spotted biscotti the other day. A coffee and a cookie. A seemingly impersonal present, but it says I know how much he loves his coffee and sweets—and how much he'll want them after that talk with his parents.

I'm still smiling a few minutes later as I wait for the coffee to brew. When footsteps sound at the doorway, I glimpse a figure that looks like Connolly. My smile grows . . . until I see Rian's dark hair.

"Wow," he says as he walks in. "I don't think anyone's ever been less happy to see me."

"Sorry, I thought—"

"—I was Aiden. I know. I'm sure he's gotten the same reaction many times, people mistaking *him* for *me*."

"Ego runs in the family, doesn't it?"

He grins. "Connollys are very aware of their many blessings. Some of us use them to build a million-dollar start-up. And some of us use them to start up the motors of a million girls."

He waggles his brows, and I can't help but smile even as I shake my head. I turn back to making coffee.

"I suck at entrepreneurship," he says. "And Aiden sucks at relationships. We play to our strengths. I try to overcome my weaknesses, which led to this whole mess. But at least I try. My brother? Not so much. It's business, business, and more business. He walks into a party and doesn't even notice the gauntlet of women checking him out because all he sees are the networking opportunities."

"Mmm-hmm." I add a dollop of cream to Aiden's coffee.

"What I'm trying to say is . . ." Rian throws up his hands. "Oh, hell. I'm here to make a plea on my annoying and exasperating brother's behalf. Don't let him walk away, Kennedy."

I freeze and then force myself to press the brewer for a second cup.

"He's going to walk away," Rian continues. "Because he's Aiden. I don't care how smart he is. In some things, he's an idiot. If you don't skywrite 'I'm interested,' he's going to tell himself this was just business. He'll let you go."

"If that's what he wants—"

"Of course it isn't what he wants. The way he acts around you? The way he talks? The way he relaxes? He barely does that with me. Which is a whole other story, I know—we have our problems. But the point is that you bring out something in my brother, something he needs, something he *really* needs. Hell, apparently, he even lets you drive his *car*."

I stir Connolly's coffee.

"That's for him, isn't it?" he says. "You're making him a coffee because you know that after talking to our parents, he'll need one the way other guys need a drink. You've fixed it exactly right. You've even got him a cookie—one small enough that he won't refuse. You can't tell me you want him to walk away."

"No, but if he *can* walk away, maybe he should."

Rian growls in frustration. "You may know Aiden well enough

to fix him a coffee, but you obviously don't know him *that* well. He doesn't take risks, Kennedy."

"Maybe he needs to start."

"Or maybe you could."

I shake my head. "Believe me, I have no problem taking risks."

"Then this one should be easy. Just—"

"I thought I heard voices," Vanessa says as she walks in. She stops. "Did I interrupt something?"

I shake my head. "I was just making Aiden a coffee."

"Ah, well, hold that thought. Rian? Can you get your brother? I heard Hope stirring, and I know everyone will want to be on their way. I'm determined to feed you all first. Can you give me a hand with that, Kennedy?"

Rian shoots me a look, but I duck it. He throws up his hands and strides off to get his brother.

————

WE'VE EATEN AND TALKED. There will be fallout from what happened in that farmhouse, but Vanessa and Marius will handle it. This was, after all, about them. We were the mortals caught in the riptide of their ancient dramas, and they don't expect we'll hear any more from the villains in this piece. We've served our purpose and been discarded.

We aren't as summarily dismissed by Vanessa and Marius. They owe us for our help and for what we suffered—Connolly's near-death experience and my curse. We have their ear and their favor.

After we eat, I announce plans to wander the gardens while the others finish up. Am I hoping Connolly will join me? Of course. But he's busy answering messages on his phone, and soon I'm walking through the front gardens alone. When a courier appears at the gate, I wander over.

"May I help you?" I say.

"Package for a Kennedy Bennett," she says.

I hesitate.

She frowns. "This is the address I was given."

"And I'm Kennedy. I just wasn't expecting a package here."

After that, she understandably requires ID, which I show and sign for the envelope. It is indeed to me, at Vanessa's address, with a very narrow delivery window.

Huh.

I rip open the seal and pull out a greeting card. It's a generic *Congratulations!* card with a cartoon cat throwing confetti.

Inside, scrawling script says: "Congrats on passing your college entrance exam! Please await further instructions on the admission process. Course selection begins soon." Signed, "your dear great-great-great-great-great granny M."

"Huh," I say, aloud this time. "That's . . . disconcerting."

"What's disconcerting?"

I turn to see Connolly walking toward me. I wave the card and share it with him.

"Do I even want to know what she means?" I say.

"Probably not. But I'm sure you'll find out soon enough." He shoves his hands into his pockets. "I wanted to say good-bye before we all take off."

And here it is. The moment of truth, when I'll know where he stands, what this is between us.

The answer, apparently, is nothing. Because that's what he says. Nothing. Oh, he talks, meaningless banalities about how much he enjoyed working with me. It's the sort of thing you say to someone you've been paired with on a project. Not what you say to someone you carried from a burning building.

Rian warned me about this. I thought he was wrong. I was special, after all. Connolly was different around me—that's why Rian came to plead his case. Surely, Connolly wouldn't just walk away.

But that's exactly what he's going to do, and when I see it coming, I see the truth of my own words to Rian.

If he *can* walk away, maybe he should.

Or is that my own bruised ego talking? I know Connolly feels more. I didn't need Rian to say so, though that should be all the extra confirmation I require.

Connolly finishes his platitudes, and I know he's ready to go. I need to say something, however simple. Maybe joke about whether he wants me to delete his number.

What if he says yes?

He's glancing toward the house, pivoting in that direction—

"Oh," he says, turning back sharply. "I almost forgot about your shop. The insurance and the police report. I can help you through that. We should be able to get you up and running in a few days."

"My lease ends next month, and I just emailed to say I'm not renewing. I'm moving back to Unstable and opening a shop there."

"You're moving . . . ?" Hands shoved into his pockets again. "Yes, of course. I knew you weren't happy in Boston, and this scare with your sisters would have only strengthened your ties to home. Plus, given the damage to your stock, it's the logical time to make the move, so . . ." He clears his throat. "Yes, completely understandable."

A beat pause. "However, my offer stands. Regardless of where you end up, there's still an insurance claim to process. I would be happy to help with that. Unless you'd prefer I didn't." A faint smile. "I'm sure you're quite sick of me by now."

"Never. And I would love your help with the claim."

He brightens. "Excellent. With the move, you'll want the claim handled expediently. The delayed police report might prove a slight bump, but I can get you past all that as painlessly as possible. After all, you did save my life."

"Uh, no, pretty sure that was Jonathan and Marius."

"You dragged me out of a burning house."

"Because you collapsed from carrying me through that burning house." I lift my hands. "Don't argue. You owe me nothing. I will, however, greedily accept any help offered. Also, you'd mentioned the idea of me expanding my business. I'm not quite ready to go international, but I wouldn't mind using some goodwill I built with Vanessa and Marius to grow my business. I could use your help navigating the gray market." I finger the envelope, hoping I don't look as nervous as I feel. "You did mention you'd be willing to do that . . ."

"Absolutely. It's an excellent idea. I've had thoughts on that—what you could do with a business like yours. In fact, I've been seeking investment opportunities . . ." He catches my look. "Or I could just offer my expertise if that's preferable. However, if any capital investment is required, my terms would be better than any bank's." He catches my look, and the corners of his mouth quirk. "Sorry. I'll stop that. If you need it, you will let me know. For now, may I suggest we arrange a time to talk about it?"

"Sure. Yes. Let's do that." Oh God, I sound like an overeager puppy, don't I? "I mean, I'm sure your schedule will be very busy—and mine will be, too, with moving arrangements—so we should firm up a time to talk."

"Is tomorrow too soon?"

"Not at all."

"Coffee then? I do believe I owe you a coffee." A smile my way. "And a cut-up brownie."

I laugh. "I might hold you to that. I do like my brownies cut up."

"Then let me suggest this little place I like, not far from your shop, on the other side of the Common. It's off the tourist path and has—in my opinion—the best coffee in Boston. Would ten tomorrow morning be too early? I could pick you up . . ."

He continues talking, one hand deftly guiding me deeper into the gardens. We walk, and we talk, making plans for the future.

Is it exactly the sort of future I'd hoped for where Connolly is concerned?

Maybe. At least in the short term. Rian may have hoped for a different resolution, but Connolly and I aren't there yet. It's like watching an action movie where the couple trade a few sparks amidst the danger, only to declare their undying love in the final scene.

I understand the constraints of a two-hour script, but I'm not really a fan of insta-love. I prefer the endings where the two former strangers make plans to stay in touch, maybe take on a joint project. I can peer into the future and give them an eventual happily-ever-after.

A week ago, I don't think I'd have been okay with this. I'd have wanted more than a coffee "date" to discuss business. But I need to be more careful now with the curse inside me. When it comes to romance, there's no more leaping before I look—not if I care about someone. And I care about Connolly.

I need to take this slow and allow for the chance that maybe it shouldn't ever be more than friendship. I'll figure it out. Be sure first. The important thing is that Connolly isn't walking out of my life. He found his doorway back in, and he leapt at it. That's all I need . . . at least for now.

COMING NEXT

I hope you enjoyed Cursed Luck! The story doesn't end there. Book two—**High Jinx**—will be out in 2022. Watch my website for details!

There will be a *Cursed Luck* series novella coming even sooner. It's Memorial Day weekend in Unstable, and Kennedy has invited Aiden and Rian. She's also invited Vanessa, who narrates the story. There's nothing Vanessa likes more than matchmaking, and the three Bennett sisters are ripe for her skills. Goddess of Summer Love will be out July 1, 2021 as part of an anthology, **Hex on the Beach**, also containing novellas by Jeaniene Frost and Melissa Marr.

ABOUT THE AUTHOR

Kelley Armstrong believes experience is the best teacher, though she's been told this shouldn't apply to writing her murder scenes. To craft her books, she has studied aikido, archery and fencing. She sucks at all of them. She has also crawled through very shallow cave systems and climbed half a mountain before chickening out. She is however an expert coffee drinker and a true connoisseur of chocolate-chip cookies.

Visit her online:
www.KelleyArmstrong.com
mail@kelleyarmstrong.com

f facebook.com/KelleyArmstrongAuthor
🐦 twitter.com/KelleyArmstrong
📷 instagram.com/KelleyArmstrongAuthor

Lightning Source UK Ltd.
Milton Keynes UK
UKHW041543310521
384682UK00001B/138